HE'S A SERIAL KIDN~~APPER, RAISED IN~~ AN UNDERGROUND CULT. NOW, HE IS THE ONLY ONE WHO CAN STOP THE END OF THE WORLD.

Adam is a Rescuer, a man who takes children out of what he deems bad situations by convincing parents to give them up. He takes the children to his underground world, where they are welcomed and raised by The Family and their leader, a man they call Father. After his latest mission, Adam learns Father is ready to trigger a catastrophic event that could end life above ground. The more Adam learns about what it takes to make his underground utopia thrive, the more he begins to doubt his beliefs. Now, Adam must decide if the above ground world is worth saving.

Praise for Kingdom Come

"In *Kingdom Come*, Nora Murray combines a parallel universe with brainwashing and shoves it deeply underground in our own world, in our own time. Readers will run on twisted paths alongside Adam and the well-intentioned followers of "Father", as their meticulously put-together world falls apart and they are forced to face the reality of what they've done." – *Kathie Giorgio, author of The Home For Wayward Clocks and If You Tame Me*

"Murray writes a remarkable portrait of cult life through fantasy. *Kingdom Come* is deliciously disturbing."—*Julie Beekman, Author, Two Trees, A Memoir*

i

Kingdom Come is the book we need in these chaotic times. Combining a wonderfully inventive world for escapism and a heartfelt look at what it truly means to believe in God and follow His words, this book is truly unique. The story is at times chilling in its realism, but that same realism is what makes the characters' journey so heart-warming. This page-turner is a must-read!"—*Carrie Newberry, Author of Pick Your Teeth With My Bones*

Excerpt

Adam reminded himself to smile as he approached the little girl. "Wow, you're fast!"

"Mommy and I race a lot. She says I can be a track star when I grow up."

"I bet," he said. Of course, the mother's only reason for teaching the girl how to do something well was for personal glory.

"Are we there yet? I'm hungry."

"We just ate at the restaurant, and you had a snack before we went into the tunnel."

She tilted her head back. "That was hours ago!"

"It was less than an hour ago, but we'll be there soon."

It wasn't just her, most of the children he rescued behaved exactly the same way. He tried to carry them when he could, but parts of the hike included narrow or steep passes that were safer to navigate with both people on foot. It almost made him wish he could just drive them to The Family, but he knew that was impossible. Their home must remain a secret. He couldn't risk being followed, and an hour hiking through the woods and then another hour in a hidden tunnel was the best way to keep that secret.

Kingdom Come

Nora Murray

Moonshine Cove Publishing, LLC

Abbeville, South Carolina U.S.A.

First Moonshine Cove edition
April 2021

ISBN: 9781952439070

Library of Congress LCCN: 2021905701

For Mom and Dad, who always believed in me, and made
me believe in myself

Acknowledgment

First, (at the risk of sounding cliche) I need to thank God for the multitude of blessings in my life. I do believe in Him and His message of love and hope. I pray I live my life in His service.

So many incredible people made this book, and my dream of having it published, a reality. I'm just going to thank them in order of who I met first to keep it simple:

My parents, brother and sisters who supported, encouraged and motivated me my entire life. That includes giving me the confidence to send this book out into the world. My parents always said I could do anything, and they never once made me question that they believed in what they said. My siblings can motivate me through encouragement, or by bringing out my stubbornness. Somehow, they always know the best motivator for whatever the situation and use it to full effect.

Kathie Giorgio, Michael Giorgio, Carrie Newberry and all the amazing writers at AllWriters' Workplace and Workshop, LLC. They workshopped this book with me from the beginning all the way to the end, encouraged me to pick it back up after I took a few years off to have those babies, and gave me years of laughter and friendship.

JP Murray, my perfect partner. He keeps my on my toes, always laughing, and never once questioned my crazy dream to write a novel. None of this would be possible with out his love, support and understanding that he did not marry a woman who cleans.

Joseph and Cecelia, there isn't enough space to explain how much you two mean to me. Thank you for being all that you are, and (since this is acknowledging those who helped with this book) somehow knowing this was important to mommy. Even as toddlers, they understood Thursday night bedtime was nonnegotiable so mom could work, while every other night was flexible. I still don't know how that happened, but those kids are awesome. The two of you are proof that there is good in this world that is worth standing up for and speaking out to protect. Please remember that love and hope are always the better option over hate and fear.

Last, but definitely not least, the publishers and editors at Moonshine Cove. Thank you for liking this book enough to publish it and get it out into the world. I was so excited the day it was accepted, my kids had to tell me to "calm down." I didn't, but they were cool about it.

About the Author

Nora Murray grew up near Milwaukee, Wisconsin, the proud member of both a large Irish-Catholic family, and a family led by socially conscious educators. A combination she says formed her faith, work ethic and convictions.

With a journalism degree from UW-Madison, she worked as an award-winning television news producer for several years before switching to public relations. She lives in Summerfield, North Carolina, where she continues writing anything and everything, including her next novel.

Nora lives with her supportive and hilarious husband, her sweet and strong-willed children, and crazy but lovable dogs.

When she isn't working or spending time with family, she enjoys reading, "thinking seriously" about exercising and drinking coffee.

http://authornoramurray.com/

1

Adam looked down at the four-year old girl tugging at his arm. The tunnel was dim, but light enough for him to see the pride-filled grin on her face.

"I'm the best dancer in my class, Daddy says so. Do you want to see me twirl?" She twirled before he could answer. "See? I'm the best, but this isn't the best twirling dress. I have a pink one at home and that's the best for twirling because the skirt flies up and twirls with me. Do you think Daddy could bring that dress when he picks me up? I could show you then."

Adam focused on his breathing to keep calm. The kid wouldn't stop talking, and he didn't know how much more of it he could take. The fact that his socks were still wet from their hike through the woods wasn't helping much either, and considering how cold the tunnel they now walked through was, they wouldn't dry out anytime soon. He tried to remember why he chose her, the trauma she must have gone through before now. He hoped it would help bring back some of his compassion.

The girl kept asking when her dad was going to pick her up. She must have seen his picture before they left the restaurant and started the hike. Infernal TVs. Why would anyone want one of those things in a restaurant anyway? Yet another problem with that society. The world really would be a better place when they got a chance to start over.

Adam used his most soothing voice to try to keep her quiet. "I don't know if your dad will be able to bring the dress, but that was a beautiful twirl."

He led her through the tunnel, lit by blue lights that were spaced about ten yards apart. It wasn't bright, but it was enough to make sure you could see what was ahead of you. Not that there ever was anything. The tunnel was empty. He was grateful he didn't have to worry about her tripping anymore. Earlier, when they were moving through the forest, he was convinced she was going to sprain an ankle or fall down a hill for the lack of attention she gave to where she was going.

Adam knew he shouldn't take his frustration out on the kids he rescued. He was a Rescuer, he was there to help them, and it wasn't their fault they didn't understand. Still, every time he went back to the surface, he became agitated. Angry even, that he and the others had to hide underground, while those sheep were able to walk around in the sun. They wasted all the gifts bestowed on them by God. Oiling themselves on beaches and falling asleep on the sand. Not looking up to appreciate the beauty of the sun, not watching the waves dance with the sand on the coastline. And then they would leave just before the sun glided down past the horizon, painting a new sky full of different colors every night.

Instead, they ran inside, put on clothes that only pretended to cover their bodies, glopped on who knows what kind of chemicals into their hair, some even painted their faces with unnatural colors. They went into their cement blocks, the ones they killed all the trees, flowers and grass for, and acted like fools.

Adam never actually went into the bars or nightclubs. He knew if he saw what went on inside, he wouldn't be able to control his anger. What they did when they left was proof enough of that. They draped themselves over one another. Clearly trying to either keep themselves or their friends from falling onto the pavement. They laughed at half-sentences. He supposed that was necessary, because they never spoke coherently once they came back outside.

Still, it was probably fair that those people had the opportunity to enjoy the time they had before they were all wiped out for good. That was the only thought that gave him any comfort. He was a compassionate person, after all. He could show mercy.

Was she still talking?

"Sometimes my mom comes with my dad when he picks me up and we go for burgers and ice cream. Do you think they'll come pick me up together?"

"I don't know, maybe." It was better to lie to her at this stage. When she still thought she was going home. When she still trusted what her dad told her when he turned her over to Adam. The children he rescued always thought they only had to stay with him for a few days, that they would see their parents again, that their parents loved them more than anything in the world. Adam guessed the last part was true.

"I'm going to get chocolate and vanilla," she said. "Mommy always lets me get both." She paused for a minute. "Why couldn't Mommy watch me?"

"She was busy."

"What was she doing?"

Probably fornicating with any number of people, he thought. "I don't know." He tried to think if there was any way to get her to move faster. "Hey!" he said with all the fake enthusiasm he could muster. "Do you want to race?" That usually worked.

She jumped up and down. "Where's goal?"

Adam looked down the tunnel. He couldn't make her run too far or she would tire, fall and hurt herself. He saw a red, blinking security light about 40 yards away. It was pushing it, but he was willing to risk it for some silence. "See that light down there?"

"It's far."

"I know, but you're a big girl now. You can make it. You ready?"

No child was willing to deny they were a "big kid."

She looked at him, at the light, then back at him. "Okay, but your legs are longer. I get a head start."

"That sounds fair. Ready?"

"Ready!" she screeched and jumped into the air.

"Okay, 1 ... 2 ... 3 ... GO!" He watched her take off, her arms flailing in the air. She looked back to see if he was following her.

11

"I'm coming!" he said, starting a slow jog. If you looked like you were running, they thought you actually were. She screamed and laughed, trying to run faster. Oh no, he forgot to check her shoelaces. Adam looked down at her scurrying feet and saw the telltale tabs of Velcro sticking out on the side, perfect. Normally, he hated anything unnatural, but they did come in handy every now and then. He justified the hypocrisy with the thought that if parents hadn't given into the commercialism and so-called advancements, their children wouldn't need rescuing.

She reached the light, panting and smiling. She was pretty fast for her age. He made a note to tell Father when he delivered her.

Adam reminded himself to smile as he approached her. "Wow, you're fast!"

"Mommy and I race a lot. She says I can be a track star when I grow up."

"I bet," he said. Of course, the mother's only reason for teaching the girl how to do something well was for personal glory.

"Are we there yet? I'm hungry."

"We just ate at the restaurant, and you had a snack before we went into the tunnel."

She tilted her head back. "That was hours ago!"

Adam knew she was too young to tell time, but he also guessed she knew she was exaggerating. It's true the hike through the woods was about an hour, but he also knew they were about halfway down the tunnel which meant they snacked 20 to 30 minutes ago. "It was less than an hour ago, but we'll be there soon."

It always baffled him how kids could have so much energy all day, until you needed them to actually do something. The road trip to the National Park, where he left the car to be picked up by someone hired by Father, was a nightmare. A full day of her constantly kicking his seat, singing songs, asking questions and never getting tired. He even let her out for an hour to run and play in a playground before putting her back in the car, hoping she would finally nap. She didn't. When they got to the restaurant inside the park, she talked all through lunch and wanted to dance around the lobby, but the moment they were in the woods, she started to complain that her legs hurt. It wasn't just her, most of the children he rescued behaved exactly the same way. He tried to carry them when he could, but parts of the hike included narrow or steep passes that were safer to navigate with both people on foot. It almost made him wish he could just drive them to The Family, but he knew that was impossible. Their home must remain a secret. He couldn't risk being followed, and an hour hiking through the woods and then another hour in a hidden tunnel was the best way to keep that secret.

"Can you carry me?"

"Sure." This was what he was actually hoping for. If he carried her, he could move faster. He wasn't physically tired yet, but he was desperate to get home. He picked her up and swung her onto his back.

"Wow," she said. "You're stronger than Daddy!"

In more ways than one, Adam thought. Her father was weak. Her father had the chance to see his daughter again. Her father had the chance to prove he was worthy of joining them when the time came. Instead, her father chose the easy path. The path of self-elimination, instead of waiting to follow through on God's plan for him. The television reporter said police found his body around ten o'clock that morning. About five hours after he gave his daughter to Adam.

Of course, no one knew where the kid was. Police from around the state were looking for her. They had volunteers, dogs, even helicopters scanning areas with any connection to her father. Fools.

Adam felt her head drop onto his shoulder. Finally. She would sleep the rest of the way. He pushed her long brown hair to the side, so it wouldn't tickle his nose, and picked up the pace.

2

Adam managed to make it home before she woke. The large red door's color and glimmering gold trim was a welcoming beacon in the middle of the grey underground labyrinth. He wished there was a way to knock without waking the kid, but he knew from experience there wasn't. He lifted the large golden leaf in the middle of the door and let it fall.

The girl's head snapped up the moment the knocker hit the door. "Are we here?"

"Yes, we've arrived," Adam said.

He lowered her to the ground and looked intently at her face. This was the moment that made the journey worthwhile. He didn't want to miss it. She looked back at him, waiting for something to happen.

The door opened, drawing her gaze away. Her eyes seemed to double in size, along with her smile, as the light from inside illuminated her face. Pure amazement. It was the only thanks he needed.

Adam let himself look away and back into his home. The golden archway, standing just inside the door, reflected the bright lights from the ceiling, intensifying the illumination and heat, acting as their very own sun. There were two other arches just like it to the east and west. Each stood in front of doors identical to the one he and the kid just walked through, welcoming Family members into their underground world. The gate to the north was larger, framing the waterfall that brought life to everything in what Adam considered their own paradise. The falls fed the clear rivers that flowed through the land, allowing the grass, flowers and a few fruits and vegetables to thrive. The flora brought brilliant colors, delicious smells and life to the underground world.

From where Adam stood, he could only see one wall. The rock created the illusion of a mountain reaching into the sky. The sky, of course, was also rock, but Father managed to hide the lights and air ducts with gems and reflective stones that created a sparkling white ceiling. It appeared as though all the stars in the night sky clustered together just for them.

Adam knew he would never cease to marvel at the world Father created. Truly, God had a hand in allowing them to build this world. It was almost as beautiful as the one The Almighty Himself made, before humans destroyed it. The only difference was the lack of sunrise or sunset. That beauty, only He could create.

Adam felt calm return to his body, and with it, his true self. No longer a bitter and angry criminal, but a peaceful, enlightened and patient being. He would have to pray for forgiveness for losing himself outside of these walls.

A group of three welcoming Children, all wearing their brown robes and rope sandals, ran up to Adam and their new, soon-to-be, sister.

"Hi!" one Child, Rose, said to the kid before hugging her. Rose released her and looked up at Adam. "Sir, may we take her to the changing room? Father is expected soon."

Adam smiled down at Rose. "You may. But remember, knowledge must be given at the appropriate times. When God allows it."

"Yes, sir," said Rose. She then grabbed the girl's wrist with a friendly pull and smile. "Come on! You're going to love it here."

"Are you coming?" the newly rescued child asked Adam. She seemed unsure of her new friends.

"Not right now," he said. "You go and have fun. I promised there would be plenty of children to play with."

"Will you come get me when my daddy gets here?" she asked.

He closed his eyes for a moment. He couldn't lie to her within these walls. He took a deep breath and knelt down so she could look directly into his eyes. "You have nothing to worry about now." He smiled.

She smiled back. "Okay." She then ran off with the other Children, all laughing together.

Adam took another deep, cleansing breath. That was how it should be, and how those Children would continue to be. Soon, the girl would become one of them. She would be happy. She would be without a memory of her past life. She would stop asking for the father who was weak, but still helped save her. She would stop wondering about her unworthy mother.

He looked down at the ground and was reminded of his own appearance. He was still in his surface clothes; tennis shoes, jeans and a black t-shirt. Longing to be in his own robes, he headed for the Rescuers' huts.

The two other Rescuers were already at the changing hut when he arrived. They all prearranged times to arrive so their tunnel entrances could go unnoticed.

Sister Clare was reading Father's spiritual book just outside of the hut, her back turned to the door so there was no chance of accidentally seeing one of the others changing. The Family wasn't allowed to read the actual Bible. Father kept it from them for their own good. Too much divisiveness and violence came from misinterpretations of the Good Word. Instead, Father selected the most important passages for Family members to read and put them in a separate book with explanations so no one could be confused or disagree over the true meaning. Adam couldn't deny he was curious to read the Word of God, but he was also grateful to Father for his protection of them all.

Brother Jonas exited the changing hut, letting out a sigh of relief. "Feels good to be home." He looked up and grinned when he saw Adam. "Hey, Adam! Welcome back."

"Hi, Jonas." Adam returned the smile. "When did you get home?"

"Not long ago," said Jonas. "I can't stand to be in those street clothes any longer than necessary."

"I'm with you. I'm going to change now. When is Father expected?"

Jonas shrugged. "I think he's just waiting for the three of us."

"And you two keep making him wait." Clare turned around and sat upright with the book on her lap. The picture of a good student, with her blonde hair pulled back straight into a ponytail, lips pursed, and sharp blue eyes anxious to continue learning.

"Sorry, Sister," said Adam. He went inside to his locker, took out his robes and sandals and took them to the changing room.

Normally, men and women wouldn't share such an intimate space, but there was limited space underground and the Rescuer's items for above ground were unique. It wasn't ideal, but Jonas and Adam were careful never to use the changing hut when Clare was inside. Father said he trusted them and Adam knew his brother and sister took that trust as seriously as he did.

He heard Jonas and Clare talking while he changed.

"Lighten up, Clare," said Jonas. "We've all had a long couple of weeks. Now is the time to relax and get back to our lives."

"How do you expect us to do that with you two dilly-dallying around the hut?" answered Clare. "We can't get back to our lives without seeing Father, and we can't see Father until we're all ready to present our new Family members."

"Yeah," said Jonas. "Well, get ready, because my kid is amazing. He's going to wipe the floor with your kids."

Adam grinned as he undressed. Jonas always tried to make rescuing children a game. Clare found it distasteful. Adam agreed with her at first, but after he got to know Jonas better, he realized it was Jonas' way of lightening the mood. Adam appreciated that, although he did wish Jonas would show Clare a little more respect.

Clare raised her voice. "How many times do I have to tell you it's not a competition?"

17

"You just say that, because you never win. At least you remembered to rescue someone this year."

Adam felt the blow to Clare in his own chest. "That's not fair, Jonas," said Adam loudly so they could hear him outside.

"Oh, come on," said Jonas. "She knows I'm kidding. It just takes some of us longer to catch on than others." Adam heard a short pause before he heard a more considerate tone coming from his brother. "Seriously, Clare. It was a joke. Even the perfect Adam came home empty-handed his second year."

It was true. After Adam's first disaster of a rescue mission eight years ago, he was afraid of making another mistake. He couldn't bring himself to rescue any children that second year. Before Adam became a Rescuer, the Elders of The Family rescued children, including Adam, Jonas and Clare, but after a while Father decided it wasn't safe for them to continue, especially as they aged and weren't up for the physical aspects of the job. When Adam came home without a child his second year, Father decided more than one Rescuer was still necessary to keep The Family growing. Jonas started rescuing children during Adam's third year on the job, and Clare was added a year later. She successfully rescued a child the first year. The following two years, she came back empty-handed, but managed to rescue a child last year and apparently, this year as well.

Adam hoped Clare was okay when he heard Jonas resume his bragging.

"My kid is great this year. He questions everything. He's got so much energy and life in him. He'll be a great athlete with the right teaching."

"All children are energetic." Clare sighed. "All children are exceptional with the right encouragement. That's why we bring them here. So they can get the encouragement they wouldn't otherwise receive."

"Some are more exceptional than others."

Adam slipped the smooth brown cloth over his head and let it drape down to his ankles. He felt the soft fabric caress his arms, and gave himself a second to enjoy the sensation before tying the rope belt and slipping on his sandals. He felt safe.

The argument continued after he walked out of the changing room.

"Come on, Clare." Jonas let his head tilt to the side toward his shoulder. "You have to admit some children are more exceptional than others. Just look at us."

"What?" Every now and then, Jonas still found ways to surprise Adam.

"The three of us," said Jonas. "We're the favorites. We're trusted to go to the outside world and interact with the sinners. We stood out from the others. That's why we're the only three Rescuers."

"No," said Adam. "There are only three Rescuers because more would be too obvious in the outside world."

"What you're saying is prideful," added Clare to Jonas. "You can't think that way. You should pray about it tonight."

"All I know is not everyone can do our job," said Jonas.

"And I couldn't do the Teachers' job," said Adam. "Or the Builders', or the Farmers'."

"Only because you weren't trained for it, because someone saw something else in you."

"Yes, Father finds the gifts in everyone to help them find their rightful place in the world. No one is better than any other."

"Whatever. Let's get going, we're going to be late." Jonas looked at Clare. "Don't want to keep Father waiting any longer."

"No, we don't." Clare nodded.

The three walked in silence to the transition rooms where their kids would be waiting.

3

Adam found his girl talking to the same group of welcoming Children just outside of the transition room. They were telling her about their lessons.

"I'm the best with the staff," said one boy, Nicholas, who was about 10 years old. "I can already spin it for a whole minute."

There was that "best" word again. Children on the outside were trained to be so prideful, but Adam hated to see it here, where they were meant to be better than the people above ground. He thought about Jonas' comments outside of the changing huts. Perhaps Adam should talk to Father about how to help set a better example for them all. To remind them that while they had different talents, that didn't make them better than anyone else. They were all servants of God.

"Why do you spin it?" asked Adam's girl.

Adam interrupted before Nicholas could answer. "So, how do you like your robe?" he asked her.

"It's really soft," she said, "but I'd like it better if it was pink. Mommy says I look good in pink."

"Mommy?" asked a younger child. "Who's that?"

"It's about time for Father to arrive," Adam interrupted again. The Children were safe now, but it was best for them not to be reminded of the outside world. That was the biggest danger of "Welcoming Day." Fortunately, the Teachers would be able to answer all the Children's questions over the next week, and then the subject would be forgotten.

"Why don't you all go take your seats," said Adam. "And you," he turned to the kid, "you are one of the guests of honor today."

"What does that mean?" she asked.

"It means you get to sit up front, next to me and Father," he said. "You'll be the center of attention."

"Okay." She shrugged her shoulders.

They started to walk up to the platform together and Jonas joined them. He was leading a young boy who Adam hoped was at least three years old, but looked younger. The boy had dark hair and a dirty face.

"He's got spunk," said Jonas. "He's already been in his first fight. Of course, he shouldn't be fighting without permission, but he doesn't know that yet." Jonas patted the boy on the back.

"No, he shouldn't," said Adam.

They approached the wooden platform, set up under the Northern Gate, right in front of the waterfall. It was simple, with a few flowers decorating the sides, but under the gate and in front of the fall, it could take anyone's breath away. Clare was already sitting with her girl when the four reached the stage.

"Uh oh," said Jonas. "That means we're late again."

Clare stared out at the crowd. Her girl was staring back at Clare, but didn't say a word. Adam sat his girl down on the other side of Clare, and took his seat at the end. Jonas sat next to Clare's kid, with his boy on his right.

Adam looked out at the crowd. The whole Family was there, taking their seats on benches placed on the grass and talking excitedly about the three kids sitting in front of them. An addition to their Family. Adam looked out at all the faces he knew and loved. The Farmers washed their faces and hands for the occasion, no dirt to be seen. They were also allowed above ground to harvest the food for The Family, but only interacted briefly with the migrant workers in the fields, who rarely spoke any English. The five Builders took one final lap around the stage to make sure it was sturdy. It always made Adam wonder why they did the final walk after people were already sitting on it. The Warriors, by far the largest group in The Family with about 50 members, playfully shoved one another, always looking for a new challenge. The Teachers worked to calm the approximately dozen children, all of whom the current Rescuers saved, with the help of a few teenagers who finally grew out of their rambunctious stages. Most of the younger Family members, including Adam, were rescued as children themselves by the Elders of The Family, but didn't remember the details. No Child did. The Elders started this world with Father, building it into what it was today, fulfilling God's will and preparing the way for Adam's generation to take over. Finally, the Cooks took their seats. Adam was sure they just finished putting the final touches on tonight's feast. His mouth watered, thinking about it.

"Is this a pageant?" asked Adam's girl. "I can't be in a pageant right now," she started to sound panicked, "I don't have my pink dress."

Adam turned to her. "It's not a pageant."

"Then why are we on a stage?"

"I told you," said Adam, "you are our guest of honor. This is just how we welcome people to our home."

"This isn't a home." She sounded very sure of herself. "This is a stage."

"Trust me," he said. "You will understand everything soon enough. You just need to be patient."

She crossed her arms. "I hate it when grown-ups say that."

Adam closed his eyes and tried to calm his mind. Father's arrival was imminent and he didn't want to appear distracted.

Moments later, the waterfall gushed with a surge of water, and then just as suddenly stopped as Father walked out from behind the rock and onto the platform.

Father strode up to the microphone. His gold robe glistened almost as brilliantly as the great gate they sat under. Adam knew Father his entire life, or at least as much as he could remember of his 26 years. In that time, the great man gained a few extra wrinkles on his tanned skin and his hair changed from a light brown to a shocking silver, but when Father spoke, it didn't seem like he'd aged a day.

Father looked out at all his children, old and young, and smiled. "My children, I am so pleased to see all of your wonderful faces. It's hard to believe it's been a year since some of you first arrived, sitting up on this very stage." Father took a moment to acknowledge the three newly rescued children before turning back to the rest of The Family. "Now, you know what an important day that was in your life. It was the day you became part of our Family, the day you were given a chance at eternal and everlasting life, the day you were rescued." Father paused again to look out on the nearly 100 pairs of eyes staring back at him. "I know many of you don't remember that day. Please, don't let that worry you, because you remember what's important. What we've taught you ever since. We've given you the word of God, a purpose in life and goals to attain. Today, I am honored to give those gifts to the newest members of our Family. As the good book says, 'Therefore, my dear friends, as you have always obeyed, not only in my presence, but now much more in my absence, continue to work out your salvation with fear and trembling, for it is God who works in you to will and to act in order to fulfill His good purpose.'"

Father turned back to the six people sitting on the stage. Adam took his girl's hand and they stood up. Clare and Jonas followed suit with their rescues.

Then, Father took three rosaries from under the podium and walked over to his new Family members. "Welcome, young ones," Father said, placing one rosary on Adam's kid, kissing her on the forehead and moving down the line to Clare's girl.

"Is this necklace for me?" whispered the kid to Adam.

"Yes, it's a gift."

"I like necklaces." She smiled.

Adam smiled back, put his finger to his lips and then pointed down the line where Father was placing the last rosary on Jonas' boy who started playing with the beads.

Father walked back to the podium and looked out at the crowd. "We look forward to a long and happy existence with all of you.

Now, it's time for you to start your journey." Father gestured to the other end of the stage, where the three Teachers waited for the kids.

Adam knelt down to look his girl in the eyes. "Okay, now it's time for you to go with one of those nice ladies. They'll take good care of you."

"But where are they going to take me?" she asked. They all asked that.

"They're just going to get you settled in," he answered.

"Why do I need to be settled? Daddy said he was going to get me soon."

"I know, but I already told you, you don't have to worry about anything here." Adam was determined not to lie. He never had to before.

"Will I see you soon?" she asked.

"You will see me soon enough." He hugged her for the first time. In truth, it would be weeks before she saw anyone other than three select Teachers and Father, but it was best not to share too much information. His answer seemed to calm her, and she went to the last Teacher waiting at the end of the stage. The other two kids already left. A familiar sadness hit Adam, knowing that when she did return, she would have no memory of him or anything before that day. Adam stood up straight and faced forward. A few moments later, Father started to speak again. "And now, let us welcome home our Rescuers. Braving the Godless and terrifying world above to save those three young souls."

The Family applauded respectfully. Adam looked out at the crowd, now standing on the lush green grass, recognizing the six Children he personally rescued ever since he was allowed to go out on his own. Brother Samuel, his first rescue, winked. Adam nodded back. Samuel's rescue may not have been perfect, but he was turning into a good man, he would be an asset to The Family.

"Now, my children," said Father, "make your preparations for the Welcoming Feast. Today is a day of joy and celebration." He turned to the three Rescuers and opened his arms. "Allow me to personally say welcome home, my children. You have been missed."

"Thank you, Father," the three said in unison.

"I'm anxious to hear about our new Family members. Let's step into my chambers while the others prepare the feast."

The three Rescuers nodded and followed Father behind the waterfall to an elevator that would take them back above ground where Father lived and protected them.

4

The Rescuers waited for Father in his study, while he changed out of his golden robes. He only liked to wear them for short periods of time, during special occasions.

Adam looked around the study. He never ceased to marvel at the number of books that covered the walls. The masterfully crafted mahogany bookshelves reached from floor to ceiling over three of the walls, except for the door. The door was lined with detailed carvings of angels and holy figures, and the knob was sparkling gold. The fourth wall was actually a window that allowed Father to look out at the fields and mountains that surrounded the house.

Adam remembered when The Family only consisted of himself and Father, when they stayed in an apartment, also above ground, and had to wear street clothes at all times in order to blend in. The apartment they lived in was smaller than the study he was currently standing in. Back then, Adam had to go to the library to read. Adam spent hours there, while Father was busy making preparations to expand The Family and their home. Father allowed Adam to read anything he desired, as long as he reported back everything he learned. Then Father would explain which books were telling Adam the truth, and which books were trying to convert Adam to evil thinking. That way, Father explained, Adam could understand the way of evil, and be better prepared to fight against it. Adam even had the opportunity to hold the Bible, once, but Father insisted it was too dangerous for Adam to interpret the holy words himself. Instead, Father shared his book with passages and explanations from the Bible. As far as Adam knew, only Father and the Elders read the Bible before they formed The Family, and no other member of The Family even saw a copy of the real thing. Adam considered himself blessed. It was a better education than any above ground school could give, he was sure of it, and the same education the children of The Family received now, in addition to the other religious books provided by Father.

Adam was pulled away from his thoughts by Clare's raised voice.

"It's not a competition!" Clare glared at Jonas.

"Okay, fine," Jonas said. "It's not a competition, because my kid is clearly the winner."

"How can you two still be having this conversation?" Adam asked.

"I'm sorry, Brother," said Jonas, "but did you see how fast my kid left the stage? He couldn't wait to start the Transition."

"Did you tell him about the Transition?" Adam grinned at himself.

"Of course not," said Jonas.

"Well, then how could he be excited to start it?" Adam asked, pleased with his trap.

Clare let out a short burst of laughter.

"That's not the point." Jonas looked at Clare. "He could sense things were about to change for him for the better. That's how smart he is." Jonas looked back at Adam. "Not like your kid who needed to be coddled before leaving."

Adam shook his head. "She is curious, and isn't afraid to ask the questions on her mind. Those are both admirable and important qualities."

"We'll see," said Jonas.

Clare winked at Adam. He felt a sense of excitement at her approval, and then chastised himself for feeling pride. He would need some time to reflect on his feelings this week in order to re-center.

The three turned when Father entered the room. He was back in his regular robes, similar to those the Rescuers wore, but he had a gold rope around his waist, and a large jeweled cross around his neck. He sat down in a leather chair behind a large wooden desk, and gestured for the Rescuers to sit on the three seats opposite him.

"Well, my children," Father said. "Tell me about the new members of our Family." Father looked at Jonas, signaling him to go first.

Jonas took on his serious tone when Father was in the room. "He was formerly known as Devon. I rescued him from his depressed mother, who was having trouble giving him the proper care after her husband passed away."

"That is a noble effort on her part," interrupted Father. "What made you feel she was unfit to care for the boy?"

"She looked for comfort, not in the Lord, but in the bottle. When I first saw her, she was dragging the boy away from a spirited game of tag on his school playground. He wanted to continue his physical education, but she wanted to get him home so she could go out and defile herself. At least, that seemed to be the pattern I observed during the past few weeks."

Father nodded, and Jonas continued. "A few hours later, she left the house in a very revealing costume. Later, I saw her vomiting in the street. Her so-called friends took her home, and left her fumbling for her keys at the door. Eventually, another person, I assume a babysitter, let her in and left. I waited for the street to empty, and looked in the house windows. The mother was sitting at the table, crying, with another bottle of alcohol in her hand. I knocked on the door, and she let me in with a blurry stare. I simply explained I could give her energetic son a better life. She agreed before falling asleep on the table, and I took the boy while he slept."

"Your motivations are noble, but are you not worried the mother would change her mind after the effects of alcohol wore off?" asked Father.

"No," replied Jonas. "She spoke of the boy as a burden to her friends and then to me. Even if she does change her mind, I doubt she will be able to remember me or our conversation."

"Very well," said Father. "I worry about some of your practices, Jonas, but you have been an admirable Rescuer, and I feel this boy will be a welcome addition to our family."

"He will, Father," said Jonas. "I was able to spend some time with him on the journey home. As you know, we had several days of driving before our return. He is full of energy and courage. I feel he will grow to be an excellent Warrior, if given the correct guidance."

"He may enjoy violence too much for that," said Father. "I noticed he was in a fight before today's ceremony."

"That comes with his spirit, Father. He was easily controlled on our journey and is capable of following directions."

"Time will tell." Father turned to Sister Clare. "Now, let me hear from my daughter. Who is the young woman you rescued?"

Clare looked at Father, but Adam knew she wasn't looking into his eyes as she should. It was a communication skill she never perfected. "Formerly known as Jennifer. I found the child and her mother leaving an abused women's shelter that I watched for several weeks. The mother was returning to her husband, despite warnings from the center's staff. I introduced myself to the mother at a bus stop. I complimented the child, who was showing an interest in the clouds."

Jonas let out a snicker at Clare's report.

"Jonas," Father said without taking his eyes off of Clare. "There is nothing wrong with showing interest in the clouds. They are a creation of God and therefore worthy of our attention. Please show more respect to your sister."

"Yes, Father."

"Continue, my child," said Father to Clare.

"The girl was asking where the clouds came from, but her mother wouldn't answer her. The woman was clearly distracted by her own thoughts and needs, and not paying attention to the child. When I complimented her daughter's curiosity, the woman thanked me and then started to cry. I suggested comfort at a nearby coffee shop where we discussed the woman's concern for her daughter's future. I explained the life I could give her daughter, and she agreed to turn the child over to me."

"And what of the girl's father?" asked Father.

"The mother and I agreed she would tell the father that protective services kept the girl. She didn't seem to think he would ask many questions, because most of his attention, both positive and negative, was focused on his wife. I gave her money to stay in a hotel that night to give me and the child time to get out of the area."

"Very well done," said Father. "And you believe the girl's father will believe the protective services story?"

"He has no reason not to."

"And what do you propose we do with our new daughter?"

"It is not my place to judge. God will lead you and the Teachers to determine her best use in our Family."

"Very good," said Father. Adam was impressed too. He didn't know why Clare came home without rescuing a child for those two years, but he knew it wasn't lack of ability. She was amazing.

Father turned one last time and faced Adam. "And now, my Adam. I see you also brought us a new daughter."

"Yes, Father."

"And I recognize the girl. Unlike the rescues of your brother and sister, your child is appearing on national news."

"She was getting attention before the rescue, Father," said Adam. "I admit, it was not an easy rescue, but I believe attention, in regards to her disappearance, will stay on the girl's father."

"It seems to be going that way," said Father. "How did you choose this child?"

"Through the news stories we spoke of. The father took the girl, formerly known as Kayla, from her mother because he didn't agree with the way the child was being raised. As you must have learned, the mother was parading the girl in front of audiences as an object in beauty contests. The girl's father also believed his estranged wife's new boyfriend was taking unholy liberties with the girl. The father was trying to protect his daughter, but couldn't while he was being hunted."

Adam paused, waiting for a question, but Father just looked back. Adam continued his story. "I found the father before local police did.

It's not hard to beat them in cases like this, because they don't understand the parents' true motivations. I found the girl and her father, and convinced him I could protect her better than he could. He said he couldn't live without her, and I explained that because his motives seemed pure, he might earn a spot for himself in our Family in time. This seemed to appease him, and he gave me the girl. Unfortunately, it appears he later took his own life." Adam would never understand why these parents gave up so easily. No matter how often he told them they had a chance to join their children, none of them ever had. Instead, they took their own lives or, as Father informed Adam, went down an unholy path making them unworthy.

"Yes, and because the girl is a young beauty queen, the national media can't show her picture enough." Father finally spoke.

"I put her in boys' clothes for the portion of our journey above ground, and used a baseball cap to hide her face and tuck away her hair. No one recognized her or gave either of us a second look. She does like to talk, and questions everything, but never caused a scene in public."

"Even though it is a sinful practice, the talent she possessed and the skills she learned while performing on stage could prove useful in the future. You have done well." Father then stood up and looked at all three of his Rescuers. "Three very different personalities, all chosen to do the same important work, and all proving successful in his or her own way; this is what gives The Family its diversity and strength. I am proud of all of you. Now go, celebrate your return with your brothers and sisters, and then get the rest you so deserve."

"Thank you, Father," the three Rescuers said together. They stood, walked out of the office and entered the elevator that would take them back behind the waterfall, and back underground to their home.

5

The celebration dinner was just as splendid as ever. Since their world was underground, they could always eat out on the dining field lawn. With their artificial breeze, warmth and sky it was always the perfect night to eat "outside." Adam allowed himself to enjoy juicy turkey, a baked potato and freshly steamed vegetables. Of course, all of it came from the land just above their home. No chemicals, no machines, there was nothing unnatural about the food.

Adam missed the pureness of these meals when he was away, but now was careful not to be gluttonous. He filled his plate, it was a celebration, after all, but was sure to not take more than would fill his stomach. He looked down the table where Clare appeared to be in a serious conversation with the Teachers. She always enjoyed getting their interpretations of the books she was reading. Adam envied her hunger for knowledge and understanding, even though they were all warned too much thought could be dangerous. "Lest we forget, it was a desire for more wisdom that cast us out of Eden," Father once explained.

At the other end, Jonas was speaking with some of the Warriors. They were laughing, and taking turns in an arm-wrestling competition. The competition was friendly, and no one gloated after winning. Instead, they gave each other tips on how to improve strength and technique. Adam worried Jonas was taking too much interest in the Warriors. All three Rescuers had their own interests, but it was their job to study all aspects of life within The Family while they were home. While they were the smallest group, and all groups were equally important for The Family's survival, the Rescuers were lucky for this very reason. On any given day, when they weren't preparing for their next mission, they could work in the fields with the Farmers, sit in on a lesson with the Teachers, work out with the

Warriors, fix anything that was broken with the Builders, prepare meals with the Cooks, or brush up on their first-aid with the Healers. Father told them that one day, it would be on their shoulders to carry on The Family, and they needed to know as much as they could. Adam and Clare worked together to make sure they were balancing their studies, but Jonas spent most of his days working with Warriors and would study agriculture and academic learning in his spare time at night. Adam decided he would pray for Jonas to find his way.

Adam sat amongst the Children. They helped to calm him and reminded him all the time spent above ground really was worthwhile. He listened to their conversations about living virtuous lives and serving the Lord, and he allowed himself to picture his newest rescue joining in the conversation.

Once all the food was served, and all Family members appeared to be in their place, Adam stood and waited a few moments for everyone to calm down. Adam had been saying the meal prayer since he was 17, when Father stopped eating with The Family. He said it was better for him to be separate from The Family, that the children were nervous around him. Adam argued separation would only make that feeling worse, but Father said it was more important for The Family to work together without him, and that this was the best way. Adam never really liked the plan, he missed eating meals with Father and talking to him about his ideas, but he also knew better than to question Father's final decisions.

"Let us pray," said Adam, taking the small hands of the children next to him. Everyone else then joined hands as Adam recited The Lord's Prayer, then he continued. "Lord, we want to thank you for bringing us all back together again safely, so that we may enjoy each other's company and praise your name. Thank you for another successful harvest so that we may eat another year. Thank you for our newest family members; may their transition be swift so they return to us quickly and help us grow to better serve you. Amen."

Adam sat down, and everyone was free to begin the meal.

"How was the mission?" asked Brother Samuel from across the table once Adam sat down. The 17-year old usually made it a point to join Adam during mixed meal times. Adam enjoyed Samuel's company, but the conversation always started with some question about the outside world. Questions Adam wasn't really allowed to answer. The Family knew the basics of what Rescuers did. They went above ground and rescued children, coming home on a pre-arranged date to keep everyone safe. What they didn't know was how the children were rescued. How the Rescuers had to move to different locations across the country so they wouldn't be recognized, find children with promise but who were also in dangerous or unfortunate situations that might destroy that potential, determine the right way to approach a parent and then, the most difficult task of all, convince at least one parent to give up his or her child. It took time, planning and practice. It's not that The Family would disagree with what the Rescuers did, but Father did not want too many of them thinking too much about the outside world or what type of life they might have had before joining The Family. The less they thought of that trauma, the better. That's why Father made a point to help them forget during the transition, so they could better focus on doing God's work. The Rescuers were chosen because Father trusted them not to be distracted or tempted by those thoughts and the outside world.

"I always enjoy doing God's work." Adam gave his usual response.

"Yeah, I know." Samuel sighed and looked down at his food. He tried to get more information out of Adam for years. "I just think it would be interesting to see the outside world again, I have no memories of it."

"You will when the time is right," said Adam. "When the world will be ready for our way of life. Until that time, enjoy your life here and believe me when I tell you, you aren't missing much."

Samuel was living in a foster home when Adam found him. The then nine-year old boy was running for help after his foster parents had gotten into a fight. The boy told Adam he thought his mother was dead, and father was dying. Seeing the frightened blue eyes, under greasy blond hair and an unwashed face, Adam scooped up the boy, calmed him and brought him to The Family. He never learned what happened to the boy's foster parents.

When Adam brought Samuel back, he was chastised for rescuing a child who was so old. Father reminded Adam that the kids should be between three and four years of age, five was pushing the limit. It was easier for them to transition if they were younger. Adam was told Samuel's transition was difficult, but eventually successful and Adam was glad, since he hated the thought of disappointing Father. Of course, Samuel didn't remember any of this, and Adam couldn't tell him.

Samuel stared back at Adam. "I am grateful for the life you have given me. I know things must be bad up there, but I also wonder about the beauty it must hold. We learn so much about the great thinkers that lived in that world. There must have been something that inspired them." Samuel was one of the few Family members who knew who rescued him, because Samuel asked. It wasn't exactly a secret, but not important enough for every child to be informed, and few cared enough to ask.

"God inspired them," said Adam. "And He can inspire minds down here just as well, if not better than the minds up there."

"I know you are right," said Samuel. "I just wonder how inspired I will be as a Builder."

"You've been assigned to the Builders?" Adam asked. Most Children were given a track to train when they turned 17. They became fully involved in The Family's work when they turned 18. Adam was encouraged in the knowledge that Samuel would now have an official role. "That is a noble and important path. You will do well." It was true. Samuel had a good mind, and would be able to understand the intricacies of the mechanics and electronics that went into making their underground world function. Adam secretly hoped Samuel would be placed as a Farmer so the boy could enjoy some of the outdoors and the Lord's creation. Perhaps quenching Samuel's thirst to know the outside world, but he also knew the risk of it increasing Samuel's curiosity. A risk Father might not have been willing to take.

"I hope so," said Samuel. "I like the theories behind many of the designs, but the actual practice is difficult."

"You will learn soon enough."

"Yes," said Samuel, staring at his food.

"Trust Father," said Adam, sensing some hesitation in his brother. "We all have a place, and our Family has thrived under his judgement."

"You're right," said Samuel.

Adam gave a reassuring nod and both returned to eating their meals.

For the rest of the meal, Adam spoke with other Children sitting around him. He enjoyed hearing them talk about their studies, seeing the wonder in their eyes as they discovered new truths. Sometimes, he wished he could've been a Teacher, so he could experience this joy every day. He wished he could enrich their minds, instead of frightening them and then having to calm them down for the journey home. He hated it when his rescues cried after being separated from their parents. Adam forced himself to stop this train of thought. It wasn't his place to question his duty or position. He finished his meal and excused himself from the table.

Adam walked alone to his hut. He hadn't been home in weeks, and he was anxious for a real night's rest. This particular rescue mission took a lot out of him. Tracking down the girl's father took extra effort. Normally, he would just watch hot spots for likely candidates, similar to how Jonas and Clare found their children, but the news story tugged at Adam's heart and he wanted to help that girl. Father always handled the logistics, renting cars and leaving them in parking lots, providing aliases with fake identification and some cash to help them move around, but once they were out in the world, it was up to the Rescuers to find the children and bring them to their new home without being caught. For Adam, that meant living in rescue missions or sleeping outdoors. Living as a homeless person allowed him to fly under the radar and very few people paid attention to him. It also allowed him to assess the character of parents while determining if they deserved to keep their children. It wasn't until the last week when he would check into the motel Father would reserve for him so Adam could shower and make himself presentable to speak with the parents directly. Father picked the regions and public places to help ensure no parents of formerly rescued children, or anyone else who might recognize him, would be nearby.

The lights that simulated day in Adam's underground home dimmed and now gave the impression of twilight. It was just light enough for Adam to see Clare entering her hut. It was next to his, a few yards from the tunnel entrance that brought him home. Each Rescuer had their own hut, but they lived next to each other. Just like the Teachers, Farmers, Builders, Cooks, Healers and Warriors had their own blocks of huts. The Children lived together in dormitory huts near the Teachers on the other side of the tunnel entrance. The Warriors lived on the other side of the western archway, also next to Father's waterfall. On the other side of the waterfall lived the Builders, Healers and Cooks. Finally, the Farmers lived near the eastern tunnel that delivered them to the fields.

Adam was surprised he hadn't noticed Clare leave the banquet, but supposed she was just as tired as he was. He fought the urge to go talk to her, she would consider it inappropriate this late at night, and walked directly to his own hut.

Adam felt his way toward his bed and the lamp next to it when he entered the dark room. It was a small lamp, but it filled Adam's room with light. His room was neatly organized with the bed and nightstand against one wall, and a desk and chair on the opposite side. A door next to the desk led to Adam's bathroom. A wardrobe stood on the other side of the door, holding Adam's few possessions, including extra robes, books, and the rock that Father said convinced him to rescue Adam and start a new Family.

Adam lay on the bed. His eyelids started to feel heavy, when there was a knock at his door. He got up to answer it. Sister Clare was standing in the doorway.

"Hello, sister," said Adam. He tried to conceal his surprise. Sister Clare rarely visited him, and never at night. Not only that, but Adam couldn't remember ever seeing her with her hair down; it flowed down to her chest. Adam forced himself to look away from her hair and back to her eyes, which were strained.

"Hello, brother," she answered. "May I trouble you for a few moments?"

Adam smiled. "You are never trouble." He walked out of his hut. "Would you care to walk?"

Clare nodded and walked alongside Adam in the direction of the gardens near the Farmer's huts. "I'm concerned about Brother Jonas."

Adam felt his heart skip a beat. "How so?"

"He seems to become more obsessed with the Warriors every year," Clare said. "And now he's starting to rescue children through," she paused for a moment "questionable practices. I worry he's becoming too aggressive for a Rescuer."

Adam nodded. "I admit, I have been concerned with the amount of time Jonas spends with the Warriors, but I cannot question his tactics above ground. That is for Father to judge, and he praised Jonas tonight."

"Yes, but even Father said he wasn't completely comfortable with the way Jonas rescued that boy. I feel, as his fellow Rescuers, it is our duty to steer him back on the correct path."

"You may be right," said Adam. "But I fear taking any action without consulting with Father. As he said tonight, we three are different for good reason."

"You can talk to him," said Clare. "He will listen to you, and guide us."

"You seem very eager to help Brother Jonas," said Adam. He felt his heart speed up. "Is there a reason you're taking extra interest in his activities?"

"I just want what is best for my ..." Clare paused and looked down at the floor, "brother."

Adam stopped walking and turned to her so he could look in her eyes. Her face was turning red and her eyes were shaking as though she was about to cry. It was a look he usually saw in children he rescued, not his sister. Adam tried to remember a time when Clare was this upset, but nothing came to him. She was usually so quiet and reserved, unless talking about books, but then her face would light up and smile.

"My dear sister," said Adam softly. "I had no idea you cared for him so. To be honest, I thought you were, at best, indifferent to Brother Jonas."

"I was." Clare's voice cracked. "But I now know I need to take more interest in all my brothers and sisters."

Hearing her voice, Adam thought he would cry himself. "I will talk to Father tomorrow," he promised. He wasn't sure it was the best decision, but he knew he didn't want to see Clare like this ever again.

"Thank you, brother," said Clare, taking a deep, shaky breath. "You are too good to me."

"I care for my brothers and sisters too," was the only answer Adam could think to give. He considered hugging her, but stopped himself, not wanting to frighten her, and instead gave what he hoped was a reassuring smile.

"I've taken too much of your time, I'm sure you want to sleep. I know I could use some rest."

They walked in silence back to their huts, stopping at Sister Clare's door.

"Sleep well, sister," said Adam.

Clare nodded and walked inside without another word. Once she was inside, Adam returned to his own bed. He felt bothered by

Sister Clare's request, but hadn't it been the same thought he had less than an hour ago? He decided to pray. Adam knelt next to his bed and asked God for guidance. He prayed for an understanding into his seemingly unexplainable feelings, for guidance on how best to help Brother Jonas, and for Sister Clare to have some peace of mind. He ended the prayer as he ended all of his prayers, "And give me the strength to lead in a way that honors You, My Lord, if and when the time comes."

Finally, Adam undressed and got under his covers. He turned off the light and expected to drift off to sleep right away. Instead, he was up for hours, thinking of Sister Clare's face fighting back tears.

6

At first, Adam didn't want to open his eyes. He thought he was still in the outside world, and didn't want to welcome the day. He was tired, and just wanted to stay in bed. Then, he felt the morning light creep through his window and uncover the familiar and friendly space. Normally, Adam would be elated by the prospect of his first full day home, but he was still troubled by the task ahead of him. He agreed Jonas needed to refocus his energies, but how would he present it to Father? He also worried about the change in Clare's concern over Jonas, but decided that was the least of his troubles, plus he didn't have a clear plan of action for that problem.

Adam knew he had to clear his mind before talking to Father. He got out of bed, stretched and pulled out his exercise wear, shorts and a sleeveless top made from the same material as his robes. He would run barefoot, and appreciate the cleanliness and softness of his home. Exercise always helped him think.

His spirits lightened the instant he stepped outside. The lights simulated the sun's morning rise, and there was a pink hue to the morning. How could he possibly be troubled when there was so much beauty in his world? The rest of The Family would be up soon for breakfast and to begin their days. Adam planned to eat alone, as he usually did, and knew if he started now, he would also have most of the exercise yard to himself.

The yard was on the other side of the fields, near the Warrior huts, about three miles away if he went diagonally and past the chapel that marked the center of their underground world. If he ran that way, he would avoid passing any of the other huts too closely and waking someone. Adam started his jog, letting his mind clear and feeling his body relax as his feet pounded the ground. The air wasn't as clean as he remembered it. It felt stale and heavy.

Adam had a flash of running along a beach in the outer world. He went out at sunrise as usual, when only one or two others would be there. The wind would push back his hair, cooling his head like a mother nursing a sick child. The crashing waves, morning birds and beat of his feet against the sand created the perfect soundtrack to forget where he was and his reason for being there. It was the only time of day he didn't miss home. On that particular morning he remembered, there was a service of some kind being held on the beach. For the first time, Adam heard someone other than Father preaching the Lord's word. Only this man's message was one of hope, of forgiveness and charity.

"But love your enemies, do good to them, and lend to them without expecting to get anything back. Then your reward will be great, and you will be children of the Most High, because he is kind to the ungrateful and wicked. Be merciful just as your Father is merciful." It was those lines that stuck with Adam. He hadn't heard them before, and knew they were not in Father's book.

Father always said the Lord loved his sheep, but this message was different. At the time, Adam had to force himself to stop listening, remembering that those in the outer world tended to corrupt the Lord's message for their own self-interests and he couldn't allow himself to be tempted into their sinful ways.

Once again, Adam shocked himself back to reality and eliminated the warm, fluttery feeling in his chest. If he was missing any part of the outside world, he was clearly out of balance. That was a world of sinfulness and confusion, he was in a world of safety and clarity. Adam tried to focus on the rustling grains in the underground fields, and the sounds of Children waking. But the grains only moved when others walked through them, and the Children were taught to start their mornings with silent reflection. The morning was as silent as a tomb.

A few Warriors were already in the yard when he arrived; doing their morning calisthenics. Adam, still wanting solitude, ran to the other end of the yard to begin his workout. He didn't allow himself any breaks, or time to think. His thoughts disturbed him, and this was his chance for escape. After about fifty push-ups, he entered the obstacle course where he ran tires, scaled walls, crawled across a rope bridge, and ended the workout by swimming twenty laps in a small lake. It was a light workout, but Adam was out of shape after being above ground. He ran back to his hut to shower and eat. Now he was ready to take on the day.

Adam ate his breakfast of eggs, toast and freshly squeezed orange juice in his hut while reading passages from Father's book of daily reflections. The goodness of The Lord gave him strength; knowing he was doing God's work gave him purpose; and believing he was following in Christ's footsteps gave him courage.

"The Lord is my shepherd, I shall not be in want.
He makes me lie down in green pastures,
 he leads me beside quiet waters, he restores my soul.
He guides me in paths of righteousness for his name's sake.
Even though I walk through the valley of the shadow of death,
I will fear no evil, for you are with me,
your rod and your staff, they comfort me.
You prepare a table for me in the presence of my enemies.
You anoint my head with oil; my cup overflows.
Surely goodness and love will follow me all the days of my life,
and I will dwell in the house of the Lord forever."

Adam took a deep breath, reminding himself he did have green pastures and calm waters in his underground home, and above him lay the valley of death where he did eat with his enemies. Now, was the time to dwell with the Lord.

Adam left his hut, determined to rid himself of the uneasiness that set in since his homecoming, and to return to his path with the same unquestioning loyalty he had just days before.

He turned toward the waterfall. He was one of the few Family members allowed into Father's chambers uninvited. As he walked, he saw Sister Clare returning from the gathering area.

"Good morning, sister," he said.

"Good morning, brother. Are you on your way to breakfast? It's a little late for you."

"No, I ate in my hut this morning. I'm off to speak with Father."

"Thank you. I'm sorry I came to you so troubled last night. I should be stronger in my faith." Clare's eyes began to shimmer and she looked at the ground, but when she looked up, her cheeks were dry. He was grateful he didn't have to watch her cry.

"It was no trouble. The Family is here to support each other in times of crisis. If I'm being honest, I'm troubled by Brother Jonas' inclination toward the Warriors as well. I know Father will help calm both our worries."

"I pray you are right," she said. Her mouth twitched into a tight smile. "Now, I must begin my studies. The Teachers suggested I read some of Father's selected bible passages to help clear my mind and forget my troubles."

"It's good advice." Adam put his hand on her shoulder, wanting to touch and calm her. He just wanted to help ease her pain. "I find particular comfort in Psalm 23."

"That's my favorite as well." She looked into his eyes. "Please, let me know what Father says. I fear no amount of study will calm me until you return."

Adam felt as though she punched him in the chest. This wasn't the Clare he knew. She never questioned the ability of the Lord's word to bring answers or, at least, solace in times of need. Was her worry over Jonas so great? Or was there something else troubling her?

"Is there anything else you wish to discuss, before I go?" He hoped there was.

"No, but please find me when you return. I plan to study in my hut today."

"Very well, bless you, sister."

"And you, brother." She turned and walked to her hut without another word. Her back was straight, her stride determined, but her shoulders were uneven, as though carrying a burden that just became too heavy.

7

The study was empty when Adam entered. He knew Father was awake; he was the one who taught Adam to start the day with the sun. Adam rang the bell by the study door and waited for Father to make it through the rest of the house. Father entered a few minutes later, wearing the same casual robes he had the night before.

"Good morning, my son." Father embraced Adam before going behind his desk to sit down. "What is it that brings you to me this morning?"

"Brother Jonas, Father."

"Brother Jonas sent you to me?" Father raised an eyebrow.

"No, I came to speak with you about Brother Jonas."

"If you have problems with any member of The Family, you should try to solve them with that person before coming to me. You know that, Adam." Father held Adam's eyes in a steady stare.

Adam knew this would be Father's response. The two talked often, and Adam knew how Father expected him to address concerns or disputes. Normally, Adam would have prayed more and possibly discussed his concerns with Brother Jonas, but Clare's distress made the issue feel more immediate.

"Yes, Father, but I'm not sure if there is a problem, and if there is, I need guidance in how to approach it."

"You should pray," answered Father.

"I have, Father, but I feel I need your guidance in this matter."

"Very well." Father sat back in his chair. "I will hear what you have to say, but I may not counsel you. Not unless I feel it is something you truly cannot handle on your own."

"Thank you, Father," said Adam. He took a deep breath. "I fear Brother Jonas is too involved with the Warriors. He is not balancing his studies, and I worry that the Warrior training is affecting his work as a Rescuer. He is becoming more forceful, which you yourself questioned last night. However, you also said we three were chosen for our differences."

"Do not all three of you unbalance your studies? Sister Clare spends more time reading than anything else. And you, my son, choose solitude over the exchange of ideas or camaraderie of sport."

"Yes, Father. This is why I came to you. I'm not sure it is my place to question how another Rescuer spends his time. If not for Sister Clare sharing in my concern, I may have given myself more time for prayer."

"And why does her distress move up your timetable?"

"Is it not my duty to show concern for fellow Family members?" asked Adam. It seemed to be the correct response.

"Yes, but you say patience and prayer would be your first choice. Why not advise her of the same?"

It was a good point. One Adam hadn't thought of. He just wanted to make Sister Clare's pain go away. "She seems to be hurting more than I would expect. It could affect her studies and therefore her ability to do our work." Adam felt more convinced of this reasoning as he said it out loud, giving him courage to continue. "Add that to my fear that Jonas' actions may also affect his work, I felt it was important to act quickly instead of cautiously."

Father stared at Adam, expressionless. They sat in silence, which Adam was used to doing. Father liked to think things through before speaking.

"What you say may be right in regards to Sister Clare. She has reason to take an extra interest in Brother Jonas, and that is my doing. However, Brother Jonas' actions are my doing as well. They have both been given separate tasks, outside of their Rescuer duties."

Adam sat straighter in his chair. They were given extra duties? Duties he did not share or even know of?

Father smiled. "Do not fear, my son. This does not change your destiny. You will still lead our Family when the time comes for me to carry out the Lord's work, and as I said to you before your most recent mission, that time is approaching. In considering that, I have added to your fellow Rescuers' duties to assist with the transition."

Adam's shoulders fell slightly, but he stopped them before he could be accused of slouching. "I cannot replace you, but if it is God's will, I will do my best to obey. However, if Brother Jonas and Sister Clare's orders are intended to help me, why do I not know what those duties entail?"

"Just as you need time to prepare for your future, so do your brother and sister. I was giving them time to adjust to their new obligations, and allow them to share with you in their own time." Father walked around the desk to put a hand on Adam's shoulder. "For now, you may go and tell Sister Clare she isn't to worry about Brother Jonas. His focus is where it needs to be. You may also tell her that I plan to speak with him myself about his rescuing tactics, to keep them from veering off the path."

"Thank you, Father," said Adam.

"Take care," said Father, patting Adam's arm and walking back around the desk. "All will be known and make sense in time."

Adam nodded and stood.

"Go in peace, my son."

The two shook hands and left, Father out of the great oak door, Adam back down the elevator to the waterfall.

8

Instead of the comfort and clarity he learned to expect from his interactions with Father, Adam felt just as, if not more, conflicted than before. While Adam always believed he was willing to follow Father's instructions without question, this was the first time that belief was tested. Father always explained every belief, reason and logic for the things he asked Adam to do or believe himself. Now, Adam was being asked to truly believe that Father knew best. Adam knew he needed to pass this test, but how?

He promised Sister Clare he would go straight to her after he spoke with Father. Perhaps she could help him sort through his feelings. Maybe she would even tell him what her extra duties were, and therefore help him see the purpose that was eluding him. But would that truly prove his faith, or just allow him to work around his current deficiency? What if she didn't confide in him? What if she did and it put his faith into further question? Adam felt his stomach harden and drop. There were too many risks in going to see Sister Clare. This was a time for personal reflection and prayer. He would talk to her once he was stronger, and perhaps then he could help her along on her journey. On the other hand, how could he break his promise to her?

Adam made it inside his hut, without running into anyone. If Sister Clare saw him arrive, she hadn't made herself known. Then the thought occurred to him. What if she saw him break his promise and walk into his hut? Would it make her worry more? Would she regret coming to him for comfort?

He wasn't ready to speak to her about everything, but he couldn't let her worry either. He would say just enough to calm her, and suggest they talk more later, after he had time for reflection.

Adam walked back out of his hut and toward Sister Clare's. He knew he made the right decision when her door opened, before he could even knock.

"I was worried you forgot about me." Clare's eyes were large and bloodshot. She had been crying.

Adam felt a pain in his chest. He put a hand on Clare's shoulder. "Of course not. I was just coming to tell you that Father says not to worry. Brother Jonas is following Father's orders."

"Father ordered him to work with the Warriors?" Clare scrunched her eyes and turned toward the exercise yard.

"Apparently so," said Adam, tilting his head to get into her peripheral vision.

"But why?" asked Clare. She turned to Adam.

"Father said Jonas will tell us if he wishes." Adam straightened back up. "That is all I can tell you for now." There was so much more Adam wanted to discuss with her, but he knew he had to clear his mind first.

Clare seemed to catch on. "Does that mean Father told you more about Jonas?"

He told me more about you too. "We discussed a number of things," Adam said.

"But you can't or won't tell me?" Clare looked at the ground.

"I am actually anxious to discuss them with you." Now Adam hunched down to catch her eye. "But I don't know my own feelings on the subjects, and wish to pray before I do."

"You need to pray on them?" Clare lifted her head slowly. "Is it that bad?"

"No, not at all." This wasn't going at all the way he hoped. "I just need to organize my thoughts. It takes me a while to realign my mind after being on the outside." This wasn't true, but Adam couldn't tell her the real reason he needed time to think.

"No, you don't," Clare said. Apparently, she knew him better than he realized. "You are always ready for discussions when we return. As soon as you walk through the gates, you are back at home."

"It's different this time."

"Why? What happened?" Clare's voice almost squeaked. Was that panic?

"Nothing, nothing." Now it was Adam's turn to look at the ground. "I just need some time to think." He looked back up at the eyes that seemed to have grown even bigger. "I promise to discuss everything with you, as soon as I know what it is I want to discuss. You have nothing to worry about."

He forced a smile, and she returned a weak one to him.

"Listen," said Adam. He knew he needed time, but he also didn't want to leave her looking so worried. She was usually so confident in her faith. "Why don't we go pray together; the small chapel is usually empty, we can go there."

"That would be nice," said Clare. Her shoulders seemed to relax.

The small chapel was about a mile from the Rescuers' huts. Adam and Clare walked down the path that bordered the mountain wall in silence. Adam walked with his back straight and eyes forward, blocking Clare from the rest of their world. Not that he needed to, everyone was busy with their own lessons in the afternoon. The Farmers would be above ground in the fields, the Teachers studying at the large church or teaching their students out in the yards, the Builders working on whatever chores needed to be done, and the Warriors exercising. All were far from the mountain, and the Rescuers' huts.

Despite their solitude, Adam hoped to portray a sense of purpose, so if anyone did cross their paths, they would stay undisturbed. Adam stole glances at Clare, trying to think of something to say, but she only looked at the ground, her shoulders hunched. He wanted to find a way to comfort her, but he wasn't sure how. He thought of grabbing her hand, but didn't want to scare her. He never held anyone's hand, except when praying or when he led children away from their parents.

They reached the small chapel, which was empty as usual. It was available to anyone who wished for quiet reflection, however most Family members used the large church which was closer to the huts. The small chapel was out of the way of everything, allowing for the solitude Adam loved, but also made it inconvenient to get to. Sometimes, Adam wondered if the other Family members even knew it existed. The Farmers certainly didn't come out this way, and Adam took it upon himself to keep the area around the chapel groomed. He even planted flowers outside the doors, and kept the garden free of weeds.

"I forgot how beautiful it is here," said Clare.

Adam smiled at her. "The perfect place to clear your mind."

She gave him a small smile back, but at least it didn't seem forced. Adam's mind flashed to an image of Clare laughing on a bright sunny day. Her whole body seemed relaxed and uninhibited, not strained as if she was trying to keep her body from falling apart. Just the thought of her happiness made him feel lighter, and he hoped to see that look on her face again.

Adam opened the chapel door, and allowed Clare to walk in ahead of him. Her scent of soap and a fresh fragrance he couldn't quite place floated up to him. He caught himself breathing deeply.

He followed her in and watched as she walked to the front pew and knelt down, her back straight, head down and hands folded. That was usually the pew Adam prayed in, right in front of the crucifix. Now, he didn't know where to go. He wanted to stay close to her, but worried she wouldn't welcome his presence. This was, after all, a place of solitude.

Clare looked up and back at Adam. "Will you join me?"

Adam gave a stiff nod and walked to the pew. The light was softer inside, filtered by the stained-glass windows along the stone walls. Adam always pictured Heaven looking similar to this, simple surroundings beautified by soft colorful light; a place to be at one with yourself and with God. Now that Clare was here with him, he realized it might not be so bad to have others with you in Heaven.

Maybe the idea of loved ones joining you at the gates wasn't so ridiculous.

The light seemed to soften Clare too, the creases that lived on her forehead over the last day were gone, but her body remained rigid. He knelt down, took her hand (they were praying, after all) and bowed his head. Her skin was cool and soft. She gave his hand a light squeeze and began her silent prayer.

Adam started to do the same, beginning as he always did with a silent "Our Father," but his questions continued to interrupt his prayers. What tasks had Father charged Sister Clare with? Why would the task increase her interest in their brother? Was she told to mentor him? No. That was not a Rescuer's duty, and the three of them were equals, no one above another. It wouldn't be for her to care for Jonas, because The Family was already charged with caring for one another. Perhaps it would have been to encourage Brother Jonas to refocus himself, but Father said Jonas' studies with the Warriors were Father's wish. He wouldn't ask Clare to distract from that.

Nothing made sense to Adam. He tried to get back to his prayers, but he heard Sister Clare take a shaky breath. He opened his eyes. One of her hands was still in his, but her other arm cradled her head against the back of the pew. She was crying.

Adam fought the panic urging him to jump up and run away. He knew she was close to crying this past day, but he never actually saw it happen. What should he do now? How could he make it better if he didn't know what was causing her so much distress? It couldn't only be Jonas, could it? The thought caused a sensation in his chest that he couldn't quite place, and his heart raced faster. No, it had to be more than Jonas.

Adam released her hand so he could stroke her hair just once, and rest his hand between her shoulder blades, allowing a small shift in decorum to remind her he was there. "Sister, what is it? What is troubling you so?"

She looked up at him, the tears streaking her face continued to fall. She opened her mouth, but no words came. Instead, a small scream, as though from deep inside her, exploded out and she buried her face in his chest, shaking more violently than before. Adam put his arms around her and kept silent. He couldn't even begin to understand what would cause such suffering in a person. He understood sadness. He felt it and witnessed it in others, including Clare, but this was something different. Over the years, teachers and friends left them, but he was able to console himself (as had Clare) with the thought that they were now with the Heavenly Father.

He knew enough to know if he had nothing to say, not to say anything at all. He hoped her head on his chest provided her with some comfort, whether it was appropriate or not. He certainly didn't mind. The two knelt in silence, until Clare's tears stopped flowing, her breathing calmed and she was finally able to lift her head from his chest.

"Thank you for being so kind," she said.

Adam gently cupped her face in his hands and wiped her cheeks with his thumbs. He wasn't thinking of consequences or what was appropriate anymore. He could feel they were past that. "Of course."

She put her hands on his wrists, then slowly pushed herself away from him. "I'm sorry. You must think I'm silly."

Adam wanted to reach out to her again, but stayed where he was, maybe he pushed her too far. "I could never think that of you. But, please tell me, why are you so troubled?"

"I don't know." Clare stood, and turned away from him. "I should feel honored for being chosen, but ever since Father gave me the task, I have felt nothing but sadness and shame."

"Emotions are nothing to be ashamed of," Adam quoted Father, "only actions."

"Yes." Clare nodded, still looking away.

"Sister?" Adam's heart was now pounding so hard, he was convinced she could hear it. "What task were you given?"

Clare finally looked back at him. "Did Father not tell you?"

Adam stood up. "No, he said you would tell me if you wished. If you don't want me to know, I will respect that, but I feel I would be of better service if I had more information." Adam hoped that last part was true.

"I'm to marry Brother Jonas at the end of the summer." Her voice cracked and she turned away again.

Adam's chest and stomach tightened simultaneously. He had to focus on his breathing, and forced his eyes to look at the pew banister. Did she say marry? That couldn't be right. No one was married in The Family. They were a family. New members were rescued and brought into the fold. They were celibate and lived pure lives so as to not confuse their personal desires with the desires of God. What purpose would a marriage serve? But it was a task given by Father. There must be a reason.

Adam found his voice. "Why?"

The word came out louder than Adam intended, and Clare jumped.

"I'm sorry." Adam took another breath. "I'm just surprised. Did Father give a reason?"

Clare's surprise faded and sadness returned to her face. She shook her head. "He said it's time for The Family to move forward. That ..." she started to cry again. "That ... our children ..."

Adam's ears filled with a buzzing noise. Did she just say children? He looked at her face. She didn't appear to be talking any longer, just crying. He took her in his arms again, leading her head to his chest. He couldn't hear anymore, and didn't want to. This was more than he was ready for. More than she was apparently ready for. Still, it was Father's wish. Then it hit him. Adam realized he was hugging his brother's future wife. Father didn't talk about marriage much, since it wasn't part of their lives underground, but Adam knew it was a holy union. One to be respected and honored.

Adam swallowed hard, moved his hands to Clare's shoulders, stepped back and forced himself to look at her. "This is a surprise.

One that has you understandably shaken, I admit I'm a little thrown myself. Let's return to our huts and rest."

Clare nodded, but the tears didn't stop. Adam hugged her again, quickly this time, and they stood in the small chapel for a few more minutes before making the slow and silent trip back.

9

Adam paid close attention to Brother Jonas and Sister Clare over the next week, while also trying to subtly distance himself from both. He knew he needed to discuss the situation with Jonas, but also knew he needed to settle his own mind first.

Jonas, of course, spent most of his time training with the Warriors as they exercised, practiced shooting drills and sparred in hand-to-hand combat, so it was easy for Adam to avoid him. Clare was more difficult as she varied her work, and Adam wouldn't decide how he would spend his day until he knew where Clare would be.

If he didn't know Jonas and Clare were scheduled to be married, he wouldn't have noticed any difference in their behaviors. They studied, exercised, helped when needed and ate as they should, but never with each other. They never had before, but Adam felt that now they might want to spend more time together. Isn't that how man and wife worked? On the surface, the couples who appeared happy seemed to spend time together. Adam knew using people above ground as examples was flawed, because they were so flawed, but he didn't have anything else to reference.

The more Adam considered it, the more he realized he didn't know how a husband and wife behaved. He never saw a real functioning marriage before. Father discussed it briefly when Adam was training to be a Rescuer. He was told people paired up, and while marriage should be a holy union forever between a husband and wife, many times one or both sinned against the other, and therefore, against God. Father said marriage was a wonderful sacrament when honored, but it could also be a distraction which was why it was not part of The Family's life. Until now.

Clare and Jonas, of course, cared for one another; just as they cared for everyone in The Family. Maybe that was enough. But then why wouldn't Adam be set with a partner? Did he want a partner? Not necessarily. There did seem to be some significance to the "Husband" and "Wife" titles that made the individuals receiving them matter, although Adam couldn't pinpoint what it was. It must be there, otherwise why would he and Sister Clare have such strong emotions about it?

Adam still hadn't talked to Jonas about his new task. Jonas definitely didn't seem as put upon as Sister Clare, he seemed the same confident and active man as he was before the assignment.

There was also the expectation of children. That fact sent Adam's thoughts into a tailspin. He knew how babies were created, but they were never created within The Family. Sexual desires were impure. When boys' bodies started to change, their urges were explained to them as distractions from Satan to keep them from focusing on God's work. Women were beautiful, and had the ability to create life. They were to be respected for that ability, but no action should be taken against the purity of female Family members. Several times, more than he cared to admit, Adam found a way to relieve those urges without anyone else's help, but he knew it was wrong. He punished himself with a fast and prayer each time, and attempted to discipline himself not to do it again.

Sex was only for procreation, an action that was not necessary for The Family because they had Rescuers who helped them grow by finding new members every year. Why now were Jonas and Clare expected to procreate? They rescued children as often as Adam did. They were already doing their part.

Adam found he was still thinking about Clare and Jonas during church that Sunday. The three Rescuers sat on the altar behind Father as he preached to The Family, organized in the pews by age group.

Adam tried to focus on Father's words of warning against the sins of the outer world and how they twisted the Word of God to justify sinful ways, but his eyes continued to drift to his brother and sister who sat still and silent, staring ahead. What were they thinking?

He didn't even hear Father's final thanks for The Family and prayer to continue leading them down the right path. He only knew the service was over when Jonas and Clare stood, and he knew he should too.

Once Father left the chapel, the other Family members started speaking again and preparing for the Sabbath.

"Hey, brother," said Jonas, giving Adam a slight nudge. "Are you okay?"

"Yes," Adam said, shaking himself back to the present. Clare was already walking out the doors. "Sorry, I was lost in thought."

"Yeah." Jonas nodded. "I've been there. Actually, I was hoping to talk to you about something, but if you've got too much on your mind, it can wait."

Adam feared what Jonas might have to say, but he couldn't deny a brother in need. "No," Adam said as he and Jonas walked out of the church and away from the crowds. "Not at all. What is on your mind?"

"It's the new responsibilities Father wants me to take on," said Jonas.

That was exactly what Adam feared.

"I know you know about Clare and me. Clare told me she confided in you."

"Yes." Adam focused his eyes on the ground as they walked. Apparently, Jonas and Clare were talking and Adam somehow missed it. Perhaps it was the day he worked above ground with the Farmers, weeding the fields, enjoying the sunlight and allowing the hard labor to take over his thoughts as worries.

"I'm glad she did," said Jonas, forcing Adam's thoughts back to the conversation. "It makes me feel like we're all in this together."

Adam stopped walking and stared at Jonas. "What do you mean?"

"I never even thought of marrying a woman, let alone Clare. Don't get me wrong," Jonas added quickly, "Clare is great; she can banter almost as well as a man." Jonas paused for a split second.

"You know what I mean. There's nothing wrong with women, they just don't seem to like to talk to me much, and to be honest, I never really know what to say to them. Anyway, Clare is great, but I'm not really sure what it will mean to be married to her. Will we share a hut? I like my own space."

Jonas appeared to be rambling to himself, but Adam cut in, he couldn't stop himself. "Clare mentioned something about children."

Jonas closed his eyes at the words. "I know. That's what Father said. He said The Family can no longer depend on rescues to sustain our way of life, and that in some cases, families could help refocus attention to God."

Adam thought he heard a slip of bitterness when Jonas said "some cases," but allowed Jonas his emotions for now.

"What does he mean by sustaining our way of life?" Adam asked. Jonas seemed more able to discuss the details than Clare, and Adam was eager to understand. He was also relieved that Jonas seemed as excited about the plan as Clare was.

Jonas straightened, widened his eyes and put a hand on Adam's shoulder. "That's what we asked him! He said there won't be many children to rescue soon and that it was our responsibility to continue life in God's image."

"Is the outer world coming to an end so soon?" Adam tried to think if Father gave any indication of the ending being so near. Father said the time was approaching for Adam to take over, but Adam assumed the transition would take years, and even when he did take over, he believed there would still be rescues. What was happening?

"Apparently," said Jonas. "I don't know, Father always said we would be called to fulfil God's plan, but I never really gave it much thought. I guess, if I'm being honest, I never really thought it would happen. A failing of my own faith, I suppose."

If Adam was honest, he also didn't give much thought to the end of the outside world, but now was not the time for a philosophical debate. Adam needed practical and actionable information.

"Is that also why Father wants you working with the Warriors?"

Jonas nodded. "He wants me to eventually become the captain and take control of all training."

"You will do well in that position."

"Hopefully, we won't ever need them."

"Yes." A new thought came to Adam. "I'm sorry to say this, Jonas, but you seem more serious than usual. Why no jokes?"

"I don't seem to find any of this funny. Like I said, I'm fond of Sister Clare, but I never thought of her as anything more than a fellow Rescuer. The thought of binding myself to her," Jonas paused and closed his eyes, "of creating children with her," he swallowed. "It's a task I never thought would be asked of me."

Adam was relieved Jonas was as confused as he was by the news. "If you both feel so strongly about this, why didn't you say something to Father?"

"Well, he kept talking about what an honor it was to be chosen. I felt like questioning the decision would disappoint him. I think Clare felt the same way."

"So, you intend to go through with it and never say anything?"

"Not exactly. Clare and I talked. Once we realized neither of us was thrilled about the idea, we hoped maybe you could talk to Father for us."

"Me?" Adam stepped back from Jonas. "This has nothing to do with me. I've merely acted as a sounding board for you and Sister Clare."

"Yes, but you and Father have a closer bond than anyone. You were the first child he rescued. You will be our leader. You may be able to reach the underlying reason for this decision and find an alternative. That or," Jonas paused and squinted his eyes, "you'll be able to explain it to us in a way that convinces us it's the right decision."

"You shouldn't need to be convinced it is the right decision. If Father says it's an honor, it is." Adam realized he was saying the words while trying to convince himself of it at the same time, but the need to defend Father was always stronger than any other desire.

"But you just asked why we didn't question it. Now, you're saying it's wrong to question?"

"It's normal for you to question Father directly, but to question him behind his back, to expect others to solve your questions of faith, that is wrong."

Jonas kicked the ground. "I know. We just thought Father would take the news better if it came from you. We really don't want to do this."

Adam put a hand on Jonas' shoulder. He didn't want them to get married either. "If it will make you feel better, I will go with you and Clare to speak with Father. We will discuss his plans as a family. However, if he feels it inappropriate for me to be there and sends me away, you and Sister Clare must be prepared to have an honest conversation with him yourselves."

Jonas smiled for the first time in their conversation. "Thank you, brother. I will tell Clare the good news. We hope to speak to Father first thing tomorrow."

"First thing tomorrow?" Adam was hoping for more time to prepare his arguments. Once Father made a decision, it was almost impossible to change it. "Why so soon, brother?"

"He plans to announce the wedding at dinner tomorrow. We have to change his mind before then."

Adam shook his head. "Very well. First thing tomorrow, but remember, brother, it's likely he won't change his mind." Adam said it, hoping it wasn't true.

"Perhaps," said Jonas. "I'm going to go tell Clare, I'll see you at sunrise," and he ran off.

Adam walked back to his hut. He planned to spend the day in prayer, hoping to make up for his distracted mind of the past week. Now, there was no time for that. He had to stop this wedding. He could make up for the distractions after he spoke with Father.

10

Adam hunched over the book of bible passages written by Father, but he could no longer make out any of the words. Everything was a blur and the usually soft light of his lamp stung his eyes. He sat up and rubbed his eyes, but it only made them water so he couldn't see anything. He lost all track of time, but he was positive he was running out of it. He couldn't find anything that would secure Jonas' and Clare's freedom. There were very few mentions of marriage at all in Father's writings. The only mention was at the beginning of time when God joined Adam and Eve and that "what God has joined together, let no man separate," and in the ten commandments. Adam wondered if there would be more in the full Bible, rather than what Father selected for The Family's book, but he stopped that line of thinking knowing it was a path to evil. Father selected these passages for a reason, and there was a reason The Family didn't read the rest. Adam refocused. He had to stop the wedding before it happened and there was no going back.

Adam looked out his window and saw the gray light of morning slinking across the artificial sky. Time was up, and he failed. Now all Adam could do was hope Father would have mercy on them and cancel the wedding. The look of Clare's tear-streaked face flashed across Adam's thoughts.

"Lord, please don't ever force me to see that face again," Adam prayed silently.

The knock on his door shook him out of his prayer.

"We're sorry if we woke you," said Jonas as soon as Adam opened his door. "We couldn't sleep, so we thought we'd come over and strategize."

Adam looked at his brother and sister. Jonas stood tall and stiff, his eyes were bloodshot from exhaustion and, Adam realized, this was the first time he ever saw Jonas unshaven.

Clare looked worse. Pale with sunken cheeks, and when she lifted her head from staring at the ground, Adam saw the dark circles that pooled under her eyes. But her hair was still in a neat bun.

Then he saw they were holding hands.

"You two have been together all night?" Adam tried to keep judgement or whatever it was he felt creeping up his throat out of his voice.

"We were studying in the church." Jonas shook his head and let go of Clare's hand. "We were looking for anything that might get us out of this."

Adam moved away from the door to let them inside. "You didn't wake me. I couldn't sleep either."

Jonas refused to sit in the chair Adam offered him. "Is that a good thing or a bad thing?"

"I haven't found anything that would ensure the end of your wedding." Adam tried to focus his eyes on Jonas. Still, he could sense Clare's disappointment as she slowly lowered herself onto the chair instead.

"So, there's no hope," said Jonas, not letting go of his perfect posture.

"There is always hope." Adam forced himself to look at both of them when he said this. "It's possible Father will hear your request and grant your wish. I can't imagine he wants to cause either of you unnecessary distress."

"Why else would he ask this of us?" Clare's weak voice echoed in Adam's ears. It was the first time he heard her voice since they were in the chapel together.

"He may have thought you would see it as an honor and a blessing." Adam's desperate need to comfort her forced him to kneel down and hold her hands. "It may never have occurred to him that you two wouldn't want to get married."

Jonas let out a sarcastic snort.

Adam stood up, anger and frustration rising in his chest. He didn't agree with what was happening, but he couldn't permit Jonas to be disrespectful. "That attitude will not help your cause, Brother Jonas," Adam said through gritted teeth. "You need to make it clear that you don't want to do this because you feel it is wrong; not because you feel like acting an insolent child and disobeying Father just to disobey him."

"Why would he ever think we would want to do this?" Jonas raised his voice. "It's clearly a punishment. I just don't know what I did wrong to deserve it."

"What you did wrong?" Clare stood up, some color returning to her cheeks. "What about me? I have done everything ever asked of me, and now he expects me to bear your children. When all I've ever wanted was a quiet life of study and reflection."

"He knows neither of us want this," said Jonas. "It's some sick and twisted game he's playing."

Adam pushed Jonas. "You are teetering on blasphemy!" He struggled to keep his voice low in case anyone was out early in the morning.

Jonas looked up, his face red, but his eyes looked hurt. "What am I supposed to believe?"

Clare started to cry.

Adam took a deep breath to calm himself. "You are supposed to believe that Father is wiser than you. That he is doing what is best for The Family."

"Then why agree to help us?" asked Jonas.

"Because while he is great, he is not God." Adam put a hand on Clare's shaking shoulders. "He is capable of making mistakes."

"Yeah, well." Jonas crossed his arms. "Let's just hope he knows that."

"Jonas." Adam wasn't angry anymore, but he spoke sternly. "I apologize for losing my temper, but you must lose that attitude. It's important if you have any hope of stopping this marriage."

Clare stopped crying and looked up at Adam. "Do you really think he'll change his mind?"

"If he believes your reasons for not wanting to marry are pure, and not only for selfish reasons, then yes, I do think he will listen to you with an open heart and mind." Adam squeezed Clare's shoulder. "He does love us. If nothing else, hold onto that."

Clare nodded, straightening her posture and her wrinkled shirt. "Yes, that's true." She looked at Jonas. "We cannot lose faith, simply because we disagree. God doesn't give us anything we can't handle."

"Well, I can't handle this," said Jonas.

"Then God won't make you go through with it," said Clare.

Jonas walked over to Adam and Clare, putting his arm around Adam. "Then let's go do this." He let his lips move into the first small grin of the morning.

Adam gave a short nod. "Good. Why don't you both go clean up and try to get a little sleep. We will have full light in about an hour. We will meet at the waterfall and break our fast above ground with Father."

11

Adam forced himself to wait in his hut for the full hour. He needed to keep control of the situation. Jonas and Clare were too emotional, and risked sending the wrong signals to Father. Adam needed to be the one to keep a clear head.

As expected, Jonas and Clare were waiting for him at the waterfall. He knew neither tried to sleep, but they changed their clothes and Jonas was back to his clean-shaven self.

"Are you ready?" asked Adam.

"As ready as we'll ever be," said Jonas.

"Good, just remember to keep a cool head." Adam tried to give Jonas a meaningful look.

Jonas raised his hands in mock surrender. "I'll let you do most of the talking."

Adam allowed himself to smile. At least Jonas was feeling more confident, it helped Adam feel better about what they were about to do. He grabbed both Jonas' and Clare's hands and the three walked behind the waterfall and into the elevator.

When they arrived in Father's office, he was already sitting at a small table, set for breakfast for four.

Adam was surprised by the morning addition. "Are you expecting someone, Father?"

Father looked up from his newspaper. "The three of you, as a matter of fact. Honestly, I didn't think you'd be able to wait this long to come to me. The eggs may be a little cold."

Adam felt both Jonas and Clare tighten around him. "How did you know we would be here?" Adam tried to settle the fear and nerves that were bubbling up inside of him.

"My sons, my daughter." Father smiled kindly at them. "I know you." He paused. "Now, please sit before the eggs really do get cold."

Adam didn't know how to respond, so he walked to the table, sat down and started filling his plate with eggs, bacon, toast and fruit. It wasn't until he was half through his food that he realized Jonas and Clare made it to the table and were eating as well.

Adam was uncomfortable, not knowing how Father would react to the knowledge they were plotting against him. But he didn't seem angry. Adam kept eating, trying to bury his anxiety with food.

After everyone finished their silent meal, Father spoke again. "Now, you want to talk to me about the upcoming nuptials."

Adam looked at Jonas and Clare, sitting on either side of him. Then he looked Father in the eye. "Father, we know you are wise and want what is best for The Family."

"Yes."

"We understand and appreciate that. However, it is causing my brother and sister great torment. They have grown up, being taught that they should devote themselves to God. Now they're being asked to marry and split some of that devotion."

"They are not being asked to split their devotion." Father shook his head. "On the contrary, the wedding is a public demonstration of their devotion. It shows they are willing to put their own desires aside to do what is best for our Family and God. This marriage will strengthen their faith and allow them to grow spiritually together."

"Yes." Adam could feel his voice starting to shake. He knew Father would always out-argue him, but Adam believed he was in the right this one time. "But this marriage." He searched for the right words. "It is causing such distress in both of them. I fear they will not be able to grow together."

"They must take control of those emotions." Father switched his focus to Jonas and Clare. "I know this is scary right now." He spoke in a calm voice. "But you will grow to learn it is for the best."

An image of a younger Father in a dark room flashed in Adam's memory. He felt sick to his stomach.

Clare's weak voice took Adam out of the memory. "It doesn't feel that way."

"I know," said Father. "But have I ever led you down the wrong path before?"

Clare looked back down at the floor.

"And Jonas, I have supported you since you were a child. Can you not do this for me?"

Jonas returned Father's stare. "It just doesn't feel like the honor you say it is. Instead, it feels unnatural. Against God's will."

"I know, but it will come to feel natural because it is. Once Clare bears you a child, you will know what an honor it is."

"Why not me?" Adam couldn't stop himself from shouting. The shocked look on everyone's face gave him a moment to collect himself. "I mean," he cleared his throat and started again. "If I am to lead, and this is the future of our Family, why not have me marry Clare?" Adam glanced at Clare and saw her face grow even paler than he ever imagined was possible. "Or someone," he added quickly.

"My son," said Father. "I told you I have plans for you."

"You want to get married?" said Clare.

"I, well ..." Adam didn't have an answer he could give them.

The corner of Father's mouth twitched up. "My son, I suppose you do deserve an explanation." He stood up. "I didn't choose a wife for you, because I need you to be a father to all of our children. You can't risk people thinking you have favorites. You, like me, must love everyone equally."

Adam looked at Jonas, who patted him lightly on the back. He couldn't bring himself to look at Clare.

"I know it is a lot for you all to take in, right now," said Father. "However, I have faith the three of you will see my vision in time. Adam will be a second father to The Family, their spiritual and moral leader. Jonas will act as a more down-to-earth mentor; the one who encourages The Family on a daily basis, and protects them. He will take charge of the Warriors, and lead them into battle when the time is right. Finally, Clare will be mother, caregiver and teacher to them. I believe raising her own biological children will serve to bring out more of those mothering instincts. I also believe that Children born of Clare and Jonas will be ideal leaders of the future."

A sense of great responsibility and panic were battling inside of Adam. "Why now?" Yes, he always knew he would take over for Father, but to be a second Father? The weight of responsibility came crushing down on him and he had to fight his own muscles to stay upright. When he allowed the thought of leading to cross his mind, he pictured checking the electrical circuits with the Builders and rationing food with the Farmers. Taking over as The Family's spiritual leader was one thing he never considered.

Father smiled. "I could never hide anything from you. The time to bring our message to the world is near. After the wedding, I will leave and it will be time for you, Adam, to take my place."

Adam's heart began to race. Deep down, he knew he never truly believed this day would come, he never expected Father to leave, and certainly not this quickly. "But I'm not ready," said Adam. "I haven't been fully trained."

"You are the most devoted of God's servants, and most loyal to me, no one is more prepared to take this on than you."

Adam shook his head. It wasn't true, there must be someone better suited. "What about one of the other Elders? They are respected, and built this world with you. Surely one of them could—"

Father cut him off by raising a hand. "The Elders agree that you should lead. They joined me to help build a better world and to help them on their spiritual paths, but they also know the outside world corrupted their hearts. Only your generation and the one you rescued are pure enough to take us to the next step."

"But why must you leave?" asked Adam in a whisper.

"The outside world needs cleansing," said Father. "It is our calling to do God's will and set things right."

70

This news surprised Adam. As much as he disliked that world, and all it stood for, he didn't believe their work there was done. "It can't be time yet. There are still so many we haven't rescued."

"How many would be enough for you, my son? We can't save them all. Trust in God to do that." Father looked at his three children. "The three of you have done well. Now it is time for The Family to create life of its own. Adam, once I'm gone, it will be up to you to match the couples in our Family. Clare and Jonas will serve as an example to the rest of them. It will be vital for the future of humanity that our Family grow."

Adam couldn't look at Jonas and Clare to see their reactions. He was too busy trying to control his own. It couldn't be time yet. There were still good people worth saving. Yes, he knew the people born into their new world would better serve God, and it should be an honor to play such an important part of making that future a reality, but it wasn't. Adam worked to control his breathing while listening to Father.

"I know this is a great responsibility and a lot of information for all three of you. That is why I was hoping to spread it out. Start with the wedding and go from there. I forgot to account for your emotions about it all. That was my mistake. But my decisions are not wrong."

No one else spoke. Father was going to leave. The end and beginning were near. Adam was supposed to lead everyone to create a better future. Clare needed to marry Jonas. The three of them never had to leave The Family again, they had to lead them. Adam had to lead them.

"I suggest a day of rest for the three of you, perhaps some prayer, but mainly sleep. You all look exhausted and there will be time for prayer in the coming days. I will see you at the banquet tonight." Father ushered them back to the elevator.

The banquet tonight, Adam thought. The banquet when Jonas' and Clare's marriage will be announced. They failed to stop it, he failed to stop all of it. The elevator ride back below ground was silent.

He looked at Jonas who was staring straight ahead at the doors, stone-faced. Clare was hunched, not making a sound and not looking at anyone.

"I'm sorry." Adam choked out the words. "I didn't know." He trailed off, he didn't know what he was going to say. There was nothing to say.

Clare grabbed his hand and started to shake.

Jonas just shook his head. "You tried, brother. Father hit you with some big news, all of us with some big news. We must do our duties."

"Yeah, well," Adam said as the elevator doors opened. "Let's all try to get some rest."

Jonas nodded and walked away, past the huts and toward the training fields. Clare kept hold of Adam's hand, not saying a word. He walked her to her hut, but she still didn't let go.

Adam wanted to comfort her. "Sister, try to rest. You may feel better once you get some sleep."

Clare just shook her head. "Please don't leave me."

Adam didn't want to leave her. He opened her door and led her inside. He knew he shouldn't be in there alone with her, but for the first time, he didn't let that stop him. They sat on the bed, because it was the only place they could stay close.

"It may not be so bad." Adam felt a lump rising in his throat. "When I see couples on the surface, some of them seem happy. Children also seem to bring joy, when raised properly."

"They choose their partners on the surface," Clare whispered. She hadn't stopped looking at the floor since Father said it was time for Adam to take over.

"Jonas is a good man. He won't hurt you, and I will always be here for you."

This made Clare look at him. "You will make a great leader."

"I don't think I ever expected to have to. It always seemed like there was more work to do."

Clare nodded. "It doesn't feel right, but how do we stop it?"

Adam shook his head. "We can't. It's up to Father and God."

Clare put her head in her hands, took some deep breaths and seemed to calm herself.

"Did you mean what you said?" Clare asked. "Do you want to marry?"

The question made Adam stop. He hadn't realized it until he said it in the office, but yes, he did want to be married. He never thought about it before, because he never considered it an option. But when he learned about Clare and Jonas, it almost tore out his heart. He wanted to be the one marrying Clare, but he couldn't say it. Not now.

"It doesn't matter now."

"When you said that." Clare spoke timidly, halting her speech as she spoke. "Just for a moment, I thought, maybe marriage wouldn't be so bad. If I married you."

"Clare." Now Adam was whispering.

"I know why it can't happen now," Clare interrupted. "You are the best choice for leader." Adam could see her working to straighten herself up and compose her speech. "I will fulfill my duty. I won't let you down."

Adam hugged her and she lay down on the bed. He made a move to leave, but she gripped his hand tighter. "Would you stay a little longer?"

He didn't know what to say. He knew it was wrong, men and women weren't supposed to lay together, they weren't even supposed to touch outside of a friendly hug or handshake, but he didn't want to let her go.

"Just until I fall asleep. Please?" She looked straight into his eyes and he couldn't say no.

"Just until you fall asleep," repeated Adam.

He planned to sit still, but his own fatigue started to take over. Adam allowed himself to feel the softness of Clare's skin and the warmth of her body. A sense of security and peace he knew he had no right to feel glided through him as he fell asleep, holding her in his arms.

12

Adam jerked awake in a sweat. He looked around, not recognizing his surroundings, heart pounding. He looked down and remembered he was lying in bed with Clare, they were in her hut and the sun was setting. The sight and memory started to calm him as she stirred and looked up at him.

"Is everything okay?" Clare asked in a sleepy voice, resting her hand on his arm.

Adam swung his legs around so his feet were on the floor, and he was sitting on the bed. He rested his head in his hands and closed his eyes, trying to remember what he was dreaming about, and forget how it made him feel.

"Just a bad dream." That was an understatement, it was the worst dream Adam could remember ever having, but he didn't know why. It was a dark room with images flashing on a wall. In the dream, Adam wanted to look away from the images, but he couldn't. The pictures were benign. His name, a picture of him and Father in a park, the bible, a woman yelling ... it was that picture, that image that caused him the most pain, but who was the woman? A knock at the door forced Adam out of his trance.

"Clare, we should get going." Jonas' voice came from the other side of the door.

Adam looked over at Clare who was now sitting next to him, rubbing his back with one hand. Her hair, normally in a neat bun, was disheveled; her robe was wrinkled; and there was a crease on her cheek where it had been resting on Adam's robe all day.

"I'll be out in a few minutes," Clare responded. "I just woke up."

"Okay, but hurry," said Jonas. "I'm guessing Father won't be too happy if we're late. I'll go check on Adam."

Without thinking, Adam walked to the door and opened it. Jonas stood there, cleanly shaven, hair neatly combed and standing tall and strong as if reporting for duty. "No need," said Adam. "I'm right here."

Adam looked at Jonas' eyes widen. Then he realized the mistake he made. How would he explain why he was in Jonas' betrothed's room?

Before Adam could think of what to say, the corners of Jonas' mouth twitched and he patted Adam on the shoulder. "No worries, brother. I'll wait out here, you two get ready."

Adam nodded, still stunned at his lack of propriety and walked to his hut. Jonas stood outside Clare's door like a soldier, waiting for them both. Adam wondered if he'd ever see Jonas relaxed again.

The three Rescuers walked to the banquet in silence, Jonas in the middle, rigid and straight-faced, Clare was back to looking at the ground, and Adam, not knowing what to do, just walked with the other two, hoping something would come to him. Part of Adam had the undying urge to run, just run, away from The Family, Father and all responsibility. Then there was the other part of him that felt protective of Clare, of Jonas, and of all the Children he rescued over the years. They were his responsibility. He had to stay to care for them. Now that he thought about it, that was probably why Father chose him as his heir. It made sense, even if Adam didn't like it.

When they arrived at the banquet, the seats were almost full. As tradition at any meal that included Father, there was one long wooden table set for Father and the three Rescuers, facing the other tables that would accommodate the rest of The Family. Father's chair was in the center with red velvet cushions, a jeweled back and gold trim. The Rescuers sat in similar, but smaller chairs, Adam on Father's right side and Jonas and Clare on his left. The rest of The Family sat at equally beautiful wooden tables, but instead of golden chairs, they sat on wooden benches. What was on the tables, however, was the same, filled with fresh foods from their own gardens, crystal pitchers of water and fine china plates. This would be a feast.

Adam, Jonas and Clare each stood next to their seats. Adam wanted to reassure his brother and sister somehow, but the words wouldn't come to him. He couldn't even manage a forced smile.

Instead, he stood and waited. The rest of The Family stood when the Rescuers arrived, because it was always the cue for Father to enter. Which he did, again dressed in his fine robes. His hands were raised to his shoulders and he held them open as if taking in all the good God was bestowing on him. Once he arrived at his seat, he nodded at the three Rescuers and lowered his hands, signaling it was okay for everyone to be seated.

"My children," said Father, once everyone was in their seats. "This is a joyous occasion. I have made a decision that will surprise, and perhaps shock many of you, but I know that in time, you will be as overjoyed about the changes in our Family as I am."

If the dinner hadn't already piqued The Family's interest, this certainly did. Adam watched as everyone sat up a little straighter, craned their heads a little higher. He fought the urge to shake his head; they should always give Father this much attention.

"I have prayed long and hard about this," Father continued. "Through that prayer, I have come to the belief that God wants our Family to find new ways to grow. By producing natural Children of our own."

The Family members couldn't stop themselves. Adam heard the chorus of a nearly simultaneous whispered "What?" from every person sitting below. They turned to one another, in a seemingly confused attempt to find someone who could clarify what was just revealed.

They all knew how children were created, Father insisted they know and learn the basics of how the outside world worked and how the people in it twisted God's design to fit their own selfish desires. That was one reason The Family didn't create Children of their own before, to remove the temptation. Of course, they also wanted to save as many innocent children as possible from what was to come.

The only people not whispering were the Elders. Instead, they sat in silence, looking at one another. Apparently, Father informed them of his plan earlier, which didn't surprise Adam. The Elders and the Rescuers were always informed of changes first.

"I told you this may shock many of you. Fear not, my children. We will move into this transition slowly." He walked over to Jonas and Clare, putting a hand on each of their shoulders. "These two brave Rescuers are now taking on an even more important and holy task. I will marry them at the end of the summer, and they will continue their efforts to grow our family, but while staying here with all of us."

Adam waited for more whispers, but none came. He looked up from the table to find a sea of faces with mixed emotions of shock, disgust and excitement. A lot of emotions, but no more words.

"As I said, it may take time for some of you to come around to this idea, but I trust, with prayer, the Lord will speak to you as he did to me, and convince you this is the right thing to do." Father then walked over to Adam. "To help you, I've asked Brother Adam to spend more time with you all to help comfort and provide guidance through this transition. Look to him as a father when I cannot be with you."

Adam looked up at Father. He knew Father was easing The Family into the transition of leadership, but who was going to help Adam? Thoughts and feelings rushed through Adam's mind as Father squeezed his shoulder. It would've felt like a reassuring squeeze if it hadn't hurt so much.

"Now, my children," said Father, "let's eat and rejoice in this wonderful news."

With that, the rest of The Family started filling their plates, and discussing this major turn of events in their lives.

"I know you desire more time, my son," said Father as he sat down.

Adam looked at him and just nodded.

Father nodded back. "I wish to talk to you tomorrow, but for now, please try to enjoy this fabulous meal. You'll see I had the Cooks make roast beef, your favorite."

Adam looked at the table. He hadn't even noticed the menu. He took a healthy helping of what really was his favorite food. He just wasn't sure how he would manage to eat it.

Normally, Father and the Rescuers would talk during the meal, but Adam couldn't think of anything more to say. He looked out at the rest of The Family throughout the meal, knowing they were talking about the changes as they continued to glance at the upper table.

Adam was grateful when Father finished his meal quickly and announced his departure, because it meant Adam could leave shortly after. As soon as Father was out of sight, Adam stood up to leave. He noticed Jonas and Clare did the same and the three walked off the stage.

They were greeted by the Elders at the bottom step.

"Congratulations to you all," said Sister Agnes, the Elder Cook. "Oh, the thought of being around newborn babies again." She paused to look up with a huge smile on her face. "It's such a blessing."

"Thank you," said Jonas stoically.

"You too, Adam," said Brother Caleb, the Elder Farmer. "You will lead us well."

"I pray you are right," said Adam.

"We have no doubt," said Sister Catherine, the Elder Healer. "We are so proud of the man you've become, and were so pleased when Father told us the news."

Adam nodded, not knowing how to respond.

Brother Joseph, the Elder Builder looked intensely at Adam. "How do you feel?"

"A little nervous, but I trust Father's judgement," said Adam.

Brother Joseph continued to stare at him. "You will be fine, and we will be here to help you."

The rest of the Elders smiled and gave encouraging nods of agreement.

"Thank you," said Adam.

"Well, I'm sure you've had quite the day and could use some sleep," said Agnes. "We can wrap things up here for you and give you some space, at least until tomorrow."

"Thank you," said Clare.

The Rescuers walked back to their huts in silence. Adam couldn't stop thinking about how much everything was going to change. The Elders' excitement hadn't calmed him. He still didn't feel ready, but there was something else. He couldn't figure out what it was, but it felt as though a thought was trying to fight its way into his mind, but couldn't get in. He told himself he needed sleep and went to bed as soon as he entered his hut

13

Adam woke early the next morning to go for a run. He needed to think, to clear his mind. The Rescuers tried and failed to stop the wedding, and now Adam was to start his transition into becoming the new leader. There was nothing more to do.

Adam wasn't sure why he felt he was being punished. He always knew when the time came, Father would need to leave and Adam would need to lead. Was he starting to have pity for those above ground? As much as he despised most of them, he did accidently catch himself smiling at a seemingly happy family playing by the ocean, be comforted when he saw individuals show kindness to a stranger, or find false hope in people preaching God's word. In those few brief moments, he would allow himself to think there was a chance for that world to be redeemed, and Father would never need to leave.

They were selfish thoughts. They were thoughts that came from the temptations and manipulations of the outside world. The very reasons only three Rescuers were allowed to go there. The others didn't have the training to resist the evil that lurked above ground. They were safe underground where those questions couldn't pollute their minds. Maybe Father was leaving just in time, before the outside world finally did get to Adam and taint his soul against The Family and Father.

As Adam ran, he forced himself to remember why rescues were necessary. The evil of the outside world. Fathers who abused or were incapable of protecting their children the way those precious children needed to be protected. Oddly, he realized, he never rescued a child from a mother. Just the thought of taking a child directly from their mother made Adam inexplicably sad. It was just easier for him to separate a child from his or her parents when Adam didn't have to face the mother.

Adam didn't remember his own birth mother or birth father, for that matter. No rescued child did. Adam did know that it was his mother who gave him to Father, the first child rescued and brought to their world. Actually, Adam had to wait while Father and the Elders built their world, but once it was complete, he was brought to live underground and witnessed the growth of The Family. He was always grateful to have those memories, and smiled, thinking of the day Elders rescued Clare and Jonas, giving Adam his first childhood friends. Now, he felt those friends were being taken away from him somehow, but he also knew that feeling was wrong.

Adam snapped out of his thoughts just long enough to realize he was nearing the Children's huts, about three miles from his own. He was about to turn around when he saw a few of the Children run out of their hut toward their exercise area. He stopped and watched as they climbed up to the monkey bars and easily swung from each bar to the next, before reaching the other side, jumping down and running to the merry-go-round where they took turns jumping off and spinning the wheel. Adam recognized young Isaac and Miriam, two of his own rescues. There was a look of pure joy on their faces, and it warmed Adam's heart. They could play without supervision here. No one would harm them, they would not harm one another and if an accident did occur the Teachers' huts were close enough to hear any cries. The Children were safe.

"A perfect moment," said a familiar voice from behind Adam.

Adam was startled, but tried not to visibly jump. He turned, to see the man in robes, but covering his face with the hood. Then, he brought down his hood to reveal he was Father. Adam couldn't remember the last time he saw Father wandering in their world without a ceremonious reason.

"Surprised?" asked Father.

"A little. I wasn't expecting to see you here."

"From time to time, I come here in the early morning to watch the Children. They are a good reminder for why we are here."

Adam allowed himself a small smile. "I was just thinking the same thing."

Father gave a knowing nod. "Will you walk with me?"

"Of course." Adam took one last glance at the Children, still lost in their game and not noticing their audience, before he turned and followed Father.

"I sense you have reservations about the timing of my departure." Father never was one to waste time on small talk.

Adam was surprised to find he was relieved Father knew Adam's sinful thoughts. Perhaps it meant Father wouldn't judge him too harshly.

"There are just so many people out there," said Adam. "I know it is likely the evil of the world, but I'm having trouble believing more can't be saved. With more time, perhaps we could change more hearts."

Father nodded. "You have one of the best hearts of anyone I've met, my son. It is why I know you will care for our Family when I am gone, but it is also why you would never be able to do what needs to be done. As much as you love God, you don't trust Him enough to end that world."

Adam's shame filled him. Father was right. "I pray that will change, that I will be capable of putting God's needs first."

Father stepped in front of Adam, forcing eye contact. "God created you just the way He needs you to be. You do not have the strength to make the final preparations, because you are not meant to make them; I am. You were made perfectly for the role you will play, and all I ask is you trust that and not interfere with the work the rest of us must do."

Adam closed his eyes and took a deep breath. "I won't stand in your way."

"Good man." Father put his arm around Adam and continued their walk. "Now, while God made you for this purpose, it will be a challenge. I know the three of you normally take time to be with The Family, but soon, you would begin making preparations for your next rescue. Now, you must instead spend that time setting yourself up as a second father to our Family."

Adam looked at Father, not fully understanding what he was saying.

Father smiled. "They already see and respect you as a leader, but you do tend to keep to yourself. Once they realize I am leaving, and that you are all they have, they will need to truly love you as well, and that, my son, needs to be earned."

"We all love one another," said Adam, hurt at the thought that The Family might not love him.

"We do," nodded Father, "but as I said, you are special. They love you, but not the way they need to. The only way they will follow you without question is if they get to know who you are and trust that you have their individual best interests at heart. Usually, that trust is earned from infancy, or in our case, their rescue, but now they all feel that for me. You are in the awkward position of filling my shoes."

"No one will ever love me as they do you," said Adam, surprised. He never knew this was what Father had in mind. "Other than the Lord himself, you are our Father. I am simply a place-holder until we find you again."

"That may not be enough to keep this Family together," said Father. "I will likely be gone for years. I need you to try, Adam. It is three months until the wedding. That is three months when I will step back and allow you to comfort them in one of the most confusing times they can remember. It should be enough to at least avoid panic and fear when they discover I am leaving."

Adam's stomach rumbled. Would Father really be gone for years? Adam was terrified at the thought, and embarrassed that he hadn't considered the end of the world would take such a long time. He knew he couldn't replace Father, but he also knew how important it was to keep The Family together; otherwise, all was lost. It wasn't a matter of if he could do it, because there was no other option. Adam would not let his Family down.

They stopped walking and Adam stood up straight with the confidence he lacked. "I won't ever be you, but I will be the man our Family deserves."

"Very good, my son." Father put a hand on Adam's shoulder. "We will talk more and I promise to guide you when I can as we move forward. Now, if you will excuse me, I have to check on our new Family members, they are almost ready to join the rest of you." The thought of getting to see the newly rescued Children lifted Adam's spirits. It always surprised Adam how much he missed them during their first few weeks away.

"How is the girl I rescued?" asked Adam.

Father gave a short nod. "You were right, she is spirited, but I think she will fit in well with The Family soon enough."

"Thank you, Father," said Adam, and he watched Father walk past the Teachers' huts and toward the wall of rock where the rescued Children lived until it was time for them to join The Family. Adam almost felt a sense of relief that no one would be separated from The Family back there again. One of the many good things, he reminded himself, that were sure to come. He just needed to keep his faith.

Adam walked back toward his hut, thinking of the young girl he rescued, and how he would actually be happy to see her again. He always enjoyed seeing the ones he rescued once they were taught the ways of The Family. Of course, they never remembered him, but he always felt a special responsibility toward them and took extra care to make sure they found their place.

That reminded him of Brother Samuel and the struggles he seemed to be having. Adam was so preoccupied with Jonas and Clare, he forgot all of his other duties. He made a mental note to check in with Samuel and create a new routine for himself. Maybe if he focused on his own mission, it would help him accept the changes that were to come.

Adam found Brother Samuel that afternoon, reading under a tree near the exercise area where Jonas and the Warriors were practicing their hand-to-hand combat skills. It must have been the boy's day off since the Builders always needed someone available to fix anything that might need fixing. Adam gave Jonas a short nod from across the field to say hello, before sitting down next to Samuel.

"Don't you find the sword play distracting?" Adam asked while still looking toward the Warriors. They were one field over from the clanging swords.

"Not really." Samuel looked up from his book and over at Adam. "It's actually a nice escape when our reality seems a bit overwhelming."

Adam was taken aback. No one ever called their way of life overwhelming, at least not until the Rescuers were given their new duties. Their world was perfect. The boy was clearly more confused than Adam realized, but he knew judgement would push the boy farther away. He worked to keep his voice as calm as possible. "Overwhelming? How so?"

"Sometimes I struggle with what God's message really is." Samuel looked at the ground, his shoulders slouched forward. "He asks us to love everyone, and to help our fellow man."

"Right." Adam nodded, listening closely.

"And that if someone is a sinner, the best way to help them is to bring them to the Lord so that they can stop their evil ways."

"Also true. That is why Father and the Elders started our world, to provide a place for sinners to repent. It was only after so many denied the opportunity that we started rescuing Children, so they could be saved before evil won their souls."

"But, if that is true, then there shouldn't be any sin here."

"Humans are not perfect, we all sin." Adam wondered how and why Samuel was coming up with these questions. "But here, we avoid so many of the temptations of the outside world. The sins here are few, and easily repented."

"What if a sinner isn't sorry?" Samuel's voice cracked as though he were holding back tears.

"Is there a sinner you have in mind?" Adam was getting concerned. What sin was so bad that it made Samuel this upset? Samuel seemed truly troubled, and if a member of The Family really was unrepentant, Adam wanted to help.

"Not exactly." Samuel shook his head. "It's just that I understand if someone breaks the Ten Commandments, that is a sin, but there are so many other acts that we consider sinful, that I question."

"Can you give me any examples?" Adam started to relax. This was an area he could handle. He knew the rules, he knew how to follow them, and he knew that his love, combined with the love of God, could help anyone.

"Well, one that has been on the top of my mind lately is sex." Samuel looked up when he said the last word. Adam realized this was first test since last night's announcement.

"Lust itself is a sin," continued Samuel. "It distracts us from the path God wishes us to follow. That much I understand, but what if you love someone, is it still wrong? Marriage is a holy union, just like Father said when he announced the marriage between Brother Jonas and Sister Clare, and as a holy union, they are allowed to have sex and create life, so not all sex can be bad."

"Well." Adam forced the idea of Jonas and Clare out of the equation. He needed to pray himself to come to terms with that union, but he also needed to calm the questions and fears that it brought to the rest of The Family. Samuel was genuinely confused and concerned. Adam could tell by the jumbled look of sorrow and hope in the boy's eyes. "I suppose that is true, if marriage and children is the path God wishes you to follow, then sex is not a sin." Adam was feeling better after his answer. Maybe he understood things better than even he knew.

"But Jonas and Clare don't love each other."

Adam felt as though Samuel struck him in the chest, and thought he might fall over. It was a good thing he was already sitting. How could this boy possibly know that they didn't love one another? And how could Adam answer the question that was plaguing him as well?

Adam tried to buy himself some time. "Why do you say that?"

"You could see it last night. Neither looked happy about the marriage. Is that what God really wants? For them to be unhappy? That is what I struggle with. If it is God's will for them to marry, why can they not marry someone they love? Someone who will make them happy?"

Adam closed his eyes and took a deep breath. This boy was smarter than anyone gave him credit for, and Adam needed to provide comfort and clarity, not fear and doubt. He opened his eyes and said what he believed Father would say.

"We cannot always know God's plan. He loves us and always wants what is best for us. Perhaps that romantic love is the distraction we need to avoid. We must trust that even though we may not believe His wishes are for the best at the time, that His wisdom will come through eventually."

"I guess so." Samuel did not sound convinced. "But if we cannot always know God's plan, how do we know this is what He wants for them?"

"Because Father said so." The answer always worked for him before, but this time, it sounded weak and uncertain.

"Right." Samuel looked back at his book and started reading.

"That's not good enough for you, is it?" Adam wasn't going to let it slide, Samuel was his responsibility. They all were now. If he couldn't pass this test, how would he pass the rest?

Samuel put the book back down. "I know it's wrong to question Father. I just don't know why it's wrong. Does that make any sense?"

Adam never thought of it that way. He always believed Father knew what was best, that he knew the will of God, but he never considered what gave Father that knowledge or power. Now that the question was being asked, Adam didn't know what to say. He looked into Samuel's eyes and saw a desperate need for an answer.

"While we can't always know God's plan, we can ask Him for guidance. Would you pray with me?"

Samuel shook his head, closed his eyes tight and bit his lips. Adam could see the boy was still fighting off tears. "I've been praying and I'm getting no answers. I don't know what to do."

Adam put a hand on Samuel's shoulder. "For now, cry. There is no reason to fight your feelings. You are confused and there is nothing wrong with that."

Adam sat under the tree, one arm around Samuel, while the boy cried into his shoulder.

When he was finished, Samuel sat up, wiped his eyes and looked at Adam. "Thank you. I suppose patience is the answer."

"For now, but we will find the answers you seek," said Adam. "This news caught many off guard, but I have faith we will find the right path together."

"Thank you. I think what I need now is a distraction. Perhaps I'll see if any of the huts need repairs. Hitting a nail would feel pretty good right now."

"Isn't today your day off?" Adam asked. He just assumed it was since Builders rarely relaxed on days they were working.

"It is, but I like the work, and I'm not getting much rest anyway. I'm sure one of the others would appreciate a break after taking down last night's banquet."

Adam remembered Father's instructions to spend more time with all the members of The Family.

"Do you mind if I join you? I have some time."

"You want to work with the Builders?" Samuel seemed surprised.

"Father asked me to take on greater leadership, now that my Rescuer services are no longer needed, and to spend more time with everyone in The Family. I didn't have plans for today, and now it seems God provided me with some."

"Sounds great," Samuel said with what appeared to be a genuine smile.

The two stood up to leave when Adam saw Jonas jogging toward them. "Where are you two off to?" Jonas asked when he was in speaking distance.

Adam smiled at Jonas, who was covered in dirt and sweat from a hard workout. "We were about to join the other Builders."

"You didn't want to join us? It's your day off." Jonas directed the question to Samuel. It wasn't uncommon for Family members to join other groups as a means of release or relaxation on their days off.

"No, thanks," Samuel answered, looking at the ground, which was unusual. Samuel normally didn't have trouble looking everyone in the eye. "You all seem to be in full Warrior mode. I'm a Builder."

Jonas smiled, putting his hand on Samuel's shoulder, trying to make eye contact. "I bet you would make a great Warrior."

"Thank you." Samuel shrugged off Jonas' hand. "But I'd rather not join the full war game today."

"Suit yourself." Jonas cleared his throat. Then he looked at Adam. "How about you, Adam?"

Adam felt an awkward tension standing between his two brothers. Jonas seemed okay, but why was Samuel avoiding all contact with Jonas? "I appreciate the offer, but perhaps tomorrow?"

"You're on." Jonas gave one final glance at Samuel who didn't return the look, turned and left.

Adam and Samuel started back toward the Builder's huts. "Did I sense some troubles between you and Brother Jonas?"

"What?" Samuel looked up at him, and then back at the ground. "Oh, no. We had a small disagreement after dinner last night, nothing of any significance."

"May I ask what it was about?

"It was unimportant. I would be embarrassed to trouble you with it."

"No problem is too small or unimportant if it bothers you."

Samuel didn't respond, and Adam guessed it was the end of the conversation, but he wasn't going to give up that easily.

"You do not have to tell me anything you wish to keep to yourself, but please remember that we are a Family and here to support one another. I am here if you need me."

"I know," Samuel sighed. "You are the best mentor I could hope for."

Adam smiled. It gave him a small glimmer of hope he could take on his new role in time. "As long as you remember to come to me when you are ready to talk."

Samuel nodded. "I promise."

The two walked the rest of the way to the Builders' huts in silence. Adam tried to think of anything else he could say that would be reassuring, but without knowing the extent of Samuel's troubles, he worried he would say the wrong thing. Instead, he said a silent prayer to God that Samuel would somehow show Adam the best way to help.

Brother Joseph was the only Builder still at the huts when Adam and Samuel arrived. Joseph was the Elder of the Builders, and one of the originals who worked with Father to develop the plans for the underground world. Brother Micah the Warrior Elder and Sister Eva the Teacher Elder died years ago. An Elder couldn't be replaced, because it was their role in forming the world that gave them that distinction, but other members of The Family worked to serve as leaders and mentors to their groups. The Elder Healer, Cook, Farmer and Brother Joseph were still with them. The Elders also rescued children years earlier, but stopped when Father worried they were getting distracted and taking too many risks. Adam knew Joseph was only a few years older than Father, but he seemed much older, no longer able to physically do most of the Builders' work. Still, he was respected and continued to train the new Builders when they were assigned to him, like Samuel.

"Good morning, brothers," said Joseph as they approached. "How are you occupying your time this fine day?"

"We were hoping you could help us with that, brother," said Samuel.

"It's your day off. You should find some time for the Lord and reflection."

"I spent some time doing just that with Brother Adam. During that time, I determined I would better reflect with a tool in my hand."

Joseph gave a small grin. "That, I can relate to." Then he turned to Adam. "Will you be helping him?"

"If there is work to do," said Adam.

"Well, it so happens the Lord brought you at an opportune time," said Joseph. "Most of the Builders are busy today, and I just received a message from the Farmers that the passage above ground is beginning to rust. It's making it hard for them to open the hatch. Adam, would you mind showing Samuel where it is and the two of you can clean it off and oil it? Shouldn't take too long, so you can both make it in time for lunch."

"We'd be happy to," said Adam. It made sense Samuel wouldn't know where the tunnel openings were yet, since only the Farmers and Rescuers were allowed to use them. The Builders would fix them, but those needs were rare and Samuel was new to the trade.

Adam and Samuel went to the tool shed and collected the supplies they needed. As they were leaving, Brother Joseph lightly touched Adam's robe. "Brother." Adam stopped. Samuel didn't seem to notice and kept walking.

"There is something I need to know," said Joseph. "Are you preparing to take over?"

Adam was surprised by the question, but then again, Joseph was one of the Elders. Unsure of exactly what to do, Adam simply nodded. He noticed Joseph was quiet the night before when he spoke with the other Elders, now he wondered if this was the reason. If Joseph had more on his mind than he was letting on.

Joseph nodded back. "I had a feeling, thank you." He let go of Adam's robe.

Slightly shaken from the interaction, Adam caught up to Samuel who was waiting. Adam led him to the eastern tunnel, behind the Farmer huts, that accessed the fields.

The field tunnel was different than the tunnels the Rescuers used to travel to and from the outside world. The Rescuer tunnels were dark, with a few lights to allow them to see the way, but not light enough for the children to really comprehend where they were going. The tunnels to the fields, on the other hand, were bright, and rather than dark metal, they had clean, white walls with a rubber floor to make it more comfortable for Farmers to walk after a long day of work.

Adam watched Samuel look around the tunnel, his eyes squinting as though he were working to determine the answer to a complicated problem.

"Are you okay?" asked Adam.

Samuel looked at Adam as though he was surprised to see him there. "Oh, sorry. Yes, everything is fine. I've just never been in the tunnels before."

Adam knew that wasn't technically true. Adam vividly remembered the young boy who walked alongside him down the dark metallic tunnel. Samuel was unlike all the other rescued children. Of course, Adam didn't know it at the time. Instead of being scared or full of questions, Samuel was just sad. He stayed silent, holding Adam's hand, and walked through the tunnel until they arrived. At the time, there weren't many other children around, because the elder members stopped rescuing children for a few years before that time. Therefore, Adam took him to the Teachers before the ceremony. The rest went as usual, and Samuel returned to The Family a month later, not remembering anything, but eventually seemed to be happy and blended in. It always gave Adam confidence that he was doing the right thing. That, and Father's reassurance, of course.

They arrived at the tunnel's exit. It wasn't far from their world, maybe a mile, and Adam allowed Samuel to climb up the ladder to start cleaning the hinges and around the edges.

"It is pretty rusty up here," said Samuel. "I'll mention to Brother Joseph that these may need some regular maintenance."

"Good idea," said Adam. The truth was he didn't know much about what the Builders did. He made a note to pay more attention to how everything operated.

"I think I've got it." Samuel, handed Adam the rust cleaner and a dirty cloth. "Would you please hand me the oil?"

Adam put the rust-cleaning supplies down and handed Samuel the oil. Samuel greased the hinges and the wheel-like handle.

"I guess we just need to try it out," said Samuel, handing Adam the oil. "You want to do it?"

"No," Adam said, not giving it much thought. "You're already up there, go ahead."

Samuel let out a deep breath Adam hadn't realized the boy was holding in. "Okay, here goes."

Adam watched Samuel turn the wheel, open the latch and the sunlight shined in as the hatch opened.

"Wow," Samuel breathed out just loud enough for Adam to hear it.

Adam realized this would be the first time Samuel saw the outside world since his rescue. Suddenly, he wondered if Samuel should be allowed to go outside, but it was too late now. Besides, other Builders must have gone out in the past when hatches needed repairs, so why would Adam need to stop Samuel?

"I'm just going to oil the outside handle and make sure the Farmers can get back in," said Samuel.

"Okay, just be quick, and check for any other people who may be around before you get out." Adam felt his heart begin to race, but why? Samuel wasn't going any farther than the Farmers did.

Samuel looked around. "It's clear." He lifted himself out into the sunlight.

Adam waited. It seemed like it was taking Samuel much longer to oil the outside than the inside. Should he go out there? The wheel turned again and Samuel slowly lowered himself back down, closing the hatch.

Samuel returned to the ground and packed the oil. "It was more beautiful than I expected." Samuel spoke to the ground, not looking at Adam.

"Created by the Lord himself. There is one thing you need to remember," Adam looked into Samuel's eyes. "What you saw was the land God created, that Father is protecting. It doesn't all look like that, it isn't all beautiful. Much of it is dirty and evil. That is why we need to rescue the Children."

"But we aren't doing that anymore, are we?"

"No," said Adam. Now he was looking at the floor. That fact hurt him as well. They were leaving so many children to suffer who knew what fate. Perhaps he could change the plan once he had a better understanding of what was to come. There was so much they still needed to do. He needed to stop thinking this way. Father knew what was best, and God would look after them to make sure everything turned out right. "At least, not for now."

"Right," said Samuel.

Again, they walked in silence. Adam feared any more words could break a very fragile understanding that he wasn't entirely sure was even there. Once again, he doubted his ability to lead when he didn't fully agree with the plan himself. He knew that was his own weakness and failure, not Father's.

"Thanks for the help," said Samuel as they returned the tools to the tool shed.

"Samuel." Brother Joseph walked up to them, carrying a stack of books.

"Yes, brother."

"I have some texts I would like you to study," said Joseph.

Samuel looked at the books. "Computer Coding? I haven't heard of this before."

Adam stepped back in surprise and felt his heart pound in his chest. What was Brother Joseph doing? The Children were taught a basic understanding of computers in case they were ever to come upon one in the future, and electronics to see if they had the potential to become Builders, but coding was far beyond anything even Adam learned. It was generally understood no one in The Family would ever need a complete understanding of technology, since it would be limited if or when they ever returned above ground. After God cleansed it of its evils.

"That's why it is important for you to study it," said Joseph.

Samuel opened the books. His eyes widened. "This is fascinating."

"Not all Builders are studying this, and I would prefer you keep the information to yourself for the time being," Joseph said, allowing himself a quick glance at Adam. "It's not information we need day-to-day, but it may be very useful in the future."

"Yes, brother," said Samuel, appearing more engrossed in the text than what Brother Joseph was saying. Samuel walked away, toward his new hut, looking through the books. Adam realized the new hut was built for Samuel. Now that he was a Builder, he was allowed to move out of the Children's dorms. Adam allowed himself a small amount of pride for the boy for doing so well, but then the worry returned.

Once Samuel entered his hut, Brother Joseph turned to face Adam. "If Father is leaving, I can't be the only one who understands how to keep this place running. He's smart enough to comprehend it."

"Father said no more information than is necessary to survive after the end of that world," said Adam. "Computers and technology will be gone so we may live the way God intended. He doesn't need to know any of that information."

"I know. Unfortunately, we still depend on it to survive down here. Until we can move back above ground, and, without Father, I can't guarantee I will be able to do it on my own."

"There must be another way." Adam was trying to control the volume and tone of his voice. He didn't want to draw attention to the argument. "Why not ask me or Brother Jonas or Clare? We already know some of the information. You don't need Samuel."

"How do you know what we need? How much do you know about the risks we may face?"

This silenced Adam for a moment, and he felt heat rise from his neck into his cheeks. It was true, he didn't know as much as he should. He never really expected it to happen, so he never really bothered to study the details.

"Does Father know?" Adam resigned himself to the fact he wasn't going to win the argument.

"I'll tell him. I've voiced my plans to train someone ahead of time in the past. I'll let him know I'm putting the plans into action."

Adam hesitated. As the future leader, he felt the need to admonish Joseph for not clearing the plan with Father first, but he had to admit that more than one person knowing how to keep their world going did seem smart. Besides, if it was truly a problem for Samuel to learn, Father would take any necessary precautions once Joseph spoke to him.

"Very well. Let me know if there is anything I can do to help. Perhaps you would allow me to study the texts as well, for my own understanding."

Joseph's shoulders relaxed. "Thank you, brother. I'll see if I can get some additional texts for you tomorrow. You may be a better leader than I anticipated."

Adam nodded, choosing to take the comment as a compliment, and headed to lunch.

14

Adam passed Clare on his way to lunch. She was reading the book of scriptures, her hair back in its usual bun, her brow creased in concentration. For a moment, she looked like the Clare he always knew.

"Good afternoon, sister." Adam managed a smile.

She jumped; clearly she hadn't noticed him. "Oh. Good afternoon, brother. I'm sorry, I didn't see you there. Where are you off to?"

"I was just on my way to lunch. Would you care to walk with me?"

Clare looked surprised. "That would be lovely, thank you." She stood, and they walked a few steps in silence. Clare spoke again. "How are you today?"

Adam stole a glance in her direction. She was looking at him expectantly. "Distracting myself," he admitted. "But working for the betterment of our Family gives me purpose, hope."

She nodded and looked forward again. "Yes, my experiences here are always what helped me deal with whatever I encountered above ground. A reminder that there is good in the world, and that the work we do matters."

Exactly how Adam felt. "Precisely." He allowed himself to look at Clare. "I'm trying to remind myself that whatever personal challenges we may face, The Family will help us get through it all."

"We will get through it all together." Clare squeezed his hand before they arrived at the dining area.

Only a few people were there, but Adam knew it wouldn't be long before the rest of The Family arrived. He took a deep breath and took a seat next to the group. "Good afternoon, my brothers and sisters."

They each welcomed him and Clare with a warm good afternoon, and helped them fill their plates with grilled chicken, asparagus and baked potatoes. He smiled and thanked them. They allowed him to enjoy a few bites of his lunch before speaking.

"It's lovely to see you this afternoon, sister," said Sister Sarah, a Teacher only a few years younger than Adam.

Adam looked over at Clare, who smiled at Sarah. "Nice to see you as well, sister."

"That was a surprising announcement Father made last night," said Sarah. "How long have you known?"

"Not much longer than you." Clare focused her eyes on her food.

"So how is the harvest looking?" Adam tried to turn the conversation to Brother Caleb, the Elder Farmer, who was pretending not to listen to Sarah's question, although not convincingly.

"Not too bad." Caleb looked up from his plate. "The new Farmers have a lot of energy. It gives my old back a rest. I'm going up after lunch to oversee the outside help and we should have enough extra corn to make a good-sized delivery to the food pantry."

The outside help were migrant workers who helped harvest the crops and care for the animals above ground. The Family Farmers didn't spend much time with them, they focused mainly on smaller crops that fed The Family. Only the older members worked with the outsiders to ensure the other crops were taken care of. Those crops were used as back-up in case The Family's crops didn't produce enough. If there was extra, which was usually the case, the food was donated to the needy around the country. It was important to do good for others, even if the others didn't always deserve it.

"So, how do you feel?" Sarah was still questioning Clare. "Jonas is very handsome, but he's also," she paused, looking around as if the word she was looking for would appear out of thin air. "Jonas," she finally said a little louder than before.

"I will do my duty," said Clare, still not looking up from her food.

Adam patted Clare's knee under the table. He hoped it was subtle. He wondered if Jonas was getting similar questions, and remembered Samuel's questions earlier that day. He looked around as a few other Family members arrived for lunch, but no sign of Jonas or Samuel. He guessed Jonas was still with the Warriors and Samuel was reading his new texts.

"How are the Children, Sister Sarah?" He realized Sarah was going to need a more direct distraction.

"They are doing well." Sarah turned her friendly face toward Adam. "If you have time, you should visit soon. We will welcome the new Family members in a few weeks."

Adam nodded. The introductions were traditionally a quiet ceremony, but still important ones. The Children were brought to breakfast, and introduced first to the people sitting around them. Then, other Family members would introduce themselves as they finished breakfast.

"Having you visit us would be a great honor," said Sarah. "You as well, sister." Sarah turned her attention back to Clare. "Your young Abigail is a deep thinker. She reads more than any child I have seen." Sarah referred to the child Clare rescued the year before.

Clare smiled. "Yes, I always believed she had great potential."

"No doubt, your own child will be similar, given your love of books," said Sarah. "Unless the child takes after Jonas."

Everyone at the table stopped eating, but Adam was the only one who looked up at Sarah. He was surprised she brought up the reality of Clare and Jonas' future so quickly and blatantly, but then again, isn't that what Father told The Family to do?

"What?" Sarah looked around at them all, her face coloring slightly. "We need to talk about it at some point."

Still no one spoke.

"Look." Sarah, put her hand on Clare's. "I'm just saying we're here for you. It's no question why Father chose you for this sacrifice. You are his most loyal daughter, but that doesn't mean this is going to be easy for you."

Clare looked up at Sarah, tears in her eyes. "Thank you." She looked down, cleared her throat and shook her head. "I'm sorry." She looked up again at everyone. "I'm going to finish my meal in my hut." She squeezed Sarah's hand. "I appreciate what you said, I just need a little more time before I know what support I need."

Sarah nodded. "I understand, I'm sorry if I upset you. It wasn't my intention."

Clare shook her head. "No. It is good to ask. It's just I'm not sure I have all the answers yet, but thank you for your kind words." Clare smiled and walked away.

"Brave girl," said Caleb after Clare left.

"Still, it is an honor," said Sarah. "Adam, do you know if Father has similar plans for the rest of us?"

"I believe that Father will announce his plans in his own time," said Adam, confident his answer was still the right one.

"You're right. I just hoped that since you seem to be taking on more responsibilities, you might have more information."

"Understandable." Adam took a deep breath. He wanted to change the subject, he wanted to tell Sarah it was inappropriate to pelt Clare with questions, but how could he? Father told Clare, Jonas and especially Adam to be leaders and to help The Family through this transition. Clare was right, answering questions was undoubtably an important part of that transition. Adam needed to take on the role of leader, of father. "How do you all feel about the announcement?"

Caleb looked Adam in the eye, a questioning look on his face. After a few moments, he said, "I suppose it needed to happen at some point. Guess I never expected to see it myself."

Adam nodded and turned his attention to Sarah. "What about you?"

She shrugged. "I mean, at first, I was very uncomfortable. It seemed wrong, against everything we believed."

"And now?"

"Now, I think if this is the future, maybe we should just embrace it. I ..." She looked at her food. "I admit to having some sinful thoughts in the past. Now, I have a little hope that maybe they weren't as bad as I thought they were."

Adam looked at his sister, the red in her cheeks getting darker. Maybe he wasn't the only one who had these thoughts. Maybe his feelings for Clare weren't special. Maybe this was Father's way of bringing new hope to The Family, even if it meant crushing Adam's. Again, he was reminded of Samuel. It seemed they all had similar experiences, but the news was making them reflect on those feelings differently. Samuel was sad and confused, Adam was lonely and frustrated, and Sarah was hopeful. Adam prayed he could help most of The Family see it Sarah's way.

Adam put a hand on Sarah's head, bent his own and prayed, "Lord God, thank you for giving my sister hope and forgiveness. Help us to remind one another that none of us are perfect, and as long as we dedicate our lives to your service, we can do no wrong. Help her to know she is loved, and has the same support of The Family that she offered to her fellow sister just this afternoon." The words flowed out of Adam, he wasn't entirely sure where they came from, but when he saw the relief cross Sister Sarah's face, he believed they were the right ones.

"Thank you, brother," she said, returning to her meal.

Adam looked at Caleb, who simply smiled back. The two men spent the rest of the meal talking about crops. Sister Sarah listened politely.

15

After lunch, Adam said goodbye to Caleb before walking with Sarah to the schoolyard.

"The Children will be so pleased you are visiting," said Sarah. "It makes them feel extra special."

"Why is that?"

"They know how important and busy you are. They know it is a special honor to get to spend part of their day with you."

Adam frowned. "I am no more or less important than any other member of The Family. Including them."

"I know that's what you all say. But the three of you sit alongside Father during every important announcement. The Children know they owe their salvation to the three of you. How can you say you are no more or less important?"

"Father would say he is not any more or less important than anyone else. So sitting beside him does not mean anything more. We follow his guidance, and he helps us to stay on the right path. The Farmers feed us, the Teachers give us the knowledge we need to do what's right, and the Children remind us of why we are working toward a better future. We all play our parts."

"I suppose that is what he would say," nodded Sarah. "Still, the Children will be excited to see you."

"I am excited to see them. Sarah's comments concerned him, but he knew now wasn't the time to argue. It was an issue he would address later, perhaps when he was in charge. Now that Sarah mentioned it, it was a bit odd that they sat apart from everyone else, but then again, they were about to be in charge.

"So has Father mentioned who your future wife may be?"

Adam felt himself jump and look over at Sarah, who was blushing now. "My future what?" Adam wasn't ready for that question.

102

"Your future wife." Sarah was looking up at him.

"Who said I was going to marry?" Adam felt heat rising from his neck into his cheeks.

"Everyone. Now that Father is pairing people together, and it seems he is starting with the Rescuers. We just assumed you would be next."

Adam shook his head. "I will not be paired."

"Oh." Sarah's eyes widened. "That seems awfully unfair."

"Why do you say that?"

"Because, if this continues, the rest of us will have mates. How could you not feel a little left out?"

"I suppose only time will tell." If he was being totally honest, he already felt left out. The pain of Clare's and Jonas' coming nuptials was still difficult to think about. The dull pain in his chest returned.

"I suppose," said Sarah. Then she looked ahead. "Oh good, the Children are still playing outside. You can say hello before their classes." She gave him a wink. "Maybe you could encourage them to pay close attention in class today. It will make my job a little easier."

"Of course." Adam forced himself to smile at her, but the smile became easy and genuine, as ten Children ran to greet him, shouting his name. "Hello, Children. How are you all today?"

"With God's grace, we are wonderful," replied Benjamin, a boy of about eight who Jonas rescued four years earlier.

Adam gave an approving nod. "I'm glad to hear it. Are you all ready to study hard and give the best of yourself to the Lord?"

"Yes!" They all shouted in unison.

Adam looked up over the small crowd. He knew it was too soon for the new Children to be in class, but a small part of him wished to see them.

"Will you study with us?" asked Benjamin.

"For a little while, if it's okay with Sister Sarah." Adam looked over at Sarah.

"Of course."

The crowd of Children cheered, each finding a finger or piece of cloth on Adam to grab onto in order to push or pull him into the classroom. Adam enjoyed this middle-aged group of children. They could communicate their thoughts better than the youngest who would be somewhere playing and learning scripture verses in another hut, and yet were beginning serious thought like the teenagers who would be preparing for their future roles in The Family.

Adam sat in the back row and watched the afternoon lessons unfold. They started appropriately with The Lord's Prayer, and then into math where the children were learning multiplication and division. They wouldn't get much farther unless they were going to be Builders or Healers. After that lesson, they moved into modern history, when the Children were taught of the evils and downfalls of the world above. How they moved away from God for their own self-interest and pleasure.

Sister Sarah explained how children above ground spend more time asking for, and then discarding, frivolous trinkets and idols instead of caring for others as God asks them to do. "It is this cycle of self-interest and greed that leads them to never be happy or satisfied, always looking for something else to fulfill them," explained Sarah. "However, we know that only God can truly fill our hearts. That is why we are so fortunate to be here, away from those temptations, living happy and fulfilled lives."

Adam smiled. The Children were truly lucky to live in this world. They had simple toys, of course, blocks, dolls and some wooden trucks, but nothing that lit up or made noise like above ground. The Children in Adam's world played together, read and shared everything they had instead of living in the world of consumption and greed.

Adam looked at the Children who were listening attentively. Not making a sound. He was grateful they were safe, but what about all of the others who weren't? He flashed back to Samuel's question earlier in the day. "Why don't we question Father?"

He shook himself out of the thought. It was dangerous to think that way. His whole body was warning him against it, he felt sweat begin to form on his brow and his hands shook. He took a deep breath to calm himself and focused back on the end of the lesson.

"Okay, Children," Sarah, said. "Line up and Brother Xavier will take you to the Warriors."

The Children cheered, then ran outside to wait before beginning their physical education.

"A fine lesson," said Adam when the last Child left the room.

"Thank you," she said, still watching the Children. "It's nice to be reminded each day as to why we are here. To make this world better for them."

"Yes. It's a good reminder for me too." Adam walked her out, and waved goodbye to the Children as he headed back to his hut. He was shaken by his own thoughts, and needed to re-center. The Children reminded him why it was important they all stay on the right path. Now it was time to be certain he could keep them all on it.

16

Adam woke up, feeling calm. His time for reflection the day before did him good, and he knew the path forward. Dinner the night before was uneventful, with similar conversations and questions he faced at lunch, and he overheard Jonas deflecting a few jokes about marriage from the Warriors. He noticed Clare did not come to dinner, and he guessed she decided to take her meal in her hut.

Adam was more certain than ever that he needed to talk to Father. He needed help, and while he was open and ready to take on any challenge Father and The Lord entrusted him with, he wasn't above asking for guidance.

He rose to prepare for his morning workout and noticed an envelope on the floor near the door. He recognized the envelope immediately; it was how Father normally sent messages when he didn't want to speak in front of the entire Family.

Adam opened the letter. It was a simple request to join Father in his study as soon as possible. For a moment, Adam wondered if Father knew he was having doubts about his new responsibilities, but calmed himself, realizing that was what he wanted to talk to Father about anyway. He dressed quickly and went to Father's study.

"Good morning, my son," said Father as soon as Adam walked through the elevator doors. He was dressed in casual robes.

"Good morning, Father. I came as soon as I received your message."

"I have no doubt. I wanted to assure you Brother Joseph did speak to me about the new responsibilities given to Brother Samuel. Joseph mentioned you had some reservations."

Adam's pulse quickened. He hoped he did the right thing by not reporting the news to Father immediately himself. He knew honesty was the best policy, no matter what the consequences. "I'm glad to hear it, Father. I trusted Brother Joseph, as an Elder, would know what was best. I wanted him to have the opportunity to tell you himself."

Father nodded. "He appreciated the gesture. That small decision has created a new sense of trust in you for him. I am proud."

Adam relaxed his shoulders. "Thank you, Father. I worried you might be upset I did not come to you immediately."

"I trust you would have if Joseph had not followed through himself. He also mentioned you told him you were preparing to take over."

The tension returned to Adam's shoulders. "I did not want to lie."

Father looked up and took a deep breath. "Yes, you truly are a good man. It's why I love you so. Come, sit with me." Father walked to one of the chairs that surrounded the table in the middle of the room and sat, motioning for Adam to take the chair next to him. "I do not want you to lose that honesty. However, you must gain a better understanding of what truths need to be told, and what truths may need to remain secret for the good of our Family. Now, Brother Joseph is one of my oldest and most trusted companions, and truth be told, I planned to tell the other Elders of your future today, so there is no danger in what you shared. However, please do not tell anyone else."

"I won't, Father. Brother Joseph caught me off guard. I won't let it happen again."

"Good man." Father patted Adam's shoulder. "As for your request for the texts Samuel received. I am glad you are showing more interest in the workings of The Family. However, I do not want too many of those books circulating. I asked Brother Joseph to share them with you when Samuel has finished his studies."

"Then, you approve of Samuel having that information?"

"It's not the decision I would have made myself. However, now that Samuel has it, there is no reason to give it to anyone else. I did

107

ask Joseph to speak to me or you before assigning any future tasks that are out of the ordinary."

"Father." This was the perfect opportunity for Adam to bring up the issue that was weighing heavily on him. "I was hoping we could find some time for you to show me some of the ins and outs of how The Family works. I know you said I need to spend more time with them, and I will, but I was at a disadvantage with Brother Joseph yesterday, and again when one of my sisters asked when I would marry. I was honest and said I would not be paired, but I would prefer not to be caught off guard again. It was simply luck that she didn't press me for the reason I wouldn't be paired."

Father nodded. "I suppose some more time together would be wise. Why don't you come to me tomorrow after lunch? That will give me time to tell the other Elders, and they will help me with your training."

"Thank you, Father." Adam was already feeling better about the situation. He embraced Father and left to start his day.

17

Adam left Father's office, determined to take on his new position with the focus that the role required. He would spend the rest of the day preparing to be his best self in order to serve The Family.

He exercised as usual and took his morning meal in his hut. He would spend more time with other Family members, but he did not want to allow himself to be distracted. He would reset himself so that he could meet Father the next day with a clear head and the correct motivations.

After breakfast, he walked to the small chapel where he usually found peace. Although this time, the moment he walked in, he was reminded of the last time he was there. When he was with Clare. Images of her face and pain flashed in his mind. He forced them out. Now was not the time to think about her. That dream was not possible, but leading The Family down the right path, keeping them safe, following through on Father's dream, that was possible as long as he did not allow himself to be misguided by envy or lust.

It was lust. He realized that. It couldn't be love, or Father would have matched Adam with Clare, not Jonas. Father wouldn't purposely keep two people apart who were in love. No, he was keeping them from allowing lust to corrupt their lives. Adam was certain of it.

He took a deep breath, knelt in front of the altar and prayed. He began with prayers of thanks for all God gave him, for allowing Adam to be part of The Family and for trusting him with the responsibility he was about to take on. Then, Adam moved to requests. He prayed for the strength and wisdom to do what needed to be done, to follow through on Father's, and ultimately God's, wishes. Finally, Adam attempted to listen, to allow God to show him the best path. Clare's face flashed through his mind, then images of a woman he recognized, but who he did not know. Both images brought on intense feelings of love and heartbreaking loss. Who was that woman? He dreamt about her before. It disturbed Adam and he tried to refocus his attention on God. Now there were thoughts of the young children he rescued, their parents' tears, Father looking down on him with love as a child, the Children of The Family looking up at him expectantly and tugging at his robes. Images of his life and new responsibilities.

When Adam finally decided to stand, his legs were numb. He stretched them, wincing at the sharp, needle prick-like pains that shot up his feet to his hips. His thoughts troubled him, because they didn't provide answers. He supposed expecting immediate answers from God was unfair and lazy on his part. He had a path, work with Father and the Elders to fulfil his duty. He needed to give it time, and forget about the work he did in the past. He would not be able to rescue anyone else. Their fates were sealed. He needed to do what he could down here, and forget about the outside world.

Adam looked at the windows and the light was still bright. His stomach rumbled and once his legs allowed him, he walked to the dining area just before the Cooks started to clear away the afternoon meal.

"We were worried," said Sister Jean as Adam strode up to the table. "It's not like you to miss a meal."

"I was deep in prayer, sister," said Adam, feeling guilty for being late and disappointed that there might not be much left.

Jean nodded. "Well, we set a plate out to the side for you." She motioned to a plate with a turkey sandwich and fruit at the end of the table.

"Thank you for thinking of me." Adam felt an overwhelming sense of love and gratitude swell inside of him. A much needed reminder that this was a Family. They looked after and cared for one another. Thought about one another. This was worth any sacrifice asked of him. Wasn't it?

Sister Jean gave a kind nod and continued cleaning up the rest of the meal. Adam sat at a table to eat his food, feeling relaxed and clear-headed. He knew he needed to spend more time with other Family members, but he did enjoy these quiet days to himself. When he was done, he cleared his own dish, bringing it into the kitchen where some of the Cooks were scrubbing the remaining dishes, while others were starting work on the evening meal.

Walking back to his hut, he began making a list of things he needed to be sure to discuss with Father: How much food does The Family consume per month or year? How much do they keep in reserve in the event of ruined crops? Is there a list of routine repairs he needed to ensure the Builders completed? How should he evaluate the work of the Teachers? How would he know what position a specific Child was best suited for when the time came to assign them? When would it be safe to send Farmers back above ground? Would the rest of The Family ever be allowed above ground? Who operated the lights underground? Who would ensure they were safe above ground if they all needed to remain underground after Father left? What needed to be done in the event of an emergency? What should he consider when matching future couples?

Adam's head started to spin, there was so much he needed to learn. Up to this point, he spent most of his time exercising, reflecting and preparing for his next rescue mission. There were always logistics to work out, cover stories, determining the safest area for him to go without risking running into anyone related to a past rescue and other minor details that took time. When he did have free time, he would work alongside other members of The Family, attempting to share his time equally so he could understand their jobs and what was needed in future Family members, but he never gave much thought to the work that went on above ground to keep those jobs moving.

Based on the amount of work it took to plan one rescue mission, he imagined there was so much more behind making their little world run smoothly.

Before Adam realized where he was going, he found himself in front of the small chapel where he already spent his morning. It felt selfish to spend more time in solitude and reflection, but he also believed it was the only place that would calm his mind. When he walked in, he realized God must be punishing him.

Adam just stared at Clare kneeling in the front pew. He heard her whispering what he could only assume were prayers, and stayed at the back of the chapel, not wanting to disrupt her worship. He found he couldn't look away from her. Light from outside shone through the stained-glass windows, engulfing her in a rainbow of light. It was one of the most beautiful sights Adam ever saw. She looked up and back at him, but his trance wasn't fully broken until she spoke.

"Would you care to join me, brother?"

"Do you mind?"

"Not at all." Clare reached out a hand, beckoning him to come kneel next to her.

He knelt and bowed his head, ready for silent prayer, when he heard her speak again.

"Dear Lord, blessed are we who know you, and know you want only what is best for your children. Help us to keep faith, Lord. Even when we do not fully understand the path You send us on. Help us to follow Your path in faith and courage, knowing even the challenges we face are for Your glory. Amen."

"Amen," said Adam, looking back over at Clare. Her eyes were closed, and her head remained bowed. They both stayed that way for a few moments more, before Clare moved to sit on the pew behind them. Adam followed her lead.

"I hope you don't mind me using your chapel." Clare looked up at the large stained-glass window at the front. "It seems to be the only place I can find true peace lately."

"It's not my chapel."

Clare looked at him with an odd grin. "We both know that's not true."

Adam was ready to protest again, but her look disarmed him, and he felt himself smile back. "I'm pleased to find you here, and thank you for letting me join you in prayer."

Clare nodded and looked back at the front window. "It feels like everything is moving so fast out there. The new Children will assimilate into The Family soon, your preparations, the wedding..." her voice trailed off as she said the word wedding.

"You still struggle with Father's decision," Adam said, hoping she knew it was without judgment.

"I have faith it is for the best," she said. "I just wish my faith was a little stronger. People keep asking me questions about the ceremony, about Jonas, about what it feels like to be chosen as the first true mother in The Family, and honestly, I don't have any answers for them. I have nothing to do with the ceremony. I've never even been to a wedding. I don't have a clue as to what it is supposed to entail. There is very little in our scripture to reference. I believe Father is taking care of most of the arrangements, which is probably for the best. Jonas and I see each other at meals, but no more than we did before. I have no idea how we are supposed to start building our lives together, if that is even what we are supposed to be doing. Maybe Father doesn't expect that of us, but it feels like we should be something more than what we were before. I just don't know what that is. As for being a mother..." Again, she stopped herself. Part of Adam was glad, he wasn't ready to discuss that topic either.

"I'm sorry you are in so much pain," he said.

"Thank you." Her shoulders seemed to relax. "It is getting better. I accept my role and the part I am meant to play. Now I just have to find a way to be happy with it."

Adam let out small sigh. "I understand. I know the confidence and faith Father is giving me by choosing me to lead The Family. That should be enough for me, but I find I am just scared, and the more I think about it, the more I realize how unprepared I am to take on the role."

"You will do a marvelous job. Everyone respects you." Clare placed her hand on Adam's arm.

Adam tried to ignore the tingling sensation on his skin that surrounded her hand. "I pray you are right." He put his hand on top of hers. It didn't calm the tingling sensation, but he didn't want to let go. "Father will begin more official training tomorrow. I'm sure I will feel better soon. Perhaps you could ask for additional guidance."

"Perhaps. I will allow myself a little more prayer first."

Adam smiled. Clare was always more pious than he. She likely would have been the better choice to lead, but she would also make an excellent mother.

A hard lump formed in Adam's throat. He attempted to clear it with a cough and stood up. "Well, in that case, I will leave you to your prayers."

Clare stood up quickly. "I hope I did not offend you."

"Of course not." Adam was surprised by her comment. "You could never offend me, sister. I simply have some work I should attend to. Perhaps I will see you at dinner."

"Yes, I look forward to it."

Adam nodded and left. This was exactly what he didn't need. Distractions. He needed to plot out the list of what he needed to know before Father left, and he needed to know how much time he had to learn it all. Too much time was already spent on worrying about Clare and Jonas, and no additional time would change that future. Adam needed to concentrate on what he could improve.

He spent the remainder of the afternoon, plotting out a more organized list of questions and what he believed would be important. He knew Father would have a plan as well, but Adam liked to be prepared. He couldn't follow blindly anymore. He needed to be ready to lead.

18

Adam walked out of his hut to dinner, when he saw Jonas coming toward him.

"Oh good," said Jonas as he reached Adam's hut. "I hope you are on your way to dinner."

"I am, why?"

"Because it's apparently the week of surprise announcements.".

Adam felt his heart drop. "What?"

"Don't worry," said Jonas, leading Adam toward Clare's door. "It's not a surprise for us. I just received word that Father is making the announcement about you tonight. Everyone is running around in a panic because they weren't expecting him, and heaven forbid he has to eat what was perfectly fine for us an hour ago." Jonas knocked on Clare's door.

Adam tried to settle himself. He knew the announcement was coming, but why so soon? Father just told Adam not to share the news with anyone. Father just announced the wedding, shouldn't there be more time to process that before Father announced he was leaving them all? Would any amount of time be enough?

"Where is she? We are going to miss all the chaos." Jonas' eagerness brought Adam back to the present.

"They just like to make things nice for him." He never liked Jonas' seemingly ungrateful attitude for the hard work of other Family members, especially now that he would need Jonas to help him lead.

"I know," said Jonas, waiting for Clare to answer. "But you have to admit, it's funny, seeing Sister Isabel turn those seven shades of red." He knocked on her door a second time.

Adam couldn't stop a short laugh from escaping his lips. Those seven shades were slightly amusing.

"May I help you gentlemen?" asked Clare after she opened the door. She dabbed a hand towel on her face, as though she just finished washing it.

"There you are," said Jonas. "Now that the gang's all together, we can go to dinner."

"We're all going together?" Clare looked at Jonas and then Adam. "Why?"

Jonas gave Adam's back a hard thump. "Our brother here is officially being promoted," he said in an almost jovial tone. Was Jonas actually happy about Adam's promotion? This seemed like excessive excitement over Isabel's discomfort. Even for Jonas.

"Oh." Clare, pursed her lips together. "Well, let me just finish washing up." She went back into the hut. He caught a whiff of the marvelously natural and floral scent of her hair.

"Okay, but be quick. If we take much longer, Sister Isabel might actually have time to make an extra course."

Adam took a deep breath. Why didn't Father tell him the announcement would be tonight? He expected the announcement would come soon, but he hoped it would be after a bit of training. It was one thing for the Elders to know, but the entire Family worried about Father's departure was entirely different. Well, Father knew best.

"Are you ready?" Clare's voice once again disrupted Adam's inner thoughts.

"If it pleases God," said Adam. It was the only response that came to mind at that moment.

"Well, it pleases me," said Jonas. "Come on, I'm hungry."

Once again, the three walked in silence to the dining area, Adam just trying to get his thoughts in order before Father's announcement.

Adam allowed himself to enjoy a bit of Jonas' disappointment when they arrived to find the dining area set up and decorated for Father's announcement. True, it didn't have nearly the number of flowers usually displayed for a major event, but the stage was up, tablecloths and napkins were neatly laid out and the gold-trimmed dishes were on the table.

"How do they get it ready so quickly?" Jonas asked aloud.

"They are mindful of their duties and ready to take on any challenge sent their way," Clare said, a small smile on her face. Adam guessed she was enjoying Jonas' disappointment as well.

The three took their places at the table on the stage, and the rest of The Family followed suit, sitting at the long tables on the ground. Adam looked at the beautifully adorned platters of ham, green beans and mashed potatoes. A smaller meal than they might have on a regularly scheduled event, but still one of Father's favorites.

Everyone stopped talking as Father walked onto the stage, his golden robe sparkling. He stood before his Family with arms open wide and started with a prayer.

"Dear Lord, Our Heavenly Father, may the food we are about to consume bless and strengthen our bodies to better serve you and one another. Amen."

The Family repeated the "Amen," then looked expectantly at Father, assuming the reason for his presence would be explained.

"My children, it is always a pleasure to see you all together, happy and healthy. I want to thank the Cooks and Builders for putting together such a marvelous feast and presentation on such short notice. I know you are all wondering the reason for my presence, and I will share that with you shortly, but for now, let us enjoy this beautiful meal and the pleasure of one another's company."

The Family waited a few moments, as if they expected there to be more, but began their own meals once they saw Father sit down and put some potatoes on his plate.

"I apologize for the impromptu announcement," said Father.

Adam looked up to find Father looking at him.

"The Elders are excited about your new position, but they want to ensure you have enough time to train. They want to be involved as soon as possible, and I agreed. They also didn't want to hide anything from the rest of The Family and we all decided an earlier announcement was best. I hoped to prepare you more, but we all agreed that you are ready."

"Thank you, Father," said Adam, moved and surprised by Father's explanation. "I pray I do not disappoint you."

Father patted Adam's hand. "You won't. Besides, I trust your brother and sister, who are pretending not to listen to what we are saying at the moment, will help you as well."

Adam looked up to see red creep across Clare's face on the other side of Father.

Jonas laughed and pounded a hand on Adam's back. "Of course, we will."

"As best we can." Clare gave a small nod. "Although we too have faith in our brother."

Adam's heart raced as his eyes met Clare's. Her reddened cheeks made her look even more beautiful than usual. Adam quickly looked down and his plate. "Thank you, all of you."

"Your training will still begin tomorrow," said Father. "Although I feel it wise you come to me in the morning instead of the afternoon. We will meet with the Elders, and determine how best to organize your days, moving forward. Likely it will involve you spending half a day with one Elder and the other half with me answering any questions you may have."

"What about the areas that no longer have Elders?" asked Adam. Adam wished there was a little more support.

Father nodded. "I will speak with you on each of those areas myself, and then you may work with the leaders in each group. Jonas, for example, will, of course, work alongside you with the Warriors."

"We'll have some fun," said Jonas. "I think you will be proud of the work we're doing."

"Pride is a sin, my son," said Father. "However, I am pleased with the progress you are making."

"Thank you, Father," said Jonas. He gave Adam a wink.

Adam relaxed. At least he knew Jonas was behind him. He wasn't alone.

"The wedding plans are also coming along quite well," said Father to Jonas.

Adam saw Jonas' previously relaxed shoulders tighten as he felt his own stomach fight against the food he attempted to swallow. He looked at Clare, who wore a strange smile.

"I look forward to discussing the details with you both soon," said Father as he ate heartily. "Why don't the two of you plan to have dinner with me in my study tomorrow night? I will be working with Adam most of the day, but I don't want you to think I have forgotten you."

"Of course not, Father," said Clare in almost a whisper.

"We don't want to be too much of a burden, Father," Jonas said. "We know how important Adam's transition is, and understand if the wedding needs to be postponed."

"Don't be silly," said Father, a little too enthusiastically, in Adam's opinion. "Your wedding is equally important for the survival of our Family."

"Great."

"The three of you give me hope that all will be as it was meant to be." Father took a few more bites of his food before standing to address the rest of The Family.

Adam gently pushed his food away. He wasn't hungry anymore. He avoided looking at Clare and Jonas. They were going to be there for him, but he couldn't help them.

"My children," said Father, again with arms opened wide. "I want to let you know about some additional changes coming to our Family."

Adam looked to see everyone sit up a little straighter in their seats. It was a big week of changes for everyone.

"Very soon, the time will come for me to take an extended absence from you."

A collective gasp filled the room.

"Now, now. I know this comes as a surprise to many of you, but I assure you I have known this to be a part of God's plan all along. I must leave, as the end of the outside world draws near, in order to pave the way for the safety and true purpose of this Family. I am not leaving you alone. Your Brother Adam will take my place as guide and leader until my return."

Adam looked at their faces, hoping to convey a sense of confidence he did not yet have. They looked back at him. He looked to the Elders, who gave him reassuring nods; at least he assumed they were trying to reassure him. He supposed the fact they weren't shaking their heads was something.

"Now, I know you may have questions right now, and if not, you will likely have questions moving forward. Brother Adam will be working alongside me, the Elders and other leaders to make this transition as smooth as possible and I encourage you to address those questions to any of us starting tomorrow. For now, take some time to pray and reflect on how you may best help our Family thrive as we move to this new stage of our purpose. I love you all, my children."

With that, Father walked down the back steps of the stage, leaving all eyes on Adam. He desperately wanted to leave, but also knew that this was his first test.

He stood, staying behind the table, and lifted his arms as if to embrace them all just like Father, but no words came to him. Instead, he bowed his head to pray. "Dear Lord. I pray for wisdom and understanding to help me lead this Family and its people, all of whom I hold so dear. Help us all to embrace the changes and challenges before us, knowing we face them in service to You. I pray my Family knows I am here for them always, and though I am taking on a new role, I am doing so in service to You and to them, so that we may all grow stronger together. Amen."

He heard the chorus of "Amens" after he spoke. He looked back up to see smiling faces looking back at him. Not wanting to push his luck, he left, off the side steps as he always had, instead of following Father through the back curtains. Adam decided then and there that he would always leave from the side, not elevating himself higher than needed. He went to his hut to sleep, knowing everything would be different when he woke up.

19

It was a long morning, but Adam felt it was worthwhile. The day started with breakfast in Father's study, so Father could explain how he worked with the Elders and used them as advisors when making big decisions. The Elders arrived shortly after the morning meal to discuss Adam's training, and it was agreed Adam would spend each morning with a different Elder, starting with the Farmers, then the Cooks, Healers and the Builders. Then Father would work with him regarding the Teachers and Warriors before Adam met with each of those groups individually.

The plan was for Father to remain away from The Family until the wedding. After that, it wouldn't be long until he departed, and he wanted to be sure The Family gave Adam the respect and authority he would require to take over.

Adam was relieved to see the Elders didn't have trouble with the idea of him taking over instead of one of them. After all, they were members of The Family for far longer, and helped create the world they all lived in. He took it as a sign that they believed this was God's plan. He was also encouraged by the faith the Elders seemed to have in him. He worked with them all over the years when he wasn't preparing for a rescue mission, and perhaps there wasn't much more to learn. As soon as the thought occurred to him, he knew it was only wishful thinking. He needed to prepare for a long road.

It was past lunch time when they concluded. Father determined it was enough for the day, and he would meet with Adam the next day, after his morning with the Farmers.

One thought Adam couldn't shake was the faith they were all putting in him to keep all The Family members on God's path. To ensure everyone was fully dedicated to The Family's purpose to create a better world for God. He couldn't help but think of Samuel and the boy's concerns just days before. He needed to find time to talk with him again. To make sure he was okay.

Adam felt it was as if God was answering his prayers, when he found Samuel walking near the Rescuers' huts. The boy stopped short when he saw Adam approaching.

"Hello," said Adam. "I've been meaning to speak with you."

"Oh." Samuel quickly looked around and then back at Adam. "I'm sorry, did we have plans to meet?"

"No, no, I just had a question for you." Adam stopped himself as he took a closer look at his brother. Samuel's eyes were red and puffy, and his brow was furrowed. He was clearly upset. "Are you okay?"

"Yes, of course." Samuel straightened up and cleared his throat. "My allergies seem to be acting up a bit."

"Okay," said Adam. Samuel was lying to him, something he didn't think anyone in The Family would ever do. They never had a reason to lie to each other. Now Adam knew he had to have a more serious talk with Samuel. No more questioning their beliefs, this was going too far. Adam gestured toward his hut. "Why don't we go inside for a quick chat?"

"I really should be getting to lunch."

"I insist. Besides, lunch has passed. Fortunately, I have some food coming that I will be happy to share."

Samuel looked in the direction of the dining area, then back at Adam. "Very well," he said and followed Adam into the hut.

"Now, Samuel," Adam started as soon as they both sat down. "I have heard of allergies appearing later in life, but if you are really suffering, it is the most severe case I have ever seen in this Family." They lived in doors with very few animals or plants with pollen. There were a few cases from Children who arrived with allergies to dust, but even that was very minor. Adam knew Samuel didn't have allergies.

"I suppose there is a first time for everything," Samuel looked at the ground.

"Including a first time for you to lie to me." Samuel's head to snapped up. "I forgive you, because you are clearly upset. But it also stresses the point that something is very wrong and you need to talk to someone. If I am not the right person, surely we can find someone else."

"There is no one I can talk to," Samuel answered pitifully.

"There are more than one hundred people in this Family. How can none of them be the right person to talk to? What is troubling you so?"

Samuel's entire body shook as he started to cry again. "I don't belong here," he said into his chest, covering his face with his hands.

It was exactly what Adam feared, but even though he considered the possibility, he didn't have an answer for it. Instead, he knelt next to Samuel.

"Why do you say that? Of course you belong here. You are a part of this Family, you are one of us."

Samuel looked up. "I don't think I want to be in The Family anymore."

Adam had to steady himself. How was that possible? "What do you mean?"

"I love you, and everyone here," Samuel said through raspy breaths. "But I don't think I believe everything you do. I think I want to be above ground, with the others."

"It is an awful and sinful world up there. I have told you about its evils. Why would you want to be a part of that?"

"Because maybe I can do some good there. Maybe I can help them, instead of waiting down here for all of them to die."

"But they are going to die." Based on what Father said, this was going to happen sooner rather than later, but he didn't want to focus on the timeline. "It is God's will, and none of us can stop that. They will be judged and sent to heaven or hell. A few will live, and stay on earth. It is then that we will be able to help them and guide them down the right path, but not before."

"But what about the lost souls that will die before we join them?" Samuel looked angry now. "Why can't we help guide them down the right path now?"

The questions frightened Adam, not because he didn't know how to answer them, he just spent the morning being reminded of the answers, but because Samuel didn't. From the moment Children joined The Family, they were taught of the evils of the world above ground, they knew they were saved because they hadn't travelled too far down the path of evil. The message was interwoven in almost every lesson. A pang of guilt hit Adam. Maybe Samuel was too old to be rescued. Maybe he needed more time to learn the lessons. Then, Adam shook himself out of that thought. It wouldn't help Samuel, and Children understood the basics after the first year of teaching. Samuel had plenty of time to learn.

"Because they won't listen." Adam decided to remind Samuel of his education, and why most of the people above ground couldn't be saved. "Father explained all of this to us. Most have to die, for the rest to understand the consequences of following their own desires over the Lord's. Only then will their hearts and minds be open to the truth."

"That's what Father says."

"Yes. Why do you question his word?"

"Because no one else does. Jesus was questioned and threatened daily, but no one questions Father."

Adam knew the answer, it was because Father knew God's will and The Family knew that to question His word was blasphemy. Of course, Jesus knew God's will as well, but His mission was different from Father's. Plus, the people who questioned Christ were bad. That was the whole point of learning those stories. However, Adam also knew the answer wouldn't satisfy his brother. Maybe he should have insisted on continuing his training with Father this afternoon. For now, he chose to sit silently. He feared he reached the limits of his ability to help Samuel. He was a failure.

"Will you let me go?" Samuel looked at Adam again.

"What? Where?"

"Above ground, once you are in charge. May I go? Just so I can see for myself what it is like."

"You shouldn't need to see for yourself. You need to have faith."

"I'm out of faith."

Adam sighed. The answers Adam had weren't what his brother needed to hear. Nothing would comfort Samuel, and Adam couldn't understand why. "I must pray on this," Adam said. As far as he knew, no one ever asked to leave The Family before. No one left unless called to be with the Lord.

Samuel nodded.

"I may also need to consult with Father. If I do, I will not lie to him. I will need to tell him everything. Do I have your permission to do so?" Adam tried to make eye contact with Samuel.

"Yes," whispered Samuel, stubbornly staring at the floor. "It is my only hope."

"Very well. I will speak with him tomorrow."

Samuel closed his eyes and breathed what sounded like a sigh of relief. "Thank you."

"Don't thank me yet. The food should be here soon. Do you wish to stay?"

"No, thank you. You have given me hope. That is more than enough to fill me for the day."

Samuel stood up without saying another word and left. Adam fell to his knees and prayed for the strength to help the lost soul that just left his hut. He never saw anyone so lost or alone, especially in his own Family, especially someone he wanted to help so desperately.

A knock at his door interrupted his thoughts. It was his lunch. He thanked Sister Agatha, the Cook who delivered it, and ate in silence, building his determination to bring Samuel back to the fold.

20

Adam pictured his morning with the Farmers to be enjoyed outside in the fields, but he neglected to anticipate how different his leadership would need to be, compared to Father's.

Instead of going with the Farmers above ground, Adam got a few pats on the back and "We have faith in you, brother," before he was left alone with Brother Caleb to discuss the realities of their food supply. Brother Caleb never wasted words, which Adam usually appreciated, but now he wished the Elder would slow down a bit and allow Adam to process the information being piled onto him.

"This is where we've been stockpiling the food," said Caleb as they walked through a bunker housed next to the Farmers' tunnel exit. "We have about 15,000 pounds of flour, sugar and other dry goods stored already. I'd have liked another year or two to get the number up, just as a precaution, but if this is the Lord's plan, who am I to complain?"

Adam nodded, looking around the room filled with bags of flour, corn, rice and jars of vegetables. He guessed it stretched back to near where the tunnel began, because he couldn't see the far end. It should be enough food to feed them for a year. He hoped they wouldn't be stuck underground much longer than that. Surely Father would return before the end of a year.

"We've done some canning, but the hope is the greenhouses underground will still provide us with fresh fruits and vegetables," Caleb continued. "They won't be as large as the Cooks like, but if we have to sit underground for a year, they can figure out how to use smaller tomatoes."

"What about meat?" Adam finally found his voice. "Will you bring animals down here?"

"We may try a milk cow or two for some of the dairy foods, but the stench would make it almost unlivable down here if we brought any more. Plus, I'm not sure how long we could keep the grass going to sustain them. We've been freezing meats back there." Caleb motioned to another door on the other side of the pantry. "You want to take a look?"

Adam nodded, realizing that likely meant the animals would be left above ground to fend for themselves. Wouldn't they need them back eventually? He forced himself to focus, knowing Father would handle everything after he returned. It was Adam's job to keep things going underground until then.

The frigid air stung Adam's face when Caleb first opened the door. Adam stuck his head inside where he saw large ribs, shelving holding steaks, ground beef, plucked chickens and pork.

Nodding again, Adam stepped out of the freezer, welcoming the warmth of the pantry.

"Well, we won't starve," said Adam. He realized he was nodding like one of those bobblehead knickknacks people above ground took so much pleasure in for no apparent reason. He needed to focus.

"No, as long as the Cooks limit the number of feasts, we should have plenty for a year, and possibly a little more, if needed."

"You think we'll need to be down here longer?" The only reason they planned to wait after whatever was going to happen happened was to give Father time to calm things down above ground so they would face fewer human risks. Surely if most of the humans were gone, it wouldn't take too long.

"I like to hope for the best and prepare for the worst," answered Caleb.

Adam agreed it was the best policy, and they left the storage area to inspect the greenhouses and the pens where the milk cow would potentially stay.

Adam let out a breath he didn't realize he was holding as he walked to the waterfall for his lunch with Father. All this talk about his leading The Family and he never really stopped to think about the reason why. The world above was going to end, and Adam needed to keep everyone safe underground so they could start it all over. Nothing would be able to operate the way it did now. Samuel couldn't go above ground when Adam was in charge, because no one could go above ground without risking his or her life. Even Adam would spend the entire year underground, not out rescuing children or even helping the Farmers outside in the fields. He would be underground, leading.

The door opened into Father's study before Adam remembered he was on the elevator.

"Come in, my son." Father's voice surprised Adam out of his thoughts. "How was your morning?" Father sat at a small wooden table that was already set with fruit and sandwiches for lunch. He extended his arm to the chair beside him, inviting Adam to sit.

"Filled with important information and useful reminders," answered Adam.

Father smiled as Adam sat at the table. "How do you feel about those reminders?"

"I may have been counting on everyone to take care of themselves more than I realized." No reason in hiding his doubts now, he needed Father to talk him out of them. "You set up our Family to work seamlessly as one, but it won't work the same way, once what is meant to be will be."

Father gave Adam an understanding look. "It's true, it won't be the same. The Family will struggle with the changes. I fear the Farmers will have the most trouble, since they are accustomed to going above ground. They will miss it. As much as I have tried to make our home as wonderful as the world above should be, I am not God and cannot equal His creation."

"There will be many challenges," agreed Adam, reminding himself not to crave nature's beauty too much. Besides, Father will have made it more beautiful, more in the way God intended the world to be, once most of the sinners were gone and The Family was allowed to help Father rebuild. "I just pray I am up to the task."

"You will be. As long as you can keep our Family's faith in God alive and well, nothing will stop you all from serving the Lord's purpose."

Adam felt a lump rise in his throat and his heart began to pound in his chest. "I am already failing you, Father."

"How so, my son?"

"It's Brother Samuel. He's struggling with questions, and I have been trying to help him, but I fear I'm making things worse. How will I keep the entire Family strong in our darkest hour, if I can't help one man while you are still here to guide me?"

"Let's not get too far ahead of ourselves," said Father in a soothing voice. "What questions have you tried to answer for your brother?"

"He's questioning his role in The Family, and if he belongs here. I have talked with him, but he keeps questioning our beliefs and way of life. I am ashamed to admit, I have not answered all his questions to his satisfaction. I have not settled his fears, although they should be easy fears to calm."

Father put his hand on Adam's. "What are his fears?"

Adam took a deep breath. He knew he was doing the right thing, but he was still worried about telling Father that his rule was being questioned. "He questions our rules and why we follow them."

Father nodded. "He questions me."

Adam bowed his head. "Yes, Father. He questions why we follow you over any others." He allowed himself to look back up at Father and was surprised to see him grinning. Still, somehow, Father also seemed sad.

"He is a bright boy, but he lacks perspective. That's why I didn't make him a Rescuer."

Adam was surprised at the revelation. "You believed he could be a Rescuer?"

"He has the mind and skill for it. He had the ability to make you question your beliefs, if only for a short while, my most loyal son. He would easily convince parents that turning over their children would be in the child's best interest."

Adam couldn't argue with that. "Then why haven't you?"

"Well, for one, we don't need Rescuers anymore, and just as I said, he lacks perspective. He isn't secure in his faith, and therefore, he himself could be swayed from the cause. I believe we would lose him if he ever ventured out on his own."

"He asked to go above ground when you leave," said Adam. "He already knows your departure means the end of that world is near, what do I say?"

"If I knew, I would have told you by now. I would talk to him myself, but since I'm the one he's questioning, I don't believe that would help."

Adam was surprised and a little confused. Father was supposed to have the answers. He always did before.

"What I do know is we must calm his fears before I leave."

Adam stayed silent, waiting for Father to talk himself into a solution.

"He thinks too much. You've seen for yourself what happens when he's left alone with his thoughts. Imagine the danger it would put him in if we allowed him to voice these opinions to the Farmers or Builders or even Cooks. None of them would be as understanding as you. And even if he did find a sympathetic ear, do you really want that discord spreading through The Family? I see the pain you are in as you battle with Brother Samuel and his questions. Would you want any of the others to go through that? They aren't as strong in their faith as you are; it would be even worse for them."

Adam knew it was true, and Father was right, Adam didn't wish that doubt on any of them.

"He must be put back on the path." Father took a deep breath and closed his eyes. "Let him shadow you when you meet with the Teachers and Warriors. Those being led by Family closer to his age.

131

Perhaps it will give him some perspective of what we do, particularly with the Children. You could also take some time to really teach him the evils of the world above."

"How would I do that?"

"Share your experiences. You, Brother Jonas and Sister Clare know better than anyone the depravity of the world. Help him to understand how blessed he is to be with us."

Adam's chest tightened as he thought of the evils he witnessed. He thought of adults tasked with caring for innocent children but hurting them instead. He thought of the images of war and starving children left of fend for themselves. He thought of the cruelty even young children learned, causing pain to others. "It's hard to describe."

"I know you don't like to remember, but you have it in you to save your brother."

"Yes, Father."

"Good," said Father. "Now, the Farmers, tell me more about what you learned."

21

That evening, Adam ventured out in search of Jonas and Clare, hoping to catch them before dinner. Adam started by knocking on Jonas' door.

"Good evening, brother," said Jonas, smiling when he opened the door.

"Good evening," said Adam. "I'm sorry to trouble you, brother, but I have a favor to ask."

Jonas moved out of the doorway and gestured for Adam to enter. Adam looked around Jonas' hut. It was designed the same way Adam's was, one room connected to a bathroom, but the layout was where the similarities stopped. Jonas slept on the floor, without a mattress. He had a few books on warfare lying on the floor next to his pillow and a pile of bed linens. Instead of a desk and bookshelves, Jonas had various weapons, including axes, swords and maces, either hanging or simply leaning against the walls. Adam searched for a place to sit, but realized he was out of luck and joined Jonas, cross-legged on the floor. Adam realized, even though they lived next door, this was his first time inside Jonas' hut, other than the first day Jonas became a Rescuer and Adam welcomed him to the team. He thought of Clare's love of reading and orderliness. How would Jonas and Clare combine their living styles? Adam didn't think Clare would be very happy, tripping over weapons. Would Jonas allow her to stow them somewhere? She'd probably want a bed as well. He shook his head to stop the thoughts that weren't productive.

"Sorry I don't have a chair. I try not to spend too much time in here, unless I'm sleeping, so I keep the luxuries out."

"You are a good warrior, and discipline yourself well," replied Adam. It wasn't his place to judge how a man lived.

"So, what's this favor?" asked Jonas.

"I need help with a member of The Family, Brother Samuel, to be exact."

Jonas sat up a little straighter. "What is the matter with him?"

"He's losing his way," said Adam, trying not to give too much of Samuel's confidence away. "Father and I have a plan to help get him back on the right path, but I'd like your and Sister Clare's help, if you're not too busy with the wedding plans." Adam trusted Jonas wouldn't want to talk about the wedding any more than he did, but felt it was only polite to acknowledge that Jonas did, currently, have a lot on his plate.

Jonas let out a sarcastic snort. "Yeah, no worries on that front. Father basically said all we need to do is spend more time together and he'll handle the wedding arrangements. Still, I can't help you with Sam. I've already tried."

Adam fought the dueling pain of the thought of Jonas and Clare spending more time together and the surprise that Samuel confided in someone other than Adam. He tried to focus on the issue he had control over.

"You know of Samuel's troubles?" Adam asked.

"That he basically hates Father and wants out of The Family? Yes."

"Why didn't you say anything?"

"I didn't see what good it would do." Jonas shrugged. "He said he talked you already and it's not like he'll listen to Father."

"He wants to leave. He wants me to let him go above ground. You know as well as I do, he can't do that."

"I may know better than you," Jonas looked toward the wall.

"What does that mean?" Adam wasn't sure if he was upset that Jonas thought he knew more than Adam, or afraid that it was true. Adam remembered the day under the tree when Samuel seemed upset with Jonas. Was this what they were fighting about?

Jonas looked back at Adam, eyes shining. "It means I'm afraid we can't stop him. He's not a Warrior, he won't just follow orders. He'll wait for your answer, but when you tell him no ..." Jonas' voice trailed off and he looked at the ground.

Adam wondered if Jonas was right. Would Samuel just leave without permission? Their world worked because everyone worked together and followed the rules, but Samuel was fighting against everything they believed. "We need to help him. Father seems to think that if he shadows me as I work with you and the Teachers, it will put him on the right path. That, and trying to explain to him what the world is really like up there."

Jonas shook his head, still not looking at Adam. "I've already tried telling him. He won't believe me. He's determined to see it for himself."

"He hasn't always been like this," Adam said, realizing it himself. "What is it that changed him? Why start questioning now?"

"He's unhappy."

"But why? What is there to be unhappy about?"

Jonas finally looked up again and his eyes met Adam's. "Are you happy, brother?"

"What do you mean?" Adam inched back away from his brother, surprised that the light-hearted Jonas he knew held so much intensity inside.

"How involved are you in the wedding plans?" Jonas' voice shook. "Should we hold the ceremony in that little chapel at the other end of the field?"

Now it was Adam's turn to look at the ground. Jonas knew of the sin hiding in Adam's heart. There was no other reason for him to bring up the chapel.

"I'm sorry, brother. I know my feelings are wrong, but please know I would never do anything to hurt you. I'm doing all I can to rid myself of my sinful thoughts, but I swear to you I have not and will not act on them. I want only love and happiness for you and everyone in our Family."

Jonas laughed past what might have been tears. Adam watched, not knowing what else to do. Jonas seemed to be struggling with his own demons. Adam wondered if Jonas really did have feelings for Clare, in which case, Adam's feelings would hurt Jonas even more. Adam felt a twinge in his chest. He was so busy fighting the wedding, believing neither his brother or sister wanted it, he never stopped to consider Jonas was just doing what Clare asked.

"I'm so sorry, brother," said Adam. Not sure what else to say. "I believed I was hiding my sinful thoughts."

"Oh, my brother," said Jonas once he composed himself. "We really do make quite the trio, but don't worry. No one else has noticed. I just know you better than most."

Adam took some comfort in Jonas' words, but he still worried about his brother. "She will be a good wife to you. I will do my best to keep my distance, if it causes you pain."

Jonas shook his head. "You do not cause me pain, brother. I know she will be a good wife, and I will do my best to be a good husband to her."

"Good." Adam fought the urge to run out the door.

"And, brother, I only want your happiness as well. It's just not in the cards for any of us."

Adam thought to question Jonas' last statement, but he didn't have the will to continue the conversation.

"What do we do about Samuel?" asked Adam.

Jonas closed his eyes tightly. "Follow Father's plan. It's the only one we have."

22

Adam hadn't the energy to talk to Clare about helping him after his conversation with Jonas. Instead, he decided he would spend a day with Samuel first and determine how best Clare could help, if at all.

The next morning, he found Samuel sitting down at one of the breakfast tables with some of the other Builders.

"My brother," Adam said, putting a hand on Samuel's shoulder. "Do you mind if I have a word with you?"

"Of course, brother," said Samuel, nearly jumping up from his seat.

Adam walked Samuel to the outskirts of the dining field to avoid anyone else overhearing the conversation.

"I've thought about your request." Adam looked at Samuel's hopeful face. It broke his heart. "I'm sorry, I can't allow you to go above ground." Adam saw the light start to go out in Samuel's eyes. "At least not right away," Adam added quickly. He knew he shouldn't have said it, but it wasn't exactly a lie. If he did have time to help Samuel with his faith, then maybe by the time it was safe to go back to the other world, Samuel would be prepared for it. The plan was for them all to go up eventually anyway.

Samuel looked at him, not hopeful, but not disappointed either. "What do you mean, not right away?"

"I mean, when Father leaves, there will be much work to do, and I expect you to be a large part of that work. We will need to band together more than ever to keep our Family safe."

"Why? What will change when he's gone?"

Adam thought about the question. He knew it wouldn't be safe for anyone to go above ground, but no one other than the Rescuers and Elders knew that. Father was going to start the end of the world, and that was a scary thought even for the most faithful followers.

There didn't seem to be much of a reason to tell the whole Family since it was thought it wouldn't impact their lives. The Farmers would face a large adjustment, but Caleb was confident they would take the change in stride. Working under the "need to know" policy, that was all Adam really knew. That, and what he was now learning from the Elders. The thought reminded him Samuel was already being drawn into the plan.

"Once Father leaves, we will need more help to keep things running down here. That's why Brother Joseph gave you that book, correct? To learn and help him when the time comes?"

Samuel's eyes widened, then he looked at the ground. "But that's what you will be here for." Then he whispered, "And Jonas and Clare. Why would you need me here?"

"We will need everyone. It will be a large change with several challenges. However, I know they will be challenges we can overcome as long as we all work together."

"I suppose," Samuel said.

"Your happiness is important to me. And I do worry that you aren't receiving the fulfilment our positions are supposed to give us. So, I was wondering if you would consider working with me instead?"

Adam gave this a lot of thought after speaking with Jonas. He couldn't tell Samuel the real reason he wanted him close, but if it was an assignment to help The Family, he might be more willing to go along. Plus, with all of the changes, Adam knew he would need more help than Jonas and Clare could provide, especially after they were married. Samuel was already studying the computer code and more advanced aspects of keeping The Family safe. His knowledge would be helpful.

"Work with you? What does that mean?"

"I will be following the Teachers and Warriors over the next several days as part of my preparation to fill in for Father. It's a lot to take in and, quite frankly, I could use another set of ears. I would ask Jonas and Clare, but they have additional duties of their own."

138

Samuel gave a snort and Adam cringed. The last sentence didn't come out the way he intended.

"After all, Jonas is taking charge of the Warriors and Clare is taking a more hands-on role with the younger Family members," Adam added.

"I suppose, but why me?"

"You're smart and I trust you," said Adam.

Samuel gave a short nod.

"Thank you, brother," Adam said taking the nod as an agreement. "We will join the Teachers after breakfast. Our new Family members are rejoining us today."

"Okay," said Samuel.

They walked back, Samuel rejoining the Builders at his table, and Adam walking to the front. The stage wasn't set up since Father wouldn't be joining them, but the Builders put out a small pedestal for Adam. Normally, Father would be the one welcoming the newest Family members, but this was now part of the transition to Adam's leadership.

"Brothers and Sisters," Adam shouted to get everyone's attention. "Good morning! I won't take too much of your time, so you can get back to the delicious breakfast the Cooks have prepared for us all this morning, but first, I want to welcome back our newest Family members." Adam looked at the table just in front of him where the Children sat with their breakfasts. The three children Adam, Clare and Jonas rescued almost three weeks earlier. "Rebecca, Jeremiah and Chloe, welcome. You are loved, you are safe, you are Family." Adam smiled at them, then he looked up at the rest of The Family. "I encourage you all to take time to get to know these young people. They are each one of us now."

Adam got down and walked over to the Children. Sister Sarah stood and formerly introduced Adam to the three of them.

"Brother Adam, this is Jeremiah, Chloe and Rebecca."

Adam shook hands with Jeremiah and Chloe, then bent down to look Rebecca in the eyes. "Hello, Rebecca. It's nice to see you." He knew he shouldn't show favoritism, but he always had a soft spot for the Children he rescued himself.

The young girl he rescued looked different, as they usually did. She was thinner and paler, due to the more nutritious foods they were given and the lack of sunlight underground. Her eyes seemed darker, but Adam assumed that was due to the change in wardrobe from the flashy and gaudy dresses the girl wore before to the more appropriate robes she wore now.

"You too, sir." Rebecca bowed her head slightly.

He thought of when he first met her, how she wouldn't stop talking and trying to get Adam and her father to watch her newest dance routine. Now, she had more humility. Adam searched her face for some flicker of recognition, but as always, there was none, just confusion and a little sadness. She didn't remember him at all. "And it's okay if you don't remember how you came to us," he said, trying to comfort her. They were always a little nervous their first day.

She gave a small smile. "Are you sure? I don't want to seem ungrateful for the gift God has given me."

Adam shook his head and put a hand on her shoulder. "Fear not, young one. None of us remember our rescue, but you will come to know us all in time. I trust we will be great friends." He gave her shoulder a small squeeze just before turning to the other two. "Just as I will be good friends with the two of you. We are a Family here, and we share in God's love together."

The three nodded and smiled. "To become our best selves, for the good of the world," they said together.

"That's right." Adam gave Sarah a quick glance. "Now, I don't want to keep you from your meal or your lessons." He stood up and faced all of the Children sitting at the table, looking up at him. "Study hard, and remember to become the best servant of God you can be, you must put all of yourself into your studies. I shall be seeing you again later today."

The Children smiled and went back to their meals. Adam turned to Sarah, who was still standing next to him. "When may we expect you?" she asked.

"After breakfast. I plan to see how the studies go, and if you have time, I'd very much like to speak with you about your days and what you may need from me in Father's absence."

"Well, we usually just send the reports on each of the Children to Father and he instructs us on any changes we may need to make for a specific child, once he believes he knows the path that child will take."

"Very well. What is in the reports?"

"How quickly they learn the information, the subjects they're strongest in and any concerning questions that may arise."

"What do you mean by concerning questions?"

"Mainly if they question God and the rules. It doesn't happen often, and we can answer most of them, but if a child seems particularly upset or confused, Father will take the child under his wing to answer the more difficult questions."

"Very well," said Adam, not wanting to show his surprise. He didn't realize Father oversaw some children's' education, other than his own. Maybe he wasn't as special in Father's eyes as Jonas and Clare believed. Although, he hadn't noticed Father spending additional time with any of the Children in particular. How did he miss it, and what did they talk about? Adam made a mental note to ask Father.

"Brother Samuel will be with me as well." Adam decided to change the subject.

"Oh?"

"Yes, he will be helping me with the transition. I just wanted you to know."

"Thank you. I should get back to the Children, we will see you shortly."

Adam nodded and went to get his own meal.

23

After an uneventful breakfast, Adam found Samuel and they walked to the classroom where the Children had their lessons.

They observed the class, which Adam thought went very well. The Children were studying the story of Doubting Thomas and all seemed to understand that it is best to live by unquestioning faith than to need to see evidence for themselves.

At the end of the lesson, Adam looked over at Samuel. Samuel's face was red and he was shaking his head.

Adam escorted Samuel out of the room quickly and silently, giving a wave of thanks to Sarah as they left.

"What is the matter?" asked Adam.

"It's just so well done!" Samuel was somehow finding a way to whisper and yell at the same time. "These Children come, and the first thing we teach them is not to question, just believe in everything we tell them."

"We tell them to believe in God. He is the true path to our salvation."

"But the only path we have to God is through Father. Isn't that also true? Or have you forgotten the lesson that comes next? That to question Father is to question God. There isn't a scripture for that, but it gets thrown in there."

Adam took a deep breath. "Samuel, I know you are upset, and I know you don't want to tell me why, but following Father has made us a Family. It has made most of us happy and is keeping us all safe."

"Says Father, says you, but I'm still not clear on what you're keeping us safe from. Did you see those Children this morning?"

"Of course I did. We just sat through an entire lesson."

"No, Jeremiah, Chloe, Rebecca." He emphasized Rebecca's name. "Didn't you see the change in them? Their light is gone. They're dead inside. Can't you see it?"

Adam stood straight. "They are not dead inside." It took all his energy not to yell. "They have been reborn. Just as you were. Just as I was. It takes some time to readjust, but they will, just as we did."

"Just as we did." Samuel let out a small laugh. "Adam, we all grew up to be robots. We aren't individuals working together as a Family. We're all mindless, unquestioning cogs in a machine, working for some purpose, but no one seems to know what it is."

"How can you say that?" Adam was starting to feel dizzy. "You know we are working toward God's plan." His heart raced. He knew that answer wouldn't be enough for Samuel, but he also knew Samuel couldn't know more. Only the Rescuers, Elders and Father were allowed to know what would really happen when Father left. Adam realized, even though he had more information, he didn't know it all. He reminded himself he knew as much as he needed to, and so did Samuel.

"The vague plan with no details. How can you not see it?" Samuel pointed back at the classroom. "They all answer the questions exactly the same way we did. Doesn't that strike you as odd? If we were individuals, wouldn't we at least change the wording a little?"

"It's a lesson, they are repeating what Sister Sarah taught them. And if we are all mindless pieces of a machine, how is this conversation occurring?" It helped make his point, but the answer frightened Adam. Why was Samuel so different?

Samuel fell to his knees and started to weep. "I don't know. I told you, I don't belong here."

Adam bent down and put an arm around his brother. "You do, but you've lost your way. We will help you find the way back."

"I don't know that I want to find the way back. I just want to leave."

"It isn't safe to leave. But I swear to you that when it is, if it is still your desire to be apart from us, I will let you go." This time, Adam meant it. He couldn't let Samuel go out to a certain death, but he wouldn't allow someone he loved to live in this pain longer than necessary.

"Why isn't it safe? You keep saying that. Jonas says it, but why? Millions of people live out there and they are fine."

"They aren't fine," said Adam.

"I know, I know, they live without God."

"It isn't just that. I believe that is the cause of most of their troubles, true, but it is those troubles that make it unsafe. They hurt one another. They steal, they cheat and they spend more time judging than helping one another. They refuse to see the fault in themselves, and instead do all they can to hurt others who disagree with them. Down here, we work for one another. Up there, it is a lonely and terrifying place."

"I guess I should have been named Thomas. I need to see it to believe it."

"I've seen it. Why is my word not good enough?"

"I know it should be."

Adam looked up at the underground sky. He should spend another hour or so with the Teachers before meeting with Father, but he couldn't bring Samuel with him. Adam thought back to his conversation with Father. What if Samuel did start asking his questions to others? Adam couldn't allow this to spread. He didn't have much confidence in his ability to handle the situation, but he knew he needed to do that much.

"Go, take some time to rest. I also understand Brother Joseph gave you some additional studying materials. Read those this afternoon, spend some time in prayer and we will meet with the Healers tomorrow."

Samuel nodded and walked in the direction of his hut, not saying another word.

24

Adam managed to eat his breakfast quickly the next day before speaking with Clare. He spent the previous day thinking about Samuel and how every answer Adam gave seemed to only strengthen his brother's conviction against Father and The Family. He remembered Sister Sarah said Father took on Children with more difficult questions under his wing. When he asked Father about it, Father said he wanted to save that particular discussion for another day, but also that it wouldn't help Samuel at this point. After further discussing his fears with Father, they both agreed Sister Clare's perspective and patience might be more effective. Still, Father reminded Adam it would take more than one morning to answer such difficult questions.

Adam found Clare leaving her hut, presumably off to break her own fast. "Good morning, Sister," said Adam, trying not to focus too hard on her bright eyes or smooth skin that glowed with the freshness of the new day.

"Good morning." She smiled back. "Would you care to join me for breakfast?"

"No, thank you," he said. "I already ate, but I was hoping to speak with you briefly."

"Of course," she said. "I understand you just came from there, but will you walk with me?"

"Thank you." Adam thought of offering her his arm, but then changed his mind. It was probably best he limit physical contact until he stopped wanting it so badly.

"So," she said, walking with her hands clasped in front of her. There wouldn't be any accidental contact from her either. "What did you want to talk about?"

"It's Brother Samuel," said Adam, refocusing his own mind on the task at hand.

"Brother Samuel?" Clare furrowed her brow.

"He has lost his way. Questioning our way of life. He wants to go up to the surface. I'm hoping you could help me bring him back into the fold."

"What types of questions?"

"Mainly, why we follow Father without question. None of my answers seem to satisfy him. Father would like the situation settled before he leaves."

"He's asking for a lot." Clare let out a deep breath.

"I know. That's why I need your help."

"We should get Jonas too."

"He can't help. Apparently, he and Samuel aren't on the best of terms. Jonas worries he will be more of a distraction than a help."

Clare went back to looking confused.

"He wouldn't give me the details, but the way he said it, I trust his judgment," Adam said before Clare could ask the question.

"All right." She shook her head. "What can I do?" Adam was momentarily distracted by the flash of purpose that came to her eyes. They were determined, she seemed to stand up straighter, even though she didn't slouch. She was beautiful, and Adam knew if anyone could help Samuel, it was Clare.

They talked the rest of the way about Samuel's struggles and Clare promised she would speak to him when the time seemed right. She wouldn't rush it, but she wouldn't put it off either. Adam promised to update her if there were any changes before the discussion.

25

The following days with Samuel gave Adam some hope. Adam asked Jonas and Clare to help keep an eye on Samuel when he couldn't, and although Samuel's solitude was worrisome, they agreed at this point, it was probably best he wasn't talking to many others. The days spent with the Healers, Cooks and Builders went smoothly without any outburst from Samuel, and Adam gained a new respect for the amount of knowledge The Family had to keep their world going every day.

Because they were the only medical professionals, the Healers needed to be well-versed in all types of medicine and kept a close eye on everyone throughout the day, trying to catch any warning signs of injury or illness in hopes of preventing any major complications.

The Builders' title didn't do them justice, overseeing the electronics, security systems, air and water flow, plumbing, medical equipment, farming equipment and communications. It was a big job that Joseph managed without most of The Family realizing anything was being done to sustain their world.

The day Adam was scheduled to oversee the Warriors, Samuel asked for a day to return to the Builders.

"I'm worried I've been neglecting my duties," Samuel said when Adam asked why he wanted to stay behind. "I'm a Builder. I should be working with Brother Joseph. Our day with them reminded me of how much important work needs to be done."

"So, you've accepted your role in The Family and wish to continue your work?" Adam asked with a glimmer of hope jumping up in his chest.

"No, Brother," said Samuel. He looked Adam directly in the eyes. "If anything, our time has made me even more curious as to why we put in so much effort to live down here away from the rest of the world. How can avoiding God's creation be worth all of this?"

The hope in Adam's chest dived into his stomach and died quickly. All the moments that filled Adam with pride and love filled Samuel with doubt and frustration. How did Samuel move so far off the path? Adam knew he had the perspective of knowing how horrific the world above ground was, but other members of The Family didn't need that perspective. Why was Samuel so different? Clare needed to talk to him soon.

Adam took a deep breath and returned Samuel's stare. The moment to calm his thoughts brought a glimmer of clarity. The boy was lying to him again to avoid Brother Jonas. Apparently, Jonas wasn't exaggerating the rift between the two. Adam was tempted to force Samuel to come along so they could mend the rift, but he was trying to fix enough of Samuel's problems at the moment and a Family tiff seemed to be the least of them. "Very well. You may return to the Builders, but I may need your assistance again in the future. I did ask you to accompany me for a reason."

"Yes, Brother." Samuel nodded.

"And I want you to have lunch with Sister Clare."

Samuel stepped back as though Adam physically pushed him and looked away. "Why?"

"Because I feel she may be more capable than I to answer some of your questions and concerns. She spends much of her time studying the good word."

"You are to be our new leader," said Samuel, still not looking back at Adam. "If you can't settle my mind, I doubt anyone can."

"It's true I will work to run the day to day reality of our Family. But Father also made it clear that Jonas and Clare would be by my side. I feel this is the perfect example of how we will work as a team." Adam paused to put a hand on Samuel's shoulder. "I believe she can help."

Samuel shrugged off Adam's hand. "I suppose I have no choice," he said, and walked away before Adam had time to respond.

Samuel's response troubled Adam as he walked to meet Jonas at the workout fields. Was asking the boy to have lunch with Clare really such a terrible thing? He never imagined anyone would consider spending time with Clare, or anyone in their Family, such an inconvenience.

He hoped to see Clare on the way to meeting the Warriors in order to warn her that Samuel may or may not be looking for her at lunch, but he didn't. He would look for her again before joining Father to discuss the day.

Adam arrived at the workout fields to find all the Warriors lined up evenly spaced, backs straight, heads up, and Jonas with a huge grin on his face.

"Troops are ready for inspection, sir," said Jonas with a too-cheerful tone.

It took all of Adam's energy not to laugh; he managed to get away with just a smile. "Jonas, I'm supposed to be observing your daily activities. I've never seen you all lined up like this."

"Because it's never been done before, and yet we did it perfectly. That's how good we are."

The rest of the Warriors let out a proud cheer, fists pumping in the air.

"All right, troops," said Jonas. "Enough fun. I want five laps and then we battle with swords."

Adam stood next to Jonas while the Warriors turned and started their run. "Was that really necessary?"

"They were a little nervous about you coming. It helped to lighten the mood. Plus, I did want to make the point that they are well-trained machines. They can do anything we ask them to without much question or trouble."

"Good to know, I suppose." After days with Samuel, unquestioning obedience made Adam feel relieved, but there was something else struggling to inch its way into his mind. He pushed it back and returned to the task at hand.

"By the way, where is your shadow?" asked Jonas.

Adam looked at the ground. His shadow was exactly where it should have been. "What do you mean?"

"Samuel. He's been following you everywhere you go."

"He asked for the day off. I don't think our time together has made any difference in the slightest. I asked him to spend his lunch with Clare to talk through some of his concerns, but he acted like I just asked him to clean out the sewers."

"Well, that is one of his jobs," said Jonas with a slightly less cheerful smile.

"You know what I mean. I just don't understand why he would be so upset by it."

"Of course, you don't. Anyway, talking to Clare may actually be what's best for him. All we can do is wait and see."

"Yes," Adam said. "So what is on our agenda for the day?"

"Well, honestly, there isn't much for you to learn by watching them work out. I mean, you've done that before and you know they are fit and ready for combat."

"Okay. Well, with the other groups, they've shown me what they do more behind the scenes that the rest of The Family usually doesn't see. Do you want to show me that?"

"Not really, but Father says you should see it anyway." Jonas' shoulders seemed to drop down a bit when he said it. He remained quiet for several seconds until he said, "I told him it was not a good idea, but he insisted. I know you won't like it."

Adam was surprised. Why wouldn't Jonas want to show him what the Warriors did? Their main purpose was to protect The Family after God's work was done above ground. He couldn't imagine there was much they needed to do now.

"We can go over the armory inventory first," said Jonas.

"Is that going to be vital to our survival while Father is gone?" asked Adam, knowing the answer was no. They had more weapons than they ever thought they would need.

"Okay, fine." Jonas let out a sigh. "Let's go."

Jonas led Adam to another tunnel, one that Adam knew was there, but never saw anyone actually use before. It was similar to the Rescuers' tunnel, cement on all sides, damp and dark, with only a few blue lights to guide the way.

There was an exit earlier in the tunnel than Adam expected where they stopped.

Jonas pulled out a white handkerchief from a pocket in his robes. "I warned them we would be coming, but this is just to be extra safe."

"Warned who?" Adam asked, but Jonas was already climbing the metal ladder to the upper exit. When he reached the top, he put his hand with the handkerchief through the door, waved it and then stepped out.

"Come on out," Jonas' voice said through the hole.

Adam climbed out into the sunshine. Truth be told, he was excited to be out in the fresh air again. He didn't know when he would have opportunity to feel God's sun on his skin, once Father left.

Adam looked around. They were just past the fields where the Farmers worked, at the edge of the wooded area that surrounded Father's land. Mountains climbed overhead on the horizon.

"This way," yelled Jonas, who already started walking toward the trees.

Adam followed, taking in the beauty that surrounded him. The sun was out, he could smell the grass and the flowers around him, and he took in a deep breath of the cool air. Once in the woods, Jonas let out a whistle and two Warriors, Brother Michael and Sister Abigail, swung down from the trees and landed gracefully on the ground, rifles in their hands.

Adam took a moment to try and comprehend what he was seeing. He never knew the Warriors were allowed outside, let alone that they were outside and armed.

"Report?" Jonas asked in a very official-sounding tone.

"Boring as ever, sir," said Brother Michael. "Not even a squirrel for target practice."

"He's kidding, sir," said Abigail quickly. "We would never hunt without permission."

"At ease, soldier," said Jonas. "I know you can be trusted."

Abigail gave a serious nod, but Michael smiled and winked at Jonas.

Jonas turned to Adam. "These are two of our sentries. We station two near every exit for security."

Adam looked at the sentries again, and realized they carried more than just rifles. There were grenades, additional bullets, binoculars and each had at least two large knives strapped to a belt around their robes. "What are they protecting us from? How haven't I seen you out here before?"

This time, Abigail answered. "We hide in the trees. No one is meant to see us, so we may protect The Family from threats outside and in." Her chin rose a little higher in the air.

"And in?" Adam directed his question at Jonas.

"How do you patrol, soldiers?" asked Jonas, staring forward and seemingly ignoring Adam's question.

"In the trees," answered Michael. "We travel swiftly and silently, ensuring it is only us and the wildlife traveling through."

Adam looked up into the canopy. When he squinted, he could make out what appeared to be ropes and bridges in the treetops. They were well hidden, anyone would need to look closely for them to notice.

"And if you are not?" asked Jonas.

"We eliminate the threat."

"Thank you. Back to your posts."

The sentries nodded and scaled back up the trees like squirrels, until Adam lost sight of them.

"What was that?" Adam said. There was an odd feeling in his chest, not pain, but more like something pushing against his ribs, trying to escape.

Jonas nodded his head to the side, signaling they should walk back toward the fields. Once they were out of the tree-line, Jonas spoke again. "That is what the Warriors do. We protect The Family from any and all threats."

"What does that mean?"

Jonas rolled his eyes. "See, I really wanted Father to tell you all of this, but he insisted that you and I work on our communication. We protect The Family, ensuring that no one from the outside gets in, and no one from the inside, other than the Rescuers, of course, gets out."

"How? How do you ensure that?" Adam asked the question, knowing he didn't want the answer. Now, it was his heart that was beating so fast, it felt as if it were expanding out of his chest.

"We kill them, brother. You know that, why are you making me say it?" Jonas stood like one of the Warriors now, back straight, eyes forward, emotion leaving his voice.

"You mean you're trained to kill them. Has anyone ever had to shoot?"

"It happens. Not often, but it does."

"Outsiders? How do they get this far?" Adam worried that it would be harder to protect The Family than he realized. He counted on the remoteness of their home to provide extra protection.

Jonas looked straight into Adam's eyes. "Not outsiders."

Adam was sitting on the ground before he felt his knees bend. "Who?" he asked. He couldn't imagine Family members disappeared without him realizing it.

"I don't know everyone. I wasn't always in charge, but I'm told Brother Micah and Sister Eva tried to leave several years ago."

Adam focused on his breathing. That couldn't be true. Brother Micah, the Elder for the Warriors, died of a heart attack and Sister Eva, the Elder of the Teachers, accidentally tripped over a cord and fell on her head. The Builders were tasked with a major safety audit after the accident.

"This can't be right," said Adam. He knew he needed to focus on one thought at a time, but there were too many, moving too quickly through his mind. Memories of Brother Micah smiling while he

153

trained Adam to fight, Sister Eva applauding him when he answered a question correctly. Why would they leave? How could anyone hurt them? He felt the wind shift as Jonas sat down next to him.

"It's all for the greater good. They threatened our way of life. They went against Father's will. It needed to be done to keep our way of life moving forward."

Adam grabbed the first thought slow enough to catch. "This can't continue."

"Of course not. Once Father leaves, he's taking care of everything. The sentries will be safe underground with the rest of us."

Adam closed his eyes in an attempt to stop the spinning in his head. He felt nauseous.

"Yeah," he heard Jonas say. "I told Father this was all you would be able to handle for the day. He said he'd be ready for you early."

Adam felt Jonas' hands on his shoulders, helping Adam to stand again. He led Adam back down into the tunnel, returning to Father's world.

26

Once they arrived at the workout fields, Jonas pointed Adam in the direction of the waterfall. Adam, out of habit, walked behind the water and into the elevator. He didn't understand how it was possible to justify killing their own. They were a Family. They were supposed to be safe here.

Thoughts of Samuel trying to leave flashed through Adam's mind. Now, it was even more important that they calm the boy's fears and doubts. Adam wouldn't be able to bear it if something happened to Samuel, especially if it was at the hands of The Family. Adam thought about when he allowed Samuel to go above ground and fix the tunnel. How much danger had he put his brother in? He shook the fear from his mind. There must be fail-safes for such actions. Adam knew it wasn't the first time a Builder briefly went above ground. Maybe Brother Joseph knew how to keep them safe. Adam found himself missing the days when he didn't know how worried he should have been.

The elevator door opened, and Adam saw Father sitting on a chair, waiting for him. "Sit down, my son," said Father. "I'm sure you have many questions."

Adam sat down, although everything in his body was telling him to stand up and move. "How can it be true?" he asked.

"It is an evil necessity. It breaks my heart, but if we are to serve the purpose given to us by God, certain precautions must be taken."

"But we are killing our own," said Adam, still trying to wrap his mind around the thought. Jonas knew two Family members died, but were there more? Adam could think of five other deaths that were apparently from natural causes; they were all older, but what was true?

"We are all members of the human race," said Father. "God's creation. You are settled on the fact that most of us must die to allow

God's vision to reach its full potential, so why do you struggle with this?"

"Because we were supposed to be safe here. We are a Family. We are to carry out that purpose." Adam, struggled to keep his voice calm. "We aren't supposed to kill one another."

"I wish you were right. Unfortunately, some of us fall off the path. It is perhaps even more insidious that it occurs in such an environment, where God surrounds us so, but it happens."

"Why did you tell me this? It's not as if it will be needed once you leave. Why tell me now?"

"Because I need you to understand the lengths you must be willing to go to in order to keep our Family and our mission safe. It won't just be pep talks and rationing food. There may be difficult choices to make, and I need you to understand that following through on our mission takes top priority, regardless of the consequences to those we love."

Adam felt the tears streaming down his face. He struggled to breathe through the sobs, praying that decision would never be laid at his feet.

Father lifted Adam's chin. "Son, I love you. You are safe as long as you follow me."

A sense of calm swept over Adam. He closed his eyes, took a deep breath and looked back up. "Yes, Father." It was all he could say.

"Very good, Now, you've had a long day and it isn't even ten o'clock. Go to your hut, rest and reflect. All will feel better after some time alone with God."

"Yes, Father." It was an automatic response, but it felt right. He left and went to sleep in his hut.

27

When Adam woke from his rest, he looked out the window and saw by the artificial sun that it was just past lunch time. After his morning, it was difficult to believe the day was only half over. He realized he must have fallen asleep the moment he lay down on his bed. His stomach growled and hunger overpowered his desire to stay away from people.

He walked down to the dining field, hoping to grab some food and take it to his hut, when he saw Samuel and Clare sitting together and engaged in what seemed like a lively discussion.

"I still don't understand why it's such a big deal," said Samuel as Adam approached. "If we are so superior down here, why can't we tell other people about it? Why can't we teach them our ways?"

"Samuel, we've been over this." Clare sighed. "You are picturing people above ground as loving and reasonable people. They aren't like that. They are selfish, arrogant and afraid of anything they don't understand. Trying to convince them there is a different way of life, trying to tell them life is better if they only live on what they need instead of what they want ..." Clare looked up, noticing Adam. "Oh, hello, Brother."

"Hello," said Adam, nodding to them both. "I'm sorry I interrupted such an interesting discussion."

"As you requested," Samuel said. "I just have trouble believing it can be that bad." He looked back at Clare.

"Because you've never been there," said Clare as Adam sat next to her. He needed to hear her speak.

"But I was," said Samuel. "I just can't remember most of it. Maybe if I went back out, I could talk to some of them. Make more of them see that following God is the way to improve their lives and the lives of others."

Clare closed her eyes for a moment before answering. "The best of them will laugh at you, the worst will hurt you and the few that agree with you will most likely offer you substances that damage your thinking or body. That's why we have to rescue the Children. We need to get to them before that world has time to infect them with these skewed morals and values."

"How do you know that? When you first bring the Children here, they're scared. They don't want to leave that world. That must mean there is some good in it."

"They are scared because it's new to them and they don't understand what is happening. They're young and can't understand, but their parents make the decision for them, they decide what's best for them."

"That's another thing. How do you decide who to take? What power do the three of you have to determine who is worthy of salvation and who is not?"

"Father," said Clare. "He taught us well. How to look for children with talents that will benefit God's purpose through The Family, but who are also in danger in the outside world."

"Then why not just take them? Why bother asking the apparently evil parents' permission? Or for that matter, take one without parents. From what you tell me, there are plenty up there to choose from, living in terrible conditions who could benefit from our world."

"That would be easier in some respects, yes," said Clare.

Adam was amazed by her patience. He was glad she was helping to answer the questions with such understanding, and relieved that he at least made one correct decision. Adam could already feel frustration rising in himself.

"Unfortunately, those without parents have likely undergone so much trauma, they cannot serve The Family," Clare continued. "While we would like to help them, the ultimate purpose is to serve God. As for asking parental permission, it prevents other complications later on and keeps law enforcement focusing on the parent who turned them over to us instead of looking for us."

"I just think we could do more."

"We can't."

"Why?"

"Because I've tried," said Clare with enough force to cause both Adam and Samuel to sit back. Apparently, she wasn't as patient as Adam believed. "After my first rescue mission, I started thinking the same way you are now. Believing that we could do more. I wasted missions, trying to talk to people instead of saving children, and ..." Clare shuddered and stopped herself from talking. Adam instinctively put an arm around her shoulders to stop the shivers.

"We are doing God's work here," said Adam, hoping to give Clare the rest she needed. "Why is that not enough?"

Samuel continued to stare at Clare. "Because it doesn't feel like God's work anymore."

"What changed?"

"Everything," said Samuel before he stood up and left the table.

Adam watched him go, wanting to follow him, but not wanting to leave a shaking Clare. "Are you okay?" he asked in a near whisper.

She sat up, taking a deep breath. "Yes, thank you."

"I didn't know that you tried to save more."

"I didn't want anyone to know. I worried Father would take away my position. That I wouldn't be allowed out in the world to rescue children."

Adam's entire body felt rigid and cold as he remembered what he learned from Jonas earlier in the day. "Did you tell any of them about us?" He tried to sound calm.

"No, never. I've always known how important it is to keep our secret, but I also felt as Samuel does. That we should be saving more, and if he is anything like I was, he won't change his mind without seeing it for himself. I'm sorry I couldn't be more help to you."

"That's okay," said Adam, breathing more gently now that Clare no longer seemed to be at risk.

159

Clare looked up at him. "Are you okay? You look pale."

"I'm fine," said Adam, clearing his throat. "It's just been a long day."

"Did Jonas give you a hard time with the Warriors this morning? I told him to go easy on you. You've got a lot on your plate."

"You two talk about me?" asked Adam, feeling both happy they thought of him and sick that they were together without him.

She nodded. "The transition is more interesting than the wedding, which is what we're supposed to be talking about, but neither of us really wants to discuss that. It will be a big change when Father leaves. I hope you know we are both here to support you."

"I do," said Adam, who was fighting off the desire to run every time the word wedding was mentioned. He forgot it was only a week away, spending all of his time focusing on what would come after that. He needed to talk to Clare.

"What does Jonas say will happen once Father leaves?"

She shook her head. "Not much. He mainly jokes about how he hopes you won't start forcing everyone to get up with you before the sun."

Adam forced a smile. "No, that's my time. You all can sleep in. Other than his jokes, does he say anything?"

"No," said Clare. "But I think he's a little nervous. The Warriors are going to have to fight, after all, and he takes that very seriously."

"Right." Adam reminded himself that the Warriors were trained to protect The Family, they trained to fight anyone who threatened them after Father triggered mass destruction. Their world was remote enough that it should protect them from the outside world, and, now that Adam realized what the Warriors other duties were, everyone would be locked in with no chance to escape until Father released them for the final battles, and for the entire Family to show the new world their way of life. The non-Family members who were left were likely to become desperate until Father, and then The Family, could get them under control. The Warriors were willing to give their own lives for The Family ... as long as they followed the rules. Samuel's frustration might not be completely unfounded. That line of thinking was cut off by Clare's voice.

"He did say something odd the other day," Clare said, seeming to regain her composure. "He said, 'At least we'll be fighting the true enemy.' As if they were fighting someone else. I asked him about it, but he laughed it off. He said he was talking about the training dummies, but there was something in the way he said it that made me remember."

Adam hugged Clare. She gave him exactly what he needed, the knowledge that he wasn't the only person struggling with the Warriors' current task. "Thank you."

"You're welcome," she said. "Do you know what he meant?"

"I think so, and we can talk about it more later, For now, I should let you finish your lunch. I have a few more things I need to do."

"Very well. Don't forget your own lunch."

Adam allowed himself a small smile. Clare would never stop looking out for everyone. He assured her he would, but first he needed to find Samuel.

Adam walked to Samuel's hut. He wouldn't give up on the boy, despite Clare's belief that Samuel would need to see the reality of the outside world before he changed his mind. Adam knocked on the door, no answer, but Adam heard rustling inside.

"Samuel," said Adam as gently as he could into the door. "Please, open up. I promise I won't take too much of your time." Adam heard more movement on the inside of the hut.

"Yes, Brother?" Samuel asked after opening the door.

"May I come in?"

"I suppose," said Samuel. Adam felt annoyance creeping into his chest. Samuel was not even attempting to be respectful. Adam walked into the hut that looked like all the others, a bed that was neatly made, desk with a few papers and the book about coding Brother Joseph asked him to read, but no other books, exercise equipment or tools, which most Builders kept in their rooms.

"Look, I realize you are likely tired of all of us telling you how terrible the outside world is and not letting you see it for yourself," Adam said, standing at the end of the bed. "If I could let you out, I would, but it just isn't a possibility right now. It's not safe."

"According to you," said Samuel who stood as well.

Adam closed his eyes for a moment to calm and focus his attention on his purpose and not on his feelings for this conversation. Even he didn't truly understand how dangerous it was until this very morning. "Yes, according to me, and Clare, and Jonas, and Father. All the people who have been out there and understand it, who have suffered the evils there. Why is it not enough?"

"Because you aren't the only ones." Samuel seemed to stop himself from saying more and looked down at the floor.

The tightness is Adam's chest returned. "Who else?" asked Adam, hoping he misunderstood what Samuel was saying.

"No one. Never mind," Samuel mumbled to the floor.

Adam didn't want to push the issue, he already learned more than he ever wanted to in one day, but he also knew this was too important.

"Samuel, if someone is going above ground without permission, it is important, for their sake, that you tell me right now." Adam hoped he sounded caring and not terrified.

"Why?" Samuel's gaze was now hard and shooting directly at Adam. "So you can tell Father? Have them punished somehow?"

"No." Adam realized as he said it that he was telling the truth. He realized he feared what the punishment might be. "No, so I can talk to them and be sure they are safe."

Samuel's hard gaze turned to one of sorrow. "No one is leaving," he whispered, and took a deep breath, falling onto his bed. "But I did break the rules."

"What rules?" Adam asked slowly.

"I," Samuel paused and shook his head. "I spoke to the workers who help the Farmers."

Adam released the air he was holding prisoner in his lungs. "Oh, the workers ... wait, how?" The migrant workers usually spent their days in fields separated from the Farmers, not to mention the fact that Samuel was a Builder. Would the Warriors really allow Samuel to sneak away? How did the Farmers not notice he was gone?

"Well, I didn't exactly speak to them," said Samuel hesitantly. "They spoke a different language, but I was working in the fields, trying my hand at being a Farmer when Father was debating what to do with me permanently. I saw them working a few fields over and snuck away to watch. I wanted to see the evil of the outside world for myself, but when I saw them, they weren't evil at all. They worked hard, they laughed, if someone was tired, the other workers allowed them to rest, they seemed to be just like us."

Adam nodded. It still didn't fully explain how Samuel got away, but he was safe, so Adam would focus on the issue at hand. Adam remembered seeing kindness and generosity in the outside world and being confused by it at first. It took time for him to realize that the kindness was short-lived and usually given for personal gain. He remembered vividly the group of people sharing a pleasant meal at an outdoor restaurant, encouraging a friend who seemed sad. It wasn't until after that friend left that Adam heard the cruelty and judgement the others suddenly shared freely.

"I went over to speak with them," said Samuel. "They were nervous, but after I worked alongside them for a while, the smiles returned and they seemed to relax. I asked them if they believed in God and Jesus Christ. They perked up when I mentioned the Lord and one showed me a Bible. I looked at it."

Samuel paused there and Adam held his breath. Samuel saw the Holy Word, a privilege only Father experienced in The Family, as far as Adam knew. Adam knew it was forbidden to look at the Bible, he should rebuke Samuel for reading the Word which could easily be misinterpreted, but he was also anxious to hear what Samuel read.

Samuel must have sensed or seen Adam's willingness to hear more, because a look of excitement crossed his face, and he sat up and continued speaking. "Brother, it was incredible. There are passages in there that talk about love and forgiveness for all. That the purpose of Christ's sacrifice is to save all, not just a select few. That no one can reach the full glory of God, and therefore no one is better than anyone else, all are forgiven through Christ." Samuel stopped to take a breath, and Adam released his, feeling a small pinprick of warmth begin to grow. Then the warmth froze.

"Wait," said Adam. "How could you read it if they spoke a different language?"

Samuel shook his head. "I have to believe it was a miracle. They had a Bible in English with them. They gave it to me." Then Samuel's face froze.

"They gave it to you?" asked Adam as his heart began to race again. "What did you do with it?"

"I ..." Samuel appeared to look for something on the ground, color spreading across his pale face.

"Did you keep it?" asked Adam, not really wanting to know the answer.

Samuel's eyes started to fill with tears. "I couldn't give it away," he choked out. "It was too wonderful. Please." Now Samuel was standing and holding Adam's hand. "Please, don't tell Father. He will make me give it up. It's the only thing that is giving me any hope."

Adam worked to fight his own tears, and the desire to start looking for the book himself. Even if he could just hold it. No, he reminded himself. He'd avoided looking at Bibles in the outside world, and despite the renewed desire to see it after hearing Samuel's description, he would fight the temptation here as well. Look at the trouble it was causing Samuel, and the danger it was putting them all in. Still, he couldn't let Samuel keep it, could he? "It's dangerous to try to interpret the Lord's word on your own. People up there, they fight over it all the time. They can't agree on what it means. They kill one another over it. It would be better for all of us if you got rid of it."

Samuel shook his head. "Isn't that what we're doing? Hiding, waiting for the rest of them to die because Father knows better than everyone else?"

"He has protected us," said Adam, but the words sounded hollow. He tried again. "He's doing what he was called on by God to do."

"That's what he says."

"Samuel." Adam couldn't think straight. Nothing was making sense, except the urgent need to keep his brother safe. "This is a dangerous path. I don't want you to give away your hope, especially now that I know it is the word of God, but you are risking our entire way of life."

"Then just let me leave. I'd rather live in a world that says I'm just as good or bad as everyone else, than here where I'm made to feel as though I'm a danger to everyone I care about."

"Who says you are a danger?" This was new and surprising. As far as Adam knew, Samuel wasn't talking to anyone else other than Jonas about his questions and no one mentioned their concerns about Samuel's questions directly to him. "I believe interpreting the book on your own may be dangerous, not you."

"Never mind. Please, just leave me alone."

Before Adam could respond, Jonas walked through Samuel's door. "Listen, Sam, I know you said ..." Jonas took a step back and straightened his back when he saw Adam. "What's going on here?"

Adam's fear rose. If Jonas learned of Samuel's insubordination, what would he do? What were the Warriors instructed to do?

"I was just speaking to our brother about the world above," Adam said. "Trying to explain to him that while the evils are sometimes carefully hidden, they have corrupted the earth."

"Still on that?" Jonas relaxed his shoulders slightly.

"Why are you here?" Samuel's icy tone surprised Adam, even after he thought nothing more could shock him for the day.

"I wanted to talk to you about something," said Jonas in a matter-of-fact way.

"Don't you have to prepare for your wedding? It's just a few days away."

Jonas cleared his throat. "No, Father has that all handled."

"Right. Look," Samuel said, switching his glance from Jonas to Adam. "I appreciate everything, but I'm tired. I'd like some time to rest and reflect."

Adam wondered what that meant. Would Samuel be reading the Bible? Should Adam stop him? He couldn't risk saying anything in front of Jonas. "I understand, but please remember what I said. We can talk more tomorrow."

"Tomorrow is the day of rest. Perhaps, another day."

"Very well, get some rest." Adam, thought he could use some time to reflect as well. He walked out, not realizing Jonas was with him until he heard footsteps coming up from behind.

"He's hopeless," said Jonas when he caught up to Adam. "He won't listen to any type of reason."

"I'm worried you may be right."

"He's going to do something stupid, Have you gotten through to him at all?"

"I'm afraid not." Adam shook his head. He knew the knowledge of what would happen if Samuel ever decided to leave on his own was on both of their minds, even if they couldn't bring themselves to say it out loud.

"Well, at least he won't have the option of leaving in a few days," said Jonas. There will be a more concrete reason he will have to understand."

"Perhaps," said Adam, wanting to believe Jonas, but not fully convinced. "Jonas," Adam's curiosity got the best of him as he toed a line that could put Samuel in more danger, "have you ever read the Bible?"

"That's forbidden," said Jonas, not revealing any emotion behind his words.

"I know," said Adam. It was procedure before moving into any hotel room to have the Bibles removed, and they tried to locate themselves as far away from churches as possible, in order to avoid any potentially harmful messages. Still, they couldn't avoid it all. "But, did you ever slip on one of your missions? I know I've been tempted."

Jonas stopped walking and Adam stood next to him. "Why do you ask?"

"I'm curious. I'm supposed to lead The Family, to follow God's will, but I've never read His word for myself."

"Oh," said Jonas. He took a moment before putting a hand on Adam's shoulder. "Listen, Brother. You are one of the best people I know. You do what is right. As far as I can tell, that is all God asks us to do, but no, I haven't read a Bible. It doesn't seem to be worth the risk."

Adam nodded. "You're right. That's how I've always felt too." He heard his stomach growl.

"Whoa," said Jonas with a smile. "That's not natural."

Adam remembered he never had lunch after stopping to talk to Clare and Samuel. "I forgot to eat lunch today."

"Well, let's get you some food before people start thinking you're smuggling animals in your robe."

"Why would anyone's mind go there?"

"Who knows where their minds go," said Jonas with a wink, and he led Adam back to the dining field.

29

"I don't know what more we can do," Clare said, sitting next to Adam in the small chapel that came to be their meeting place. The only place they could be alone. "We've told him everything. Now it's up to him to believe us."

Samuel avoided all the Rescuers in the days since Adam learned about the Bible. Adam couldn't stop thinking about what Samuel said was written inside, but he also couldn't shake the terror that came along with knowing how many rules Samuel was breaking and the possible consequences. Father was willing to kill members of The Family. The sentence still didn't seem real.

"I'm just worried about him," said Adam, not daring to tell Samuel's secret to anyone. Not even Clare. "He's going down a path that might not allow him to return. I feel there is more I could do, I just don't know what it is."

Clare squeezed Adam's hand. "You are a good man."

Adam looked at her. He wondered if this was the last time they would meet like this. He knew if he was smart it would be. He made the painful decision to remind himself why. "What about you? You have a very big day tomorrow, and you are spending this time helping me. I hope I'm not keeping you from any preparations." He chastised himself for lying. He did hope he was keeping her from something.

Clare let go of his hand. "No, nothing. My dress is ready, and Father says it will be a fairly simple event. All I have to remember is to say 'I do' when asked the big question."

"Seems simple enough."

"It does, doesn't it?"

"And you and Jonas are ready to start your lives together?"

"I don't know. He will move into my hut after the ceremony. Other than that, I don't know how things will change."

Adam could think of one very big way, but he couldn't bring himself to mention it.

"Father says children aren't necessary right away," said Clare, bringing it up for Adam. "He understands it will be a difficult transition for everyone. He says Jonas and I need to get used to each other and sharing a hut is the first step. He says the rest will follow naturally. I just pray he is right."

"He usually is." This new information actually made him feel a little better, although he was terrified of the day Clare and Jonas did get used to each other. Still, the fact she had trouble picturing it made him think it wouldn't be for a long time.

"Well." Clare stood up. "Speaking of tomorrow, I should probably get some sleep. Apparently, I'm supposed to look beautiful on my wedding day." She gave a small smile.

Adam smiled back. "You always do."

"Thank you." Clare started to blush, turned and walked out of the chapel.

Adam watched her go, then turned to the crucifix that hung in the front. "Dear Lord," he prayed. "Please, give me the strength to do what You have asked of me. Help me give Jonas and Clare all the love and support that they need to make it through this new responsibility being put upon them. Give me the strength to hide any doubts I may have, so as to help calm their own. As for Samuel, Lord, give me the wisdom to guide him as we face this new challenge. Help me to keep him in the fold. Don't let me fail him." Adam wanted to say more, but couldn't think of what to add. "Amen."

30

The morning of the wedding, Adam didn't want to get out of bed, but he couldn't lay still either. He finally decided to get in a quick workout before going to breakfast. Hopefully, that would help calm his anxiety.

The workout helped a bit; at least he felt like he had less nervous energy as he walked to breakfast. When he arrived, he noticed Sister Sarah waving in his direction. He took the empty seat next to her, surrounded by other Teachers.

"Good morning, Brother," Sarah said with a large smile on her face. "Are you excited for today's festivities?"

"Of course." Adam hated lying, but it was for the good of everyone that they believed he was fully on board with the marriage. Especially since he didn't have a good reason for being against it. "Today will be a marvelous day, and one to be celebrated for years to come."

"The Children have been working so hard these past few weeks. They are so excited to be a part of the ceremony, and nervous that they'll make a mistake. It's just adorable."

"They will be singing, correct?" asked Adam. Everyone in The Family had some role to play in the day's festivities. The Cooks and Farmers were, of course, in charge of the feast; the Builders were charged with the decorations; the Teachers, Children and anyone with sufficient musical talent had entertainment; the Warriors were escorting the bride and groom throughout the day and helped with some of the larger set-up tasks; and Father would officiate the wedding, with Adam at his side.

"Most," nodded Sarah. "Some of the older Children will be putting on a performance during dinner as well."

"I look forward to hearing them," Adam said.

"It will be a wonderful performance. Young Rebecca is helping with the costumes."

Adam was surprised by this, he remembered the little girl who almost never stopped dancing, even when she was being led down an underground tunnel. "Really? I would think she would be part of the performance. She was a talented dancer in her other life."

"Yes," said Sarah with what looked like a sad smile. "She did want to participate in the actual performance, but Fa – I mean, we felt it would help her assimilate to our way of life better by helping others shine."

Adam nodded. He felt sad for Rebecca, but it was also hard to argue the logic. Her life on the stage was one of the things her biological father wanted to take her away from, it was one of the reasons Adam rescued her.

"We are all so happy and proud for Sister Clare and Brother Jonas," added Sister Beatrice, an older Teacher sitting across from Adam. "I always hoped Clare would be a Teacher, but Father was wiser than I and made her a Rescuer. Now she will raise The Family's first newborn Child and be a teacher to us all."

"Yes." Adam smiled at the aging woman. She had such joy and hope in her eyes, Adam couldn't help but be happy for her. He started to sense Father really did know what he was doing, especially if his decisions brought this much happiness to everyone Adam cared for.

Adam listened to the rest of the wedding chatter in silence, eating his breakfast as quickly as he could. Everyone discussed the special touches they tried to put into their contributions for the bride and groom. The Teachers said they made sure to include music with violins, because that was Clare's favorite instrument. The Cooks and Farmers made sure to have plenty of beef, so that Jonas could have third or fourth helpings if he wished. And the Children asked permission to pick flowers from all of the gardens so they could hand them to Jonas and Clare after the final performance. Despite everyone's surprise and confusion over the original announcement, being involved in the wedding preparations certainly brought them together to share in the joy of the day.

When Adam finished eating, he excused himself and went directly back to his hut. He was pleased The Family was in such a joyous mood, and ashamed he wasn't sharing in it. He wanted time for some quiet reflection before the ceremony. He needed to be in great spirits before he stood before them all and watched Clare marry Jonas.

He could tell now, this was for the best. The Family always worked together for the betterment of them all, but this was different. There was an energy Adam hadn't seen in them before. He guessed this was what Father was hoping for when he put the plan into motion; a way to give the entire Family a new sense of energy and purpose, in addition to growing The Family naturally, without the rescue missions. A way to remind them they were all in this together, before they needed to take on the responsibility of healing the soon-to-be destroyed outside world.

Adam was starting to feel a little better, until he walked into his hut and saw Clare standing in his room. The shock of seeing her there overwhelmed him. Women and men weren't supposed to go into one another's huts in order to avoid temptations. Adam looked outside to make sure no one was around and shut the door, but his surprise kept him from forming any words.

"I'm sorry to come in when you weren't at home," said Clare. "But I needed to see you, and thought I would just wait here."

"All right," said Adam, finally able to make his lips move. "Is something wrong?"

"No." Clare shook her head, her eyes were wide, as though she were frightened. "It's just I need to do something, before the wedding."

"Okay," said Adam. He wanted to help her, but he was also afraid to move.

"Don't judge me."

173

"Of course—" Adam was about to say "not" when Clare stepped forward and kissed him. He looked at her for a moment, not realizing exactly what was happening. Her eyes were closed and tears were gently trickling down her cheeks. He knew he needed to stop her, but then he felt her lips. They were so soft, and her hands were light and soothing on his face. He closed his eyes and gave into the moment, wrapping his arms around her. He allowed his lips to part slowly with hers, and then come back together; just once, and then they both stepped back.

"Clare," Adam whispered, not knowing what to say, but he was fairly certain some type of apology was in order. How could he do that to Clare? To Jonas? To The Family? His mind started to spin and he put his hands on his knees to steady himself. He felt dizzy and his legs were shaking. He felt the physical proof of his sinful desire begin to show. He sat on the bed and put his pillow on his lap, hoping to steady himself in the process.

"It would have been worse after the wedding," said Clare. "I needed to see what it was like. Just once." She looked at him. Adam knew he needed to say something, but too many thoughts were running circles around his brain, too fast for him to grab any single one. Clare wiped the tears from her eyes. "I'm sorry. I promise it won't happen again."

She moved to leave, but sudden panic allowed Adam to stand and touch her arm. "No, I am sorry," he said. "Sorry you are sad. Sorry I can't make this better for you."

She smiled and hugged him. "You just did." She left without another word.

Adam didn't know if he felt better or worse after the kiss. He knew it was the best moment of his life. He loved Clare. He wanted to be the one marrying her, but it was too late. She was marrying Jonas. Maybe she didn't have to, maybe he could ask Father to change his mind and allow Adam to marry her. No, it was too late for that. The wedding was going to start soon. The Family was finally excited about the idea. What would happen to them, to all they were

174

building, if suddenly Clare were marrying someone else? Adam stopped himself there. Here he was, being selfish again. Here he was, actually considering upending his entire Family for one person. Adam knew Clare marrying Jonas was for the best, because Father deemed it so. Should he feel guilty for the kiss? For having feelings for his brother's betrothed? Of course he should. Here he was supposed to be their moral guide, the one to lead them down the right path, and he was committing one of the worst sins possible. It would never happen again.

Adam changed out of his regular robes and into his new ceremonial robes. They were white satin with a golden rope, to match Father's golden robe and white rope. Jonas and Clare would each be wearing something similar, but Jonas would be in velvet and Clare in lace instead of satin. The rest of The Family would be in their traditional clothing as usual. Adam looked down at his new robes, a symbol of the position he was being groomed to take. The responsibility hit him again, and he reminded himself he couldn't allow himself to be distracted by Clare anymore. He'd already threatened the one event that was bringing so much joy to those he was sworn to protect.

Maybe that was why she needed to marry Jonas. If she married Adam, he would be too wrapped up in her to help anyone else. A shame he would have to live with forever while others suffered. At least this way, he was the only one to suffer.

Adam resolved to throw his whole self into his new responsibilities, to helping Samuel and the rest of The Family. Caring for and worrying about Clare were now for Jonas to handle, whether any of them liked it or not. Adam would help them from a distance. He'd start by doing all he could to make this one of the happiest days of all their lives.

Adam closed his eyes, took a deep breath and set out for the church.

31

Adam surveyed the church, impressed with what he saw. The plain pews, where The Family sat every Sunday for service, were now decorated with simple, but beautiful, white and purple flowers, and a white ribbon draped along the sides. At the front, a large bouquet of flowers adorned the altar, flanked by two white candles. As usual, Christ looked down on the scene from his crucifix, just under the stained-glass window, illustrating his resurrection. Adam looked at the altar where he would stand behind Father during the ceremony. Staring out at the others, needing to put on a brave face so The Family wouldn't know how he really felt about the wedding.

The whole scene was simple, yet beautiful, just like Clare. Adam shook the thought from his mind and headed for the Sacristy where he knew Jonas would be preparing for the vows. Adam was determined, now more than ever, to be a support and guide to his brother.

Jonas was sitting, with his head in his hands, when Adam walked into the room. "Hello, Brother," Adam said softly, hoping not to startle Jonas.

Jonas looked up, his eyes puffy and red. He was still in his regular robes, the robes for the ceremony hung on the closet door. "Oh." He cleared his throat and stood up. "Hello, Brother. I wasn't expecting to see anyone before the ceremony."

"I just wanted to check on you." Adam was shocked to see Jonas crying, because he never saw it before. "Are you all right?"

"Me?" Jonas puffed out his chest and flashed a smile. "I'm always all right, you know that." He turned away from Adam. "If you'll give me just a moment, I seem to have something in my eye. I'll be right back." Jonas walked quickly to the washroom.

Adam stood uncomfortably in the middle of the room, waiting for Jonas' return. He needed to be there for his brother.

Jonas returned, having rinsed his face and straightened his hair. "What brings you here so early? The wedding isn't for another hour."

"I just wanted to check in and see if you needed anything," said Adam. "Is everything okay?"

"I'm fine. It's no secret to you that this isn't exactly what I wanted, but I've come to accept my duty."

"As we all must, but you will work to keep her happy, won't you?" He couldn't help but ask the question.

Jonas gave a small smile. "I will do my best. We certainly have our differences, and we have a knack for driving each other a little crazy, but I will do what I can to not make her miserable on purpose."

It wasn't exactly the answer Adam was hoping for, but he knew it was honest. He walked over and sat next to Jonas, remembering back, before the engagement, how he always appreciated, and was usually entertained, by how different Jonas and Clare were. On the upside, he hadn't noticed the two of them bickering since the engagement. "Well, you seem to be succeeding so far."

"Yes, I think we've come to accept that we are in this whole mess together. It has made us closer." Jonas gave a small laugh. "Although, I do admit, I have missed our arguments. It's just so easy to get her worked up."

Adam smiled at this, remembering how Jonas would make insane claims about anything, just to get a rise out of Clare. Adam always knew when Jonas was joking, but Clare didn't and the two would argue a point until Clare got frustrated and left in a huff. She was never angry for long, and the arguments were usually very entertaining. "You can still have those arguments, just maybe not as many." Adam smiled. "I think she secretly enjoyed them as well."

"I hope so. You and Clare are two of my best friends. That's one of the things that has worried me the most. I don't want to lose those friendships."

"Why would you lose our friendships? You and Clare will become closer than ever, and things between you and I won't change."

Jonas put a hand on Adam's shoulder. "I hope that is true."

"Of course it's true. Why would it change?"

"Either you know, and are too noble a man to say it, or you are in denial. I'm going with the noble side, and I pray you can forgive me for marrying Clare today."

Adam was surprised. How did Jonas know? Did Clare tell him? Were they caught? Adam's heart started to race, until he took a closer look at Jonas' face, which had a look of love and fear, not hurt or anger. Perhaps his Warrior friend was more intuitive than Adam gave him credit for. "Everything that happens today is God's will. I will not question that, nor would I judge or hold anger for any man doing what is right."

"Thank you, Brother."

Adam patted Jonas' shoulder. "I truly believe it. It was hard for all of us to accept at first, and may still take a little more time, but I am beginning to see the wisdom behind this plan."

Jonas nodded. "As am I."

"Now," Adam stood up. "What can I do for you? I've heard rumors that today is all about the bride, but surely the groom deserves some attention."

Jonas laughed. "Honestly, I can't think of anything, but I have appreciated the distraction."

"Well then, it shall continue. Would you care to arm wrestle?"

Jonas laughed harder. "With whom? I'd take your puny arm down in a second."

Adam rolled up his sleeve. "Well, we'll see about that." He sat, placed his elbow on a table and raised his hand, ready for battle.

Jonas shook his head, moving to join Adam. "All right, but don't use your broken wrist as an excuse to miss the ceremony."

"And I don't want to hear any whining that your crushed hand hurts when you have to put the ring on Clare's finger." Allowing himself to smile in the friendship with his brother, and ignoring what a ring on Clare's finger actually meant.

Jonas grabbed Adam's hand. "Winners don't whine."

32

Adam rubbed his forearm as he waited for Father's arrival. He and
Jonas' arm wrestling battle lasted ten minutes, with Jonas as the victor.
Adam took some solace in the fact that Jonas was nursing his arm as
well, and the two parted laughing and in higher spirits than when
they greeted one another.

Now, the ceremony was just a few minutes away. Adam would
have stayed with Jonas, but he needed to be at the front of the
church to welcome Father before the wedding began, and Jonas
needed to get dressed. Adam wondered if all grooms waited until the
last minute. He sat, looking out over the packed pews of Family
members, smiling and talking excitedly about the wedding. As usual,
they sat women on the left and men on the right. Then, out of the
corner of his eye, Adam saw Father enter the front side door.

Adam stood, raising his hands to the heavens, signaling for
everyone to stand. When everyone was standing and silent, Father
walked to the altar, beside Adam. The music started and Jonas
walked in from the other side, standing at the front of the aisle.
When the back doors opened, everyone turned and craned their
necks to get the best view of the bride.

Adam allowed himself to look at the doors and gasped. He heard
his reaction echo amongst the rest of The Family, and allowed
himself a quick glance at Jonas who still stood straight, with a small
smile on his face. Adam felt a stab of jealousy hit him, and guilt for
feeling jealous, as he looked back down the aisle.

The bridal robe was simple white lace with a gold rope. Clare's
hair was pulled back, but not in the tight bun Adam was used to
seeing. Instead, the front was loose, allowing small, curled tendrils to
fall on either side of her face, and flowers decorated the curls that
were allowed to rest at the back of her head. She carried a small

bouquet that matched the rest of the decorations. Adam didn't think it was possible for anyone to look more beautiful.

Clare walked forward, slowly, staring straight at Adam. She wasn't smiling, but she didn't look sad either. Adam felt his heartbeat grow stronger. He knew he had to look away, but for some reason, he didn't. Instead, he allowed himself to get lost in her eyes as she moved toward him. Clare was the first to break eye contact, when she reached the front of the church and Jonas took her arm.

The shock of reality allowed Adam to look up and around at the church. Everyone was looking at the new couple, smiling, some with tears in their eyes. Adam gulped down the pain growing in his throat. He wanted to center his thoughts and looked for Samuel. The boy was standing in the back, crying, and they didn't look like happy tears. Adam looked away, knowing how easy it would be for him to echo Samuels' reaction if he didn't focus on the task at hand: pretending to be happy for his brother and sister.

Father signaled for The Family to sit. "My children, this is truly a glorious day the Lord has made. Today, we celebrate, not only the joining of these two wonderful and deserving people, but also the future and growth of our Family. It is the beginning of a new and exciting chapter in all of our lives. One filled with love, hope and a renewed sense of loyalty to one another. It is a reminder that we are all one Family, and although Clare and Jonas will become man and wife today, we must remember that they will remain our brother and sister. Two people who love us as much as we love them, and who will help us move into our future only with your love and support. It is not an easy road they are taking, but one they both take willingly out of love for one another, and love for all of you. Remember that, and help them on their journey. What the Lord has joined together, no man must separate."

Adam tried to calm his breathing. Jonas and Clare may have agreed to the wedding, but he wouldn't say they were willing. He stopped himself, he was being too critical, possibly because of the guilt that threatened to overwhelm him. It was as though Father was

181

speaking directly to Adam, condemning him for the feelings and actions of the day.

Then Father looked at Jonas and Clare. "My precious children, remember the vows you take today are holy vows. You must honor and protect them at all costs, for the good of our Family and your own souls."

Adam felt shame wash over him as he watched both Jonas and Clare bowed their heads. He prayed they were not feeling the same way he was.

"Now, please face one another," said Father, directing Clare and Jonas to turn and hold hands. Adam knew they practiced this before, but the motions still seemed forced.

"First you, Clare," whispered Father. "Do you, Clare, take Jonas to be your husband? Will you honor, love and protect him from this day forward? For better or for worse, in sickness and in health, in joy and in sorrow until death do you part?"

Clare swallowed and looked directly at Jonas. "I do." Adam focused on what his face was doing. He couldn't let his true emotions show.

Father nodded with a look of pride before turning to Jonas. "And you, Jonas. Do you take Clare to be your wife? Will you honor, love and protect her from this day forward? For better or for worse, in sickness and in health, in joy and in sorrow until death do you part?"

"I do," nodded Jonas.

Adam allowed a quick breath while keeping the smile on his face stable. Father placed Jonas' and Clare's hands on The Family's holy book. The one Father provided them, not the Bible. Adam sensed a thought trying to nag its way to the front of his mind, but he needed all his energy to keep up appearances. His cheeks were starting to hurt.

"Then, by the power vested in me by the Almighty Lord, I now pronounce you husband and wife." Father motioned for Jonas and Clare to face the congregation. "My children, I present the beginning of our future." Adam took a deep breath and held it as Jonas and

Clare joined hands and began walking down the aisle. Had it all really happened that quickly? After all the build-up, the questions, the confusion, were Jonas and Clare really married? They were. Adam heard Father say the words. There was nothing more to be done, it was over. Adam felt the weight of reality pushing down on him.

Adam felt Father's hand on his shoulder, forcing him to lift the weight and straighten his back.

"It is time, son," said Father. "Let us go toast your brother's and sister's happiness."

Adam nodded and walked alongside Father down the aisle, the rest of The Family following behind.

33

Adam refused to let himself look at Clare during the feast or the dancing that followed. Instead, he focused on the Children's performances, allowing himself to enjoy how happy they were to be a part of the day. He felt a small pang of sadness when he remembered Rebecca wasn't taking part. He looked for her behind the stage, but guessed the Teachers had her helping elsewhere. He hoped she felt included.

At Father's urging, he toasted the happy couple, being careful to hold eye contact with Jonas, thanking them both for their service and friendship. Then, when the socializing began, he focused on The Family. Adam considered leaving after the feast with Father, but decided against it. Father never socialized much with The Family, and although Adam was to be the leader, he never wanted to put himself on the same level of importance as Father.

For the rest of the evening, Adam smiled at stories the Elders told about Jonas and Clare when they were younger, danced with the Children and engaged in conversation with the rest. He considered joining Samuel, who stood quietly at the edges of the celebration, but didn't trust himself to be any comfort to anyone. He wondered why Samuel wasn't happy about the wedding, but Samuel seemed to be opposed to everything The Family did lately.

Other than Samuel, the rest of Adam's brothers and sisters seemed delighted. Speaking to the older members, Adam noticed that, while they were happy about the marriage, their conversations looked to the future, not on the day. They were excited to see what the next step would bring them, since many of them were with Father during the building of their world and the start of The Family.

"He hasn't steered us wrong yet," a few said. "They make a handsome couple, and their children will make us all proud," said others. "Babies bring a sense of hope few other experiences in this life can," the rest agreed.

Adam wasn't thrilled with the discussion of babies, but he was also enthralled by the look in their eyes when they talked about them.

"What do you mean, babies bring hope?" Adam finally asked. Adam only spent time around children, never babies. When he did see them above ground, they were either crying or sleeping.

Sister Agnes was the one to answer the question as tears slowly welled up in her eyes. "There is nothing in this world more innocent than a newborn child. Watching them grow and learn from the people and world around them, if done right, is an incredible experience."

Brother Calvin, a Builder, stepped in. "And their children will be born in this world. Where they will be safe to play, learn and grow without the threat of outside evils. There won't be anyone to cloud their judgment, lead them down the wrong path or steal their innocence too early. The possibilities for those children are endless."

"We do what we can with the young ones you rescue," chimed in Sister Beatrice. "You bring back such marvelous children, but the torment they experience in the outside world, it is difficult to erase. And they've already reached certain milestones that can't be undone. It works in the end, just look at you; but to see what can happen if we start from scratch, that will be a true miracle to behold."

"What do you mean, erase?" The voice came from behind Adam. He turned to see Brother Samuel moving closer to them.

Sister Beatrice looked at him and smiled. "When the Children first arrive, we do what we can to help erase the trauma of their previous life, but you can't undo it all."

"How do you do that?"

Adam listened quietly. He realized he didn't know what happened to the Children during the weeks between arriving in their world, and the time the Children actually started living amongst them. He didn't need to know to lead The Family after Father left, so it wasn't part of his training.

185

"Well, I can't get into all the details now. It's boring, and this is a celebration, but we do what we can to ease their pain."

"I don't see how that could be boring, doing such good work," Samuel said. Adam sensed a hint of sarcasm in the teen's voice, but he didn't think anyone else did.

"Before you arrived, Brother Samuel, Father and a few of us Teachers did a study of the best ways to help children who had been traumatized by life. We saw the destruction the outside world did to children, and we wanted to help them the best way we could. We developed a system of best practices based on psychology, science and, of course, Father's teachings."

"What are some of those best practices?"

Beatrice looked around the rest of the circle before answering. Everyone else remained silent. "Well, primarily, it focuses on showing them love. Love they didn't experience in the outside world, which I'm sure Brother Adam can attest to."

Samuel looked at Adam.

"It's true. One of the things Rescuers are trained to look for are children who lack the needed love and support of their families to reach their full potential."

"Exactly," said Sister Beatrice. "We give them what they were lacking above ground."

"So why don't any of us remember life before. Love doesn't make you forget the bad things. It simply softens the bad feelings."

"I said we primarily focus on love, not that there is not more to it."

"Then what takes away our memories?" Samuel was getting more aggressive.

Adam put his arm around Samuel. "I think that's enough, Samuel. We are here to celebrate, not to badger Sister Beatrice, who, I will remind you, has spent her life here, caring and teaching for all The Family's children, including you and me."

Sister Beatrice gave a nod of gratitude to Adam.

"Do you know what happens?" Samuel stared at Adam now.

"I know that I bring promising, yet damaged children to come and live with us. I know when they arrive, they are filled with anxiety, questions and sadness, and when they come to officially join us all, those bad feelings are gone. I also know that it is a system that sustains us all, and one that has helped you and me grow into the men we are today. That is enough for me."

"I just have trouble believing we could all show so much potential, if life were really that bad above ground," said Samuel, refusing to take Adam's hint to drop the topic.

This was exactly what Adam and Father didn't want. Samuel expressing his concerns and doubts to other members of The Family. Adam closed his eyes. He didn't have the energy for this, not after today. "Brother, please try and enjoy the celebration. I have said I am anxious to speak with you more on a great many things, but now is not the time."

Samuel's mouth tightened as he took a deep breath through his nose. "I suppose you're right. I don't want to ruin this celebration. I'll say goodnight."

Adam watched with concern as Samuel left. It was one thing for Samuel to question and be defiant in front of Adam. It was another to show such disrespect to the elderly Family members. He seemed to be slipping away faster every day.

Brother Joseph gave Adam a strong pat on the back. "He'll come around."

"I pray you are right." Adam looked at the Elder who was also watching Samuel leave. He felt comforted by Joseph's confidence that everything would work out, but also worried he didn't know how far gone Samuel might be. "How long since you've been above ground?" Adam asked Joseph.

"Not long enough," the elder builder answered. "As soon as this world was complete, I stayed. I wanted nothing more to do with the evils above ground. I admire your strength and courage to face it as often as you do."

"Thank you."

Brother Joseph gave Adam another pat on the back before asking Sister Agnes to dance. Adam remembered he should be celebrating as well and decided to rejoin the party with Sister Beatrice as his dance partner.

34

Adam forced himself to stay at the reception after Jonas and Clare left. He didn't want to follow them back to the huts and watch the two of them enter Clare's hut together. Adam supposed it was their hut now.

Instead, Adam joined in the dancing and conversation until the other party-goers started to leave.

Walking back to his hut, Adam said a silent prayer that there would be nothing but silence coming from Jonas and Clare's hut. He wondered if it was worth trying to sleep at all.

Before he made it to the huts, Adam saw Jonas running toward him.

"He's gone," said Jonas, out of breath.

"Who's gone?" asked Adam, surprised, and a little relieved to see Jonas alone on his wedding night.

"Brother Samuel. I saw him rush off, so I went to check on him. His robes, books, everything is gone."

"Everything? Are you sure?" asked Adam. He knew it wasn't important, he knew Jonas was telling the truth, he just didn't want to believe it. Samuel was leaving The Family.

"It's not like he had a lot to pack," said Jonas, sounding slightly annoyed. "Listen, last night, he was talking about leaving on his own. I thought it was a joke, but now ..." Jonas' voice trailed off.

"We need to stop him," said Adam.

"What if it's too late?" asked Jonas. It was the first time Adam could remember hearing even a hint of panic in Jonas' voice.

"How would we know if he did?" asked Adam. "Do you have communications with the Warriors outside?"

Jonas shook his head. "Only in the Comms room. It's not like we want to broadcast that particular duty to everyone."

"Okay," said Adam, not having time to ask what the Comms room was or comment on the duty Jonas was referring to. "You go to the Comms room and learn what you can. Tell the sentries to hold fire. I will go after Samuel. Any idea what tunnel he might use?"

"He should only have access to the Farmers' tunnel. Our tunnels were already sealed off once we decided to stop rescue missions, and no one knows about the Warrior tunnel except a few select Warriors and you."

"Okay, I'll go. You just make sure no one shoots me," said Adam, without a hint of sarcasm in his voice. He couldn't believe the words were actually coming out of his mouth.

Jonas simply nodded and started running. Adam went in the other direction toward the Farmers' tunnel. He only hoped Jonas had time to issue the warning before Adam's or Samuel's head, for that matter, made it above ground.

As he ran, Adam prayed there was still time. Samuel left the wedding hours ago, and Jonas was right, none of them had many belongings to pack. His body could already be lying in the woods just outside the fields. Adam shook the image out of his mind. Samuel had to be alive.

Adam made it to the tunnel without running into anyone else. Apparently, they were worn out from the wedding and went straight to bed. He was fast, possibly the fastest person in The Family. If Samuel took time to make this decision and walked to the tunnel to avoid suspicion, there was a chance Adam could catch him. The hope faded a little more every moment Adam ran down the white tunnel without Samuel in sight. He wanted to stop and listen for the sound of Samuel running or opening the hatch, but he couldn't risk losing a second. Would Adam hear the gunshot from here? No, he needed faith Jonas would stop the Warriors. Suddenly, he saw the shadow of the ladder in the distance. Was Samuel on it? There he was. At the top.

Adam shouted, "Samuel, no!"

There was no response, but now Adam could hear the hatch open, and then close.

Adam practically slammed into the ladder, not wasting a moment to slow down and started to climb. Samuel would be running now that he knew Adam was after him.

Adam reached the hatch. Turned the wheel. Opened the door. Then he heard it. A gun shot.

On instinct, Adam ducked down behind the hatch door. No, if there was any chance they missed, he had to find Samuel. The sentries must not have listened to Jonas. Or Jonas didn't make it in time. Adam's heart sank, but he couldn't worry about Jonas now, or himself for that matter. He needed to get Samuel.

Adam crawled out of the hatch, kicked it shut and waved his arms. He should have grabbed a white cloth to wave at the sentries. He hoped his unique wedding attire and arm waving would be a signal that he was chasing Samuel, not trying to escape. Adam looked around, but didn't see a body on the ground. Maybe the bullet missed Samuel. Adam allowed a small bit of hope into his mind and ran toward the woods.

"Samuel!" Adam yelled. "Samuel, come back!" Adam made it into the woods. It was dark and he could barely see through the branches. Which way would Samuel go?

One of the Warriors, Adam couldn't tell which one, dropped down from the branches in front of him.

"Sir," she said. "I've been instructed to tell you that Brother Samuel ran off toward the east."

"Was he injured?" asked Adam.

"No, sir," she answered. "We were instructed to fire a warning shot to get him to come home, but it just made him run faster."

Adam let out a sigh of relief. Jonas did make it to the Comms room in time. "Thank you," he said. "I'll go after him. You may return to your post."

"Thank you, sir," said the Warrior. "When you do return, give three short whistles when you reach Father's border. That way, we'll know it's you."

"Thank you," said Adam. He hadn't even thought of that, and was grateful someone had. He started running in the direction Samuel went. Adam knew he could maneuver through the brush easier than Samuel could, but what path would he take? He would be hard to track in the dark.

Adam was surprised to see that Samuel wasn't leaving much of a trace. He must have slowed down to avoid sound and to not break too many branches. After traveling about half of a mile, Adam started to wish he had a flashlight or any tools to help him find his brother. Could he get some from the Warriors? No, he didn't know where they were hiding in the trees, and he couldn't risk them losing tools they might actually need. He was already breaking too many rules.

Adam continued on, knowing that Samuel would have even more trouble navigating the woods. Adam stopped, took a deep breath, and looked around. He wasn't far from the exit of his own tunnel. He realized he was taking his usual path out of habit, but there was an easier one Samuel might take. If he made it this far, it would be simpler to navigate and lead away from Father's property. They designed it that way so no one visiting the nearby national park would accidentally find themselves on Father's land. The path toward the national park was only about a mile away, and ran around the border of Father's property. Samuel was bound to find it at some point.

Adam started to run again, feeling more and more sure of himself. He reached the path, stopped and listened. He couldn't hear anything, not even animals walking around. Likely because of all of the noise Adam made, but Samuel could have contributed as well. Adam started down the path, slowly and quietly, hoping for some sign of Samuel.

35

Adam walked for an hour before stopping. He wasn't tired, but he had trouble believing Samuel wasn't, or that Samuel would have made it this far without Adam catching up. The boy could be anywhere. Adam allowed himself a moment to thank God Jonas noticed Samuel's absence while they still had time to act. Why was Jonas checking on Samuel on his wedding night? Adam decided it didn't matter. He knew Jonas and Clare weren't thrilled about the situation, and maybe Jonas was just trying to find a way to delay the inevitable. Or maybe that was wishful thinking on Adam's part.

Adam leaned his head against a tree. The sun would be up in the next few hours and he knew the hikers from the park wouldn't be far behind. He would get a few hours sleep before heading back and trying to pick up Samuel's trail in the sunlight.

Adam looked at the sky. The moon finally made it out from behind the clouds and its silver light outlined the leaves in the trees. He breathed in the cool, pine-scented night air, and took in the stars sparkling in the night sky. Adam's shoulders relaxed, and he allowed himself to believe God was giving him a moment of peace in an otherwise painful and overwhelming day. Adam knew he didn't deserve it, but he accepted the gift gratefully.

Just before dozing off, Adam heard the distinct sound of a branch breaking. He opened his eyes and turned his head just fast enough to see a head duck behind bushes approximately ten yards away. Adam jumped up and ran to the bushes before Samuel had the chance to stand back up.

"There you are!" The sternness in Adam's voice was unintentional, but he felt the anger begin to fill him mere seconds after the relief of finding Samuel.

"Hello, Brother," said Samuel in a tired and defeated voice.

Adam had so much he needed to say and ask, he couldn't think of where to begin. He decided to start with the basics. "What are you doing out here?"

"Hoping you would lead me out to the real world."

"I would lead you? You left." What was Samuel trying to do?

"I know, but I didn't know where to go. Then I saw you running and figured if I could follow you, you might lead me where I needed to go. I thought maybe God was on my side for once." Samuel sounded bitter in that last sentence.

"You were following me?" Adam asked, almost as much to himself as he did to Samuel. He had been so panicked and in such a hurry to find his brother, he hadn't stopped to think that Samuel wouldn't know where to go. If Adam just slowed down and allowed himself to think rationally, he might have found Samuel sooner.

Samuel's voice shook Adam out of lecturing himself any longer. "So, are you here to shoot me?"

"What?" Adam took a step back. Why was that Samuel's first thought?

"I know what a gunshot sounds like. I've heard the Warriors practicing. They were firing at me!"

They were firing at him during practice? No, that didn't make sense, Adam thought. He must mean the warning shot. "Do you mean when you ran away?" He wanted to be sure, it really had been a long day.

"Yes. My own brothers and sisters. They tried to kill me." Adam heard the pain and sadness in Samuel's voice. The boy wasn't even mad that they tried to kill him.

"They weren't trying to kill you. It was a warning shot. They were trying to get you to stop."

"Oh. Well, that's good. I guess."

"What are you doing?" Adam asked again. He didn't want Samuel to have time to think about why there were guns out there in the first place. "You know that no one is allowed to leave."

"Yeah, well, staying isn't really an option for me anymore, either." Samuel spoke to the ground.

Adam sat down. He had a feeling they would be there for a while. "Why? I know you have your questions, but at least you're safe and loved back home. Why do you have to leave?"

"The only thing that gave me any happiness is gone. The only person who truly understood me, who made me feel like I was part of something bigger ..." Samuel's voice faded away as he blinked tears out of his eyes. "It doesn't even matter," he whispered. He started to speak again, stopped himself and then cleared his throat. "They belong to someone else now."

The lump in Adam's throat nearly choked him. He didn't bother stopping the tears from running down his own face. It was too much. Adam understood Samuel's feelings too well. Samuel loved Clare too. Of course. She said Samuel had the same questions she did, that she looked to save everyone too. No wonder the boy ran after the wedding, why his tears and emotions reflected Adam's own. If Adam didn't have all the information he did, if he wasn't responsible for the well-being of the entire Family, he probably would have run away too.

Adam hugged Samuel, knowing no words would provide any comfort. He just held him and they cried together.

Adam was tempted to stay in the forest, away from Clare and Jonas and all of the responsibilities of The Family, but he also knew they needed to go back. At some point, Father would realize they were missing.

"We need to go back before anyone notices you are gone," said Adam.

Samuel wiped his eyes. "They were shooting at me. I think they know."

Adam shook his head. "Again, they were just warning shots. Jonas said he would cover for us as long as he could. The night watch won't be relieved until morning, and we could be back before then."

Now Samuel was looking at the ground, shaking his head. "I can't go back. Not now."

Adam knew that wasn't an option. They had to go back, but maybe not right away. Samuel was already out, he had questions, and Clare said he would need to see the evils for himself before he would believe any of them. Adam's emergency clothes were buried about two miles up the trails near the wooded camping sites, and he could get a message to The Family that they wouldn't be returning for another day. The clothes were there, in the event he felt he was being followed and didn't want to lead anyone to The Family, he would have emergency provisions and disguises to last him about a week.

He and Father had a communication protocol to alert Father to any delays as well, Adam could leave a message so no one would worry. He only needed a day or two with Samuel and they could go home. As far as he knew, Father wasn't planning to leave for at least a week after the wedding. Father might not like it, but Adam needed to do what was best for The Family. Maybe this was it. Samuel was taking extreme measures, and voicing doubts to other Family members. Maybe the questions did need an extreme response. Adam said a quick prayer that he was making a noble and not a selfish decision.

"Listen," Adam said. He pulled just far away enough so he could look into Samuel's eyes. "Since you're already out here, there are things you should see. Maybe it will help bring you some peace."

Samuel raised his eyebrows in what looked like a combination of surprise and relief in the moonlight. "Really?"

"We can't be gone long," Adam warned as gently as he could. "But clearly, talking isn't going to help you."

"Thank you, Brother."

"Let's get some sleep. It's been a long day."

Samuel nodded and looked around. "Where do we sleep?"

"Right here." Adam gestured to the ground. He knew it wouldn't be terribly comfortable, but if Samuel was as tired as he was, it wouldn't matter.

The two lay on the ground, heads resting on their arms, and fell asleep.

36

Adam woke with a deep breath. The forest air was cool and damp with the morning dew. He thought of Clare. She would be waking up next to Jonas. Jonas would get to see her hair untidy, before she had a chance to put it up in her usual bun. Jealousy and overwhelming sadness welled up at the bottom of Adam's throat. He swallowed it, sat up and stretched.

His back was sore from the hard ground, but the air began to refresh him and he looked around. The sun just barely peeked through the large trees, which were bigger and denser than anything they had at home, and sounds of birds chirping filled the air.

He turned and gently shook Samuel to wake him. They needed to get started, and Adam needed a distraction from his thoughts.

Samuel grunted, barely opening his eyes.

"Come on, Brother. We need to move before the hikers start coming. We don't have much time."

"Okay," said Samuel, stretching himself.

Adam watched, not wanting to miss what he was certain would come next.

Samuel yawned, rubbed his eyes, opened them and then opened his mouth in awe. Adam watched as the boy looked up, taking in the full size of the trees that filled the forest. Of course, Samuel saw trees from a distance while working in fields, but never up close, in the middle of them all. Adam felt a sense of joy, being able to share the beauty of God's creation with another member of The Family, but it was a joy they would need to share while walking.

"We need to move," he said, standing up, and motioning for Samuel to do the same.

Samuel nodded and stood, but then jumped back, looking around. "Wait, what's that?"

Adam looked around as well, but he didn't see or hear anything. "What?"

"Over there," whispered Samuel. "I just heard it again."

Adam looked to where Samuel was pointing, and saw the two squirrels running up the tree trunk. "It's fine, it's just squirrels."

"Oh, okay."

As they walked, Samuel looked everywhere, and Adam had to keep a close eye on his brother to make sure he didn't trip. Samuel wanted to stop at every noise and investigate what animal made it. "Adam, look! It's a frog!" he shouted, or "Do you see how high that bird was flying?" Adam indulged the delays for the first half hour, understanding this was the first time Samuel was seeing any of this outside of a book, but he started to get concerned about Samuel only seeing the beauty and not the evil of the world. They couldn't stay out here forever.

"Samuel," Adam said as Samuel stopped to watch a caterpillar move across a log. "I promise you we will have more time to explore the wonder that is nature, but we really do need to keep moving."

"Oh, right, sorry, Adam." Samuel's face turned a little red.

"No, I'm sorry. This forest truly is amazing. In fact, most of the children I bring back do exactly what you're doing now, but we can't stay here long and there is more you need to see."

"Did I?"

"Did you what?"

"Was I this fascinated the first time you brought me through these woods? To The Family?"

Adam stopped walking. Of course, Samuel didn't remember, none of the Children did, but the sadness of Samuel's voice caught him off guard. Adam thought back to when he rescued Samuel.

He knew he couldn't tell Samuel the details of his rescue, none of the Children were allowed to know that information, but Adam supposed there wasn't too much harm in answering this one question. As long as he was careful.

"It was dark. There wasn't as much to see, and you were tired." All of that was true, even if Adam was leaving out the part that Samuel was also incredibly sad. Adam never did find out why. He broke almost every rule of rescuing when he found Samuel, but it was his first time. Adam supposed he was paying for those mistakes now.

"You can't tell me anything else, can you?"

"No, I'm sorry." They needed to keep moving. He needed to get a message to Father before he started to worry. "But I do believe I did what was best for you. I've always cared about you, and I will continue to try and keep you safe."

"I understand. I'll try to keep up."

"Thank you," Adam said, trying to keep frustration out of his voice. This happened every time he came above ground. The beautiful reminder of the paradise God created for people, and how it now had to be destroyed because humans didn't deserve it. Samuel, and the other Children, missed out on all of this because of those people. Because they chose their own desires and temptations over all the Lord freely provided. Adam needed to try to calm down so that he could show the evil side of the world to Samuel. The boy wouldn't trust him if he couldn't at least appear rational.

For the most part, Samuel kept his promise, but he did get distracted by a few larger animals like deer and elk. Adam was grateful they hadn't run across any hikers yet. Their robes would surely spark curiosity and conversations. Normally, Adam would change before leaving on a mission to avoid unnecessary encounters. He needed to get Samuel out of the woods.

They reached the point where they needed to walk about a half mile west of the trail to where Adam's emergency kit was buried. The brush was thick, and Adam warned Samuel to be on the lookout for snakes in case they were poisonous. When they reached their destination, Adam used a stone to dig up the kit from under a bush of thorns. He chose the spot intentionally so campers or hikers wouldn't accidently dig it up when they needed to relieve themselves.

It was hard work, but Adam didn't mind and it gave Samuel a little extra time to enjoy their surroundings.

Adam smiled the moment he heard the sound of the rock hitting metal. He pulled up the case, got free from the thorns and opened the lid. Inside was a backpack with five t-shirts, two pairs of shorts, a pair of pants, sweatshirt, energy bars, a few bottles of water, blanket, knife, and $1,000.

He looked up and saw Samuel bent over something a few feet away. "Brother, I've got what we need."

Samuel stood up and ran over. "It's amazing here." He was smiling.

"I know." Adam handed Samuel a pair of shorts and t-shirt. "Here, take these and change out of your robes. We'll blend in better."

"Okay," said Samuel, looking at what he was handed.

Adam slid his shorts on under his robe, before taking off the robes and putting on his own shirt. He realized he didn't have boots or even tennis shoes, since the bag was meant for him when he would have already been wearing appropriate footwear. They would have to travel in their sandals.

When he looked up, Samuel was pulling at the shirt which was too big for him and made of harsher material than the robes Samuel was used to wearing.

"I know it's uncomfortable," said Adam, trying to loosen the shirt he was wearing by moving his arms around. "You'll get used to it."

"You have to wear these all the time up here?" asked Samuel, who was now scratching his back where the tag of the shorts would be.

"Yes, to fit in and stay unnoticed."

"Well, that's at least one reason to dislike coming here."

Adam allowed himself a small laugh and repacked the backpack with their robes and slung it over his shoulder. "Okay, are you ready?

Samuel nodded, still pulling at the shirt shoulders.

"Now, if we run into anyone, just let me do the talking."

"Okay. Where are we going?"

"You're going to meet other people. You'll see what they're really like."

To Adam, it looked like Samuel was about to say something, but stopped himself. Since he didn't want to risk a philosophical discussion on the hiking trail, Adam ignored it. "Breakfast," said Adam, tossing an energy bar to Samuel.

Samuel gave the bar the same look as he gave the clothes.

Adam opened his and took a bite. "They don't taste good, and I'm not entirely sure what they're made of, but they'll keep you going."

Samuel nodded, opened his bar and ate it, only letting a brief look of disgust cross his face before taking a deep breath and continuing on.

They were about a half mile from the visitor center when Adam heard a cheerful voice behind them.

"Well, good morning!"

Adam turned to see a middle-aged couple dressed in matching green and khaki outfits with large, sun-blocking hats, and carrying walking sticks. "Good morning," he said.

"Great morning to get out, isn't it?" asked the woman.

"It's beautiful," responded Adam.

"You're not really dressed for it though," said the man, motioning to the sandals Adam and Samuel were still wearing. "You could break a foot."

"We like feeling the earth. We're careful."

"Can't say I blame you. Just trying to help you learn from my mistakes. One bad trip over a boulder was all it took for me to learn that lesson."

Adam wanted to say something condescending, something that would make the man know that giving obvious and uninvited advice was obnoxious and a little rude, but he stopped himself, remembering that wouldn't help his cause. "We'll remember that for next time," said Adam, and he allowed the couple to pass them on the trail.

"Okay, well, you boys enjoy the rest of your day," said the woman, waving at them.

"You too," Adam said, waving back. He didn't start moving again until the couple was well ahead of them.

"You just lied," Samuel said when they started walking again.

"I know." Adam, kept his eyes focused straight ahead. He was used to lying above ground, but did feel ashamed, now that someone else witnessed it.

"Do you have to do that a lot?"

"More than I would like."

"You just did it so easily. I almost believed you."

Adam didn't say anything. He didn't know what to say.

"Do you only lie above ground?"

"What do you mean?" Adam turned toward Samuel.

"I mean, have you ever lied to someone in The Family?" asked Samuel.

"Of course not!" Adam was truly offended, especially since he went through such great pains not to lie underground. It wasn't always easy. "How could you ask me something like that?"

Samuel backed away slightly from Adam. "I'm sorry, Brother. It's just you did that with such ease. It made me wonder."

Adam took a deep breath, trying to calm himself. The negative effects of being above ground were already seeping into his conscious. He was feeling anger, shame and a sense of superiority. He needed to remind himself that Samuel was never above ground and that questions were to be expected. "As I have explained, sometimes we need to do things that feel wrong here, because there is no other way. I don't like lying, and avoid it when I can." He looked at Samuel to see if the boy was comprehending what he was saying; he wasn't. "This is why The Family lives underground, away from all of this. We can't live the pure and honest lives we do and survive in this world. It wouldn't work. To survive here, sometimes you have to do things that are unacceptable at home. You won't feel good about it, and you may even resent the people that force you to do it, even if they don't know what they made you do."

"Okay, I'm sorry. I will try not to question your actions."

"I understand the questions, but I need you to remember that everything I do is for our safety."

"I do."

"Thank you."

"I'm just having trouble seeing the bad."

Adam closed his eyes. He knew Samuel's silence so far was too good to last.

"The animals run and play with no boundaries, the trees are bigger than anything I've ever seen and even the grass and moss are a green I don't think any man can reproduce."

"They try," said Adam, not hiding the scorn in his voice.

"I could stay here forever."

"That would cost you."

"What do you mean?"

"People have to pay to stay in this forest. Other people make money from humans' desire to rejoin with nature, and they do it by destroying some of that nature to make room for the modern conveniences the paying public has come to expect. Some are better than others, and stay in tents or even sleep outside, but they still have to pay to do so."

"But why? Isn't God's creation there for everyone to enjoy?"

"It should be. But people here believe everything is meant to be owned and controlled. You will find very few things are actually free in this world, so be cautious. Don't take anything without knowing who owns it and what they want for it."

Samuel just nodded. Adam wondered if the message was getting through or not.

Finally, they reached the end of the trail. Adam looked at the familiar hotel that was built with wood, painted brown. He never understood why they painted wood brown, when the wood itself was always more attractive. There was only one car stopped to check in, and the rest filled the parking lot on the side. The sign in front of the hotel welcomed visitors to the national park. Adam stopped Samuel before he walked into the parking lot. "You need to be on the lookout for cars," Adam explained. "They don't always stop for people."

"I'll just follow you," said Samuel, a tinge of annoyance now in his voice.

Adam found a bench just off of the parking lot for them to sit. "What's wrong?" he asked.

"What do you mean?"

"You seem to be questioning me already, and we can't have that out here. I need to know you will do as I say in order to keep us and our Family safe," said Adam with an emphasis on the word Family. He wanted to help Samuel, but he also knew he couldn't let Samuel escape. Too much was at stake.

"I understand. It's just that you don't seem to be giving any of them a chance. You hate them."

Adam took a deep breath. "I hate how they treat the earth and themselves. You also have to understand, my feelings come after years of being surrounded by them. By watching them. They aren't feelings that just came out of thin air."

"I suppose," said Samuel. "I just haven't seen anything that would make you so angry. I've questioned our ways, I even ran away from home, but you are staying with me, trying to keep me safe. Why am I worth helping, but they aren't?"

"Samuel," said Adam, realizing more words weren't going to make a difference. "I want you to stop and watch these people get in and out of their cars."

"Okay," said Samuel.

They both looked out at the pavement that covered what was once a beautiful forest. Adam shook his head. The irony of people driving SUVs and other gas-guzzling vehicles to the forest so they could escape the city pollution never ceased to amaze or anger him.

He closed his eyes and breathed deeply, trying to calm himself. He was here to try and teach Samuel, and he obviously couldn't do that if he let his own emotions take over. He opened his eyes to a family getting out of their car. The father was yelling at the mother about why they don't eat in the car, their teenage son was wearing headphones and staring down at some type of electronic device and a younger daughter was crying because she hated being outside. Adam motioned for Samuel to look at them.

"Do you see that? That is what greed and vanity get you. A life where you cannot even enjoy the beauty that God created. They take the world for granted."

Samuel looked over at the family and then looked back at Adam. "Okay, but what about them?" Samuel pointed to a man and a woman wearing backpacks as though they were heading out on a hike, and holding hands with two younger children. All four were smiling. "Or them," said Samuel, pointing out a group of twenty-something friends filing out of the hotel toward the parking lot. They were also smiling and laughing as they walked. "Even your family," Samuel continued, pointing back at the first family Adam noticed. "They seem to be coming around."

Adam looked back. The man was now kissing the woman on the forehead, apologizing, and the son was grabbing bags out of the car, although he still had the headphones on. The girl was still crying.

"Don't you see how they are ignoring the one who seems to be in the most pain?"

"I suppose, although, she doesn't seem to be that hurt, just loud."

"Come with me." Adam took Samuel into the lodge where there was a small restaurant with televisions all around them. He chose a table near one of the televisions and ordered them each eggs, sausages and hash browns.

"It won't be as good as you're used to, but it will be better than the energy bar," said Adam, hoping breakfast would give him time to think. "I'll be right back." Adam got up before Samuel could ask any more questions. He needed to get a message to Father and didn't want to waste any more time. He went to the lodge courtesy phone, dialed the number that Father set up for the Rescuers and left the "Sorry, wrong number" message that would signal to Father he was okay, and would be home as soon as it was safe. Then he quickly returned to the table.

Adam was surprised at how different Samuel's experience in the parking lot was from his own. Samuel saw the good in everyone, while Adam only saw the bad. He wondered if that was a difference in the two of them, or one that grew in himself after being above ground so many times. Did Adam ever have a pleasant moment above ground? When he ran at sunset, he always appreciated God's creation, but became angry that it was wasted on the sinners above ground. Was that it?

Adam tried to remember his first mission, the one where he rescued Samuel. Unlike most of the rescued Children, Adam could remember being above ground before living with The Family. However, that time was always indoors with Father. Adam was rarely allowed in the world except when it was time for him and Father to move to a new location. Moving underground with The Family was the first time Adam could remember feeling settled and secure. When he was told to go back aboveground, he was scared. He was afraid of what or who he would encounter. The mission itself went fine. Adam managed to live in a small apartment for the month, watching families at city parks and finally finding Samuel, an energetic and inquisitive child who had very disinterested foster parents. Adam never actually spoke to either of the parents. One day, Samuel just ran to Adam, crying, and Adam took him. It seemed the easiest way, and Father warned Adam to never do that again. The fact that battling parents forced police to focus on one of them instead of looking for another kidnapper, he was able to remain a Rescuer. Fear and anger were always part of his experience above ground, but maybe not as strong as they were now. Adam made a note to watch his anger around Samuel

37

Adam finished his breakfast quickly, and instructed Samuel to watch the televisions while he found them a ride out of the park. Watching the people on vacation clearly wasn't going to convince his brother they weren't worth saving. This would be when they were at their best, but Samuel wouldn't know that. Adam rarely watched television himself when he was above ground. It usually only served to make him more angry, but he hoped it might do the same for his companion.

Once Samuel promised not to talk to anyone or leave without Adam, Adam went to the front desk. He hoped there would be a shuttle to one of the nearby towns. Normally, Father had a car in the parking lot waiting for Adam, but since this particular trip wasn't planned, Adam couldn't count on that.

He walked up to the concierge desk where a man in khaki pants and a green polo shirt greeted him with a smile. "Good morning, sir. How may I help you?"

"Hi, my friend and I would really love to get into one of the towns for the day. Is there any chance you have some type of transportation we could use?"

"I'm sorry, sir, no," said the concierge, not able to hide the confusion from his face. Apparently, he was never asked this question before. "How did you get here?"

"We came with friends," said Adam. "Our plan was to stay and just hike the full week, and our friends would come back for us, but now we're thinking getting out to the surrounding areas could be fun. Any suggestions?"

"You can come with us, if you'd like," said a voice from behind Adam.

Adam turned around to find another man dressed in khaki shorts and a blue polo shirt, smiling at him from under a blue baseball hat. "Thank you," said Adam, trying to keep the skepticism from his voice. "Where are you headed?"

"Whitefish," said the man. "I'll warn you though, it's about an hour and a half drive with a bunch of crazy Catholics."

Catholics? Was Adam really willing to risk putting Samuel on a bus of religious people when he needed to see the evils of the world? Or maybe it would be a good thing, because Samuel would see the hypocrisy. The Rescuers learned about other religions during their training, to prepare them for any false God talk they might encounter. Catholics were a wildcard. Some were even more strict than Father, while others didn't actually know what the difference was between Catholicism and those people pretending to praise God in the middle of a light show. Adam thought about it. It was risky, but he didn't have many options. Plus, three hours on a bus still gave them a few hours in the city and enough time to get back to The Family by the next morning. Adam hoped they could make it back that night, but if they needed to sleep in the woods one more night they could.

"I appreciate it, thank you, sir," said Adam, shaking the man's hand. "I'm Adam, and my friend is Samuel."

"It's a pleasure to meet you, Adam," said the man. "I'm Father Fitzpatrick, but you may call me John. Our bus is leaving in about a half hour, once we've had a chance to wash up from breakfast. I'll make sure there are seats for you."

Adam smiled and nodded, then headed back to Samuel. He hoped this would work.

When he got back to the table, Samuel had his head in his hands, turned away from the television.

"Everything okay?" asked Adam, paying close attention to his facial expression. He didn't want Samuel to know his apparent discomfort was part of Adam's plan.

Samuel looked up. "How can they be so awful to each other?"

Adam took a deep breath. Well, at least one part of the plan was working. "What did you see?"

"They're fighting each other in almost every part of the world. If countries aren't fighting, individuals are hurting one another for petty reasons. How have they not destroyed themselves yet?"

"It's a good question," said Adam, deciding to allow Samuel to convince himself of the evil above ground.

"I just don't understand how they can be so terrible. There must be some good. Just look around, people laughing, smiling, enjoying God's creation."

"This is where they come to escape the reality of their lives. Look around. Watch that waitress deliver that tray of food, and then watch what happens next." Adam pointed to a waitress who was carrying two plates of steaming hot food to a nearby table. She put the plates down, said a few words and left. Then, the couple at the table started eating. "Did you see that?"

"They didn't pray."

"That's right. If you watch carefully, no one here will pray at any point during their meal. They won't give thanks. In fact, if you watch long enough, at least one person will get mad about whatever is in front of them. They aren't grateful for the food, nor do they credit God for providing it to them."

"That doesn't necessarily make them evil. Maybe they are just uninformed. If we explain about God and all that he does, maybe they would start to pray."

"They know about God. Some of them even claim to follow Him, but won't pray and give thanks before their meal. Others have simply chosen not to believe. There are some here who try to bring them back on the path, and many times, those people are mocked or ignored."

"Well, what about that?" Samuel pointed to the front entrance, where a group of friends were greeting one another with hugs. "That's love. That's kindness. Isn't that worth anything?"

"Samuel." Adam paused, trying to choose the right words. "You are correct in thinking that the world isn't all bad, but we can't save everyone. We do our best, we rescue the children that can be rescued, but for our sakes and the sake of the human race, we can't do much more."

"There must be more we can do," said Samuel.

"Take the day. I truly believe you will understand."

Samuel let out a small snort and shook his head. "Don't take this the wrong way, but I'm hoping to prove you wrong."

Adam nodded. "It would be wonderful if you could." Adam surprised himself with the realization that he did want Samuel to prove him wrong. He thought of Clare's face when she talked about trying to save more people. The crushed hope. Disappointment took over Adam's surprise, he knew Samuel wouldn't prove him wrong, no matter how badly they both wanted it.

"Do you mean that?"

"Of course, I do. Samuel, I don't want it to be a bad world. It's just that my experiences here have proven otherwise. I think it would be wonderful if you could change my mind. I just don't believe it will happen." Adam took a deep breath and sat back in his chair. His chest felt tight. What else could he say to Samuel to make him understand? He looked back up to see Samuel's attention now completely focused on the television. Adam looked and saw what captured Samuel so completely. He felt his heart skip a beat. It was Father, walking with people the newscaster called "world leaders."

"Ambassador Kingston is scheduled to meet with Russian officials early next week to discuss a variety of topics, from nuclear weapons, cyber terrorism and possible trade deals with the U.S. The president says Kinsgston's business and technological expertise will prove vital in the talks," the disembodied voice said over a variety of videos featuring Father, leaving no question that she was actually talking about him, and what he would be doing tomorrow, not something he did in the past.

Adam tried to focus on his breathing while attempting to wrap his mind around what he was hearing. It was unusually difficult to do both at the same time. Was Father an ambassador of some kind with business and technological expertise? Adam only ever saw Father as a man of God, intent on doing what was right. How could he not only fit in, but be lifted up in the world he taught the entire Family to fear? The people praising him were the very people Father wanted to destroy. Adam thought about the shameful things he did to fit in during rescue missions. What did Father have to do to reach the level he was apparently at now?

Adam looked around for a newspaper. There, on the front page of a *USA Today*, was another photo of Father, or Alex Kingston.

Near the middle of the article, Adam found the information he was looking for.

> Kingston, caught after successfully hacking into several intelligence department servers, and serving several years in prison, went on to make billions through his cyber security firm, EDIN (Expert Defense of International Networks) after his early release for good behavior.

Adam stopped reading. Caught hacking? Prison? Billionaire? Adam knew Father was wealthy, he could tell just by comparing how Father lived above ground to living conditions Adam saw on his missions, but a billionaire? Adam had trouble imagining that much money. He also had trouble believing Father would keep all that money. Was it getting warm in the restaurant? Adam thought it through a little more. Father was responsible for the entire Family, it would be irresponsible to take on that responsibility if he didn't have the funds to cover them. He took a deep breath.

Still, Father was apparently a very powerful man in this world. A world Father claimed to despise. How could he live and be so successful in this world without succumbing to the evils they were supposed to be fighting against? Adam supposed if anyone could do it, Father could. He took another deep breath. But the article also called him a criminal. He was caught, put in prison, and yet he was praised. His success was based on the evils of the world. The name Kingston sounded vaguely familiar, but it frightened Adam. That couldn't be Father, but it was, the news reports confirmed it. Adam looked up, trying to stop the dizzy feeling taking over his head. It didn't work.

Adam looked over at Samuel, who was now reading the same article Adam just put down.

"What do you think?" asked Adam when Samuel put down the paper. Focusing on the task of helping Samuel helped to ground him. His breathing calmed. Adam wasn't sure he wanted to know Samuel's answer, but he was sure he needed to talk to someone about it.

"I think Father clearly knows how to keep secrets."

Was that all he had to say? Adam's heart was now beating in frustration, the heat rose from his chest to his face. "That's all you take from that?"

"Did you know his real name?" Samuel shot back. "Or even have a clue as to how rich and powerful he is? For someone who believes everything about this world is wrong, Father certainly found a way to live successfully in it."

Adam closed his eyes. He needed to focus and everything was getting blurry. Adam tried to ignore the fact that was the same initial thought he had himself. "He must have done it out of necessity. He needs to care for all of us, that can't be cheap."

"I suppose. I'm just thinking about all the lies and compromises you say you've had to make on your rescue missions, and those are only a couple of months each year. I'm just wondering what Father has to do to thrive here all year long."

Adam stood up quickly. His lungs needed more space, he wanted to escape and he was sorry he started the conversation. He admitted Samuel made good points, but they were also blasphemous. How could Samuel question Father like that? How could Adam himself question Father like that? Of course, Father found a better way to live in this world. Adam had no doubt of that, and he was mad at Samuel for trying to make him question Father again.

Adam took another deep breath, he needed to calm himself. Not only did he not know where to go, now that he was standing, but he also reminded himself he shouldn't get mad at Samuel for asking questions. The boy was wrong to question Father, but he did question and it was Adam's job to answer those questions and bring Samuel back around.

"Samuel." Adam sat back down. His eyes started to clear. "I understand you have questions, and I know I should be more understanding, but it does anger me when you question Father like that. He saved all of us, he knows what is best for us. He deserves the benefit of the doubt."

"The problem is, I don't know if I believe that he really saved us. I don't know if I believe he really knows what is best."

Adam nodded as he pushed down the scream he felt rising in his throat. "Okay, I need you to be honest with me. No holding back, no half-truths, just the complete truth. When did you start doubting Father and why? I know it wasn't always like this."

Samuel straightened his posture and looked directly at Adam. "I can try, but the full truth is I don't know exactly when it started."

"Okay," Adam forced himself to look at the boy, actually Samuel was a man now, sitting across from him. Adam only had one day to bring his brother around. He was going to need to move this along, and to do that, he needed as much information as he could get. Lecturing wasn't working. Maybe listening would.

"It started when I realized I was having," Samuel paused for a moment, "sinful thoughts. At least, sinful according to the rules Father established for us. I fell in love with a member of The Family and we started seeing each other in secret. The relationship didn't feel wrong and the closer we became, the more I thought that maybe it wasn't wrong. When Father announced Jonas and Clare's marriage, I realized I was right, loving someone isn't sinful. Once I came to that realization, I started to wonder what other rules could be broken."

Adam tried to hide his confusion. Back in the forest, he was convinced that Samuel loved Clare and that was why he ran away, but that couldn't be who Samuel was talking about now. Clare wouldn't have carried on a secret relationship. She kissed Adam. Did Adam misunderstand what was said? "But Father reversed that rule. You can be with the person you love now," said Adam, trying to clarify for himself.

"No, I can't. Only Father determines who we can be with. If it were really up to us, Jonas and Clare wouldn't be married right now. I know you can't disagree with that."

Pain hit Adam's chest. No, he couldn't, but that still didn't answer the question as to why Samuel was so convinced he couldn't be with the person he chose.

"Who is it you fell in love with?" asked Adam, praying Samuel wouldn't say Clare's name. Praying he wasn't as large a fool as he was beginning to feel.

"Adam, you have been a good friend and mentor. And believe it or not, I do hope this trip brings us both a better understanding and acceptance of our world, but I'm not ready to answer that question yet."

Adam nodded. He wouldn't force the issue. In truth, if Samuel asked him the same question, he wouldn't answer either. But now wasn't the time to dwell on that. "Okay, even if you're right about this, doesn't Father changing his mind prove he knows what's best? He recognized he was wrong about keeping us all celibate and he changed his mind. He's never claimed to be perfect."

"If he never claimed to be perfect, why is it wrong to question him?"

"Father gives us a moral path to follow and a world where we can follow it without judgment. You have no idea what a precious gift that is. Watch the people in this world. They are filled with self-doubt and fear. It causes them to do horrible things to one another."

"I guess I haven't seen enough of it yet. There are terrible things in this world, but I've seen a lot of happy people too. Happier than I've ever seen anyone in our world. I'm just starting to think it may be worth it."

Adam shook his head. He knew the trade-off wasn't worth it. Now he knew how he could help Samuel. He had to show him why their world was so much better than this one.

As Adam thought, he heard screaming coming from one of the hallways, and he worked to keep a grin off his face. "Come with me."

Samuel followed Adam into the hallway just in time to see a young boy, screaming at what Adam assumed was his father. "I don't want to walk again. I want to go swimming!"

"Why are you acting this way?" the father yelled at the crying boy. "This is supposed to be a fun family trip and you are ruining it."

"I want to swim!" the boy shouted back through his tears.

"You can swim all summer," the man yelled through gritted teeth. "Now it's time to enjoy the beauty of nature."

"I don't care about nature."

"How can you not care? This is the whole reason we came here. People come from all over the world to see these things."

"Well then, let them see them. I don't want to be here! I'm tired of walking!"

"We've barely started."

Adam turned to Samuel and led him back to the lobby. He was feeling better, calmer, as though God offered the pair to help Adam prove his point. "You see, a father and son. A pair that should show love and respect towards one another instead making a public display of anger and frustration. It's not uncommon. There is no shared moral code, the boy is spoiled and the father can't control his temper or teach the boy through love. Instead, they yell."

"But that is just one family. And they are arguing over such a small thing. How do you know there isn't usually love between them?"

"I don't, and there could be," said Adam, ignoring the twinge of frustration that poked at his gut. "But would you ever see a display like this in our Family? Have you ever seen something like that?"

"No," said Samuel with a sigh.

"No. Because we are raised and taught to treat one another with respect. We share a moral code that is backed by our beliefs. It not only strengthens our bond as a Family, but helps us find productive ways to solve any disagreements we may have." Adam waited for a response from Samuel, but none came. "Okay, let's wait here. I found us a ride into the city."

"Okay." Samuel sat down on a lobby chair and appeared to be deep in thought. "But ..." Samuel started speaking and then stopped.

"But, what?" asked Adam, hiding his annoyance that the conversation wasn't over.

"We follow the same path, and it allows us to get along, but how do we know it's the right path? We take what Father says as truth. That what he says is sinful is sinful, that what he says is good is good. We never question him."

"He takes all of his lessons from the Bible. He's not making things up as he goes, he is simply teaching us the lessons of Jesus Christ."

"Some of those lessons seem counter-intuitive."

"How so?" Adam never saw a conflict between any of the lessons from Father.

"We're taught that certain behaviors are sinful. And that those that sin will be punished by God, but we're also told to love and respect everyone. How can we do that and call them sinners at the same time?"

"We're all sinners. I have my flaws just as you do and just as Father does. The key is to do our best to avoid sinful temptation, and to ask for forgiveness when we fail. When we see sin in others, it is our job to try to help them, because that is how we love and respect them. That's why we rescue the children, to try to protect

217

them from families that have chosen the path of evil. Those that have turned away from God."

"But then aren't we punishing the parents?"

"They agree to give us their children."

"But not all of them. You only convince one parent to give up their child. Sometimes there is a second that has no knowledge that they're losing their child until it's too late."

Adam cleared his throat. No one ever questioned his rescuing tactics before. He admitted he didn't love his job, but he did believe it was important. "That second parent is usually the reason the first parent is willing to give up their child. The first parent is so desperate to save their child from the second, that they are willing to give the child up and never see them again. That is true love and sacrifice."

"So why don't we save them too?"

"We give them the option. We tell them that there is a chance they can join us if they stay on the correct path."

"But we haven't gone back to get any of them."

"They don't stay on the path."

"How do you know? Who makes that decision?"

"Father keeps an eye on them," said Adam. "And as we now know, he has the power and influence to learn a lot about them. I trust his judgment."

"It's a lot of trust to put into one person."

"Yes, it is. I believe Father earned that trust. He hasn't given me any reason to question his heart or motives."

"I guess I'm not sure he has given us reason not to question them."

Adam flashed back to the news reports. Was it just a line? Did Father know those parents would never see their children again? Adam always believed it when he made that promise. No, he couldn't start questioning Father now. He needed to focus on rescuing Samuel. Adam started to speak without really knowing what he was going to say, when he felt someone pat his shoulder. He turned to see Father Fitzpatrick smiling at him.

"You boys ready to go?" the priest asked.

"Yes, sir," said Adam. "This is my friend, Samuel."

"A pleasure to meet you, my son," said Father Fitzpatrick as he shook Samuel's hand. Adam felt himself flinch at the stranger calling Samuel his son, but regained his composure quickly. He had too many battles to fight today, and that did not need to be one of them.

"Well, right this way," said the priest, motioning toward the doors. "The rest of our party will be joining us momentarily."

"The rest of our party?" Samuel was looking between Father Fitzpatrick and Adam with a confused expression on his face. Adam realized he never got around to telling Samuel they had a ride.

"I apologize," said Adam. "Samuel, this is Father Fitzpatrick. He and his flock have a tour bus and generously offered to take us into the city."

Samuel stood up straight and nodded.

"Oh, son, you make it sound so serious. Look at the boy," said the priest, motioning to Samuel. "He looks like he's ready to salute me. At ease, my boy." Father Fitzpatrick patted Samuel's shoulder. "I've just got a few good people from my congregation who wanted to get closer to the Lord through nature, and they let me tag along."

Samuel nodded, but didn't speak.

"Well, we certainly appreciate your assistance," Adam said. He wondered if Samuel was nervous to be around a priest, but he wasn't sure why that would be the case. Maybe he was just worried about saying the wrong thing to an outsider. At least that would mean some of Adam's warnings were getting through.

"My pleasure, oh, and here they are now," said Father Fitzpatrick, turning to a group of about ten middle-aged men and women chattering as they walked down the stairs.

"These the hitchhikers you picked up, Father?" boomed one of the taller men in the group who was wearing a pink polo shirt and khaki pants. The other members of the group smiled and waved as they made their way to the bus.

"Pete Davidson, glad to meet you," said the man, taking Adam's hand and squeezing just up to the point it might have hurt.

"A pleasure," said Adam, forcing a grin to cross his face. He couldn't risk losing their ride into the city. He only had a day to convince Samuel to go home. "I'm Adam, and this is my friend Samuel."

"Fantastic," said Pete, leading Adam and Samuel toward the bus. "Where are you boys from?"

Adam took a breath; he was used to answering these types of questions, but was nervous of how Samuel would react to the half-truths he was about to tell. "Not far from here, actually," said Adam. "We hiked out here." He glanced at Samuel who was staring at the ground. Adam wondered if Samuel would say anything the entire trip. Fortunately, Pete didn't seem to notice.

"Nature lovers, hey?" said Pete as they got on the bus. "I prefer golf myself, but thought it would be good to get out and see a little more of the country outside of the city. So, if you live so close, why couldn't someone just come and get you?"

Of course, you like golf. One of the best ways to bastardize God's creation so you can walk around, avoid your family and make even more money you will only spend on yourself. Adam took a breath. He couldn't allow himself to get angry. It wouldn't serve any purpose and he wanted to show Samuel he could be open-minded. Plus, the man obviously didn't trust them, considering the question he was asking.

"They're a few hours in the opposite direction and there really isn't anyone who could come out today. We thought we could make a nice trip out of it, but our legs disagreed."

"Well, lucky for you, we came along."

"Yes, we certainly appreciate it. I was trying to get a cab when Father Fitzpatrick offered. I didn't realize there isn't much transportation in and out." Adam hoped his comment about trying to pay for a way out would satisfy this large man.

Pete nodded. "Yeah, well, I guess most people come a little more prepared."

"I suppose so," said Adam, not missing the dig for not being prepared. They were finally getting on the bus. Adam said a silent prayer that Pete wouldn't try to sit with him.

"And isn't it lucky for us, they weren't," said Father Fitzpatrick from behind Adam. "Allowing us to show God's kindness and generosity to others." Adam almost forgot he was there, and allowed himself to be grateful for the interjection.

The priest motioned for Adam to sit next to Samuel near the front of the bus while Pete walked to join the rest of his group.

Adam allowed his shoulders to relax slightly when he sat down and attempted a smile at Father Fitzpatrick who sat across the aisle from them.

"So, you boys live on a ranch," said the priest. "That sounds like hard work. Do you get the opportunity to enjoy the park much?"

"Not as much as I'd like," Samuel said. Adam was surprised to hear his voice. He turned to see Samuel looking intently at Father Fitzpatrick.

The priest nodded. "I hear ranching is hard work, but likely very fulfilling."

"I'm considering a change."

Adam felt his muscles tense. What was Samuel doing? Adam knew he needed to be careful. If he overreacted to Samuel's seemingly banal comment, he could give them away, but if he underreacted, Samuel could accidentally give them away by saying too much.

"You're considering a change?" asked Father Fitzpatrick. His posture and expression hadn't changed. "Do you know what you want to do?"

"I want to help people. My Family says that's what we're doing now, but I'm not sure I believe them. I think we could be doing more."

Father Fitzpatrick smiled and leaned back slightly. "God has a purpose for all of us. Ranching is a noble profession, and does help others. It feeds them, nourishes their bodies so that they may serve the Lord. However, if you feel called elsewhere, then that may be where God wants you to go."

A safe and diplomatic answer without any advice. Adam supposed that was a good thing, considering Father Fitzpatrick didn't know them, or was it a trick to pull them into his way of thinking, as Father always warned?

"But how do you know it's him and not selfish desires?"

Adam wanted to cut Samuel off, stop the conversation now, but he didn't know how. Normally, he was in total control, but he could tell Samuel was determined. Adam warned Samuel that people above ground would twist the Lord's word for their own purposes, but if this priest told Samuel what he wanted to hear, it could undo everything Adam was working toward. Could he risk the priest's answer?

Adam made the first argument he could think of. "The Lord does say to honor your Father."

"That is true," said Father Fitzpatrick. "And your mother, but He also commands us to serve him and to serve one another. Honoring your mother and your father does not mean you do everything they tell you, but to respect, love and care for them as we should everyone on this earth."

"Even the sinners?" asked Samuel.

What happened to the employment conversation? wondered Adam. Was Samuel trying to argue with Adam through the priest, or was he just bolstering his own ideals?

"Especially the sinners. It's our duty to show God's love to everyone so that they may know it as well. Remember, Luke Chapter 15, when the bible speaks of the shepherd leaving the 99 sheep to find the one that is lost. 'I tell you in just the same way there will be more joy in heaven over the one sinner who repents than over ninety-nine righteous people who have no need of repentance."

Adam's vision blurred. He never learned that verse, was it really in the Bible? He said, "But, so many people don't want to know it." He was holding the anger and confusion in his stomach, fighting to keep it from rising to his voice. This priest spoke as though there was still hope, and Adam knew there wasn't. Just as Father warned, this religious man was using the Bible to steer Adam and Samuel onto the wrong path.

"I believe they do, they just don't know it yet," said the priest, smiling. "You boys seem to have put an awful lot of thought to this. Samuel, do you feel you're called to the church?"

"No. I'm not sure where my calling is, but I do want to ask you something. You say God wants more than anything to save the sinners. However, I have a friend who agrees with Adam. That people don't really want to know God, they just want to live their lives for their own pleasures. Even using the Bible, the Word of God, for their own purposes. Why would God care so much about them? Doesn't that bother you?"

Hearing Clare's words brought a wave of pain to cover the anger and panic Adam was trying to contain. Of course, her words would be the only ones to hold any weight with Samuel. She should be the one here now, not Adam. She would know what to do. Maybe he should have just taken Samuel home. Maybe Father was right to keep them all underground and avoid these confusing temptations.

Father Fitzpatrick shook his head. "God loves us all, and that means he wants the sinners to repent. I cannot be mad at the Father for missing his lost children. You are also right in saying that there is disagreement and misinterpretations of the Good Word. I do not believe that is the fault of God, nor should it take away from the importance and truth of the Bible. Instead, it is proof that humans are imperfect, and cannot fully understand the ways of the Lord. That is why we must do our best to live as Christ desired. To love and care for one another, even when we disagree."

"Do you ever think it's hopeless? That most of this world is doomed?" asked Samuel. Adam needed to stop this. But how?

Father Fitzpatrick shook his head. "Romans 8:31, if God is for us, who can be against us? The Lord will do the heavy lifting. I just need to keep my faith in Him and do my work. Half of my congregation is asleep by the end of my mass, but I hope that some of the words seep into their dreams."

"How can you treat that so lightly?" said Adam. This was becoming too much. If anyone in The Family fell asleep during one of Father's sermons ... Now that Adam thought of it, no one ever did fall asleep. "It's disrespectful to you and to God. How can you allow that?"

"What would you like me to do?" Father Fitzpatrick asked, his voice carrying a hint of laughter. "Rap their knuckles with a ruler? They're adults and it's not school. Frankly, I'm just grateful they bothered showing up at all, at least trying to know Christ."

Adam looked to the front of the bus. He couldn't stand to see the priest's smile anymore. The man was obviously delusional and couldn't face the reality of the world. This was exactly why Father had to do what he was doing, because the so-called clergy were willing to sit on their hands and allow sinfulness to run rampant.

"What do you say to non-believers?" asked Samuel.

"It depends," said Father Fitzpatrick. "If they're being aggressive, I tell them I'll pray for them. If they're asking honest questions, I answer them and invite them to church. If they're talking about football, I say the true meaning of faith is being a Browns fan." The priest chuckled at his own joke.

Again, Adam was taken aback by how lightly the priest seemed to take his calling.

"How can you joke about that?" asked Samuel. Adam was glad Samuel seemed to have the same thoughts as he was.

"Because arguing with them in the middle of a friendly conversation won't help. Some people can't be helped by words, they can only be helped through actions. I show them God's love. It's when we try to make people believe through force, shame and exclusion that we turn people away from Christ."

That's why we need to start from scratch, but Adam felt sick at the same time. Was that really the only way? Of course it was. Father said it was.

Adam looked at Samuel, trying to gauge how his brother felt about the priest's opinions. Samuel was looking at the floor and shaking his head.

"But they're going to go to hell," said Samuel in a voice Adam didn't recognize. It was full of pain and panic all at the same time. "How can you sit by, joke with them and know they are good people who will go to hell?"

Father Fitzpatrick's smile faded and he leaned forward to look Samuel in the eye. "Yes, that troubled me for a long time, but I came to realize that the Lord works in many ways and uses many different tools to save people, not just me. He loves us all, and wants us all with Him. Those of us on earth will never understand all of His ways. All we can do is love one another as He commanded us to do."

Adam was only half-listening to the priest's babbling. The man struck Adam as lazy, not working harder to save his congregation. At the same time, Adam couldn't really blame him. Most people on earth were too far gone to be helped, but one of the last things the priest said caught Adam's attention.

"What do you mean by that?" he asked.

"By what?"

"Those of us on earth will never understand all of His ways."

"Just that. We do our best to follow the word of God, to be good to one another and to live by his rules, but in the end, we are not God. We are humans and therefore destined to make mistakes."

"What mistakes?"

"How do I know?" Father Fitzpatrick smiled.

Adam said, "The Bible says, 'What you hold true on earth. I will hold true in Heaven.'"

"Yes." The priest nodded. "But what church was he referring to? Different groups hold different beliefs. Who is right?"

"You're Catholic," said Adam, amazed that he had to remind the priest of that fact. "I would think you would believe Catholics are right."

"That would be awfully presumptuous of me." The priest was smiling again.

"How can you say that?" Adam's anger was now in his throat. He looked at Samuel who was staring intently at the priest. Adam couldn't tell if the boy was being taken in by the priest, or simply in shock that a leader of the church could be so weak in his faith.

Father Fitzpatrick took hold of Adam's hand. "My son, I believe in the Catholic faith. I believe in one God. I believe he sent his only son, Jesus Christ, to earth to die for our sins, and I believe in the Holy Spirit. I do what I can to spread those beliefs and the word of God in this world through my calling. I follow the rules made by His Holiness, the Pope, because I believe he does have a special connection to the Lord, but I don't believe he is the Lord."

The priest paused, but Adam couldn't find the words to respond. He was in too much disbelief. This was who led people in their faith? No wonder so many were lost.

"Even the disciples misunderstood and forgot the lessons taught to them by Christ, and he had to remind them and sometimes even scold them for their mistakes," continued Father Fitzpatrick. "They were handpicked by the Lord and he sat directly in front of them, yet they were human and imperfect. Some might argue they were chosen for their imperfections. Over the years, people have been so sure they knew the will of God, they were willing to go to war, to kill over those beliefs. We have split into so many different faiths, it's hard to keep track, and new faiths arise every day. However, all Christian denominations agree Christ is the means to salvation, and that is where I choose to start, even if I am not certain of the answers."

"You've studied the Bible." Adam fought to keep his voice calm, but he knew he was shaking. "It's your job to know the answer." Father studied the Bible, and he knew the answer. He projected confidence, and that gave The Family comfort and assurance that they were doing the right thing. How could this man take the privilege of leading others so lightly?

"It's many people's job to know the answer, Adam. Very few of them believe exactly the same thing. Naturally, I believe I am right and try to guide others down their own path. However, the moment I judge others for disagreeing with me, the moment I decide to deny God's love to others because they don't like what I have to say, that is the moment I forget God's commandment to love others the way he loves me."

"So, there is hope for the sinners," Samuel said while letting out a deep breath. "What we say is sinful may not be sinful?" He looked up with so much hope in his eyes, Adam had to steady himself.

"There are disagreements over what is sinful and what is not. What is right and what is wrong. In fact, the only thing most religions agree on is that people should be good to and love one another. Treat others the way you want to be treated. That's what I use as my guiding principle."

"Basically, don't be a dick." Pete's booming voice stopped Adam from screaming.

"Well, to start anyway," laughed Father Fitzpatrick. "Baby steps, Pete."

"We all have our bad days," Pete said. "Father, the missus was hoping to take some photos out in that flower field." Pete pointed out the window where the ground seemed to be blanketed in yellow wildflowers. "Do you mind if we make a quick stop?"

"Of course not," said Father Fitzpatrick. "That's what we're here for."

The priest got up to ask the driver to pull over, and Pete walked back, yelling, "Get out your camera, honey."

Adam barely had time to realize he was grateful to Pete for ending the conversation, and giving Adam an excuse to get some fresh air. He felt like he couldn't breathe. What just happened?

38

Adam scrambled off the bus, although he knew it was faster than necessary, and took large gulps of air. He made sure Samuel was behind him. It was a truly beautiful day. He looked around; the yellow flowers filled the field and seemed to reach all the way to the base of the mountains that pointed to Heaven. The Catholics walked through the path of flowers, smiling, laughing and taking photographs as though they didn't have a care in the world. Adam lost faith in his own legs and sat down among the flowers. He saw Samuel talking, once again, to the priest. He knew he should stop him, but he couldn't stand up. Finally, Samuel saw him and walked over.

"Are you okay, Brother?" asked Samuel.

"Just feeling dizzy." It was true, he just couldn't explain why.

"You know," said Samuel taking a seat next to Adam. "Father Fitzpatrick is not a bad man."

"I never said he was a bad man." Why were they talking about the priest?

"I saw you judging him. You don't approve."

"I may not approve of his beliefs or how he chooses to follow his calling, but I don't think he's a bad man. A bad priest, maybe, but not a bad man."

"Still, you don't want to save him."

Adam's head was already spinning. He looked down at the grass. "Samuel, he's a priest. He's saved."

"That's not what I mean. You wouldn't allow him in The Family."

"Samuel, if he knew about The Family, he would have us all arrested." Adam still didn't look up. It was something about the bus. The bus was making him feel this way. Did that even make sense? He wanted to get back on, even though he felt trapped on it moments ago. Still, he started to panic it would leave without him. It didn't make sense. Adam tried to refocus on what Samuel was saying.

"Doesn't that make you wonder why? Why would a good man have us arrested if we're doing a good thing?"

"Because, even though he is a good man, he is tainted by the warped views and beliefs of this society," explained Adam for what felt like the five hundredth time. He wanted to get back on the bus. Why? Focus on Samuel. "He wouldn't be able to see the good in what we do, because his views are clouded by a lifetime of living here. That's why we must rescue children, to get them before their innocent minds can be turned."

"What if we're the ones who have warped beliefs?"

"You can't believe that. Think of everything we've already seen. Father Fitzpatrick himself admitted some people here can't be saved. He himself gives up on people, yet he claims it's his life's work to bring them to God."

"That's not exactly what he said, and he isn't giving up on them."

"Neither are we. Unlike Father Fitzpatrick, it isn't our calling to bring these people to God. It's our job to prepare The Family for what comes after this society fails. So that when Judgment Day arrives, the human race won't be lost, and instead of a flawed and sinful society, the world will once again be ruled by God's people." Repeating the purpose, remembering why he did what he did helped Adam, but he still couldn't bring himself to look up.

"It sounds fine when you say it like that. But you leave out one key factor."

"What's that?" The conversation was helping, refocusing Adam on Father and The Family. Adam looked up at Samuel. He just needed to avoid looking at the bus.

"In order for our calling to be fulfilled, most or all of these people have to die."

Samuel said it in a whisper, but Adam felt like the boy screamed it. It was true. Father always said that when the time came, many people not protected by The Family would die, it was just a point

Adam never put much thought into. After all, it was God's plan, it wasn't meant to be questioned. Right? Adam reminded himself of the big picture, and how it was explained to him. Samuel's view was shortsighted.

"You say that like it's the end, when you know full well that it isn't. When they die, if they lived a righteous life, they go to Heaven to live an eternal and perfect existence with our Heavenly Father."

"If it's so great and we're so wonderful, then why don't we get to go?"

"We will one day, but it is our duty to create a world God can be proud of."

"You mean a world where no one is accepted or loved for who they are, but rather respected for following the rules and behaving like everyone else. Just look at me. I don't fit into a group, so I'm left on my own, to fend for myself."

"I'd hardly say you need to fend for yourself," said Adam, getting annoyed. "With The Family, you eat and sleep better than most people who live here. You are loved and cared for." The word 'billionaire' flashed through Adam's mind. Father really did provide for them, even if the way he did it was giving Adam doubt.

"I'm taken care of. There is a difference. Did you ever notice that you and Jonas are the only people that ever talk to me voluntarily? No one in The Family wants anything to do with me. They know I'm different, and that's enough for them to shun me. When you are out rescuing children, I'm alone."

"That's unacceptable," was the only response Adam could give. He hadn't noticed Samuel was being ignored, but now that it was pointed out to him, he couldn't remember a time he saw Samuel having a pleasant conversation with anyone. "It will change when we go back. You will have your questions answered and you will know where you belong. The one thing I do know is that you do belong with The Family." Adam put his hand on Samuel's shoulder, hoping to reassure him.

Adam accidentally glanced at the bus. He needed something on the bus. Something that would keep him safe. No, that wasn't possible, he didn't bring anything with him other than the backpack which he still carried. Adam's heart was pounding. The thought of going back to The Family suddenly terrified him, but it was the only thing he could think of to do. Why was he scared? As much as Adam wanted to get back on the bus, he knew now that this was a mistake. They needed to go back. Adam needed Father.

"Thank you, Adam," said Samuel, dropping his chin to his chest.

Adam put an arm around Samuel's shoulders and allowed the boy to cry. After few moments, Samuel composed himself and they looked at the mountains.

"So," said Samuel. "God really made all of this?"

"He really did," said Adam, taking a large cleansing breath. He needed to start feeling better. They had a long walk ahead of them, and he needed to be ready for Samuel to fight their return. He knew his brother wasn't ready to go back to The Family, but somehow Adam knew they didn't have a choice.

"He is great."

"There is no doubt," said a voice from behind them. It was Father Fitzpatrick. "Are you boys ready to keep going?"

Adam looked up at the bus again. His hands started to shake. He desperately wanted to get on the bus. It wasn't an option. He couldn't. It was wrong. He just didn't know why it was wrong.

"Are you okay, son?" asked the priest, a concerned look crossing his face. Adam didn't want to see his concern.

"I think it's motion sickness. Maybe we should just walk back." he said to Samuel, hoping he wouldn't vomit in front of the priest. Then he would never leave them.

"Are you sure?" asked Samuel. Adam saw the conflicting emotions of disappointment and concern crossing Samuel's face. Adam obviously wasn't hiding his symptoms very well.

Adam just nodded, swallowed the saliva building in his mouth and looked back at the mountains. Away from the bus.

"I couldn't let you do that. It's at least 10 miles back to the hotel, and I'm sorry to say, but you don't look in any condition to walk at the moment."

"The motion sickness usually ends if I stay out of vehicles for a while. I think the walk will do me some good."

"Didn't you want to go into the city?" asked Samuel. Adam knew the boy didn't want to go back. He was grateful Samuel wasn't fighting him harder.

"I did, but I don't think I can." Adam wished he knew why his body was reacting this way. Why couldn't he stop shaking?

Adam saw Samuel look up in the direction of the bus and back at Adam. "Okay, if you're sure." Samuel looked back at the priest. "I'll make sure he's okay."

"Very well," said Father Fitzpatrick. "Just follow the road and it will take you back to the lodge." He reached in his pocket and handed a small card to Samuel. "Call me if you are ever in my neck of the woods," said the priest. "The priesthood is a noble calling, if you choose to follow it."

Adam wanted to warn Samuel against listening to the man on the bus, but he was afraid to speak. The nausea was getting worse.

Adam looked back up long enough to see Samuel take the card and return a smile to Father Fitzpatrick. Adam realized Samuel might try to run again once the bus was gone. Try to escape The Family again, but then he saw concern cross his brother's face when he looked back. A rush of gratitude swept Adam. The boy wasn't lost, he was staying by Adam's side, to help him. Adam looked back down until he heard the bus drive away. A flash of a small boy crying, "Don't leave me," crossed his mind, but didn't know why.

"Are you strong enough to walk?" asked Samuel, offering a hand up to Adam once the bus was out of sight.

"I don't know," said Adam, trying to calm his heartrate down. He could feel it pounding as if trying to escape through his chest.

"I'll give you a minute." Adam saw Samuel's feet walk toward the street.

Adam's heart and lungs started to calm.

"Hey, there's a car coming," Samuel said. "Maybe we could get a ride back."

"I'm not sure that's a great idea." Adam wasn't sure if he was ready to lift his head again. Was the bus really gone?

"Yeah, they're coming fast. Doesn't look like they're interested in slowing down."

Adam heard the car. It was closing the distance at a high speed. The engine roared. He looked up to see Samuel near the road. The car was close. "Hey, that's too fast. Back up," he yelled.

"Wha..." Samuel's question was cut off with the loudest crash Adam could ever remember hearing. He watched, unable to move, as his brother's body was thrown into the car's windshield and rolled over the top. The car sped away, not even slowing.

It was seconds before Adam realized what he saw actually happened. He rushed over to Samuel's body. Samuel wasn't breathing. Adam wanted to perform CPR, but the boy's chest was bleeding so badly Adam was afraid any pressure would cause more damage.

The bus. He needed the bus. They could help. Suddenly, Adam couldn't breathe. He remembered everything. The bus. He was four or five. His mother was taking him on a trip. On the bus. They rode the bus for days. At the last stop, he found a cool blue stone he wanted his mother to see. She was tired. She was tired a lot. It was his job to take care of her, because she took care of him.

There was a nice man who looked at the rock, and told him it was actually turquoise, and that he should hold onto it. The rock was familiar. Where was it now?

At the next stop, the man bought him ice cream and his mother coffee. The man gave him money to play some games. When he came back, his mother was crying and told him he was going to stay with the man. He liked the man, but he didn't like his mother crying, and he certainly didn't want to go anywhere without her. He cried, but she told him to be a good boy and to listen to the man. He gave her his rock and stayed behind when she got back on the bus and left forever. The man tried to comfort him, asked him what he thought of the name, Adam. Father. The man was Father.

Adam was shocked out of his memories as someone pulled him off of Samuel's bleeding and broken body. "No!" shouted Adam. "No! Samuel! Help Samuel!" Adam didn't know who was carrying him away. He couldn't stop looking at Samuel. Why weren't these strangers helping Samuel? Why were they wasting their time with him? "He's hurt, can't you see that? Help him!"

"Help is on the way, brother," said a voice, "but we need to get you out of here. Now."

Adam looked up at the word, "brother." It was Sister Abigail and Brother Michael. The Warriors from the woods. How did they find him?

"We're taking you to Father," said Sister Abigail.

"What about Samuel?" asked Adam, barely able to get the words out. He could feel the heat of tears gathering behind his eyes.

"Others are coming," said Brother Michael.

"I don't understand." This was all too much, too fast. Was that really a memory? Did a car really hit Samuel? Was he okay? How did the Warriors find them? How long were they in that field?

"He's going into shock." Adam heard Abigail's voice, but didn't see her. "Get the oxygen." He felt a mask being put on his face, and then nothing.

39

Adam woke with the feeling of a giant rock sitting on his chest. His back was stiff, there was a kink in his neck from sleeping at an angle and his legs were cramped. He opened his eyes and didn't know where he was. He turned his head slowly, trying to stretch his neck as he went.

Why was he in pain? There was an accident. Was he in an accident? No. Samuel. The memories came rushing back and the pain intensified. He could feel panic rising through him, and he forced it back. Now was not the time. Where was he?

He was lying in a bed, in a dark room. The bed was small, but with a warm comforter and soft sheets. The ceilings were high. There was a crucifix above his head. That was a good sign. He looked to the other side of the room. Father was sitting in a chair, watching him.

"I'm glad to see you awake, my son," said Father.

"What happened?" asked Adam, praying that he was waking up from a terrible dream. Praying Father would tell him everything was going to be okay.

"How are you feeling?"

"I'm sore. Where are we? Where is Samuel?" Adam wanted to stand, but his whole body hurt. He was with Father, he was safe. Wasn't he? Flashes of his mother leaving and then Samuel being hit by a car crossed his mind. He needed to focus on Samuel. Was Samuel okay?

"We are back home. In my house, to be exact. Why were you and Samuel out there without permission? When I got your message, I believed you were stuck somehow, but then we find you farther away from home. What were the two of you doing?"

Adam closed his eyes. He knew Father deserved an explanation, but he needed to know if his brother was alive or dead. He also knew that if Father was avoiding the question, there was a reason.

"Samuel ran away," said Adam, hoping to get this part over as quickly as possible. Father already knew most of the lead-up to the story anyway. "I know what the Warriors are trained to do if they see anyone leaving, but Jonas and I wanted to protect Samuel. Jonas told the Warriors on guard to fire a warning shot, hoping to get Samuel to turn around. When he didn't, I went after him. I found him the next morning, but couldn't convince him to come home, and I knew allowing him to enter the world alone wasn't an option. I knew I could send you a message to tell you we were safe, and I had my emergency supplies. I hoped that if he saw the true evil that lives out there, he would understand why our way is better. I failed."

Adam couldn't stop the tears from coming. He sobbed. He couldn't stop. Father hadn't said the words, but Adam knew the answer. Samuel was dead, and it was Adam's fault.

"You went with Samuel in order to save him and bring him back to The Family?" Father's voice was still calm, but Adam wished he could see his face.

Adam nodded while he cried. "We were preparing to come back when ..." He couldn't say it. There were no more words in him. Then he felt Father's arms around his shoulders, hugging him, comforting him in a way Adam knew he didn't deserve.

"Samuel was killed in a hit and run. Brother Michael and Sister Abigail saw it, but they couldn't get there in time to stop it. Brother Jonas sent them after the two of you when you didn't return the next morning. The message you sent let us know where to start looking. An ambulance was called for Brother Samuel, but it was too late. He could not be saved."

"I failed him," cried Adam, not able to shake the feeling of a boulder sitting inside of his chest. "I was supposed to keep him safe."

"You were trying to help him. It was a noble goal, and a lesson you needed to learn. I learned the same lesson the hard way, just as you now have."

"What do you mean?"

"Samuel wasn't the first Family member to try to leave. I tried to help them, and it didn't work. That's why the Warriors patrol the boundary. I don't want to hurt those I love, but it is our duty to protect them all. What happened to Samuel is inevitable for those who stray from the path, but we can keep them from putting us all at risk before the world swallows them whole."

Adam knew Father was trying to comfort him, but the words only brought him more pain. More reminders of what they were doing for the "greater good" and how many good people were being hurt in the process. How many people did Father need to hurt to get to where he was now? Adam couldn't forget what he learned in the news reports, no matter how much he tried to push the thoughts down.

Then, Adam flashed back to the memories he experienced in the field. At least, he believed they were memories. Memories before Father rescued Adam, that was obvious, but why didn't Adam remember it before? Why didn't any of them remember it before? Samuel questioned it, but Adam always took their way of life at face value. Still, the emotions he remembered were real. The love he had for his mother was real, and she couldn't have been that bad if he loved her that much, could she? Maybe she could. The parents he rescued children from were pretty awful, but the kids always wanted to go back. Even Samuel, and he didn't even remember why.

A new wave of sadness swept over Adam.

"You lay down and rest. We'll talk more in the morning."

Adam did as he was told. He didn't have the mental or physical energy to do anything else, but after Father left, Adam still couldn't sleep.

Samuel consumed Adam's thoughts. He thought of the young and confused boy he rescued all of those years ago. The smiling and curious face that grew up, always asking questions and craving more knowledge. The seriousness he took on later in life when he couldn't get the answers he wanted to the questions he asked. He was so tortured, so desperate to find a truth that made sense to him. Adam said a silent prayer that God was answering all of Samuel's questions and that the boy finally had some peace.

40

Adam woke after what felt like only a few minutes of sleep, but the light coming through the window indicated otherwise. He remembered he was in Father's house, not quite home, but close.

Adam sat up. The physical pain he felt the night before was gone, but the emotional pain was worse than ever. He wanted to talk to Clare. She would help him figure out what to do next. How to handle the guilt and sorrow, but maybe he didn't deserve that comfort just yet. He needed to deal with this himself.

Adam rose out of bed, just as the door opened and Father walked in.

"Ah, good, you're awake. I was beginning to worry you would miss breakfast."

"What happens to Samuel now?" Adam asked, unwilling to waste time on small talk. He didn't deserve any type of rest until Samuel was cared for.

"My son, I would think you would already have the answer to that," said Father, with his eyes raised. "Samuel is with our Lord."

Adam let out a gasp of frustration; of course, he knew that. "No, I mean in this world. How will his body be returned to us?"

"Ah," said Father, nodding. "Unfortunately, that is a risk I could not find my way around. Claiming his body from police would have raised far too many questions and complications. Most likely, he will be listed as a John Doe and given a pauper's burial."

"No." Adam knew his voice was raised, but he couldn't control it. "No, Samuel is a member of our Family. He deserves to be buried with honor and respect. Those who love him deserve the right say goodbye."

"I'm sorry, my son. It's impossible."

It was too much for Adam to handle. Not only had he failed Samuel in life, but now he couldn't even care for him in death. It wasn't Samuel's fault he was on the side of the road. Adam was the one that took them off the bus and wouldn't let them get back on. It was Adam's arrogance that allowed him to think he could change Samuel's mind with one day on the outside. And now, it was Adam's fault that his brother would be buried with no name, no ceremony and no real closure.

Adam squeezed his eyes tightly, stopping more tears from blurring his vision. He needed to find another answer. Father was rich and powerful in the outside world. Adam knew that now. They could find a way.

"Let me go back," said Adam, taking a step toward Father. "They already know he and I were connected. Let me claim him. I'll bring him back myself. You don't have to travel with me."

"It's too late. If you claim him, the police will question you, and wonder why you left in the first place. I'm sure they're already looking for you. I know you are trained to elude their questions, but it's not a risk we can take. Not when we are so close to accomplishing our goals. Perhaps when our mission is complete and we are above ground we may find him, but I'm sorry, nothing can be done to retrieve him now."

How could Father speak of their goals when Samuel was dead? A vague promise that far in the future wasn't enough.

"Father," Adam started to ask the question, but was interrupted by the wave of Father's hand.

"I will give you time to grieve, my son, but unfortunately, not everything can stop for this. We still have God's work to do, and this incident has forced us to move up the timetable."

Adam was struck silent. One more thing that was his fault. Now The Family didn't even have the time to grieve Samuel because of Adam's foolishness and arrogance.

"I'm sorry, Father," said Adam, bowing his head. He was out of fight and out of thoughts.

"It's no matter," said Father, putting an arm around Adam and leading him out of the room. "I still have total confidence in you."

Adam shook his head. He couldn't stop the tears any longer. "My leadership caused Samuel's death. How can you still trust me?"

Father stopped in the middle of the hallway, put his hands on both of Adam's shoulders and leaned in so Adam was forced to look him in the eyes. "You kept Samuel in the fold far longer than I expected, and you did it with love and compassion. It is that care and support our Family will need as they handle the loss of their brother and the changes that are bound to come once I leave."

Adam nodded. He knew there was no point in arguing, but he couldn't help feeling angry at Father for saying he always knew Samuel would leave. Why didn't Father do more to save him? Adam then chastised himself for the anger and judgement he felt against Father, the man who cared for so many and brought them to God. Still, the memories of the news articles, Father's life in the outside world and Samuel's questions continued to seep into Adam's mind. Were they really doing the right thing? Had anything felt right since Samuel left? Adam shook his head. He needed to stop these evil thoughts; they were the easy way out of Adam's own guilt and self-pity. He would simply have to dig deep within himself and find the strength to do his duty to Father and the Lord.

Father led him further down the hallway. When they stopped, Adam recognized the large oak doors of Father's office. The entryway outside held a beautiful oriental rug made of reds, yellows and blues. The large windows from Father's office continued onto this area, and Adam could see the sun brightening the mountains and fields outside. Adam took his first deep breath since he woke up the night before.

Father opened the door and Adam walked into the office. The next thing he knew, a dense, heavy object rammed him into the floor and a woman was screaming. The heavy object was moving on top of Adam, he felt arms flip him around and, for a split second, saw Jonas' face before a fist slammed into Adam's jaw and his vision became temporarily blurred. Then, the arms were off of him, and a foot connected with his ribs before that too was dragged away. Adam managed to raise himself off the ground just enough to see Father and Clare pulling Jonas to the other end of the room.

"You were supposed to protect him!" Jonas yelled as Adam managed to sit up. "You promised to bring him back!"

How could Adam have forgotten Jonas and the promise? He dropped his chin to his chest. "I'm sorry, brother. I'm so sorry."

"There was nothing Adam could have done to protect Samuel," said Father. Adam looked to see both Father and Clare were still holding Jonas. Adam knew they were really there to comfort Jonas, and not to protect him. If Jonas wanted to attack Adam again, a woman and an elderly man wouldn't be able to stop him.

"It wasn't his fault," Father said to Jonas.

"You promised!" Jonas yelled back, ignoring Father.

"I know. I'm sorry."

"Jonas." It was Clare's voice now. Adam looked up. She was holding Jonas' face in her gentle hands. Adam realized, with a pang, she was comforting her husband. "Jonas, this isn't going to bring him back. This isn't helping anything."

"It's helping me."

"No. It isn't."

Jonas' body slumped over into Clare's, and she held him while he grasped onto her. Adam couldn't tell if Jonas was crying.

"Shhh," said Clare, as she stroked the back of his head. "It's going to be okay. We will find a way to get through this."

Jonas stood up. He was angry again. For the first time, Adam was able to clearly see Jonas' bloodshot and swollen eyes. He had been crying. Probably all night.

"That's easy for you to say," Jonas said, walking to the center of the room between Clare and Adam. He pointed at Clare, but spoke to Adam. "She's safe. I kept her safe. Where is Samuel? How are you supposed to lead us if you can't even keep one of us alive?"

"That's enough." This time, it was Father's voice. Quiet, but forceful. "This is an emotional time for us all, and we are likely to say things we will regret. Jonas, return to your hut and pray. You need some time alone. Thank God for the time we did have with Samuel and ask for guidance on where you go from here."

"What about training?"

"That can wait. We've had enough violence for one day."

Jonas opened his mouth as if to continue the argument, but he stopped himself and went to the elevator to return home without looking at any of them.

Adam looked back at Clare, but she was looking at Father. "I'm sorry, Father. I tried to keep him at home, but he insisted he needed to be here when you returned." Then she looked at Adam. "I had no idea he would attack you. The news hit us all hard, but Jonas doesn't deal with things the same way most of us do."

Adam couldn't move. He was only gone a day, but he missed her, and now she was apologizing to him for the pain that he caused.

Father put his hand on Clare's shoulder. "You have been by his side the way you should. Jonas does tend to deal with his emotions physically, but I feel some reflection will help him calm down a bit. Now, go take some time for yourself. You have been strong for your husband, but I know you also feel the sting of Samuel's loss."

Tears started to fall from Clare's eyes. "We all do, Father. The Family has been up all night, crying. We must do something for them."

"Spoken like a true mother," said Father with a smile. "You will help lead our Family well, my daughter. But you can't lead them if you don't take care of yourself. Go to your place of solitude, and I will find you later. We will make arrangements to help everyone say goodbye to our lost loved one."

Adam swallowed the lump rising in his throat. Father was right; if anyone could get The Family through this, it was Clare.

"Yes, Father," said Clare. She walked toward the elevator and looked at Adam. Her eyes were red too. "At least we didn't lose you too," she choked out in a whisper. "I'm glad you're home." Then she disappeared through the doors.

Adam stayed seated on the floor, wrapping his hands around the back of his head and putting his head between his knees. He wanted to disappear. It should have been him, not Samuel to never come back. Jonas was right, and for some reason, Father couldn't see it. How was Adam supposed to lead the entire Family when he couldn't even protect Samuel from the outside world? How was he supposed to guide them when the first time he faced a Family member's doubt, he failed to bring that person comfort? How was he supposed to earn trust, when he broke the most important promise he ever made?

Adam felt a sharp pain in his throat, and warm tears started to fill his eyes. He couldn't stop the tears from coming now, and they came in waves. Samuel was gone, and it was his fault.

Adam didn't know how long he cried before he felt Father's hand on his shoulder. "It is going to be okay, my son," Father said in a low, comforting voice. "We will always miss him, but he is with the Lord, he is back in his true home. I know that doesn't make the pain go away, but it should help to ease it a bit."

Adam stopped crying as he looked at Father. "It should, but it doesn't," Adam managed to choke out. "I was supposed to protect him, and I failed."

"No. You were trying to save a man who could not be saved. Samuel was there because he wanted to be. We warned him of the risks and he went anyway. You did nothing wrong."

"I was supposed to help him find his way."

"You are supposed to lead this Family, and he was keeping you from it. You cannot focus on one when they all need you. That is the lesson I hope you have now learned. The Family must always come first. If they don't, more will die."

The words sliced through Adam and sent shivers down his spine. He remembered the words of Father Fitzpatrick, how the shepherd left the ninety-nine to save the one, but he pushed away the thought. He couldn't be responsible for more deaths. He needed to focus on

The Family, forget his doubts and lead them, as Father instructed, to keep them all safe. "So, what do we do now?" asked Adam.

"I'll make preparations for Samuel's memorial, and you get some more rest," said Father. "After seeing Jonas and Clare, I think you are right that The Family needs closure, and that must come first." Father paused. "I would say you can return to your hut, but I fear you will be bombarded with questions if anyone sees you, and it may be best to keep some space between you and Jonas for the time being."

Adam couldn't argue with that, although he thought a good sound beating from Jonas might actually be better than continuing to feel the way he did. "Yes, Father." Adam decided he didn't have the energy to do anything else.

"Return to your room here and I will have someone bring you breakfast."

"Thank you, Father," said Adam, starting to leave the room.

"Try to rest," Father said, patting Adam on the back. "I will wake you when you are needed."

41

Adam awoke to someone softly shaking his shoulder. He opened his eyes, and Father's face came into focus.

"I'm sorry, son," said Father. "It's time to wake up."

Adam sat up and rubbed his eyes. Looking out the window, he guessed it was a little after noon, and just as before, the memories smacked him back into consciousness. He was back with Father, staying in Father's house because Jonas couldn't bear to be near Adam, because Adam failed to bring Samuel back home, because Samuel was dead. Adam leaned his head against the wall. Father said Adam was still the man to lead The Family, and Adam supposed now was the time he needed to prove it.

"The memorial service has been arranged for tonight, and a special feast will be held afterwards in Samuel's honor. I asked Clare to call everyone together this afternoon, and explain exactly what happened to Samuel. I didn't have much time for explanations before I left last night. Clare is speaking to everyone now, and will ask them to let you be, so you should be able to return without being mobbed with questions."

"Thank you."

"However, Jonas would like to hear the full details from you," said Father, keeping a steady gaze on Adam.

Adam nodded. "Of course."

"I told him he must remain calm, and his initial anger seems to have subsided, but if you would rather wait to talk to him, I can have a message sent, and you may stay here another night."

The thought of facing Jonas' rage was oddly comforting to Adam. At least Jonas was being honest and giving Adam the punishment he deserved. Adam knew he didn't deserve forgiveness, and he couldn't bear the thought of listening to Father give it to him the rest of the

246

day. Not when Clare was already facing The Family for him. Adam couldn't let her clean-up all of his mess. "No, I owe him an explanation."

"Very well. Clare is speaking to everyone in the church now. You should be able to make it to the Rescuer huts without being seen. Jonas is there."

"Thank you," said Adam, standing up.

"The service will start at five. That gives you about four hours before I need all three of you in the church. I know that may not be enough time, but the three of you need to put forth a united front, if only in appearance, for now."

"What do you mean?"

"Our Family was dealt a horrific blow, and they will look to the four of us for comfort and guidance. If it appears the three of you are not as one, it will only serve to confuse and hurt them more. You are their leaders now."

Adam gave Father a short nod. He understood the logic, but he dreaded having to explain it to Jonas and Clare. Asking them to ignore or push aside their own feelings at a time like this seemed like too much.

"Very well," said Father, leading Adam out of the bedroom, back to the office, and to the elevator in silence.

Adam took a few deep breaths, hoping to slow his racing heart, as he rode the elevator down.

He stepped out from behind the waterfall and looked around. The trees, rivers and grass were still there, but they seemed to have lost some of their color. They looked pale. The sound of birds chirping was missing, he lifted his head, but missed the breeze. Adam felt a jolt in his throat as he remembered Samuel's reaction to the real forest. His innocent and curious fascination with nature and all it had to offer him.

Adam took a deep and shaky breath before moving forward. The air tasted and smelled stale, there was not a single person in sight. Adam shook the sudden image of a tomb. He considered going to the church first, just to listen in on what was being said, but knew he would only be postponing the inevitable. As difficult as answering The Family's questions would be, it would be nothing compared to facing Jonas.

Adam walked to the huts. He looked longingly at his own, wishing he could go inside and sleep until the pain would go away, but he knew he couldn't. He turned to the door of what was now Clare and Jonas' hut and knocked.

"Come in," Jonas' gruff voice said from behind the door.

Adam opened the door and saw Jonas sitting still and straight on the bed. "I wasn't sure you would have the guts to show up."

Adam didn't say anything. There was nothing to say. Instead, he sat in the chair that was set up directly across from his brother. Adam looked Jonas in the eyes, prepared to take anything Jonas needed to throw at him. It was the least Adam could do.

Jonas' eyes were no longer red, but they appeared to shake. Adam wasn't sure if the shaking threatened new tears, new rage or both.

Adam wanted to let Jonas start, but after a few moments, Adam wondered if Jonas' emotions would allow him to speak. "Where do you want me to start?" asked Adam. He realized he was going to have to relive it all, and no matter where he started, it was going to be painful to say and for Jonas to hear.

"He was hit by a car?" asked Jonas. His voice was strained, but firm.

"Yes."

"Where?"

"Inside the national park." Short sentences. That was all his voice would allow. "We got off of a tour bus. He was hoping to hitchhike."

"Hitchhike?" Jonas seemed confused.

"Yes. We were going to get to the nearest city. So, I could show him the evils of the world. I wanted to convince him to come home. When I realized I couldn't ..." He couldn't finish the thought.

"You were already on a bus. Why did you get off?" Jonas' entire body seemed to shake now. "Why weren't you the one trying to get a ride?"

Adam lowered his head in shame. "It was my fault." He managed to choke out the words. "I was panicking and couldn't get back on the bus. We were coming back. I was trying to get my bearings when ..."

"When a car killed him. You should have brought him straight back. Why were you going anywhere other than home?"

"He wouldn't come. He was convinced he could help people. Save them. He was even talking to a priest about finding his purpose."

Jonas stood up quickly and leaned toward Adam. "His purpose," Jonas yelled, "was to live here with his Family, and do God's work where he was safe."

Adam shook his head, a realization coming to him for the first time. "It wasn't. He wasn't fulfilled here." Adam looked up at Jonas, not wanting to continue the explanation, but knowing he had to defend Samuel's choices. "Samuel didn't feel as though he was doing God's work here. Up there, he started to hope that he might. There was a light forming in him I hadn't seen in years. God was calling him to do something else."

"God called him to die? Is that what you're trying to tell me?" Jonas' nose was almost touching Adam's, and his knuckles were white as he gripped the arms of the chair.

"I don't know." Now, Adam was unable to shake the image of Samuel taking the card from the priest. There was an actual smile on Samuel's face. He was certain of it now. "I wish to Heaven it hadn't happened, but if you had seen him, you would understand."

"If I had seen him, he wouldn't be dead," said Jonas, pushing off the chair so hard that Adam fell backward. "If I had been up there with him, I would have brought him home. I wouldn't have taken him anywhere else."

"You would have, because he would have asked you to," said Adam, standing up slowly. He was almost grateful for the soreness returning to the spots where Jonas hit him earlier. "Samuel had a passion for God's work and it was dying down here. It started to come alive up there. I saw the boy we all knew and loved. Not the angry one, but the one who was curious about the world and wanted to help it in any way he could."

"And how did the world repay him? It killed him."

Adam stayed silent. He agreed with Jonas on that point.

Jonas paced the room, clenching and releasing his fists. Eventually, he stopped and stared at the wall opposite Adam. "Was he happy?" Jonas' voice was quiet now.

Adam shook his head. "He had hope that he could be."

Jonas sat back on the bed, but he was no longer stiff. "He was dying down here," Jonas spoke in a whisper, "but he died up there. He belonged to Heaven. Nowhere else was good enough. He was an angel."

The word angel surprised Adam, but he remembered that before their fights, Samuel admitted to being close to Jonas. In fact, Samuel said he was closest to Adam and Jonas. They were both in pain. Adam sat next to Jonas on the bed and put his arm around his brother. Jonas was no longer mad at Adam. Adam found himself wishing Jonas made it harder on him; maybe then some of the guilt would go away.

Clare eased her way into the hut. Speaking of angels, Adam caught himself thinking. He forced himself to look back at Jonas, his brother, Clare's husband, the man who was hurting so deeply because of Samuel's loss. Why did Jonas feel the loss so deeply?

The question sparked ideas and memories that swirled in Adam's mind. He jumped off the bed and looked around the room. There was a double bed, the bed was made, but on the other side of the room was a rolled-up sleeping bag on the floor and a pillow.

"You don't share a bed," said Adam almost to himself, now pacing the room. "Samuel said he would never be allowed to marry ... did he say 'she'?" Adam paused for a moment and looked up before answering his own question. "He didn't." Adam's pacing continued. He couldn't stay still. "Jonas told me he kept Clare safe, but I failed him. Jonas was looking for Samuel on your wedding night." Adam realized he was rambling, his words trying to keep up with his mind and the increasing beat of his heart. He stopped pacing and looked back up at Jonas and Clare, who both looked concerned and confused. "You loved him," said Adam to Jonas, the words spilling out of his mouth.

Jonas' face paled.

Clare's back straightened, and she put her arm around Jonas. "Of course he did, we all did."

"No," said Adam, still looking at Jonas. "You LOVED him." Adam fell to his knees and started to cry again. This was too much. Samuel was troubled because he sinned, and he didn't feel that sin was wrong. Adam hadn't known. Maybe he could have helped him. Maybe they could have worked it out underground where Samuel was safe. Adam remembered back to his Rescuer training, when they learned, in more detail, about all the sins in the world above. How they were told they would see sins that would never be seen in The Family, homosexuality being one of them. How did this happen? Adam thought about Samuel and Jonas, two of his best friends, his brothers, hiding this from him, from the whole Family. Betraying them. Samuel told him. He said there was a secret relationship. Was Adam not listening closely enough?

Adam felt Clare's arms wrap around him. It was a comfort beyond words and also a painful reminder of his own sin. Was he any better than his brothers? He coveted Jonas' wife.

"Brother," Jonas said, a hint of panic now edging his sorrow. Adam wanted to look up, but he couldn't bring himself to do it. "Please, we didn't ... I mean ..."

"Stop." It was Clare's voice now, strong and compassionate. "Jonas, you have nothing to explain." She gently guided Adam's shoulders up so that he was looking into her sweet face. "This changes nothing."

Adam looked at her. Just the sight of her helped relax him, but how could she mean what she was saying? Everything just changed. And was she really defending Jonas? The man who was supposed to be her husband? The man who caused Samuel to stray and cause all the pain they now felt? Adam stopped there. He was still partly to blame for where they were now. His choices were the final nail. Still, Jonas and Samuel sinned, and that sin caused Samuel so much pain, he ran away. "Maybe other rules can change." That's what Samuel said. He was looking for hope that what he felt for Jonas wasn't wrong. Was it?

"I know you are struggling with this," Clare said to Adam, bringing him back from his thoughts. "I struggled with it as well, at first, but it will be okay. We need to support one another now, and not let this overshadow what actually matters."

Adam still didn't understand how she could be so calm, but she sounded so confident that he allowed himself to believe her.

Clare continued. "What matters right now is that tonight, we will honor and celebrate the life of a beautiful and loving man, and we will do it together, as a Family."

Adam nodded. She was right. Now was not the time to deal with this. They needed to display a united front, just as Father said. They needed to focus on Samuel who was Adam's brother, no matter what his demons may have been.

Adam stood up and Clare took his hand, then she took Jonas'. "The three of us are meant to lead this Family through what will be a difficult time, and we can do it, but we must do it together or it will all fall apart."

Adam was impressed by the certainty and power in Clare's words. She was back to her old self, before the marriage announcement, but with more strength than he ever saw in anyone before, maybe even more than Father.

"Okay," Adam said, forcing himself to nod and look at Jonas. Jonas looked back with a blank expression. Adam wondered if Jonas was just as confused by the situation as Adam. "Well, where do we start?"

Clare let out a sigh of relief. "First, we need to get the two of you through tonight."

"And you, too," said Jonas. Adam saw Jonas squeeze Clare's hand. "You're hurting too."

Clare gave Jonas a tender smile, squeezed his hand back and led him to the bed where the two of them sat. She motioned for Adam to sit in the chair. The familiar pang of jealousy hit Adam's stomach. He assumed it was jealousy, and he reminded himself of what he just learned about Jonas and Samuel. Still, Jonas and Clare had the marriage act perfected. Adam wondered how close they became in the weeks preparing for their marriage and days since. Adam successfully avoided them by distracting himself with work and trying to help Samuel during that time; he didn't know what happened between them. Was Clare trying to help Jonas get past his sin?

Clare said, "I just spoke to the rest of The Family. They're torn up, of course, but not as surprised as I expected. They all know they are down here for protection, and know the dangers of the outside world. I explained exactly what happened, that Samuel left and you were trying to convince him to come home. That Samuel wanted to save more people above ground, but was killed by them instead. They were outraged."

"Of course, they were," said Jonas. "It is an outrage! Who runs over a man, and then just drives away?"

That was a good question. Adam hadn't really thought about the motives before, but it did seem odd. They were in a national park, who drives that fast and then runs off? The world must be worse than even he realized.

"Some questioned why Samuel left." Clare kept her voice calm. "I explained he felt a calling, but in the end, it isn't for us to question the will of God, brought to us through Father. For now, we can only pray for understanding and everlasting peace for our brother."

Adam nodded. "He at least earned that."

"Yeah," said Jonas through clenched teeth. "He did. And one day, I'll get my peace as well."

Adam didn't like the way Jonas said "peace," but knew it wasn't the time to question him. Whether Adam approved or not, Jonas was feeling a pain Adam couldn't fathom.

"They will want to hear from you at some point." Clare was addressing Adam again. "But I asked them to give you some time, for now. They understand you've been through a great deal. Father will give the eulogy tonight. As long as the three of us show up together, he is giving us this night to grieve and rest. Our leadership will be required in the days to come."

"Okay," Adam said, standing up. Clare was now rubbing Jonas' back while he rested his head in his hands. Adam didn't need to watch that. "I'm going to shower and rest a bit before tonight. I haven't even been to my hut yet."

Clare nodded. Jonas stood up and gave Adam a half-hug with a pat on the back. "Thank you, brother." Then Jonas walked out of the hut, back straight.

Adam looked at Clare. Once Jonas was gone, her shoulders loosened and her head dropped into her hands. He didn't feel the urgent need to leave anymore. "How are you?"

She shook her head and Adam could hear her start to cry.

It took him two steps to reach the bed and put his arm around Clare. He knew it was wrong, he shouldn't even be there, but for the first time, he wasn't going to let that stop him. Too much had happened. Was this what Jonas and Samuel felt?

Clare buried her face in Adam's shoulder while she cried. "It's so awful. Samuel was young and idealistic. He was trying to do the right thing and he was killed. It's not fair!" She raised her head, her voice shaking. "And Jonas! I've never seen anyone in so much pain. I'm trying to stay strong for him, but I don't know how, and it's even worse because when Father told us what happened, my first thought was relief that you were still alive."

Adam didn't know when he made the decision, but he found himself kissing Clare and he couldn't make himself stop. He held her tight to him and kissed her. He allowed himself to forget all of the terrible things that happened over the last day and let himself find a little relief in her and the fact that she was glad he was alive.

"Adam!" Clare jerked away from him, but didn't let go of his arms.

Adam caught his breath and realized they moved from sitting on the bed to laying on it. He also realized what surprised Clare. It was pressing against the jeans he hadn't had time to change out of. "I'm so sorry," he said, standing up and turning away from her. He wanted to get the sign of his desire as far away from Clare as he could.

"It's okay. I'm sorry, I've just never felt that before."

Adam let out a short laugh. That answered any questions he had about Clare's and Jonas' marriage. Their marriage. A new wave of shame and embarrassment crashed throughout Adam's entire body. He headed for the door.

"I'm so sorry. You are a married woman. You are Jonas' wife, and Samuel ..." Adam looked at Clare. "I have no right to judge or feel betrayed by anyone. I'm the worst of us all."

"You're taking the beam out of your eye," Clare whispered the sentence just loud enough for Adam to hear it, but it didn't make any sense to him.

"What?"

Clare put her hand under one of the pillows and pulled out a book Adam recognized. Samuel's bible. He needed to focus on breathing. How did she get it? Why did she keep it?

"Samuel left this for Jonas before he ran away. He wrote a note. It said we all had the right to know the truth. I wasn't going to read it, but I couldn't stop myself. There's a quote from Christ himself that I can't get out of my mind." Clare opened the Bible to a marked page

255

and read, "Why do you notice the splinter in your brother's eye, but do not perceive the wooden beam in your own eye? How can you say to your brother, 'Let me remove that splinter from your eye,' while the wooden beam is in your eye? You hypocrite, remove the wooden beam from your eye first; then you will see clearly to remove the splinter from your brother's eye." Clare stopped reading and looked at Adam.

The passage convicted Adam, yet comforted him. Christ himself was telling Adam that he was right. He didn't have the right to judge his brothers, and so he wouldn't. It was a relief.

"I'm surprised Father never shared that passage with us," said Adam. He thought again to the 99 sheep. What else didn't he know? He shook his head. He couldn't think like that. Not now.

"I'm starting to think there are so many beams around here, we don't even notice them," said Clare.

"I suppose that's why we have Father," said Adam.

Clare shook her head. "I worry he may have the largest beam of all."

"Don't say that," Adam said, a little too loud. He was terrified of where this conversation was leading. He couldn't lose Clare. "That's what Samuel said, and look where it got him. Maybe Father was right to keep that book from us."

"It's the word of God, Adam." Clare wasn't yelling back. The calm was back in her voice.

"Are the passages we do know in there? Did he lie about any of that?"

Clare bowed her head. "No. Everything he taught us is in there too."

Adam took his first deep breath since returning home. At least not everything was a lie. "He protects us. He doesn't lie."

"Jonas told me what the Warriors do when someone tries to leave," Clare said, looking back up at Adam. "Father tells them to break one of the ten commandments God personally gave us to follow. He didn't lie about it, but are you going to tell me that you're okay with it?"

"What are you saying?" Adam was holding back tears now. He had no fight left.

"I don't know." Tears returned to Clare's eyes as well. "I just know that what I feel for you doesn't feel wrong. Jonas' love for Samuel doesn't feel wrong. Allowing people to die, and me being married to Jonas, feels wrong."

Adam returned to the bed, put his arm around Clare and let her rest her head on his shoulder again. He was too tired and confused to feel anything else. "We should try to get some sleep."

Clare nodded, and lay down on the bed. Adam allowed his fingers to caress her arm briefly and kissed her forehead before going to the Rescuer showers. He tried to clean the stench of the outside world off of himself and changed into clean robes that were waiting for him in his locker. Normally, a shower and his robes helped him to relax and leave the outside world behind. This time, the robe felt heavy and irritated the skin around his neck. He pulled at the collar while walking back to his own hut. He noticed a group of people praying in the distance. He quickened his step, hoping to make it back to his hut without anyone seeing him.

When did his life get so complicated? The day Father told him he would be taking over The Family. The day he learned he could no longer simply follow orders, but was responsible for the spiritual and physical wellbeing of the people who meant most to him. The day he learned Clare was the one person who meant most to him, and that it was a sin for him to feel that way. The day Samuel started questioning their way of life. The day Adam started questioning their way of life.

The last thought was too much for Adam to take. He made it into his hut, kicked the door close behind him and fell onto his bed. He slept.

42

Jonas shook Adam awake, but didn't say a word. Neither of them did. Adam looked for signs of anger, resentment, sadness, anything on his brother's face, but there was nothing. Jonas looked vacant. Adam followed him out of the hut where Clare was waiting for both of them. She stood in the middle, took both their hands and the three of them walked in silence to the church.

They walked into the side entrance and to the rectory where their official garments were stored. Adam was surprised to see Father sitting in the room, already dressed for the memorial. Usually, Father was always the last to arrive at an event, but Adam supposed a funeral wasn't just any event, and this was the first funeral the Rescuers were asked to take part in.

"Hello, children," Father said, standing up.

The three of them stood there in silence.

"I wanted to be here to greet you. To prepare you for what is going to happen. Adam." Father looked at Adam directly. "I know I told you that you wouldn't be required to speak tonight, but from what I've seen, the rest of The Family needs to hear from you. I know this will be difficult, but it also won't be the last time you will need to put your own needs and emotions aside for the good of The Family."

Adam nodded. He didn't care. It didn't matter. He almost felt relieved, Father was going to tell him what to do and all he had to do was follow orders. He didn't need to think.

"You can keep it short. Just let them know that Samuel was looking to the outside to do God's work, he was killed by the corruption above and that the three of you will be here to keep that from happening to any of them again."

Adam was surprised by the reasoning Father gave for Samuel's escape, but he reminded himself that he didn't need to think. He nodded.

Clare put a hand on Adam's arm. "Father, I spoke to The Family earlier. They seemed okay with waiting to hear from Brother Adam."

Adam was grateful to her, but he knew Father wouldn't change his mind.

"Thank you, daughter. You look out for us all, but The Family saying what they can wait for, and us knowing what they need to move forward are two different things." Father turned back to Adam. "Just follow my lead, I know you won't let me down."

Adam simply continued to nod. He didn't know what else to do other than exactly what he was told, and the nods allowed him to avoid speaking.

"Jonas and Clare will be behind you for support."

Adam nodded.

"I'm going to greet the rest of The Family as they arrive. They need the extra comfort tonight."

Adam nodded. He remembered Father doing the same thing for the other Family members who passed away. Even the ones Adam now knew were killed by Father's orders. Adam reminded himself that didn't mean anything. The loss of a Family member was a tragedy, even if it was for the greater good. Just because Father allowed their deaths to happen, didn't mean he didn't care. Adam knew he needed that to be true.

Adam focused on what needed to be done, not the thoughts that would keep him from his duty. Once Father was gone and closed the door, Adam walked to the closet, handed Jonas and Clare their robes and the three of them put the vestments on over the robes they were already wearing. Once they were dressed, the three of them sat on the couch and waited in silence for Father to return. Adam wondered if Jonas and Clare were as numb as he felt.

They stood up when Father walked in. Father took a deep breath and opened his arms. The three of them walked to him and the four of them held each other for a moment.

"You will get through this, my children. You will come out of this stronger than you were before, and it will make you better leaders."

Adam looked at Clare and Jonas, who were nodding.

They walked out into the chapel where The Family was singing, "Amazing Grace."

Adam, Jonas and Clare stood in front of the three chairs on either side of Father's seat. Father walked to the front of the altar and motioned for everyone to be seated.

"Hello, my children. I know you are all hurting," said Father. "We aren't here to make the hurt go away, but we are here to remember your brother and be reminded that we aren't alone in this pain. That we are all here for one another."

Adam recalled the speech. It was the same one Father gave at every memorial. Adam looked out at the crowd. There were tears, but not enough. Adam pushed away the thought. Now was not the time for his grief.

"Now, let's hear from the person who knew Samuel best, the man who rescued him from a lifetime of Godlessness and who was with him on that final day."

As Father spoke, Adam had images of his time with Samuel. The curious and intelligent boy who always wanted to know more about what was happening above ground, the confused and lost man who wanted answers, and the hurt, yet hopeful man who thought there was a chance of finding those answers before the corruption and evil of the outside world took it away from him.

Adam looked up and noticed Father motioning for him to come forward. As he walked to the front, Adam swallowed the lump growing in his throat and tried to remember what he was supposed to say.

"Samuel was a servant of God. He loved all living things." Adam smiled when he remembered Samuel's first moments in the forest.

The pure joy in the perfection of God's creation. "When he was first above ground, he was so excited to see the living animals in their natural habitats. I had to pull him away from them." Adam looked up. Everyone was crying, but they seemed intrigued by what he was saying. It was slightly off script. He couldn't allow them to get excited about the world above. He remembered what he needed to say. "It was then he saw the people who live above ground. He learned of the evil in their hearts, but he had so much love in his, he was determined to save them. I wasn't able to save him, but together, we can save each other. If we stay together, and follow the teachings of God, we can protect our Family. Now, Jonas, Clare and I are more determined than ever to protect and lead you all."

He looked up again to see his Family comforting one another. He felt a twinge of hope they could get through this tragedy. Adam felt Father's hand on his shoulder. He looked back at Father's sad smile and then moved back to his chair.

Adam didn't hear much of the rest of the service. Based on how it started, he assumed it was like all the others. He stood and sat when everyone else did, but he didn't sing the songs and didn't listen to anything else Father had to say. Instead, he held onto the image of Samuel in the woods and how happy he was in those moments. Adam decided that was how he always wanted to remember him, not the angry and caged man he was with them. He made a note to tell Jonas more about the story when the time was appropriate. Then, Jonas stepped to the front of the altar. Was that a look of surprise on Father's face? The look didn't last long enough for Adam to be certain. Adam looked at Clare who stared at her husband, but who wasn't revealing any emotion other than sadness.

"I also wanted to thank you all for coming," said Jonas. "Samuel was reserved, but he loved you all. Any concerns he had were for The Family's well-being. It's not right that he is dead." Adam thought he heard a crack in Jonas' voice, but his strong brother recovered quickly. "As Adam said, he, Clare and I are more determined than ever to keep you all safe. Adam and Clare are model servants of

God. There is no question of their love and devotion to all of you and to the Lord. I know some of you may have your questions about me. That's okay, because you have the two of them. Like Adam said, we are also here to keep you safe and that is what the Warriors and I are here to do." Jonas' voice hardened. "We will keep you all safe, and ensure that what happened to Samuel will never happen to this Family again. No matter what."

Adam watched Jonas return to his chair. He appreciated the sentiment, but the way Jonas said it made Adam wonder what his brother actually meant. Was Jonas promising none of them would be killed? That wasn't a promise Jonas, or any of them, for that matter, could make. The Warriors trained for a reason. That no one would go to the surface again? Obviously not, since the plan was to eventually go above ground, but perhaps not for a long time.

A nudge from Clare broke Adam's train of thought. Everyone was standing and it was time to leave. He followed Father down the aisle and out of the front door. He, Jonas, Clare and Father spent the following hour, hugging, crying and comforting Family members as they left the church and headed to dinner. There, they ate Samuel's favorite meal, roasted chicken, mashed potatoes and grapes. Adam always thought grapes were out of place at dinner. Fruit was more appropriate during the day, but Samuel always got extra grapes and saved them for dinner. When Samuel was about twelve years old, Adam asked him why he did that, and Samuel told him that he didn't like vegetables, but he still wanted to make sure he ate all of his food groups during dinner. Samuel always had a reason for everything he did. Adam smiled after popping a grape into his mouth. It was good.

After dinner, Adam gave out more hugs, wiped away a few tears and sent his Family to bed with empty and robotic words of comfort, which seemed to do the trick.

Finally, when only a few members of the kitchen staff were left, cleaning up the tables, Father told the Rescuers they could go to bed.

"You did well today, my children. Get some rest. I will call for you tomorrow."

The three Rescuers walked to the huts. When they arrived, Jonas was the first to speak. "I am going to go for a run."

"Now?" asked Clare.

Jonas took her hand and squeezed it. "I wouldn't have made it through these past couple of days without you. I will never be able to thank you for that, but tonight, I need to be alone."

Clare hugged him and kissed his cheek. "I love you."

Adam tried not to flinch as Jonas gave her a sad smile and said, "I love you, too." Then Jonas turned to Adam and took off his vestments. "Thank you for what you said today. We'll have more to talk about later." He dropped his vestments on the ground, turned and jogged away.

Clare picked up the discarded clothes and walked into her hut.

"Good night, Clare," said Adam.

"Good night," she said before closing the door.

Adam walked into his own hut, disrobed and crawled into his bed. The day didn't feel real. Adam wondered if he would wake up in the morning and find out it was all a horrible dream. He closed his eyes and heard his door open, then shut. There was only one person it could be, but Adam didn't open his eyes. If it was a dream, he didn't want to wake, and if it wasn't, he didn't want to know. He wanted this, even if he didn't want to admit it. Clare crawled into the bed next to him, laid her head on his chest and draped an arm across his stomach. She was still wearing a robe. Adam shifted to give her more room on the bed, wrapped an arm around her shoulders. Was this really happening? Should he let it happen? Clare was right, even though it should be wrong, it didn't feel wrong. Could he give himself this? Just for a little while? The lilac scent of her hair swept over him. He never did know how she got her hair to smell like that. He didn't need to know. He fell asleep, breathing her in.

263

43

Clare was still there when Adam woke up the next morning. He
didn't want to move. He didn't want to face the day and the new
realities it would bring. He just wanted to lay there with Clare in his
arms. He knew this couldn't continue. Consummated or not, she
was Jonas' wife. As far as The Family was concerned, Clare belonged
to Jonas and Adam couldn't belong to anyone. Adam felt a pain in
his chest that he tried to rub away. He didn't want to feel bad about
this.

He felt her move and looked down. She looked up at him and
smiled, squeezed him and sat up on the bed. "We need to start the
day."

"What?"

"Last night was for us," said Clare. "Now, we need to get back to
work for everyone else."

"What does that mean?" He tried to force his mind to switch on
as quickly as hers seemed to.

"We need to set an example for The Family and try to get life
back to normal. You should go for a run."

"A run?" The thought of a run seemed so unimportant to him.
"How does that help anyone?"

"It shows that life goes on. I'm going to go make sure the
Teachers have the lesson plans ready and then head to breakfast."

Clare ran her fingers through her hair and put it up in a ponytail.
She hugged Adam, a few seconds longer than usual, opened the
door and looked around before leaving. Adam assumed Clare was
checking for anyone who might be passing by and notice her leaving
the wrong hut. Adam wondered if Jonas ever made it back to their
hut and noticed his wife missing, but realized that even if he had,
Jonas probably wouldn't care.

Adam stretched and went out for his run. The exercise did help clear his mind, but it only made room for thoughts of falling asleep and waking up next to Clare. He ran to the exercise field and saw Jonas doing push-ups. He thought about stopping, but the twinge of guilt poking at his memories made him think it was best to leave Jonas alone for the time being. Adam ran to the pond, did his laps and ran back to the hut. He showered and went to breakfast. The kitchen staff hugged him when they served his eggs, toast and grapefruit. He just sat down when Jonas sat next to him. "Eat fast, brother. Father wants to see us."

Adam stood up. "Is Clare already on her way?"

"No. Father only wants to see you and me."

It was odd. Adam couldn't remember a time Father left out only one other Rescuer in a discussion. Except, of course, when Jonas and Clare planned the wedding, but that was understandable. Adam wondered what Father would have to say to only Jonas and himself. "Let's go," said Adam.

"We don't have to go right now," said Jonas. "You can finish eating."

"I'm not hungry." It was true, and Adam wanted to know what Father had to say. Too much happened for it not to be important. Plus, he didn't feel completely comfortable sitting next to Jonas alone for too long. There were too many feelings of guilt, betrayal and confusion swirling through Adam's mind and he couldn't make sense of any of them. He knew he would need to work all of it out with Jonas eventually, but he wasn't emotionally ready to do it just now. That much he did know.

"Okay," said Jonas with a shrug and they walked to the waterfall together.

"Do you know what he wants to talk to us about?" asked Adam.

"Not really. I suppose it's time to move on." Adam thought he heard a twinge of bitterness when Jonas said "move on."

When they reached Father's office, he was already sitting behind his desk, looking at papers. "Come in, my sons," he said, not looking up from his paperwork.

They walked in and stood in front of the large desk, not saying a word.

After a few moments, Father looked up. "Well," he said, taking time to look both Adam and Jonas in the eyes. "It has certainly been an emotional couple of days."

Adam didn't say anything and didn't look at Jonas. Father's tone was different than it was since his return. Adam got the feeling he was being scolded.

Father continued to sit and look at the two men, then his face softened. "I still believe I made the right choice when I singled the two of you out as leaders. Jonas, you are strong and can be fierce when necessary. You have a rapport with the other Warriors that I would never be able to duplicate. They trust and respect you, because you are one of them." Then Father turned to Adam. "Adam, you keep a level head and weigh the pros and cons before making an important decision. Usually, this leads you to the right and just path. You think of the well-being of others before you think of yourself, and people see all that is good in you. They trust and believe in you because they know you have their best interests at heart."

Then Father stood up. "But you both have one weakness and you need to control it quickly."

Adam stole a glance at Jonas, but caught himself and looked back at Father before he could see Jonas' reaction. What was the weakness? What was upsetting Father?

"Lately, you both have allowed your emotions to get the best of you. When you were able to control your actions, I let it slide, but now you are letting those emotions lead your actions."

Did Father know about Adam and Clare? Had they been seen? Did Father know about Jonas and Samuel? Would he have allowed that to go on for as long as it did? How was any of it possible? The questions swirled through Adam's mind in rapid succession.

"I don't expect you to be perfect," said Father with a sigh of exasperation. "I know you will make mistakes, but you are starting to make mistakes that will impact the rest of The Family." Father's voice started to rise. "And mistakes that will hinder your ability to lead if you continue to make them."

Father walked to the front of his desk, continuing to look at his two successors. "I can see the two of you trying to work out how much I know. Let me be clear." His voice was low now and it started to scare Adam. "I. Know. Everything. I know about the sinful feelings you both have for people you have no right to have them for, and I know how far you have each taken those feelings. Fortunately for Jonas, although he may not see it this way, his temptation is gone. Although the unexpected outburst last night shows the effects of your sins linger."

Adam felt his jaw twitch. Based on the feelings of injustice and anger Adam was feeling toward Father's statement, he was amazed Jonas remained standing still. Samuel was dead. Their brother, Father's child. He wasn't a temptation.

"Adam's temptation, however, is living next door and apparently feels it is acceptable to sleep in his bed."

Adam's feelings of outrage switched to guilt and shame. He glanced at Jonas who stood straight, his expression revealing nothing. Father did know all, and Adam was caught. Adam felt a lump jump in his throat. The Bible. If Father knew everything, did he know about the Bible? No. Clare would be here too. Or maybe Father would deal with that temptation in a different manner. But how? Adam stopped himself. This was pointless. Adam knew he was in the wrong, and what and how Father knew was irrelevant. He knew.

"Fortunately for both of you, I believe I am the only person in The Family who knows of your indiscretions. Other than Clare, of course." Father looked at Adam when he said it, and the weight of his stare slammed into Adam's gut. Adam blamed Jonas for corrupting Samuel, and Father blamed Adam for corrupting Clare.

She was everything good and his desires and selfishness were making her stray from the path. How could he do that to her?

"It must stay that way," continued Father, "and the only way no one else will learn of the evil in your hearts is if you put a stop to your destructive behavior now. Can you imagine what would happen if anyone else learned what you did? Jonas, would the Warriors continue to work with you, let alone follow you if they knew of your desires? Adam, could people take guidance and follow your example if they knew you coveted another man's wife? Your brother's wife?" He put an emphasis on the word brother.

Adam closed his eyes and let his chin fall to his chest. He was too ashamed to look at Father.

"Jonas, you must focus on your wife. Let the brotherly love you have for her grow into something that can distract you from your other urges. And Adam, you must think of what is best for your Family. Jonas can't focus on his wife and marriage if his wife is focused on you. Help me save Jonas by letting him keep her. You, instead, need to focus on the good of The Family and helping each of them grow spiritually. We all need to shore up our faith for what is to come. Do you both understand?"

Adam swallowed the lump in his throat. Father was right. Adam didn't deserve to lead The Family. He wasn't worthy. He was flawed. He was allowing his own desires to not only corrupt himself, but now it was corrupting those around him. Those he cared about the most. How could he live with himself, let alone give advice to those he loved? What if he only hurt more people?

"Yes, Father," both Adam and Jonas said at the same time.

"Good," said Father. "Now, Adam."

Adam looked up. Father's expression softened.

"I know you are doubting yourself, my son. I know you think your indiscretions make you unworthy. In some ways, you are right, but what you don't know is that we all make mistakes, and I believe you can overcome yours. I still have faith you are the best person to lead our Family in my absence."

"I pray you are right, Father. Adam wasn't surprised Father seemed to be reading his mind. Father always could sense what he was thinking. Adam just wished the words comforted him the way they used to. Why didn't they? The realization started to hit him. The only reason he was going to lead The Family was because Father was leaving, because Father was going to trigger the end of the outside world. Millions of people were about to die. A fact Adam continued to forget. How could he keep forgetting?

"And when will that be, Father?" asked Jonas.

Father gave a small smile. "That is the other reason I summoned you both here. I leave tomorrow."

"So soon?" asked Adam. Now panic began to take over his guilt. Samuel's questions started to fill his mind. He needed more time. Maybe there was another way. His skin felt like it was trying to jump off of his body.

"I worry about what will happen if I wait much longer," said Father with a meaningful look at Adam. Was Father reading his mind again? Was Father really okay with allowing so many people to die?

Adam's shame returned; he shouldn't be questioning Father. Then, he remembered what Clare said the day before. Allowing people to die felt wrong.

"Are you certain this is the path we must take?" The question came out of Adam's mouth before he realized he was asking it.

"The world needs to be cleansed, my son. It is God's plan. I am simply the tool He will use to put it into motion."

"But ..." Adam stopped, trying to find the right words. He couldn't find them.

"You've known what was to come," said Father without any emotion in his voice or face.

"I know. But Thou shalt not kill. It's one of the ten commandments." Now, Adam's voice was starting to rise.

"I wish there was another way. I've prayed about it, and I believe this is what the Lord wants me to do. It's like Sodom and Gomorra,

269

sometimes things get so bad, you need to wipe them out. Besides, I won't be doing the actual killing. I'm simply setting in motion events that will cause them to destroy themselves. If it is not God's will for them to die, they will save themselves."

Adam fought the urge to scream. He didn't know the details, but he knew Father well enough to know the people wouldn't have great choices, once the plan was in motion. He agreed the people above ground didn't deserve all they had, but did they deserve to die? Did they really deserve to be eliminated this way? What about those who were good? The ones who did try to do God's work. They were up there, he saw them. Samuel believed in them. An image of Father Fitzpatrick smiling with Samuel flashed through Adam's mind. Then a woman Adam now knew as his mother, hugging him. In all that happened, Adam never had the chance to sort through what memories of her meant to him, but now that the plan was becoming a reality, Adam knew he needed more time. He couldn't let Father go through with the plan.

"How?" The sound of Jonas' voice made Adam jump. In the confusion of what was happening, Adam forgot Jonas was with him.

"How what, my son?"

"How will you have them kill one another?" Jonas was as still as a statue, standing at attention, eyes forward.

Father nodded. "Yes, it's a good question, but not one you need the answer to."

Adam waited. There was no way Jonas would accept that as an answer. Maybe they could work together to stop this. Convince Father to find another way.

"But it will be effective?" asked Jonas.

"Of course. It is the will of God."

"How can you be so sure?" asked Adam. "I know this was always the plan, but it doesn't feel right. Father, please. Give us some time to think of another way."

"Let no one deceive you with empty arguments, for because of these things the wrath of God is coming upon the disobedient," quoted Father. "My son, I know you are in pain, but do not allow that to take you away from God."

Adam stepped back as Father's words struck him. Was he really going against God or was he going against Father? Until this moment, he never really considered there to be a difference, but now he couldn't resist the need to see things the way Samuel wanted him to see them.

Convincing Father on his own wasn't going to work. Panic crawled into Adam's throat like an animal trying to escape a net. "Jonas," he said, now trying to forget Father was standing there. Trying to forget that he was going against the man who raised him. He focused his eyes on his brother. "We can't let this happen."

"It's happening, brother," said Jonas, still staring straight forward. "You're just going to have to deal with it."

"But Samuel," said Adam, trying to think of anything that would change Jonas' mind. "Samuel didn't want this to happen. He wanted to save them. He didn't want them to die."

"Samuel is dead," said Jonas in a dangerously calm voice. "They killed him, and justice will be served."

"This isn't justice," Adam said, desperate to reach Jonas. "This is ..." Adam stopped himself. There wasn't a word for what this was. He knew that now.

"Have you really fallen so far?" Father's voice came from near his desk.

Adam kept his eyes on Jonas. He knew if he looked at Father, he would lose his resolve.

"No, brother," said Jonas, turning to look back at Adam. "It is justice. A few days ago, I would have agreed with you, I was ready to stop this, but not anymore. Not after they killed the one good thing in my life."

Adam saw Father moving toward him out of the corner of his eye and refocused on Jonas.

"But Father made you hide your love for Samuel. He made you marry Clare. He just said Samuel's death is a blessing in disguise.

How can you still follow him?" Was Adam really saying all of this? Was he convicting Father? Adam started to feel nauseous, but he couldn't stop. This was too important.

"I am choosing what is best for my Family, and I suggest that you do the same. We'll work it all out when this is over," said Jonas.

The words were more than Adam could bear. Was he putting his own wants before The Family again? Was he going to hurt them all again? Father was standing right behind him. If Adam turned around, he could still beg forgiveness. He remembered the look on Samuel's face when he was in the woods. He remembered the tears in Clare's eyes the night before. "You mean when millions of people are dead."

"Think of it this way," said Jonas. "The good ones you want to save will ascend into heaven and receive the ultimate reward. The others will still get what they deserve."

Adam couldn't listen anymore. He didn't know what to do. Without Jonas' help, he didn't stand a chance of stopping Father's plans.

Adam felt a sharp pain in the back of his head.

44

Adam woke up with dull pain in his head, and his back was stiff. He tried to stretch, but he couldn't. He looked down. His arms and legs were strapped to a metal chair. He tried to keep calm. He looked around the room. The room was dark, except for a few glowing television screens that weren't showing anything but gray.

What was happening? He tried to calm his breathing, which he started to realize was speeding up.

"Try to keep calm, brother," came a familiar voice from behind Adam.

"Jonas, what is going on?" Adam asked once Jonas walked into his sightline.

"Well, Father wants me to refresh your memory as to why we do what we do. He has his way, but I'm hoping my way will work."

Adam waited for Jonas to continue, praying the situation wasn't as bad as it felt.

"I want to start by showing you something," said Jonas. He lifted what appeared to be a remote and pointed it at the screens.

Adam took a closer look at the monitors. They were filled with images of their world, and The Family. They were all being watched. Lines of huts, the dining area, chapels, playgrounds, fields, everything had a camera on it.

"This is how Father knows all," Jonas said. "We tell him."

"He must have other ways."

"What do you mean?"

"He learned your secrets," said Adam. "I'm guessing you didn't tell him those."

Jonas cleared his throat. "No, I didn't. I thought I knew all the blind spots, and you can see there aren't any cameras inside the

273

huts." He paused. "I suppose that's what I get for trying to outsmart Father."

Adam felt sinfully proud of making Jonas uncomfortable. Normally, he would try to protect his brother from any pain, but not now. Not when Adam was strapped to a metal chair with no idea why.

"The reason I'm showing you this," said Jonas, "is to show you that you won't be able to rally the rest of The Family. The second you try anything, it will be reported to Father and he will find a way to stop you, and that's even if you can convince anyone that Father is wrong, which is highly unlikely."

"You have so little faith in them?" Adam said, convinced the rest of The Family would be as against this plan once they knew about it. "You think they're so mindless, they will follow anything Father says?"

A sad smile glanced across Jonas' face. "Funny you should put it that way." Jonas motioned around the room. "Do you know where we are?"

Adam tried to look around. The room appeared to be a cement block with nothing but a chair and the monitors. Wait, were those metal tools on the floor? Even with all his recent tours of their world, and all his knowledge, he never saw this room before.

"No. What happens in here?" Adam asked, even though he knew he didn't want the answer.

"Brainwashing." Adam thought he heard a catch in Jonas' throat, but didn't want to give him credit for it. "I'm not entirely sure how it works. I've never had the courage to sit in and watch it happen, but I do know that every child that comes through those doors, sits in that chair, is given some type of injection, watches something on these screens, and comes out convinced that Father is all that is good in the world, and anything related to the real world above ground is evil. There are a few more just like it down the hall."

"That's why they don't remember anything," said Adam in a whisper.

"Exactly, it's too painful for them to remember, so they don't. Kids really are incredible at surviving."

"You knew they did this?" Adam turned on Jonas. "You knew this is what happened and you kept bringing children back?"

"Really, Adam?" said Jonas. "I understand you're upset by everything, but don't play dumb with me on this. What did you think happened to the kids? I let it happen because I believed this was a better place for them, and you did too. We were programmed to believe it."

"I didn't know we did this!" yelled Adam. He wanted to fight against his restraints, but he couldn't move.

"You knew you were taking them away from their families. Away from their lives. You also knew they somehow forgot everything before this, and you encouraged all of us to help keep it that way. Did you think that all happened with bunnies and chocolate?"

Adam felt a twinge in his gut. Jonas was right, Adam had suspicions and chose not to listen to them. Samuel asked him to question it, and even then, he refused to see reality. He chose to be ignorant, but he wouldn't let Jonas win that easily. "I thought I was bringing them to a better life. Not this."

"It is a better life, brother. Look at what happened to Samuel. None of this changes the life and The Family we have built down here. We are still a community of Christians, who love, respect and care for one another. None of this changes who we are."

"I'm starting to think Samuel was the only good person down here. Including me. I can't believe I allowed myself to be so blind to this."

"He *was* the only good person down here," agreed Jonas. "He almost had me convinced this was wrong. The world above killed their chance of survival when they killed him. There is no hope for them. There could be a future for the rest of us, but not the way things are now."

Adam just stared at Jonas. He didn't know how to argue anymore. "So, what am I doing down here?"

"I'm supposed to brainwash you again. Make you forget your feelings for Clare and your memories of what happened with Samuel and prepare you to lead our Family."

Adam swallowed the fear rising in his throat. How could he convince Jonas not to do this?

"I don't want to do that to you. You're my brother, and honestly, I owe Clare a chance at happiness." Jonas looked up at the screens and took his own hard swallow.

Adam wondered what emotions his brother was trying to control.

"I'm hoping you will be smart enough to help me keep your memories. Father wants me to inject you with some drug that will help reset your brainwashing in a day. Or I can knock you out, and pretend I brain washed you and let you keep your memories so you can better care for our Family. I'm hoping you will realize that, through no fault of their own, everyone out there is mindless," Jonas said, pointing to the door. "They've been brainwashed into trusting Father without question, they won't believe you if you tell them Father's plan, and if you try, they will turn against you. That can't happen. They need you, and you know they do. Father is going through with this plan, no matter what. Without you, this Family, the people we love, will be left with me as a leader. I can protect them, but I can't care for them. I can't listen to their troubles and guide them back to God, I can't be the shoulder they cry on and I can't be the moral guide that sets the example. That has to be you. Without you, they will be lost."

"What about the Warriors spying on all of us?" asked Adam, grasping for any straw of hope he could think of. "Do they know what's happening?"

"They know they are supposed to watch the monitors and report any unusual behavior. There has never been any unusual behavior, until Samuel, and they've never questioned the orders not to tell anyone else about their job."

Adam felt as though his body was full of air and it was deflating. He was powerless to stop any of this, but how could he agree to be a part of it? Then, the worst thought of all occurred to him. "What about Clare?"

"What about her?"

"Does she know?"

Jonas let out a short laugh, then his face turned to pity. "No, brother. She doesn't."

Adam let out a sigh of relief. He still had hope.

"You don't have time to convince her. We were all brainwashed. If she learns of Father's plans, she either won't believe you or will want Father's confirmation, and he won't give it to her until it's too late."

Adam shook his head in defiance. Clare was smarter than all of them put together. The brainwashing may have allowed her to turn a blind eye, just as Adam had, but she would see the truth.

"Adam, think about it," said Jonas. "Think about all the times Samuel asked you to question Father. You even had him talk to Clare, and she didn't see it then either."

Adam could feel the hope leaving his body. Jonas was right. Samuel drilled Adam with doubts and questions for weeks. Adam saw with his own eyes Father's other life above ground. Despite all of it, it never occurred to Adam to question Father, until Samuel's death. If Samuel couldn't convince Adam in all of that time, how was Adam supposed to convince Clare in a day?

"Look over there." Jonas' voice broke Adam from his thoughts. Jonas pointed at a monitor that was focused on The Family dining area. People were just sitting down to eat.

"Look at their faces, brother," Jonas said. "Remember the love you have for them. Yes, they are misguided and yes, they blindly follow a man you now see as evil, but they will also follow you blindly. You can be their salvation. You can make sure they continue to live happy and Christian lives. You can keep the smiles on their faces and love in their hearts. Please, in all of this, don't forget about them."

Adam looked at the faces. The innocent faces of all the people he loved. He found young Rebecca. The vacant expression from her first day, which he now understood, was gone and she sat, smiling and laughing with other Children. He rescued her from a terrible situation. He cringed at the thought of the life she would have had if he left her with her parents. Now, the light in her eyes was back. She was happy, wasn't she? He looked over at another group of older Family members, talking and smiling. They were more than his friends. They were good people and they didn't deserve to be betrayed, especially by him. But what was the bigger betrayal? Leaving them or letting them continue to live like this?

"I don't know," was all Adam could manage to say.

"You shouldn't be expected to. Not yet. I'm trusting you, brother."

Adam felt another sharp pain in his arm. He looked down at the needle Jonas stuck in him. Adam tried to fight the sleep, knowing it was pointless.

45

Adam didn't want to open his eyes at first, terrified of what he would see when he did.

A cool, damp rag patted his forehead. It was gentle, soothing, but could he trust it?

His back was still stiff, and his wrists and ankles were sore, but he realized he was no longer tied to the chair. In fact, it felt like he was entirely off the chair and possibly back in his own bed. He took a deep breath, willing the courage to open his eyes.

"Adam," said a soft, sweet voice. He recognized it, and for the first time in his life, it didn't comfort him. "Adam, are you okay?"

He didn't have an answer to that question.

"Adam, you need to wake up," said Clare.

He didn't move; he didn't know what to do and he didn't want to give her proof he was awake until he did know.

"I know you're awake," she said. "I don't know what's going on, and if I could let you sleep here all day, I would, but you need to get out of bed."

"Why?" asked Adam, barely recognizing the rough, gravelly voice that escaped from him.

"Father is looking for you. He says he needs to talk to you before he leaves."

That made Adam sit up. "Is he leaving now?" He put his hand to his head, hoping to stop the spinning from sitting up too quickly.

Clare sat up straight. Her hair was back up in its usual bun and she was in her usual gray smock, but she looked different. He didn't know if it was good or bad, but it was definitely different. "I don't know. Jonas said he is likely to leave soon. What happened yesterday? You both went to meet Father without me, and Jonas carried you back to bed at night. He then disappeared without any explanation until this morning when he told me Father wanted to see you."

Adam got off the bed in one motion; now was not the time to give into his physical pain. "What did he say?" Adam realized that if he remembered Jonas and the metal chair, Jonas must not have brainwashed him. He was trusting him.

"That was it," said Clare in a louder voice. She was still sitting on the bed, but her cheeks and neck were starting to turn red. "Jonas told me to wake you. He said he needed to do some work with the Warriors. What's going on?"

Adam paced the room, ignoring his sore muscles. He needed to talk to Father, but he needed to think through what he was going to say. He couldn't let himself be railroaded again. He scanned through his memories. As far as he could tell, they were all there, including the ones of his mother. Jonas wasn't doing everything Father asked him to do. Maybe there was still hope, but Adam would need to be careful.

"Adam!" Clare's voice broke through his trail of thought.

Adam stopped pacing to look at her. He didn't know where to start.

"What did I miss yesterday? Did you and Jonas fight? You were completely out last night and you've got bruises, but they don't look like defensive or offensive wounds. I asked the Healers for help, but they said Father instructed them to simply let you rest. None of this makes any sense."

Clare's eyes were welling up with tears. Adam crossed the room and hugged her. He didn't know much of anything right now, but he knew he couldn't watch her cry. It would keep him from focusing on the task at hand.

"I'm not completely sure. I know something is wrong and I need to fix it, but I'm not sure how."

"What's wrong? What do you need to fix?"

"I can't let Father go through with his plans," said Adam, realizing he didn't have the energy to lie to her. Not her.

She pulled away and looked at him. Was that relief in her eyes? Or wishful thinking on Adam's part?

Adam quickly turned when he heard his door open.

"You won't talk him out of it," said a voice from the doorway. Adam looked over and was surprised to see Brother Joseph standing there. Adam instinctively moved away from Clare, and she seemed to do the same.

"Oh, don't worry about me," said Joseph. "I won't say anything, but you need to pull yourself together. Father sent me. He wants to see you."

"I won't talk who out of it?" asked Adam, deciding to move past the major indiscretion he and Clare just committed. She shouldn't even be in his hut. Not without her husband.

"Father. You won't talk him out of his plan. You shouldn't waste your time trying. You need to come with me now and pretend like you are on board."

"Why would I need to pretend?" How did everyone know what Adam was thinking or planning? Were there cameras in his brain as well?

"Because it's wrong. And you finally realize that."

Adam didn't know what to say. Joseph, one of Father's most trusted Elders, was on Adam's side. Or was it a trick to make sure Jonas brainwashed him? Adam didn't want to give himself away, but he didn't want to turn away a powerful ally either.

"I'm not sure I understand."

"Who is saying Father's plan is wrong, and who is trying to talk him out of it?" asked Clare from beside Adam, the frustration still in her voice, with a hint of panic.

Joseph turned to Clare. "Adam is realizing that, no matter how terrible the outside world may be, our only job is to love and care for one another, not destroy our fellow humans. He also realized the only reason he hasn't thought this before is because you were all literally brainwashed as children to believe otherwise, and it was only the death of Samuel that was traumatic enough to knock Adam out of it."

"What do you mean? Samuel's death knocked Adam out of what?"

She was trying to process the information. Adam realized she was already questioning Father's plan. She said herself, allowing people to die felt wrong. The brainwashing information was entirely new to her. He wanted to explain it to her, but he knew he needed to tread carefully. He couldn't trust anyone right now.

"I'll explain everything, I promise, but for now, Adam, you need to go convince Father you are back on his side. It's all over for you if you don't."

"I'm always on Father's side," said Adam, straightening his back. He needed to tread very carefully from this point forward.

Joseph gave a sad sort of smile. "That'll do, son." Joseph walked out and Adam looked back at Clare, hoping she could help him focus his thoughts. His heart was racing. Father wasn't above tricks and tests. Still, Joseph gave Samuel the books that encouraged questions of The Family plan, and would Joseph have risked letting Clare know The Family secrets if it was just a test? How could Adam be certain of anything anymore?

"Adam." Clare's voice came out in a shaky whisper. "What's going on?"

"I want to tell you," said Adam. Forcing himself not to touch her again. He wanted to sink into her warmth and forget about the realities of the world, but there wasn't time for that. "I will tell you, but I need to go see Father. He's waiting for me."

Clare shook her head. "I'll come with you."

"No," said Adam, remembering Father's most recent warning. "This is something I need to do alone. Go find Jonas, and tell him thank you, and that the three of us need to talk as soon as I get back." Adam didn't want to send Clare to Jonas, he wasn't certain he could trust his brother, but Jonas also didn't brainwash Adam like he was told, and Clare wouldn't accept anything that didn't promise answers.

"Fine," said Clare, exhaling. "But one of you need to tell me what is going on, and soon."

"I will, I promise." Adam exited his hut, back straight, face stern. He remembered the cameras and didn't want any question, exhaustion or fear to escape from him, despite the fact they were swirling throughout his entire body.

46

Adam knew he had to think quickly and clearly. At this point, Joseph was either on Father's side and there was no hope for Adam, or Adam now had a powerful ally, and he couldn't risk ruining his one chance to set things right.

What were the lessons he needed to remember? Respect. Honor. Loyalty. The words flashed through his mind. Father is always right. Never question him. The outside world is evil. There is no good in it.

A flash of Adam's mother entered his thoughts. Adam was scared, and she was crying. She hugged him, and he felt comforted until he fell asleep. Adam shook the memory from his mind. He couldn't risk the vulnerability he felt the memory bring. He needed to be a robot.

"Good morning, my son," said Father when Adam exited the elevator.

"Good morning, Father." Adam kept his back straight, eyes forward, answers short.

"How are you feeling this morning?" asked Father.

Adam turned his head toward Father with a short jerk. "Ashamed of my sloth. I appear to have slept too long."

Father gave a cautious nod. "Yes, well, you had a tough few days. I wouldn't be too hard on yourself."

"I cannot lead The Family if I am sleeping."

"No," said Father, still not allowing any emotion to sneak into his speech. "Still, you must take care of yourself if you are to care for others." Father paused to take a sip of water, then asked, "What did finally wake you?"

It was a test. The cameras. Father knew.

Adam looked at the floor. "I do not wish to betray a fellow Family member."

"What do you mean?"

"I was shocked to find Sister Clare in my hut this morning. I believe she was just checking on my well-being, but her presence was," Adam paused, pretending to choose his words carefully, "startling."

Father nodded. "Well, she is a married woman now. Perhaps she believes that gives her additional liberties. I would advise you to correct her thinking, but do so compassionately. She is still learning her new role."

"Yes, Father," Adam said, careful to keep the anger out of his voice. He focused on controlling his breathing, hoping that would slow down his racing heart. He couldn't risk any signs that he was upset with the conversation.

"Very well. I am preparing to leave. Do you remember your lessons? Do you feel prepared to lead our Family in my absence?"

Adam looked at the wall. "I know I cannot replace you, but I will do my best to keep them safe, and with God, until your return."

"Thank you, my son," said Father, now relaxed and coming toward Adam for a hug.

Adam hugged Father back, closing his eyes and pretending it was anyone else.

"Very well," Father said, patting Adam on the back. "You may return to your duties. I will contact you when it is time for you all to join me above ground. Until that time, remember to keep everyone underground where it is safe. And allow Jonas and Clare to help you. They are vital assets."

"Yes, Father." Adam turned and walked back to the elevator, focused only on keeping his posture perfect, and walk calm. He continued to his hut, and was relieved to find it empty. Remembering Jonas said cameras weren't inside the huts, Adam collapsed onto his bed, finally allowing the tears to come. He felt alone. For the first time he could remember, he didn't know who he could trust or what he should do. He just lied, and was planning to betray, the one person who Adam never questioned, the one person he always trusted.

Now what could he do? Adam's only choice appeared to be Joseph, but could he really trust him? What were his other options? Adam didn't know how to even begin stopping Father, and there was no time to figure it out. If Joseph meant what he said earlier, he might have a plan. If he didn't, Adam would be brainwashed again, or killed. He'd be lying to himself if he didn't consider that a possibility at this point. Then again, could he live with himself if he did nothing? No. He couldn't.

Adam sat up and thought. He knew what he needed to do. He needed to trust Joseph. It was his only hope, and he needed Jonas on his side. There was no way he could fight Father and his brother.

Adam forced himself to stop crying, stood up and took a breath. What first? Probably Joseph. He needed more information, and if Joseph was just a spy, then at least The Family would still be in the hands of Jonas and Clare. They would be safe.

Adam wasn't hungry, but he knew lunch was still being served. He walked to the dining area, hoping Joseph would be there. He couldn't think of another reason to see the Builder.

As he walked up to the dining area, several Family members stopped him to say hello and to thank him for the kind words at Samuel's memorial. It was hard for Adam to comprehend that the memorial was only two days ago. So much happened since then. Adam smiled and nodded, looking for Joseph. He also kept an eye out for Jonas and Clare but didn't see either of them. He got a tray and saw Joseph sitting alone at the end of one of the long tables. Adam gathered his courage, willed his palms to stop sweating and walked over to the man who would be either Adam's partner or betrayer.

"Good afternoon, brother," said Adam. "May I join you?"

"Please do." Joseph motioned to the seat next to him. "I trust your meeting with Father went well."

"Yes," said Adam. "He plans to leave today." This would be safe to say. Father normally kept the Elders apprised of all of his plans.

"I know. I believe your meeting put him a little behind, but still on schedule."

"I'm sorry to have delayed him," said Adam, still not sure how to safely speed up the conversation.

"It won't make much of a difference. I'd like you to meet me in my hut once you've finished your lunch. There are some building plans I would like to discuss with you."

Adam nodded. Finally. "Very well."

Joseph stood and left. Adam forced himself to finish the food on his tray as quickly as possible, without making himself sick. It was hard to keep anything down, his insides felt as though they were in constant motion, but he managed to finish eating before getting up and walking calmly to Joseph's hut.

47

Adam knocked on Joseph's door and waited for Joseph's response before he walked in.

"Sit down," said Joseph. "I have a lot to catch you up on in a very little amount of time."

Adam was surprised at the change in Brother Joseph's tone and demeanor. The Elder was so calm during lunch. Now he was sweating and speaking quickly.

"I double checked for bugs this morning," said Joseph. "It was clean, so my brother is still not suspicious of me, thank Heaven."

Did he just say his brother? Adam looked at Joseph. They all called one another brother, but Father was Father. Never brother. Adam tried to look past Joseph's pale, sickly complexion, balding hair and additional wrinkles. Joseph and Father did have a similarly shaped nose and jawline. And the eyes. Adam was surprised he hadn't noticed how similar the blue eyes were.

"You and Father are biological brothers?" asked Adam. Maybe he wasn't ready for this.

"Look," said Joseph with an impatient sigh. "I appreciate that you've gone through a lot this week. More than anyone should ever have to go through, and take in more information than a mind can possibly be expected to handle at one time, but I promise this will go faster if you just let me talk without any interruptions. If we want to stop him, we need to move fast."

"Very well." Adam had many more questions, but he didn't want to risk Joseph's apparent plan. At least the man seemed to have one.

"Okay, yes, we are brothers. Honestly, that is probably the only reason he still trusts me. Father and we Elders started The Family many years ago. We wanted to create a community free from the sin and temptations of the outside world. It was working all right, until my brother decided he wanted to start rescuing children. A few of us questioned him, but he talked us into it once he came home with you."

Joseph held up a hand before the question could even leave Adam's mouth. "I promise, Adam. I will tell you that story, but not now." The older man took a deep breath. "The larger The Family became, the more power-crazed my brother became. To the point when two of the Elders tried to question and stop him, he had them killed. It was at that moment I knew it was up to me to stop him, but that I also had to wait for the right moment to do it. I've been secretly collecting evidence of his crimes and his end goal, with the intention of releasing all of it to the public before he has the chance to go through with it."

He stopped and looked at Adam. Adam wasn't sure if it was his turn to talk, but he couldn't hold it in. "What are his plans and what do you need from me?"

"Good man," said Joseph. "He's going to attack the power grid. He's an expert hacker and can do it. The joke of it is, once it happens, they'll call on him to find out who did it and how to fix it. I don't know if you're aware, but he's built quite an impressive and almost laughable reputation for himself above ground."

"I've recently learned of it, yes," said Adam, looking at the floor, remembering how horrified Samuel was by the news and how Adam tried to justify it all. How could he have been so blind?

"And you understand the implications if his plan succeeds?"

Take out the power grid? Adam thought of how much they all relied on electricity above ground. No one would be able to call for help, security systems would be shut down, hospitals would lose records and life-saving machines would stop working. There would be panic, which tended to lead to riots, where even more people would get hurt. Adam shut his eyes. That's what Father meant when he said they would destroy themselves. Plus, if Father were in charge of restoring power, he could wait until he felt sufficient damage was done before bringing anything back online.

"Why not stop him earlier? Why wait until the last minute?"

"This is the only time he will have his guard down. He can't trust anyone else to push the button. I'm sure he's had a team above ground, working on setting everything up, but he will need to actually do it. He will want to be sure he's positioned perfectly before it happens, or risk being caught up in the destruction himself. Now, he hasn't given me his full plans, but I'm willing to bet he will be in the White House when it actually goes down. Giving him an alibi and making him easily accessible to help." Joseph said "help" as if it were a slimy piece of lettuce he hadn't noticed in his salad.

"If I revealed him earlier, he would have seen the message go out, he would have had time to cover his tracks."

"So how are you going to time it now? You're down here, and apparently, he's headed to Washington. How do you know when is the right time?"

Joseph shrugged. "Like I said, he still trusts me. At least as much as he trusts anyone. I was charged with checking the plane, and I put a tracker on it. He keeps his jet at a small airport nearby. The tracker will allow me to see when he lands and know it's time to start sending."

"But he could still see what you're doing."

"That's where you come in. You help me jam the signal going out, and it should give me the minute or two I need to upload the files. Once he realizes something is wrong, he'll check the cameras, see everything is as it should be and call me to check on the signal glitch, and that should give us the time to send the files."

"There are a lot of assumptions to this plan," said Adam, not feeling at all confident. "Not the least of which, is the assumption that I have any idea how to block a signal."

"I'll walk you through it," said Joseph. "The real problem will be getting up to the office without Jonas coming after you. He still seems to be on Father's team."

"Yes," admitted Adam. Finally, a part of the conversation where he could contribute. "Samuel's death seems to have cemented any doubt Jonas had that everyone above ground should suffer."

Adam looked at Joseph, who seemed like he was about to cry.

"That poor boy," said Joseph, almost to himself. "He had such potential. If he would only have been a little more patient."

Adam was confused. Was Joseph talking about Samuel?

"It's my fault," said Joseph, now sitting on the bed. His urgency from earlier gone. "I should have told him what was going on. He was already questioning the world and I tempted him with the coding book and new possibilities, but I didn't give him hope we could end all this. I wanted to protect him."

Adam's heart pounded against his chest as if it were trying to escape. "What do you mean?" he asked slowly. He wasn't sure he wanted an answer. Did Joseph, an Elder, knowingly put that innocent man in danger just because he couldn't find a way to deal with his brother on his own?

"That book, do you remember? The one I gave Samuel?"

"Yes, the book about coding."

"I wasn't teaching him how to run our world underground. I was going to have Samuel help me with the plan. It intrigued him and he started asking about the possibility of leaving. I told him his skills were needed here. I didn't realize he would leave. If I did, maybe I could have stopped him, told him the whole plan ..."

Joseph was interrupted by the door slamming behind Adam. Adam turned to see a red-faced Jonas standing in the doorway.

Adam quickly moved his body in between Jonas and Joseph. If Adam's anger were any indication, Jonas' rage wouldn't be contained for long.

Adam heard Joseph's voice behind him, but he didn't turn. He didn't want to take his eyes off Jonas.

"I'm sorry, Jonas," said Joseph. "I tried to warn him. I told him what would happen if he tried to leave."

"You," said Jonas, sounding more like a caged lion in a zoo than himself. "You put those ideas in his head?"

Adam assumed Joseph was nodding. "I wanted to give him an outlet for his curiosity and intelligence, but it just made his desire to leave stronger. I was going to tell him more, but then he actually did leave and there wasn't enough time to save him."

Adam assumed the confusion crossing Jonas' face was similar to his own. He allowed himself to turn around.

"What are you saying?" they both asked at the same time.

Joseph's face changed from sorrow to pity. "I wish I could have protected you all more."

"What are you saying?" repeated Jonas, the rage creeping back in his voice.

"Do you really think there was a hit and run accident in the middle of a national park?" asked Joseph. "A lot of drunk drivers who like to go hiking at 10 a.m.? And it's just coincidence that two Warriors were in the car behind to grab Adam immediately?"

Adam fell to his knees. Another obvious sign of Father's corruption he failed to see. He felt Jonas move past him. When he looked up, Jonas held Brother Joseph by the collar, against the wall.

"You're lying," said Jonas.

"I wish I were."

"It can't be true." Jonas loosened his grip.

"You know it is. You, more than anyone, knows Father is not above killing anyone who gets in his way."

"Why not kill him, then?" asked Jonas, pointing at Adam. Adam tried not to feel the sting of Jonas' words.

Joseph looked at Adam. "Father needs someone he can control in charge of The Family. Sister Agnes and I are trustworthy, as far as he knows, but not brainwashed the way the rest of you were. Also, he has a soft spot for Adam because he was the first child to be rescued, the one who inspired Father to make The Family what it is today. Adam is his weakness."

Adam felt himself start to cry and he couldn't stop. He was weak. Father needed him, not because he was the best leader, but because he was easy to control. Nothing proved that more than the past few days. He fought against every opportunity to see the person Father really was and followed him blindly. He'd done it his entire life, and now it was too late to do anything about it. Samuel's death and the millions of deaths still to come were Adam's fault, because he was weak.

Jonas let go of Joseph and started to pace.

"Listen," said Joseph with a sigh. "It's complicated. We all call him Father, but he thinks of Adam as his son. The rest of us ..." Joseph paused. "We're his Family. He believes he loves us, but it isn't the same. He won't hurt Adam unless he's absolutely sure he has no other options."

The thought that Adam might have some power over Father should have made him feel better, but it didn't. Father couldn't have done any of this if he truly loved Adam. Joseph was wrong.

"So why not just poison Samuel and kill him down here? Why risk letting him escape?" Jonas asked.

"He was probably hoping it would do for you and Adam what it did for Clare."

That statement got Adam back on his feet. Jonas stood straight and tense, fists clenched.

"Years ago, Clare was questioning Father's plans, just as Samuel did. On her second rescue mission, she checked in on the family of the first child she rescued," explained Joseph.

Adam said, "She wouldn't do that. We were specifically instructed to stay away from those families."

Joseph nodded. "And for good reason, but your sister let her curiosity get the better of her. She wanted to see the impact she was making. She didn't speak to the family. When she got to the house, they were crying, there were missing posters, even after a year of the child being gone, they were grieving.

It hit her hard, and she decided there must be a better way to help more people instead of just rescuing a few children. She spent her time volunteering, working with churches and trying to spread the good word. She came back lying about how she just couldn't find any children to rescue."

Adam remembered those two years Clare came home empty-handed. Father would nod, say, "Very well," and that would be the end of it. He felt a small smile pull at the corners of his mouth. He knew she was smarter than the rest of them. He knew she could be their salvation, but what changed? She did start rescuing children again.

"How do you know all of this?" said Jonas, his muscles still tense.

"Because Father had her followed, like he has you all followed when you go above ground. He considered having her killed, but there wasn't anyone to take her place as a Rescuer, and at the time, Sister Eva took a liking to Clare and intervened on her behalf. Father decided to try to convince Clare he was right about the world, so on her third rescue mission, he hired someone to attack her."

"No," Adam yelled, louder than he intended. "He wouldn't have done that to her."

"He did. While she was ministering in a church, a man he planted there threw her against a wall. Ripped her clothes and threatened her life before anyone was able to scare him off."

"Did he ..." Jonas choked out the start to a question Adam couldn't ask.

"No, the attacker was told not to go that far. Still, it was enough to scare our sister into believing the world was too far gone. That someone could attack a messenger of the Lord in a church. She reluctantly went back to rescuing children. My guess is that since that worked for Clare, Father believed losing Samuel to evils above ground would convince the two of you that the people up there are also too far gone to save."

Adam became lost in his thoughts. The look on Clare's face when she talked to Samuel about the evils above ground. Clare relating to his questions. The image of a man attacking her and taking away even a small part of the hope and love in her sweet soul.

He felt something, either a scream or a sob, rise from center of his chest into his throat. Not wanting to do either, and instead taking control of the situation, Adam grabbed Joseph's desk chair and threw it against the doorway. The chair fell to the ground, breaking off only one leg. The sound of Jonas smashing the back of the chair with his foot provided a much more satisfying sound.

"Listen, boys," came Joseph's voice. He was holding up his hands as if to surrender.

Adam looked over at Jonas who was in attack position, face red, eyes filling with tears and fists still clenched. It was only then Adam realized his body was in a similar formation.

"You let him do this to both of them," whispered Adam. He didn't trust his voice. "You let him hurt her and kill him."

"He would have killed more if I tried to stop him earlier," said Joseph, standing up straighter, hands still raised. "Elders Eva and Micah tried to stand up to him and we know what happened to them. This was the only way."

"You could have found another way," said Jonas. "You're just too much of a coward."

Both Adam and Jonas were now moving closer toward Joseph. Adam wasn't sure what he was going to do, but he knew someone needed to be punished for all of this. Still, Joseph wasn't backing away. Instead, he seemed to gain more confidence as they talked.

"You're right. I was afraid, still am, of the psychotic man who has found a way to take out the power grids of the world, and who controls a literal army, brainwashed to do his bidding. So, you can come after me and let him win, or you can help me stop him now."

Adam and Jonas stopped moving. They towered over the older man, standing only a few inches from him. He looked up at them, determined. Adam didn't know what to do. He didn't know how to respond. It felt like choosing one evil over another.

"I need to go see Clare," said Adam.

He turned and left. It was the only action he could think to take that didn't make him sick to his stomach. Also, he needed to see her, confirm that what was done to her didn't destroy her.

As he walked, Adam felt someone come up alongside him. It was Jonas.

"I'm coming with you," said Jonas, looking over at Adam. "She is my wife, after all."

Adam nodded. It still hurt to hear the words, but he couldn't deny it. Also, now that he was out of the hut and getting a little distance from the horrors he just learned, he realized having Jonas with him would give him some credibility for seeing Clare. Less suspicious.

48

When they got to the huts, Adam stepped back, allowing Jonas to open his own door. Jonas shook his head, signaling she wasn't inside. "She's probably looking for us. She sent me to get you, and I'm guessing she got impatient. She isn't happy with either one of us right now."

Adam nodded. He remembered her face when he sent her to find Jonas. It was probably better she have time to calm down, but they'd have to talk to her soon. He walked to his hut and motioned for Jonas to follow.

"What do you think?" asked Adam once Jonas was inside and shut the door.

Jonas sat on the bed and rested his head in his hands. "I don't know. I can't think anymore. Nothing feels real, and as soon as I think I understand what is going on, some pale little bald Builder comes and tells me up is actually down."

Adam sat next to his brother. At least now they were on the same page.

"How do we know we can even trust him?" asked Jonas. "How do we know Father did all of those things?"

Adam felt a sad smile cross his face. It was the same question he asked himself earlier that day, and he hated that he knew the answer. "We don't, but based on what we know, it makes the most sense."

Jonas fell back across the bed. "Fuuuuuuuck!"

The curse word took Adam back. Of course, he'd heard the word used above ground, and knew it was considered distasteful even there. Adam's surprise must have shown on his face, because Jonas rolled his eyes.

"Seriously, brother? I'm the gay Christian cult leader, married to the love of your life, who considered brainwashing you yesterday, and you're going to judge me for cursing?"

Adam started laughing. He didn't know why, but he couldn't stop. Jonas joined him. Adam didn't know how long they were laughing, but they eventually got control of themselves and then, silence.

"Fuck," said Adam quietly. It did feel good to say.

Jonas patted him on the back. "There you go."

"Well, I guess we help Joseph," said Adam, realizing they really were running out of time.

"I don't want to," said Jonas. "He's just as bad as Father. They're brothers, for crying out loud! Who the hell were their parents?"

"Let's not even go there. I don't love the idea, either, but what are our other options?"

A soft knock on the door cut off the rest of the conversation.

"Brothers?" came a voice. It sounded like Tobias, one of the Warriors.

Adam opened the door. "How may we help you, brother?"

"Father requested the three Rescuers join him in the chapel," said Tobais.

"Thank you," said Adam. "Has Sister Clare been notified?"

"Not yet," said Tobias. "I'm headed to the education area next."

"Please don't bother yourself. We will get her. Thank you."

Tobias saluted and left.

"Now what?" Jonas said.

"He's getting ready to leave. He wouldn't leave without saying goodbye."

"What do we do?"

Adam realized Jonas must not have heard all of Joseph's plan before bursting in.

"Nothing for now. We remain his loyal servants until his departure. I act brainwashed. You act more certain than ever that Father's plan is right."

Jonas' jaw clenched, but he didn't argue. "What about Clare?"

298

"We don't tell her anything yet." He hated that this was the plan, but there wasn't another option. "We don't have time for her to process the information."

Jonas nodded, and they headed out of the hut toward the playground.

Adam spotted Clare, playing a game of Family freeze tag with the Children. The rules of the game suddenly struck him as sick. All of the Children start frozen by the evils of the outside world, until someone marked as the Rescuer unfreezes them. They then must run to the safety of The Family before the person designated as the outside evil catches them and freezes them again.

Still, the joy on Clare and the Children's faces as they ran around, laughing, shook Adam from the cold icy feeling filling his veins. She was happy. Father didn't destroy her. There was good in this world, he just had to make sure they kept that joy while ridding the evil that surrounded them.

Clare looked up, saw them and the smile on her face vanished. She put it back on to wave goodbye to the Children and marched over to them. "One of you better start talking," she said when she reached them.

Her scowl softened as she took in their expressions, but not by much. Adam's voice caught in his throat. He wanted to speak to her, but there was too much to say and he couldn't get even the simplest sentence out.

"We've been summoned to join Father in the chapel," said Jonas, extending his arm for her to take it. She simply stared at him, forcing Jonas to continue. "I promise, we will explain everything, but there isn't time now. We need you to trust us and to not question anything we are about to say or do."

Clare let out a short laugh before a look of confusion crossed her face. "Are you two serious?"

"Please." It was all Adam could say while trying to keep his face calm and emotion-free.

Clare took Jonas' arm and let them lead her to the chapel. "Is he leaving so soon?"

"We think so, but aren't certain," answered Jonas.

Adam turned and walked just in front of them. It would be easier to keep up the appearance he was back on board if he didn't have to see them touching. Besides, he had bigger things to worry about right now and didn't need the distraction.

Father was waiting for them in the chapel behind the main church. "Hello, my children." Father smiled and opened his arms to welcome them in.

"Good afternoon, Father," they all said. Adam heard the stress in his own voice, and Jonas', but at least Clare's sounded sincere. He wondered if Father could hear the difference.

"As you may have guessed, it is time for me to leave. There are just a few things I need to prepare you for before my departure." He motioned for them to sit in the pews next to him. "At some point, after I leave, you will lose power."

Adam scrunched his eyebrows together, hoping to convey confusion.

"It is nothing for you to concern yourselves with, but I know it may frighten other members of The Family. It will be up to you to keep them calm while Brother Joseph and the Builders work to restore the light and air vents."

"But if the air vents aren't working," said Adam. "How will we breathe?"

"You have enough air to last several hours, as long as everyone remains calm. That is why I am telling you now. Joseph is very capable and knows what he must do. There are flashlights and other tools to help you see and to reassure The Family that you have everything under control until the backup generator is up and working." Father looked at them all. "It is all necessary to keep you safe, trust me."

Adam nodded to keep himself from flinching.

"When will you return?" asked Clare.

"I don't know, my daughter," said Father with a loving glance.

Adam had to fight back his anger. Father didn't have the right to look at her like that. Not after what he did.

"I must prepare the outside world. I must be certain it is cleansed and ready to welcome my beloved Children into the world you all deserve."

Adam's stomach was in knots. How could he have believed all of this for so long? "As is the will of the Lord," Adam said. It was the response he knew was expected.

Father smiled. "I am so proud of my Children. I know you will keep our Family safe."

"Thank you, Father," said Jonas. Adam was surprised to hear Jonas speak as though he meant it. Then again, maybe he did. They would keep The Family safe, even if it was keeping them safe from the one man they all trusted.

They dressed in their ceremonial robes, which Father delivered to the chapel, and walked out to the sanctuary where The Family was assembled.

Father walked forward, with the three Rescuers standing behind him silently. "My Children. The day we have discussed has arrived. I must leave you."

A short collective gasp filled the room. They all knew the day was coming, but they likely never really considered it would happen this quickly.

"I will miss you," said Father. "However, I leave you in capable and loving hands. The hands of your brothers and sister who stand behind me. I know they will care for you, just as I have."

Father bowed his head in prayer, and everyone else followed suit.

"Dear Lord, thank you for blessing me with this Family. Thank you for giving me the knowledge and power to bring these chosen few together, to protect them until they may fulfill Your divine purpose. Please continue to give me strength as I face your most difficult request, so that Your will may be done. Amen."

Adam heard the dozens of voices say, "Amen," as he mouthed it for appearances. He was saying his own silent prayer to give him strength for his own mission, realizing only the will of God would determine who won the stand-off Father didn't know they were in.

Father turned to give a short blessing to each of the Rescuers, starting with Clare, then Jonas and finally Adam. Adam bowed his head and closed his eyes as Father made the sign of the cross in front of him and whispered, "In the name of the Father, the Son and the Holy Spirit."

Then, Father stopped, hugged Adam, and said, "Be well, my son," and left. Adam stood, stunned. The hug felt genuine, it caught him by surprise and actually comforted him before he remembered the circumstances. As Father walked away, Adam worked to regain his bearings. He knew he needed to keep up appearances. Still, all he wanted to do was make Father feel all the pain Adam felt the past few days. Adam tried to take comfort in the knowledge they had a plan. What was supposed to happen next? Keep up appearances.

Adam stepped forward. "My brothers and sisters. Thank you for your prayers and support. I encourage you all to continue doing God's work as He and Father ask us to do. Know the three of us are here for you if you need anything, and God Bless."

With that, the congregation exited and the three Rescuers went back to the chapel to change robes. Father, as expected, was already gone.

Jonas spoke first "So, what do we do now?"

"I suppose we go see Joseph," said Adam. Then, he remembered they weren't necessarily in a safe space. "I want to be sure he is set to handle any potential problems when the power goes out, and to see if he will need any assistance from us."

"That's a good thought," said Clare. "It would be nice to take action instead of just waiting around for something to happen, but then you both have a lot of explaining to do."

Adam felt his heart lose rhythm for a moment. Clare was following them, letting them move forward, thinking they were following Father's wishes. Thinking everything was going to plan. She didn't know the deceit they were all trying not to drown in. She didn't know anything. He needed to tell her, but it couldn't be here.

"Let's all go then," said Jonas.

Adam looked at his brother. Jonas was looking at Clare. Adam wondered if Jonas was feeling the same guilt.

They walked halfway to Joseph's hut in silence, until Clare broke in. "Okay, I'm sorry, I know there is a lot happening today, but I can't wait any longer. What is going on with you two?"

Adam looked back to see Jonas giving her hand a gentle squeeze. "Let's talk when we get to Joseph's hut," said Jonas.

Adam turned around. He wanted to comfort her, but knew it wasn't safe. This all needed to end, and it needed to end today. He quickened his pace toward Joseph's hut.

49

"Are you in?" asked Joseph when they entered his hut.

"Do we have a choice?" asked Jonas in a sarcastic tone.

"In what?" asked Clare.

"You haven't told her yet?" asked Joseph, his eyes widening.

Jonas said, "We haven't exactly had a ton of time."

"What did you do when you left here?"

"We had some stuff to sort through," said Jonas, getting louder.

"Can someone please tell me what you are all talking about?" Clare yelled.

Adam didn't blame her for losing her temper. He was impressed she kept it together this long. He looked up from staring at the floor. He was trying to collect his thoughts, but that wasn't going to happen any time soon. Everything was happening so fast.

"Clare," he said quietly. It was enough to stop Jonas and Joseph from speaking. Adam guessed they each wanted to avoid being the one to tell her. "We need to stop Father from going through with his plans."

Clare stepped back, let go of Jonas' hand, but didn't take her eyes off of Adam. "What do you mean?"

Adam shook his head, they didn't have time for her to pretend she didn't understand him. "You said it yourself the other day," said Adam. "Allowing millions of people to die doesn't feel right. The direction this Family is going doesn't feel right. It doesn't feel right, because it's wrong and we all know it."

"How do we stop him?" She looked as though she was fighting back tears. "He's so powerful, Adam. I don't think you fully understand how powerful."

Adam couldn't stop himself now. He strode over to her and hugged her. Was it possible she already knew everything? "We know, but we have to do something."

She cried and nodded against his shoulder. He felt confidence and power flowing into that shoulder and spreading throughout the rest of his body.

"Good," said Joseph. "Because the plane will take-off from the airport in about three hours which doesn't give us much time to pull all of this off."

50

Adam couldn't stop thinking about Clare as he walked toward the waterfall exit. She was back with The Family, eating dinner, while Adam, Jonas and Joseph worked to upend their entire world.

They couldn't all just disappear the first day without Father. Someone needed to continue a sense of normalcy. Adam closed his eyes, not wanting to let go of the image of her face as she lifted it off his shoulder and asked how she could help. She wasn't brainwashed. She knew Father was evil, and she was willing to help them, no matter what it would take. She was so brave and beautiful. He never should have doubted that. He would do this for her.

It was actually Clare who translated Joseph's video loop, jamming nonsense, for Adam so he would be able to do what needed to be done. Of course, she studied coding for fun. She studied everything for fun. He didn't worry about where she found the books. It wasn't important now. They considered simply sending Clare up to Father's office to do the work, but realized it would be less suspicious to anyone walking by for Adam to be going into the waterfall than Clare alone.

So, it was up to Adam. Jonas was in the control room, offering to give the Warriors surveying The Family a break for dinner. Jonas could keep an eye out for Adam, and avoid any uncomfortable questions, but no one could help Adam once he reached the office. Joseph was in his own hut, preparing to transmit all of the information about Father and The Family. Adam was supposed to find the video feed in Father's office, in a cabinet next to the desk, and connect a device that looped a video of The Family eating and leaving for dinner. A device Joseph said he saved from when they lived above ground. Adam had a walkie-talkie on him so they could all communicate any issues that arose.

306

Adam made it to the elevator without running into anyone and rode it up to the office. He couldn't stop his heart from racing. Was he really doing this? Was he really betraying Father and putting The Family's entire way of life at risk? He remembered Clare and stepped off the elevator, making sure to push the button to hold it open, just in case he needed to get out quickly.

He turned back to the office, and his heart stopped. He willed it to start again. There. Standing in the office. Was Father.

"Good evening, my son," said Father as if he summoned Adam there as usual.

Adam tried to gather himself. "Good evening, Father. I'm so relieved you are still here."

"Are you?"

Stay calm, thought Adam. He tried to look casual as he put his hands into the pocket of his robe and grab the walkie-talkie. "Yes. I've been speaking with Brother Joseph, and I have some concerns regarding the loss of power you discussed."

"I understand that, son," said Father. "However, at this point, I must ask you to simply have faith in me."

"As you and the Lord will," answered Adam. His hand was on the walkie-talkie. He needed to get out so he could warn Joseph and Jonas.

"Good," said Father. "So now, will you stop conspiring with my brother and fulfill your sacred duty?"

Adam turned off the walkie-talkie. It was the emergency signal to let his brothers know something was going terribly wrong. He stood in silence. Praying in his mind that they received the signal, that Joseph was sending the information as quickly as possible in the vain hope something would get through, that Jonas was gathering the Warriors by the entrances in preparation for whatever may come next, and that Clare was still safe.

"Yes," continued Father after a few moments of silence. "I am aware my brother, Joseph, is attempting to turn you against me. Attempting to fill your minds with ideas of grand gestures and saving the world. He is using the memory of Samuel and our tragic loss to twist reality and the good work we are doing here. I didn't want to believe it at first, but the tracker he put on my plane this morning confirmed his treachery, and the amount of time you and Jonas spent with him today confirmed yours."

"I'm just not certain the work is as good as we originally believed," said Adam. He was relieved he didn't have to lie. At this point, whatever happened next was in God's hands.

Father nodded. "I know, my son. You've always been pure of heart. That's why I needed to rescue you. I still believe you will be the perfect example of how a boy should grow into a man. That it is possible as long as we can keep you all on the correct path. It's not easy, but it is possible."

"How can you be so sure? I'm here because I considered betraying you."

"Yes, but you haven't. Not yet," said Father. "I still have faith in you."

Adam couldn't help but be touched by the words. This was the man who raised him, after all. The man who calmed his fears and trusted him with the care of their entire Family. Even after Adam turned away from him, Father still believed in Adam. Or was it a trick?

"Why did you choose me?" asked Adam, now thinking if he kept Father talking, it might give the others time to do what needed to be done. Also, this might be his last chance to hear the story. "Why did you pull me into all of this?"

"You inspired me," said Father, smiling. "You were so happy and curious about everything, with so much energy," Father sounded like a loving parent, remembering the happy life with his child. "And caring." Adam didn't want to see the loving tears welling up in Father's eyes. "You kept trying to cheer up that woman who couldn't find enough energy to give you the smile you so richly deserved. I watched you try to get her attention and love for an hour before I called you over to me and allowed you to show me the rock. You

308

were so excited to learn something new. It was that moment that I realized there actually was something I could do for the world, and it started by rescuing you. When the bus stopped, I offered your mother a meal and convinced her to let you come with me. As you have learned in your time as a Rescuer, all parents resist at first, but I convinced her and took you away. The plan took some time to form and I gathered a few trustworthy friends to help me create the world in which we now live. As you know, some remain respected Elders in our Family to this day. I realized the weapons wouldn't wipe out everyone, and if we really wanted to start over fresh, I would need an army to protect our way of life, and enough people to help us start over. So, a group of us started rescuing more children, the way I rescued you, and I worked on building our resources to sustain our world. The older they became, the less people trusted them and the harder it was to survey the children in public. So, we trained you, Jonas and Clare to do the work. And look at what we have created." He whispered the last line, raising his arms and motioning around the room. "We are finally ready to start the world over, in the way God intended it to be."

Adam couldn't respond. He couldn't think. His mind was racing. He remembered Father teaching him about the rock he found. "It's turquoise," Father told him. Getting ice cream while his mother and Father spoke. How much Adam loved her.

Adam felt the tears falling down his face. "How could she give up on me?"

"No, my son," said Father, putting a hand on Adam's shoulder. "She gave you a chance. She was running from the man who impregnated her with you. A man who threatened her life and yours. She gave you a chance to live while she foolishly went back to him."

Another memory returned to Adam, the two words his mother lived by, "Try love, my sweet boy," she would say. "No matter how bad things get, no matter how much evil you see, no matter how stuck you feel, you will find the answer if you simply try love." That's what she was doing. She did love him and wanted him safe, but she couldn't turn her back on anyone, not even his biological father. She loved too deeply. It was the opposite of everything Father taught him, but just remembering the words filled Adam with warmth and hope. Now there was one more reason to fight back.

"Do you know what happened to her?" asked Adam.

"Does it matter?" asked Father.

"I don't know." Adam wanted to know, but what would he do with the answer? Regardless of what the answer was.

"In that case, let us not trouble you with that now. I need to check on your brothers and sisters."

Father walked to the television monitor against the wall and turned it on. Adam watched in horror as images of Warriors fighting strangers dressed in black flipped across the screen. Others were running away from the attackers. Adam's entire person shook with the need to act, but he couldn't move or take his eyes off the screens. Bodies, injured and unmoving, lay on the ground. Who were they? Most were Warriors and Farmers. The Farmers were holding pitchforks and shovels, while the Warriors had swords, axes and other weapons. Adam looked for Clare. There she was. Lined up with the Teachers in front of a hut. They held hands. The Teachers looked scared. Clare looked determined, her beautiful face set tight-lipped, back straight. He guessed they were guarding the Children who were inside.

Next, Adam looked for Jonas. He was fighting alongside the other Warriors. Adam caught a brief smile cross Jonas' face when he slammed an attacker to the ground. Jonas was finally making someone pay.

"What is happening?" asked Adam in a whisper, unable to make his voice any louder. "What have you done?"

"As I said, I found the tracker on the plane. I sent it off without me and waited to see what would happen next. I don't know exactly what Joseph had planned, but I always have a backup. These are separate set of men who could come in and take care of whatever I needed. Don't worry, I know Joseph tricked the three of you. The men were instructed to do as little damage as possible while destroying my brother and all he was trying to do. Once it is over, The Family will know the evils of the outside world. They will understand it in a way I never wanted them to have to understand, but you all forced my hand."

"You are killing our Family," said Adam, praying what he was seeing wasn't real.

"Only those who get in our way," said Father. "Only those who try to stop me from fulfilling the will of God. The rest will still be here for you to lead. More frightened than ever, and therefore more convinced that what I taught them was true."

Adam turned to face Father. His voice was back. "How can this be the will of God? Killing those who love you and trust you to care for them? This is your will."

"Sacrifices must be made."

"This is what Samuel was trying to tell us. This is what he knew would happen. You can't follow God's word and teachings through hate, fear and judgement. It can only truly be done through love, understanding and forgiveness."

"That is the weak thinking that made the world the Hell it is today," said Father in a measured and even tone that frightened Adam. "It's the easy way out. Not requiring everyone to follow the law of God. Instead, letting them follow their own selfish paths, desecrating all God created."

"No. It's people like you who make others feel they can't turn to God, that there is no hope, no salvation, no sanctuary for them because they made human mistakes."

"You disappoint me, my son," said Father.

"I need to help them," said Adam, turning toward the elevator.

"No," said Father, still unmoving. "You could get hurt."

"They are getting hurt," yelled Adam. "Your children, my Family. They are dying."

"No, just Joseph and possibly a few Warriors. Once Joseph is gone, they will leave. See?" Father pointed back at the screen where the men dressed in black were leaving.

"But the wounded." Adam couldn't bear staying up in the office while his Family suffered.

"The Healers and the Warriors are perfectly capable of caring for them. I can't have you going down there and telling everyone I was behind the attack. We will take care of your memory first and then you may rejoin them all."

Adam watched the screen. Jonas and Clare were running to Joseph's hut.

"What are you going to tell them?" asked Adam, keeping Father's attention on him. "You aren't supposed to be here and I should have been."

"Yes, you should have." Adam felt the conviction Father meant for him. "It's no matter. The memory adjustment will cause you to act oddly when you first arrive back. I will inform The Family that the men came to stop me from fulfilling my purpose and you fought to protect me. When you couldn't, the men got past you and attacked them. They will be indebted to you and more certain than ever that the world above ground needs to change. My plans can wait a day or two."

Adam saw Jonas and Clare walk out of Joseph's hut. Jonas put an arm around Clare as she cried, then appeared to be speaking into the walkie-talkie. What could it hurt now? Adam thought, and pulled his own device out of his robe and turned it on.

"Please tell me you can hear me," came Jonas' voice from the machine.

"I'm here, brother," said Adam, staring ahead at Father. Father didn't move.

"Are you okay?" asked Jonas.

"I'm in the office. With Father."

Adam listened to the silence on the other end of the walkie-talkie. He looked at the television, but the picture switched to where the Healers were treating the wounded.

"How are you?" asked Adam.

"Joseph's dead. The Healers and the Warriors are working on the others. I believe everyone else survived, but it's too soon to tell."

Adam didn't let go of Father's stare. At least that was good news. There was still hope.

"Are you coming back down?" asked Jonas.

"I don't know."

"Should we come up?"

"No. Care for our Family." Adam spoke the words that were to signal they should take him for his word, and not try to help him in the office.

"May the Lord's will be done," Jonas said.

"May the Lord's will be done," said Adam, not really sure what that meant anymore. He put the walkie-talkie down.

"You see?" said Father. "Only the traitor is dead. My Children are safe."

"I betrayed you as well."

"You were deceived."

Adam remembered what Joseph said, the part Adam originally ignored. "Adam is his weakness." Now it made sense. Father wouldn't believe that Adam would intentionally and willingly go against him. He would always believe he could bring Adam back into the fold. Adam and Father continued to stare. Adam guessed they were both deciding what to do next. It wasn't until the phone rang that their eye contact was broken.

Father walked to the desk and answered the phone. "Kingston."

Adam flinched, hearing Father admit to his other name.

"What?" Father said. Father turned to look out the window. It was the first time Adam remembered Father looking genuinely surprised.

Adam looked out the window as well. The night was clear and quiet, the stars were out, some were moving toward them. That didn't make sense. As the stars came closer, Adam heard the sound and realized there were actually several helicopters headed toward them. Adam's pulse quickened and he looked back at Father who appeared to pale. Adam allowed himself a small amount of hope. Were the helicopters coming for them? Joseph wasn't sure what would happen if he managed to get the information out, but if the right people believed it, he said the action could be quick and fierce. Father said he didn't know the specifics of the plan, maybe Joseph didn't die in vain.

Father looked at Adam and spoke into the phone. Color began to return to his face. "Get over here now. We'll handle it." He hung up the phone. "You should go to one of the bedrooms and pretend to be asleep," said Father. "I will get you once it is safe."

"Why would I hide?"

"It is the only way I can protect you."

"I don't want your protection anymore."

Once again, Adam and Father were in a silent staring contest. Adam wanted more details. He wanted to ask what was happening, but he also didn't see the point. Father would either lie or use the information against Adam. It was better for Father not to know what Adam was feeling. Adam imagined he could see Father's thoughts moving through his mind. How was he going to get out of this? Or was it just wishful thinking on Adam's part that they actually pulled it off? That the messages actually made it out. He couldn't be certain. Would they really have responded so quickly? Adam looked at Father again. No matter what was happening, this was the most uncomfortable he ever saw Father. He allowed himself a small smile. "May the Lord's will be done."

He ran to the elevator, which was still open, and went downstairs before Father could respond.

51

Adam ran to Clare and Jonas near Joseph's hut. He just needed to be near them, no matter what happened next. He passed by Family members caring for the wounded, calling out to him for comfort. He told them to keep working, and that all would be explained soon as he ran by, knowing he should stop, but also knowing there wasn't really time. There was never time.

He saw Clare and Jonas in the distance, seemingly giving instructions to Warriors and Teachers. He saw Clare give Rebecca a hug before the young girl followed the Teachers and other Children to another location. Adam knew Clare would have them go somewhere they would feel cared for and safe.

When Adam reached his brother and sister, Clare threw her arms around his neck, sobbing. Jonas finished giving instructions to a few Warriors before bringing his attention back to Adam. Holding Clare, Adam looked at Jonas. "What happened?"

"From what we can tell, Joseph sent out video of the attack with the location," said Jonas. "He wasn't able to upload all of the information before they took out his computers, but it looks like the video did make it out. I don't know if anyone saw it. What's happening up there? Who were those guys?"

Adam shook his head. "Father sent them."

Clare gasped and Jonas tensed.

Adam continued his story. "He realized Joseph was working against him, but he didn't have all the information. I think that's the only reason Joseph was able to get anything out at all. There's a chance it worked, too. Helicopters are coming this way. I've never seen Father so worried."

Jonas smiled. "We can only hope." Then the smile faded. "What now?"

Adam squeezed Clare, remembering his mother's words. "We try love."

"We try what now?" asked Jonas.

"Love," said Adam, looking at his skeptical brother. "We try loving and trusting people instead of operating through hate and fear. The way Samuel wanted us to."

Jonas just shook his head. "Nice thing to say, brother. What happens when the people in those helicopters show up?"

Adam took a big breath. He knew Jonas was right, no one would be trusted, at least not right away, and Father had more credibility than the group of people living underground with missing children. It wasn't that Adam didn't understand the trouble he got them all in. Rather, it was that he didn't have time to think it all through. Still, he knew they made the right decision. He couldn't have allowed Father's plan to go through. His new optimistic viewpoint was the only way he could see moving forward without sliding back into Father's worldview.

"We just have to try," said Adam. "Listen, not to take all the credit, but when they ask, I'm in charge. I'm going to try to keep the two of you out of it as much as possible."

"You can't do that," said Clare, still holding tightly to him. "You will get blamed for everything."

"She's right," Jonas said. "Father is the leader. He needs to take the heat for this."

"I know, and I will try to make that clear, but we're the only three that know all of that. Everyone else in The Family will see Father as in the right and take his side. I can't put you two in the crosshairs."

Clare buried her face in Adam's chest and Jonas continued to shake his head. "God bless you, brother. You're too honorable for your own good, but I'll go along with it for now."

"Thank you," said Adam. He turned toward the sound of feet pounding down the tunnel.

"If we are going with the plan of love and trust," said Clare, now slowly separating herself from Adam, but still holding his hand. "Ask for a lawyer."

"What?" Adam knew what a lawyer was, of course, but he never considered needing one himself. The legal system was one thing they hadn't studied in depth since Father always assured them he would handle any legal troubles that arose. Now that Adam thought about it, that was just one more way Father put himself in control of all their destinies. "I don't know any lawyers."

Clare said, "You don't need to. Just ask for one, they are legally required to give you one."

Adam was surprised by how much Clare seemed to know about the laws above ground. His confusion must have shown because Clare shrugged and said, "There was a brief time I thought I might need a lawyer. I did some research."

The realization felt like someone stabbed Adam's chest. Clare was questioning Father years ago. She must have tried to find a way out before he had her attacked. Adam never really knew her, or how strong she really was, but he didn't have time to fix that now.

The footsteps were getting closer.

"Clare," said Adam. "Go and tell as many people as you can to cooperate with whomever comes through this tunnel, and to not say anything, other than to refer questions to me. Nothing any of them can say will help, at least not right now."

Clare nodded and ran off, stopping at those nursing their wounds and dispatching others who could move to pass the word along.

"What do I do?" Jonas said.

Adam allowed himself a small smile of relief and gratitude to his brother. "Just back me up."

Jonas gave Adam's shoulder a pat. "Always."

"And drop the gun," said Adam, just now realizing how much Jonas looked like one of the GI Joe action figures they sold in toy stores above ground.

Jonas gave Adam a sideways look and glanced down at the gun. "Fine," he said, rolling his eyes. Jonas put the gun on the ground and kicked it a few inches away. Adam knew Jonas could grab it if he really wanted to, but he didn't push the issue.

The two brothers turned toward the tunnel entrance, shoulder to shoulder and waited. There was nothing else to do. A few other Warriors saw them and started to take formation. Jonas signaled for them to drop their weapons as well. They waited.

Shortly, a new group of soldiers came through the tunnels. Instead of being dressed in black, they had uniforms with the identifier "U.S. Army" sewn on their chests. They came in with weapons of all shapes and sizes, and then everything seemed to happen very quickly.

First, the men spread throughout The Family's underground home, ordering everyone to the ground with their hands behind their heads. Adam started to shout they were not going to fight back. Two of the men stood by Adam and Jonas, told them to shut up and pointed guns at their backs.

They were clearly ready for a fight. Joseph's video of the earlier battle must have gotten through. Adam prayed the soldiers could see that the battle was over. Then he thought of Clare. He didn't know where she was, he hoped everyone had the message and were safe. The realization of how little he could control hit him hard and he started to pray that he could get them all through this as unscathed as possible.

After what felt like hours, but was more likely only a few minutes, another man came back. "On your feet."

Adam didn't have a chance to stand up himself. The two men pointing guns at Adam and Jonas lowered the firearms just enough to hoist Adam and Jonas up to a standing position. Adam looked at Jonas who stood stiff as a board with an expression that couldn't be read as anything other than hate and frustration. Adam tried to give an encouraging nod to his brother, hoping that would keep Jonas calm enough while they talked. So far, he didn't hear any gunfire and that was a good sign. Now, the soldiers were asking questions. It was the best he could hope for right now.

"Which one of you is Adam?" asked the new man.

"I am," said Adam in as calm a voice he could manage.

"Everyone is telling us to talk to you," said the man.

"That's right," said Adam. He felt his shoulders relax a bit. The message got to everyone. The Family was listening to him, at least for now. "These are innocent people. There are children here who have done nothing wrong. We will cooperate, just please don't harm any of us."

"Don't give us a reason to," said the man.

Adam simply nodded at this. He had the feeling that the less said right now, the better. He knew what the scene looked like, with injured bodies scattered throughout their world. It didn't look good.

"Well, we have a lot to get through, and a lot of questions," said the man. "I'm going to need you all to come with us."

"We understand," said Adam. "You won't have any trouble from us."

"We'll see," said the man. He motioned to the other two with the guns and they pushed Adam and Jonas forward through the tunnel.

The march through the tunnel was silent at first, until the man walking behind Jonas spoke.

"Man, did you see the set-up they had back there? What the fuck?"

"It was totally bizarre," said the man behind Adam. Adam tried not to be hurt by the comments. They were talking about his home, the place where he used to find comfort and solace. Only now did he understand how surreal it would seem to the rest of the world.

The man cleared his throat as a less intimidating group of people passed, carrying white boxes marked with red crosses and stretchers. Adam was grateful the injured Family members would get some help.

A woman in the back of the group stopped at Adam. "Any injuries?" she asked the man behind Adam.

"These two seem fine, and we need this one for questioning," said the man behind Adam.

She shined a light in Adam's eyes. "How are you feeling, sir?"

"I'm fine, but he might be hurt," said Adam, leaning his head toward Jonas.

"I'm fine," said Jonas before the woman could get to him.

Adam didn't dare turn around, but he knew the injuries to Jonas' face and arms would at least justify a quick inspection.

"Let's just take a minute to be sure," said the woman.

"Can I keep moving with him?" asked Adam's man.

"He seems fine, but I'd have Dr. Thompson give him a quick physical before he flies," said the woman.

"All right, let's go," said the man and he nudged Adam forward with the butt of his gun.

"No, wait," said Jonas' voice from behind. "I should stay with him."

"Please, sir. This will go much faster if you sit still," said the woman.

"I'm fine, Jonas," said Adam, hoping to calm his brother. "Look after everyone else." He continued to walk toward the end of the tunnel and back above ground.

Adam both missed Jonas the moment they were separated and was grateful Jonas now had a better chance of being grouped with the rest of The Family instead of with Adam. Adam was determined to keep them all safe, and he was certain being far away from him was the first step toward that safety.

He didn't say anything the rest of the walk. He didn't say anything as he was inspected by the other doctor, but he did allow his eyes to scan the area for Father. Only soldiers and the medical team filled the once empty field.

He didn't say anything as they loaded him into the helicopter, but he did take the time to look through the small groups being led out of the tunnel. Jonas was in the first pack with a bandage on a cheek and another on his right arm. Adam noticed three stretchers with people on them, but he couldn't make out the faces. He assumed Warriors since they would have jumped into the fight. Finally, he saw Clare, helping to calm the Children as they were led out into the air, some for the first time in years. They looked scared. Adam's heart sank. Did he do the right thing? It was too late to change anything now. Moving forward, he needed to be smart, he needed to think things through and he needed to do it without the help of the ones he cared about most. There was still no sign of Father. Adam wondered if he escaped or if they were questioning him inside. There was no way to know.

Adam did know he couldn't do this alone. Clare said he needed to ask for a lawyer, but could he trust these people to give him someone who would actually help? Did he have any other options?

Adam thought about his time above ground. He didn't know anyone. He wasn't supposed to. The only person outside of The Family he ever had any real contact with was Father Fitzpatrick, and Adam had been so rude to the man. Still, Father Fitzpatrick was kind, despite Adam's behavior, and he gave Samuel hope, even if it was too late. It seemed to be Adam's only option. If he was given the chance, Adam would call the hotel and pray the church group was still there.

Adam sat between two soldiers in the helicopter, but he was able to see out the sides as they flew away. He saw a caravan of trucks driving down the road toward Father's home. He guessed they were meant to transport The Family somewhere. He just wished he knew where. Clare would care for the Children. Jonas would stay strong. The Family would follow their lead and stay safe, at least for a little while. Father. Father was still out there, fighting against Adam, but believing he was doing what was best. The thought overwhelmed Adam, and all he could think to do was pray. He prayed for luck, for help, for anything that would at least even the playing field between himself and Father, because right now, Father held all the cards and no good could come from that.

52

To Adam's relief, he was given the opportunity to make a phone call once the helicopter landed at a large cement block building in the middle of — Adam had no idea where. He asked if the man had the number for the lodge at the national park. The man looked it up and Adam made the call. He thanked God when he learned Father Fitzpatrick was still there.

"Hello," said the priest in a cheerful tone.

"Father Fitzpatrick?" said Adam.

"This is he, how may I help you, son?"

"This is Adam, we met a few days ago. You were kind enough to let my friend and I join you on your bus."

"Yes, of course," said Father Fitzpatrick, sounding genuinely pleased to hear Adam's voice. "How are you, my boy? You had me a little concerned when you wouldn't get back on the bus. I'm glad to hear you apparently made it to civilization after all."

"Yes and no, Father," said Adam. "I'm in a bit of trouble that I can't fully explain, but I need a lawyer and I don't know anyone to call to help me find one."

"A lawyer? What could you possibly need a lawyer for?" The priest still sounded cheerful, but also confused.

"It is a very long story," said Adam, allowing his fatigue to come through. "I'd like to explain it all to you, but it's complicated and I'm not sure I can do it justice."

"Well, as a matter of fact, I do know a young man in the area that I'd be happy to call for you. Not knowing the trouble you're in, I'm not sure he practices the right type of law, but he's a good man. I'll give him a call. Where are you?"

Adam didn't have a clue. He turned to the man who offered him the phone and who was clearly listening in on the entire conversation.

"Where are we?" asked Adam. "A friend is going to try to get me a lawyer and needs to know where to find me."

"Tell your friend you'll be at the federal courthouse in Billings tomorrow," said the man. "If he's a lawyer, he'll know where to find you."

Adam relayed the message to Father Fitzpatrick.

"Okay, son. I'll have him there tomorrow," said the priest. "What is your last name so he knows who to ask for?"

The question stopped Adam. He didn't have a last name. He never needed one. Adam turned to the man waiting for him to finish the call. "I don't have a last name."

"You don't what?" said the man. Adam heard the echo of Father Fitzpatrick asking the same question on the phone.

"I don't have a last name. I'm just Adam."

"Okay, son," said Father Fitzpatrick. "I'll just have him ask for Adam. His name is Dave Ballinger. If you don't hear from him tomorrow, give me a call at this number. We'll be here another two days."

"Okay," said Adam. "Thank you." He hung up, feeling more agitated than he had before. He had no idea who he was.

"Okay, just Adam," said the man in the tie. "Now you've made your call. Can you help me straighten out whatever the hell is going on here?"

Adam shook his head. "You got the hell part right, sir. Unfortunately, I'm not sure I can help you until I talk to that lawyer."

"You only need a lawyer if you've done something wrong, son. People in my holding cells downstairs seem to trust you and think the world of you. Did you do something wrong?"

"I've done a lot of things wrong," said Adam. "I'm trying to fix them, but I want to do it the right way this time."

The man nodded. "All right, I'm tired and would like to see my kids, so you get your wish for tonight. Orders are to keep you away from the pack just in case."

Adam felt his heart sink. He wanted to see his Family. To know they were okay, but he understood he didn't have any of the power here. He was led to a cement cell with bars keeping him in. "Is this really necessary?" asked Adam.

"No one knows what's going on," said the man. "All they know is something weird was going on down there, someone sent us a video of a major fight, we found dozens of injured people with guns lying on the ground, surrounded by a bunch of scared people, and you seem to be in charge. Get some sleep and we'll get you to the city in the morning."

Adam knew he didn't have the right to ask any favors, but his curiosity took over. "Do you have Fa..." Adam stopped and cleared his throat to correct himself. "Do you have Mr. Kingston?"

The man in the tie stopped. "You want to tell me something about him?"

So much, Adam thought to himself, but he knew saying it wouldn't be smart. Father would be ready for that. Adam needed advice before trying to take Father on alone. Still, he didn't want to give Father a head start either. "Just don't trust him," said Adam. "I know you don't have a reason not to trust him, but don't."

The man shook his head. "The fact we found you all underneath his house is reason enough for me not to trust him. At least for now. We'll talk tomorrow." Then he left.

The bars shut and Adam sat on the metal shelf that was supposed to serve as a bed. A foam padding covered the top. The idea of sleeping agitated Adam. Instead, he sat on the bed, running through the events of the last few days and years. Trying to sort out what was good and what was bad. Trying to think of a way to keep his Family safe.

They were all being held somewhere. They were still loyal to Adam, but they thought that also meant being loyal to Father. Was he doing anything to get them out? Should Adam let him? Would Father save them or hurt them? He couldn't really risk anyone learning what they were being taught underground, could he?

Learning he knew children were being "rescued?" No. He couldn't. Too much was at stake. Father would leave them to their fates, no matter what those fates might be. At least he couldn't hurt them directly. Not now.

Father must be in trouble. Nearly a hundred people were living under his home with missing children. The man in the tie said it, that was reason enough not to trust him, for now. There was no way he could talk his way out of it. Was there? He did manage to become rich and powerful, even after prison. It would be a mistake to underestimate him. What were Adam's options? He needed Clare and Jonas. Clare was smart, she would help him think through the pros and cons. Jonas was strategic. What was Adam? Father's puppet. He couldn't do this.

Then he remembered the faces of Clare and Jonas after the attack. They asked him what was next. Despite everything, they still had faith in him. They still trusted him to lead. Maybe he wasn't just a puppet. Even if he was, he needed to start acting like a leader. He would tell the truth. At least to the lawyer. He needed to trust someone in the outside world, and Father Fitzpatrick was his best bet. He may not be the best priest, but he was a good man. Adam could trust that. He would keep as much of the blame on himself and Father as possible. There was no way they were getting out of this unscathed, but if he could paint the rest of The Family as victims, he could at least save them.

53

Adam must have fallen asleep at some point, because in the morning, a man came to put him in another helicopter that flew him to an airport, put him in a black SUV and drove him to a different building in a city this time. They only spoke to him when it was time to move, and he kept his mouth shut and did what they said.

He saw a swarm of people with cameras and microphones standing in the front of the building, shouting questions at a group of people in suits standing on the steps. He only saw press conferences on the news back when he bothered to watch them. He wondered what they were talking about today. He forgot to breathe for a moment when it occurred to him that he might be the topic of interest, or at least The Family. Would the news have gotten out that quickly? Possibly.

He was led through a door in the back of the building to a small gray room with a table, three chairs and a large mirror on one wall. He was told to sit in the chair opposite the mirror and that someone would be with him shortly.

The man from the night before eventually arrived. "Still waiting on that lawyer?"

"Yes, sir," said Adam.

The agent rubbed his face with both hands. "Listen, I'm not sure I properly introduced myself last night. There was a lot of shit going down. I'm Agent Wilcox, Homeland Security."

"Nice to meet you. I'm Adam."

"Right, just Adam because you don't have a last name, is that correct?"

Adam took a deep breath. "Agent Wilcox, I know I have a lot to explain. I know very little makes sense, but I have people I need to keep safe and to make sure I'm doing that, I really need to talk to a lawyer."

"Who do you need to keep safe?" Wilcox's voice was calm, but Adam could see his arm muscles tense. Adam guessed the agent was clenching his fists under the table to give the appearance of civility. "Who are you protecting? The dozens of people filling my holding cells who refuse to say anything other than we need to talk to you? The small army we found in an underground bunker with all of those people? The kids who are magically popping up on our missing persons database? Or the fucking U.S. Ambassador who was living above your little underground kingdom?" Wilcox was starting to lose his cool. Adam couldn't blame him, when it was all laid out in a row, it was a lot to take in at once. It was a lot for Adam to take in during the last few days. Agent Wilcox only had about 12 hours.

"Most of those people are innocent. They are good people," said Adam. "Some aren't so good. I need an attorney to help you sort them out, because no, I don't expect you to take my word for it."

"Fine," said Wilcox, turning red. "Your attorney should be here soon. He called to confirm you were here this morning."

"Thank you," said Adam.

After Wilcox left, Adam started to pace the room. He knew it was pointless, but he needed to move. He needed to do something, but he couldn't. He was trapped, stuck in this box, just waiting for someone to come talk to him, give him some update.

Finally, a man in a well-fitted black suit, tie and shiny shoes walked into the room with a briefcase. Adam held his breath. At first glance, the man reminded Adam of the version of Father he saw on the television screen. He let out a breath when he realized it wasn't Father, the eyes were closer together and the chin seemed flat. Still, Adam didn't get the sense of relief he was hoping to feel.

"Hello, young man," said the man in the suit. "I'm Dave Ballinger. Father Fitzpatrick called me and told me about your situation. I'm a defense attorney familiar with federal cases out here, and I've agreed to take on your case pro-bono. Father Fitzpatrick and I go way back, so you owe him one." Dave Ballinger sat down and opened his briefcase, then motioned for Adam to sit as well. Adam couldn't read his expression. "I'm not sure I completely understand the situation. It sounds like law enforcement is a little confused as well. That might actually work in our favor, but I'd like to hear you tell the story." For the first time since he walked in the room, Dave Ballinger looked at Adam in the eye. "Aren't you going to sit down?"

"Not yet," said Adam. "Father Fitzpatrick called you?"

"Yes," said Dave Ballinger. "He said he met you and another young man on the bus earlier this week and that you called him out of the blue for help. He didn't have the details, but based on the mood of the agents out there and the stories floating around the news media, you've got one hell of a story to tell."

Adam couldn't believe Samuel only died a few days ago. The enormity of what happened and what he still had to deal with hit Adam all at once. He sank into the chair, burying his head in his arms and cried.

After a few moments, Dave Ballinger cleared his throat and began to speak again. "Okay, well, if what the agents out there tell me is even close to true, there is a lot to go through here." His voice seemed to soften, even if he hadn't lost his suspicious tone.

"What is happening?" Adam asked. It was all he could manage to get out. He knew he would have to tell the whole story at some point, but he needed to know where his Family was, what was happening to them and if Father was free or facing the justice he deserved.

"Yeah, well, I was hoping you could tell me that, but if you are asking about the others, most are in holding cells. Apparently, when you were all being taken into custody, most of them were looking for you. Saying you were in charge. Are you the leader?"

Adam shook his head. "I was supposed to be."

"Okay, well, I'll need more than that, but for now, all the adults are being held until agents can determine who is responsible for what. You all had about a dozen missing kids with you down there."

"Are the kids okay?" asked Adam.

Dave Ballinger nodded slowly. "They're with child protective services, and being reconnected with their families."

Adam's heart skipped a beat. In his heart, he knew this would happen. He knew if they left, the Children would have to go home, but as a Rescuer, he also knew those kids were brought to The Family for a reason. "Make sure they check out the parents," he whispered.

"What do you mean by that?"

Adam collected himself. "Can I trust you?"

Dave Ballinger took a deep breath. "Legally, I'm not allowed to tell anyone anything you share with me without your permission."

"Legally?" questioned Adam. He knew what it meant, but it sounded like there was fine print to the statement. "Does that mean you still might tell someone?"

"No. As a lawyer, the law is actually very important to me."

"And Father Fitzpatrick trusts you?" Adam knew he needed to trust someone. He needed help, but he also needed to know this was the man who could actually help him.

"I trust Father Fitzpatrick," said Dave Ballinger. "He apparently believed I could help, because he called me. How much does he trust me? You would have to ask him."

Adam supposed that was as honest an answer he could expect, and the fact that Dave Ballinger seemed to be questioning whether he wanted to help Adam or not spoke well for his character. Adam wasn't sure he deserved help either, but his Family did.

"We took the kids from the parents, but we were given permission from at least one of them."

Dave Ballinger took out a legal pad and started writing. "Okay, that's something. Was the permission in writing? Do you have any legal documentation?"

Adam couldn't help but let out a small laugh. "No."

"Okay, well, why did you take the children?"

"We thought we were protecting them. Rescuing them." Adam could hear the sarcasm in his own voice when he said the word "rescuing."

"Rescuing them from what?"

"From the sins of the world," said Adam, looking down at the table. How could he have been so blinded by Father? He was ashamed.

"Why did you think they needed saving from that?" asked Dave Ballinger.

"It's what Father told us God wanted."

"Who is Father?"

Adam looked back at Dave Ballinger. "You know him as Alex Kingston."

Dave Ballinger stared back at Adam. "Fuck me." Adam couldn't help but smile. Normally, the crassness of the statement would bother him, but considering how it helped him and Jonas just a day earlier, he appreciated the appropriateness of it at this moment.

"Why do you call him Father?"

Adam sighed. "Because that is what he told us to call him and who he was to us. He was our leader and cared for us. At least, that's what we thought. What most of them still believe."

"But you don't?"

Adam shook his head. "No, and it took me too long to reach that understanding. It may be even harder for the rest of them. Do you know where Father is now? Has he said anything about me?"

"I don't know, but ..." Dave Ballinger paused. "Hold on." Dave Ballinger pulled out his phone and pushed a few buttons. "Fuck me." He looked back up at Adam. "You may not be as crazy as I thought you were."

"Only time will tell." Adam might actually like Mr. Dave Ballinger. As much as he could like anyone above ground anyway. At least the man didn't hide what he was thinking.

Dave Ballinger handed Adam the phone. Adam saw the headline:

BREAKING NEWS: Federal Authorities Raid Home of US Ambassador and Tech Genius.

Below the headline was a picture of Father, outside the home, smiling and waving. The photo alone was enough to make Adam want to break the phone, but he kept reading:

Federal authorities swarmed the home of U.S. Ambassador and computer genius Alex Kingston Tuesday night.

Investigators are not yet releasing the cause of the raid, but did confirm in a press conference that Kingston is a person of interest in an ongoing investigation.

Reporters witnessed agents from at least three different agencies, the FBI, NSA and Homeland Security, at Kingston's home last night, and he came out briefly to wave to reporters, before going back inside with officials.

This is a developing story and we will bring you more information as it becomes available.

Adam stopped reading and gave the phone back to Dave Ballinger.

"I'll probably be able to get more information," said Dave Ballinger as he took the phone back from Adam. "But listen, if you are taking on Alex Kingston, you are going to need a lot more help than I can give you."

"No. I trust Father Fitzpatrick too. Please help."

Dave Ballinger rubbed the back of his neck. "All right, we'll cross that bridge when we get to it. Why don't you start from the beginning?"

"It is a very long story."

"Yeah, I'm catching onto that, but tell me anyway."

Adam didn't really know where to start, so he decided to start when it began for him. When he met Father.

54

When Adam finished his story, Dave Ballinger sat back and used what was apparently his favorite phrase. "Fuck me."

Adam shook his head, he needed Dave Ballinger to get to work.

"Listen, Mr. Ballinger, I know he's powerful, but why am I here and he's smiling at cameras out there?"

"You don't just arrest a US Ambassador," Dave Ballinger said, shaking his head and sitting up a bit straighter. "And yeah, he's super rich and powerful. He doesn't end up in places like this."

Adam was angry, but he told himself he shouldn't be surprised. What did he really think would happen? They would send the information and just be believed? They were nobody, but apparent kidnappers. Father was trusted and powerful. Adam tried to think clearly.

"Listen, Mr. Ballinger."

"Just call me Dave."

"Okay, Dave, listen. It doesn't really matter what happens to me." Adam tried to keep his voice calm. He would battle Father and lose, but he couldn't bring the rest of The Family down with him. "You need to help all of the others. This isn't their fault. They didn't know what he was doing, they didn't even know the full story of what I was doing when I rescued the Children. They just knew what we told them. They're good people."

Adam knew he wasn't being totally honest. Some of them knew even more than Adam did, but that wasn't important now. Jonas and Clare deserved a new life.

"Listen, if what you're telling me is true, you may be able to cut a deal. Tell them what you know about Kinston, tell them everything, and you might get out. You could save yourself and everyone in those cells, but you will need to be honest."

"I'll do whatever it takes to keep them all safe."

"Okay, I'll check on the others, talk to the investigators and touch base with you in the morning. This thing is too crazy for them to let you out tonight, but you should be able to get some sleep with your friends."

"Thank you." It was all he could ask for now. This was going to be a long battle. Adam needed time to think, to pray and to get control of his emotions. He'd need to be better than himself if he was going to save his Family, and hopefully make Father answer for some of what he had done.

Dave got up to leave.

"Dave?"

Dave turned. "Yeah?"

"Ask for Clare and tell her I'm okay. Tell her we will all be okay."

"Sure thing."

After Dave left, Adam sat back and waited, but this time, it wasn't frustrating. He soaked in the last few moments of peace he would have for a long time.

EPILOGUE

The buzzer signaling the door opening frightened Adam out of his own thoughts. He didn't want to be here. He didn't want to talk to him, but the therapist at the hospital said it was important for closure. Whatever that was supposed to mean.

It was hard to believe the raid and upending of Adam's whole life started just over a year ago. So much happened. So much changed, and now Adam felt like he was returning to the past. Adam walked into the cold gray room that smelled of mold, but when he saw Father, the way the man sat and looked at Adam, Adam could have sworn they were right back in Father's office, the older man in charge of the world.

Adam focused on his steps and breathing, not wanting to give away his fear. Adam should be the one in control. Father was the one in the orange jumpsuit, shackled to a metal table, not Adam.

"Hello, my son," said Father, causing Adam to falter slightly. "It is so good to see you."

"You saw me at the trial," said Adam. The trial that was finally over after a year. The trial that sent Father and the other Elders to prison for decades. However, when the authorities learned Father recruited his secret army while serving time for his original hacking crimes, they decided it would be too dangerous to send him to just any prison. Instead, he was in solitary confinement in a maximum-security prison and only allowed visitors under strict supervision. Of course, Adam also learned Father had all the comforts of home in his larger than usual cell, thanks to friends and connections in high places. Father also made a deal with the government to help them better understand how his underground world worked in exchange for some extra comforts and freedoms, although Adam didn't exactly know what those were. Now, the only home Adam ever really knew was a government research facility. Agents gave Adam and other Family members the opportunity to go back and collect belongings, but no one owned anything. It was all Father's, plus they were raised not to place importance on material goods, so there didn't seem to be a reason to go back. Adam actually felt relief he would never need to return.

"Yes," said Father, "but I wasn't allowed to speak with you then. To tell you how proud I am that you took care of your brothers and sisters. Even during that difficult time."

"Someone had to," said Adam, angry that he felt joy in Father being proud of him. He knew he still had work to do.

"So, what are you doing now? I assume you and the others are out of the facility. Do you still see them?"

Adam didn't want answer the question. Originally, prosecutors wanted to send the entire Family to prison, but it was hard to justify locking up a bunch of brainwashed kidnapping victims. While the children were either sent back to their families, put into foster care or adopted, the older Family members like Adam, Jonas and Clare, who were adults, but also brainwashed as children, were sentenced to psychiatric facilities for a minimum of six months. As far as Adam knew, he was the only one still being treated. The others were released to try and rebuild their lives.

"We are all doing the best we can, under the circumstances," said Adam.

"Ah, my son," said Father, leaning back in his seat. "I'm sure you feel lost. That is why I built The Family in the first place. To create a world without fear and confusion. Perhaps I allowed you into the outside world for too long. Perhaps that is what turned you against me, I don't know, but it pains me to see you now. I pray you will find your way back to what is right."

Father's words pushed back Adam's shame and fear, allowing his anger to boil up from his legs to his chest. He jumped up from his seat and started to pace the room.

"Way back to what is right? I have no way of determining what that is anymore. You took that from me. I can't trust my own judgements, because of how long I let you manipulate and lie to me. Allowing me to think that I was doing good, when, in reality, I was just helping you hurt everyone I cared about."

"I'm sorry you feel that way," said Father. "I do not believe that is what we were doing."

"Of course, you don't," said Adam, wanting to stop Father from saying another word. "You created a world where everyone agreed with your way of life, because you didn't give them any options. The ones that were strong enough to question you ended up dead. You convinced all of us that it was best for the world, but it was just what was best for you."

"That's not ..." Father leaned forward and started to speak, but Adam stopped him again.

"No. You don't get to talk anymore. You had me convinced we were doing God's work, had us all convinced. Do you know what you actually did? Most of my brothers and sisters don't even believe in God anymore. You turned them away from Him."

It was true. During the therapy sessions, when his brothers and sisters were still at the facility with him, Adam listened as they let out their anger, not just against Father, but against God. Father intertwined the two so closely, his brothers and sisters couldn't tell them apart.

Father shook his head. "But you still believe?" he asked, his voice shaking just slightly.

It was the first time Adam could remember Father coming close to tears, but he was too angry to feel compassion. "Not because of you. Don't for a second think I still believe because of you."

Adam likely would have turned away from God if it wasn't for Clare, and Samuel. Clare never gave up on God, holding tightly to the Bible Samuel left behind. She would talk Adam back to God every time he questioned his faith. She also reminded him of the hope the book gave Samuel, and Adam remembered the weight that seemed to lift off his brother after speaking with the priest. God and Father were not the same, and it wasn't right to blame God for Father's actions.

Adam began to feel the weight lift off him. He could do this.

"Listen, I just came here for one reason," Adam said, calming his voice. "That's to say goodbye. My therapist seems to think that will help me move on, and maybe it will or won't, but I need you to know that this is over. I will not come to visit you again."

"We will see, my son," said Father, regaining his composure and speaking in a tone that seemed to imply he knew more than Adam did.

In the past, the tone would have unnerved Adam, but this time, Adam felt nothing. He allowed himself a small smile with the realization he could be free of this man and turned to the door. "I'm done here," said Adam to the guard. The door opened and Adam walked out, not bothering to look back at Father.

Adam took a deep, cleansing breath as he walked out into the sun. He looked out past the fence and saw Jonas waiting for him.

"How did it go?" asked Jonas when Adam reached him.

"Better than expected," said Adam as they both opened their doors and got in the car.

It was Jonas' car. One he bought after getting a job for an armored truck company. Originally, Jonas wanted to join the army or a police force, but despite being found innocent, his history of kidnapping children kept him from pursuing those careers.

"Does that mean you can leave that hell hole and come live with me?" asked Jonas.

Adam smiled. Jonas left the facility as soon as his six months were up, and then seemed to make it his life's mission to get Adam to join him.

"First, it's not a hell hole," said Adam. Another part of Father's sentence was he needed to pay for all The Family members' therapy. The facility turned out to be very luxurious with a pool and spa. It actually made Adam a little uncomfortable to have so much comfort.

"Second, no, but I do think I'm closer. I'm still not sure I can trust myself to live a good life out in the real world."

"Who can? You're being too hard on yourself. No one knows for sure if they're doing the right thing, all we can do is try our best, but you can't even do that if you don't let yourself live."

"How do you even start?" Adam was genuinely curious. "I mean, we thought we were doing the right thing before and look at the mess we made."

"First, we. Were. Brainwashed." Jonas took his eyes off the road just long enough to emphasize his words with a nod in Adam's direction. "Second, you start with the Bible." Jonas paused for a moment to let that sink in and then continued. "The fruit of the Spirit is love, joy, peace, patience, kindness, generosity, faithfulness, gentleness, self-control. Against such, there is no law. Galatians 5:22 to 23."

Adam just stared at his brother. He couldn't believe Jonas of all people was quoting the Bible to him. Let alone a verse Adam never heard before.

Jonas smiled and shrugged. "I've been talking to Clare."

Adam gave a sad smile. Of course, Clare was still helping her brothers and sisters, and of course, she found the perfect passage to help them move forward if they would listen.

Clare left the facility about a month after Jonas. She was now at a convent, studying to become a nun. The Catholic Church immediately ruled she and Jonas were never actually married and allowed them to separate as friends without any guilt.

Jonas said, "She still cares about you. You know that, right?"

"I do." During the trial, and even after, Adam and Clare considered being together, but there was too much happening and too many emotions to handle all at once. Adam still loved her, but he respected her decision. She was clearly called to a higher purpose. Clare was marrying God, and Adam supposed if he was going to lose her to anyone, it might as well be the Lord.

"So, anyway, I've been meaning to tell you, I was promoted to a driver. I'll make a little extra money and get a little more responsibility."

"That's wonderful, congratulations," said Adam, grateful for the topic change.

"Thank you. So, since I will be making more money, I can afford to rent a bigger place, that is, if I had a roommate to help me out."

Adam sighed. "I would just hold you back. I'm not sure I'm ready to just live my life like nothing happened."

"You don't forget what happened. You learn from it and you forgive yourself. That's about the only thing those quacks at the facility said that made any sense."

"Yeah. I'm just not sure I deserve forgiveness yet."

"Look in the glove compartment."

"What?" asked Adam.

"Just look."

Adam opened the glove compartment and found a handful of handwritten cards inside. All addressed to him, from children he rescued and then helped return home.

Adam looked through the cards while Jonas talked.

"Agent Wilcox gave them to me to pass on to you. Some of the Children wanted to reach out, but they didn't know where you were, so they sent them to Homeland Security. They're okay. Some are back with their families, and others were placed in good homes. Plus, you know as well as I do that, even though our methods were wrong, some of those kids really are better off now."

"I can't think like that. It's a slippery slope." Still, Adam had to admit the colorful cards made him smile. He stopped at a picture of Rebecca, or she was probably called Kayla again. She was smiling with her mom. The mom left her questionable boyfriend after Rebecca/Kayla disappeared. On the back of the picture, Rebecca/Kayla colored a picture of herself dancing. The thought of the little girl's face lighting up again as she danced made Adam smile. Then, Adam opened the letter from her mother. It was painful and heartwarming, all at the same time. Her mother said she would never be able to forgive Adam or her ex-husband for taking her daughter, but she would always be grateful that her daughter was at least kept safe and returned to her. She informed him this would be the first and last communication he would have with her daughter, they needed to move on, but she felt she owed him one goodbye. Adam didn't want to be forgiven for his crime and was humbled by her gratitude and kindness. In the end, even though it took him too long, he did do the right thing.

Adam couldn't stop the wave of emotions and relief from spilling out of him. Jonas patted Adam on the shoulder while Adam cried.

"What would I even do?" asked Adam when the tears finally finished. "I'm not qualified for anything."

"No, but you're smart and a hard worker. You always liked working outside. You could join a construction crew or maybe we could find a farm for you to help out on. I'm making a decent living now. You wouldn't have to make much, right away."

"I can't depend on you," said Adam. "You should live your own life and stop worrying about me."

"We all owe you. You saved us. If it weren't for you, I would have gone along with Father's plan out of anger and Clare still wouldn't know the whole story. As for the rest of The Family? They're out there, living their lives, too. Like you should be."

Adam nodded. Maybe he was ready to leave. Maybe it would be okay. The thought of working outdoors was appealing, as was getting out of the facility. Maybe it was worth a try. He would need to pray on it, ask God what the best path was.

The thought surprised Adam, Clare and the memories of Samuel kept Adam's belief in God alive, but this was the first time he allowed himself to think he could keep his faith. The thought comforted him. He could still pray and look to God for answers without letting Father win. Instead, Adam could focus on what Samuel wanted to emphasize, love, compassion and forgiveness.

Adam felt as though a weight was lifted from his chest and heart. He could breathe easier. He thought about getting his own Bible and smiled.

"What's with the face?" asked Jonas, glancing over from the driver seat.

Adam let himself let out a small laugh. "I guess I just feel good right now. Thanks, brother."

Jonas patted Adam's shoulder. "It's about time."

Adam nodded and, for the first time, allowed himself to dream about a future all his own.

CPSIA information can be obtained
at www.ICGtesting.com
Printed in the USA
LVHW090452300421
686058LV00009B/806

9 781952 439070